For Jade,
Than

Secrets

Best wishes
Michael

By

Michael Letterman

This novel is a work of fiction.

Some events in this novel are based on research and discovery of historical facts, fully available through various public domain methods.

Any resemblance to persons living or dead is purely coincidental.

As a child, I wanted to be a pirate. Many of the characters in the novel are *my* plunder!

Dedication

For Jan, who stands beside me and always believes.

For Jan, who nursed me back to health from malaria, a remnant of a slightly darker side of my past and a reminder, there are some things you do in life that always follow you. It goes without saying, this book would have never been written had it not been for you.

For Jane Austin who created our memorable passage from Mr. Darcy in *Pride and Prejudice.*

"You must know... surely, you must know it was all for you. You are too generous to trifle with me. I believe you spoke with my aunt last night, and it has taught me to hope as I'd scarcely allowed myself before. If your feelings are still what they were last April, tell me so at once. My affections and wishes have not changed, but one word from you will silence me forever. If, however, your feelings have changed, I will have to tell you: you have bewitched me, body and soul, and I love, I love, I love you. I never wish to be parted from you from this day on."

Jan, you bewitched me body and soul!

You must know... surely, you must know it was all for you!

Happy 6th anniversary!

All my love,

Michael Letterman
October 23, 2015

"If Tomorrow Never Comes"

Performed by Garth Brooks Written by Kent Evan Blazy

Sometimes late at night
I lie awake and watch her sleeping
She's lost in peaceful dreams
So I turn out the lights and lay there in the dark
And the thought crosses my mind
If I never wake up in the morning
Would she ever doubt
The way I feel about her in my heart

If tomorrow never comes
Will she know how much I loved her
Did I try in every way to show her every day
That she's my only one
And if my time on earth were through
And she must face this world without me
Is the love I gave her in the past
Gonna be enough to last
If tomorrow never comes

'Cause I've lost loved ones in my life
Who never knew how much I loved them
Now I live with the regret
That my true feelings for them never were revealed
So I made a promise to myself
To say each day how much she means to me
And avoid that circumstance
Where there's no second chance to tell her how I feel

'Cause if tomorrow never comes
Will she know how much I loved her
Did I try in every way to show her every day
That she's my only one
And if my time on earth were through
And she must face this world without me
Is the love I gave her in the past
Gonna be enough to last
If tomorrow never comes

So tell that someone that you love
Just what you're thinking of
If tomorrow never comes

Historic Quotes

Be on your guard; stand firm in the faith; be men of courage; be strong.

Saul of Tarsus
Who after his conversion would later become
The Apostle Paul
I Corinthians 16:13

The test of our progress is not whether we add more to the abundance of those who have much it is whether we provide enough for those who have little.

Franklin D. Roosevelt

History, despite its wrenching pain, cannot be unlived, but if faced with courage, need not be lived again.

Maya Angelou

In the long term we can hope that religion will change the nature of man and reduce conflict. But history is not encouraging in this respect. The bloodiest wars in history have been religious wars.

Richard M. Nixon

Aut si quid est in vita in aeternum resonat!
What we do in life echoes in eternity!

Marcus Aurelius (121 AD ~180 AD)

There are moments when Nature reveals the passion hidden beneath the careless calm of her ordinary moods--violent spring flashing white on almond-blossom through the purple clouds; a snowy, moonlit peak, with its single star, soaring up to the passionate blue; or against the flames of sunset, an old yew-tree standing dark guardian of some fiery secret.

JOHN GALSWORTHY, *The Forsyte Saga*

The Caribbean
1700 A.D.

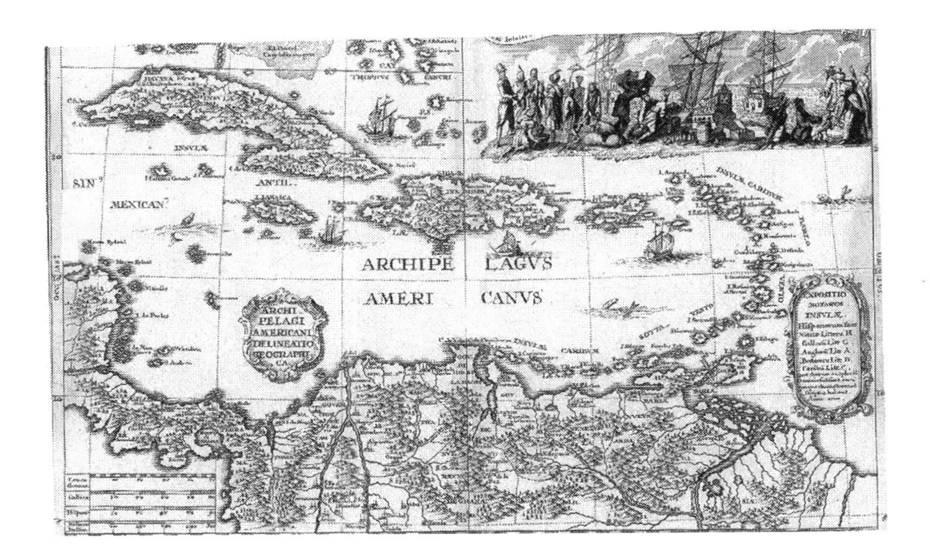

I love the Caribbean. The oceans are like blue glass where one can see the grains of sand. I'm at home in Port Royal, New Providence, or on the sands of an isolated and deserted beach.

In my mind the islands are the gateway to the sea, which conceals all secrets, and allows a man time to contemplate upon the cause of all things and therein to find peace, a state so often sought after and so rarely found.

- Michael Letterman -

The Fight Between the Lions

It is interesting this wisdom appears as wolves in Cherokee history and lions in the Maasai tribe in Africa.

An old Maasai grandfather was teaching his grandson about life.
"A fight is going on inside me," he said to the boy.
"It is a terrible fight and it is between two lions. One is evil - he is anger, envy, sorrow, regret, greed, arrogance, self-pity, guilt, resentment, inferiority, lies, false pride, superiority, and ego."
He continued, "The other is good - he is joy, peace, love, hope, serenity, humility, kindness, benevolence, empathy, generosity, truth, compassion, and faith. The same fight is going on inside you - and inside every other person, too."
The grandson thought about it for a minute and then asked his grandfather, "Which lion will win?"
The grandfather simply replied, "The one you feed."

Foreword

"Perhaps it is true. Although mankind is perceived to be the highest species in the animal kingdom, perhaps they are little more than wolves, after all. Or perhaps the wolf is the greater of the species, as it follows the law of the jungle – strike first and then give tongue!"

The dawn was beginning to break when Mowgli went down the hillside alone, to meet those mysterious things that are called men.

Rudyard Kipling

Chapter 1

"Almost in every kingdom the most ancient families have been at first princes' bastards."

Robert Burton

It was February 10, 1684 and the worst winter recorded to date. 1684 and 1685 heralded deep snow, with falls of continual snow affecting London. This lasted for five weeks, along with the freezing of the Thames. The heavy snow and frost continued for many months. The coldest year ever recorded saw the severe snowy winter end around mid April, at which time arctic sea ice had extended around the entire coast of Iceland.

Snow and ice built up everywhere. Ice on coasts built up to eight inches in parts. All people were affected very badly by the crushing winter. The cold brought famine to the poor, as livestock perished, and crops failed. Dubbed by many as the "Little Ice Age", the weather continued to ruin harvests as wet weather then took over from the cold. The Thames remained frozen for months, leaving ships to port in warmer waters. The wealthy froze in their castles, as did the poor in their thatch huts. It would take England years to completely recover.

The winter wasn't the only thing amiss this evening. In the shadow of the massive castle belonging to the Duke of Kensington, a small servants cottage was aglow from the fireplace and the extra lanterns.

Two well-dressed men warmed themselves by the fireplace. Henry Rockfort, son of Lord Charles and the Eighth Duke of Rockfort extended his hands closer to the fire. His best friend Bernard Howard, the Seventh Duke of Norfolk stood with him. Every once in a while Henry would react to the cries of pain beyond the bedroom door and pace back and forth across the floor of the small cottage.

"Here, old friend," Bernard said quietly. "Have a glass of rum to boost your spirits. Women have been having children since the world began!"

His speech was slurred.

"Are you sure my wife does not know?" Henry said. "I have no wish to start, yet another scandal!"

"Scandal?" Bernard said as he laughed. "Another servant girl pregnant by her Lord and Master? All of England is full of such!"

"Beatrice may not care," Henry replied. "But I love the woman behind that door!"

"I know," Bernard said as he gently placed a hand on his friend's shoulder. "We are forced to marry to increase our wealth and riches. Love is for fools."

"Then I am indeed a fool," Henry retorted. "I have a wife that hates me and a simpleton son that will require someone to help him run the affairs of the estate. I have found more comfort in the arms of Josephine than I have ever found anywhere else. This child is my heir, although illegitimate. If England changes, some day he could inherit my entire fortune! Have we not married too closely for too long?"

"Indeed," Bernard replied as he generously sniffed a small sample of snuff. "Beatrice was your first cousin, if I recall."

"First bitch," Henry replied.

Another scream from behind the door, followed by the wailing cry of a small child brought both men back from their conversation.

Henry started toward the door, but was met by an elderly midwife.

"You have a son, my Lord," the woman replied as she placed the squalling infant into Lord Henry's arms. "He is perfect!"

"Hello my son," Henry whispered as he held the crying infant. "Someday, I swear you will have my name!"

"And the mother?" Henry asked.

The midwife looked toward the floor and then at another woman that silently slid through the door and closed it.

"Dammit woman! Answer me!" Lord Rockfort hissed in anger.

Only the cold wind blowing outside responded.

Finally the old woman spoke.

"I am sorry my Lord. She was so young and so weak. She breathed her last bringing this little one into the world."

Lord Rockfort handed her the child and burst through the bedroom door. On the bed lay a beautiful young woman, the perspiration drying on her face. There was no breathing. But her beauty was still unmistakable, despite the difficulty of the birth.

Henry dropped to his knees beside the bed and buried his face on her breast.

"What will I do without you?" he whispered. "What will we do?"

"The child requires a name," the midwife spoke from the doorway.

"Record his name as Henry Rockfort, the Ninth Duke of Kensington," Henry replied.

"Do you think that is wise?" Bernard asked from the safety of the main room. Henry's temper was well known.

"He is my son!" Henry resounded.

"I understand," Bernard said gently.

"What can I do and where am I to take him?" Henry replied. "He cannot stay here. Beatrice will have him killed if I am away!"

Bernard thought for a moment.

"Do you remember the Battle of Sole Bay?" Bernard asked quietly.

"How could I forget that bloody hell?" Henry replied. "As part of the Kings Battalion, we were forced to combine with the Coldstream Guards to achieve victory!"

"I was not thinking of just the battle," Bernard said again as he stared into the fire, closed his eyes and reopened them. He took another drink of rum in an attempt to drive away the screams and anguish of men dying in battle.

"Do you remember stepping in front of the pistol and taking the ball that was destined for me?"

"How can I forget," Henry said as he rubbed his left shoulder. "I have a constant reminder."

"You saved my life and it is now time for me to make good on that debt," Bernard said. "I propose that I take the child and raise him as a high servant. I will see that he is well educated and trained for a trade, just in case your inheritance does not fall to him. You can see him any time you wish!"

"The child is hungry," Henry observed.

"I have a wet nurse at my estate," Bernard said. "He will be well taken care of."

"You would do this for this child? My bastard?" Henry asked.

Words failed him.

"Yes," Bernard replied. "And I would do this for my honorable friend that saved my life."

Henry nodded his thanks.

"Let it be so," Henry said. "The new Henry Rockfort, Ninth Duke of Kensington will be raised at Norfolk Castle."

The two men shook hands. The fate of the child had already been decided and was in motion.

Chapter 2

"It would be nice to say the rich people, the fancy people, all behaved like bastards and the poor slobs all came through like heroes. But as a matter of fact, sometimes the poor slobs behave like slobs and the great, noble, privileged characters come off very well, indeed."

Walter Lord

The walls of Norfolk Castle stood against the icy winter wind as it had for centuries. Norfolk Castle was the site of one of several original Roman forts constructed to hold Calvary as a defense against Saxon raids up the rivers of the east and south coasts of southern Britain, also known as the *Saxon Shore*. The Howard family inherited the property when the First Duke of Norfolk was cited for bravery in defense of his king during what would later be dubbed as *The War of Roses.*

The final victory went to a claimant of the Lancastrian party, Henry Tudor who defeated the last Yorkist king, Richard III at the Battle of Bosworth Field. After assuming the throne as Henry VII, Henry Tudor married Elizabeth of York, the eldest daughter and heiress of Edward IV thereby uniting the two claims. The House of Tudor would rule England and Wales until 1603.

The inside of the castle, for the wealthy, was a stark contrast to the poor servant's quarters in the lower rear of the castle. The main quarters were rich with draperies, statues, and suits of armor. Beautiful pictures and tapestries decorated the walls. One painting in particular was of Lord Leitermon, an unlucky Captain in the Yorkist army. He was captured at the Battle of Bosworth Field. He was taken to London, beheaded, drawn, and quartered. Afterwards, his remains were placed on display for all to see. All that bore the name of Leitermon had a price placed on their head and a sentence of death. Their lands were forfeit to the crown and avoiding death became their constant companion. Many fled to Ireland. Others fled to the New World. The Howard family had a lineage that traced back to the Leitermon family, a fact that was kept secret, except for this old painting.

The carriage belonging to Lord Bernard Howard pulled through the main gate and the driver prepared to pull directly in front of the main entrance to allow his Lord and the old woman carrying a small infant to disembark.

Lord Howard rapped on the top of the carriage with his cane. The top of the cane was solid ivory with a touch of gold.

"Peter, be a good fellow and pull to the rear entrance of the castle," Lord Howard said.

The driver immediately passed the main entrance and took the longer road that would take them to the rear of the castle. There, Lord Howard and the old woman disembarked with the baby sputtering his disgust at the cold weather.

Once again, Lord Henry used his cane, this time to rap on a somewhat incongruous door that led to the quarters of unmarried female servants. The door was answered, by a young woman of about twenty years of age. She immediately dropped her eyes when she saw Lord Howard.

"My Lord," she said as she managed a slight curtsy. "What brings you to our poor door at this hour?"

"I have a special task for you," Lord Howard replied. "This child needs someone to feed it and raise it as if it were their own. I know your baby died in childbirth just a few days ago."

"Yes, my Lord," the young woman replied sadly. "He was so small it was not meant to be."

"Perhaps God has sent you another," Bernard said quietly as he took the baby from the midwife and handed the child to her. The baby, feeling the warmth of her skin, immediately began searching for a breast upon which to feed.

"He is starving," she exclaimed. "Of course I will take care of him."

"Very well," Lord Howard replied. "Nobody must ever know this was not your child!"

He produced six gold guineas from his pocket. He gave two each to the young woman, the elderly midwife, and the driver.

"Take her back to her home," Lord Howard told his driver as he motioned toward the midwife.

"Listen to me, all of you," Lord Howard said sternly. "This child is my repayment for death atonement! Do all of you understand what that means?"

Everyone murmured his or her assent.

"Tonight never happened."

His voice was low and stern. "If anyone breathes a word of this evenings events, I will personally see them horsewhipped naked in front of the castle. Does everyone understand?"

Then he turned toward the young woman, the baby now greedily feeding against the young breast.

"Ellen, perhaps this will help you overcome your grief," Bernard whispered tenderly. "I must go now. Perhaps I will come to see you again in a few weeks? By the way a special friend of mine may want to visit the child from time to time. Would that upset you?"

"That would be fine, my Lord," Ellen said as she managed a half curtsy.

"There, it's all settled," Lord Howard, replied as he touched the brim of his hat. "Oh, here. Let me remove the locket from the blanket. It is part of his birthright. I'll keep it until he is old enough to have it. Good evening!"

Ellen watched him climb back into the carriage that would take the old midwife home. She was certain it would drop him off at the front entrance. It drove off into the blinding snow.

Ellen stopped for a moment and watched him go as the snow built up on her hair and the baby's blanket.. This was the best that life could offer a woman of her young age. Being the servant in a great house was much better than freezing in a thatch cottage.

"Good evening for you, Lord Howard," she whispered bitterly. "Especially since me' dead child was your bastard, my Lord!"

She closed the door against the wind and blinding snow and scuttled back to her quarters as Henry Rockfort, the Ninth Duke of Kensington continued to greedily drink his fill at her breast.

Chapter 3

"A baby is something you carry inside you for nine months, in your arms for three years, and in your heart until the day you die."

Mary Mason

Seasons passed. At the age of three, young Henry knew naught of his plight or his somewhat controversial birth. All he knew was comfort in the arms of his new mother, Ellen Jennings. Lord Howard was right. Henry had become her child.

Something changed within Lord Howard the evening he handed the crying infant to her. He no longer came to the servant quarters to satisfy his needs. The servants that attended his Lordship and her Ladyship told a different story. It was the story of a man that had come to realize and treasure that which he had. His wife, Lady Sarah, the Duchess of Norfolk, learned to accept her husband's advances, and according to some servants that heard them making love behind the thick walls, reported that she seemed to enjoy it.

Lady Sarah had become somewhat sickly within the past few weeks and Lord Howard sent to London for the finest physician to tend to his wife. The couple was now almost inseparable, except for business events that took him abroad infrequently.

This evening, as Lord Howard read the *London Gazette,* sipping a glass of Cognac, the Butler presented the doctor to him.

"May I present Doctor Ashcroft sir?" the First Footman said, with a somewhat nasal annunciation.

"Of course," Lord Howard replied. "Doctor, may I offer you some refreshment? Tea or would you prefer something stronger?"

"No, I am fine," Doctor Ashcroft, replied as he waved him off. "I must return to London. Your wife is fine, Lord Howard and her situation will be resolved in about seven months, as close as I can tell."

"What do you mean, seven months?" Lord Howard asked.

"I mean sir, your wife is approximately 2 months pregnant," Doctor Ashcroft replied with a smile. "If all goes well, you will be a father soon! Now sir, if you will excuse me?"

Doctor Ashcroft was taken aback as the ever strict and proper Lord Howard rushed past him, to the staircase, taking the stairs two at a time until he burst through his wife's door.

"Is it true?" Bernard asked Sarah. "Are you with child?"

"I am," Lady Howard replied with a laugh. "It would seem my dear that *you* finally got it right!"

Chapter 4

"Friends are the siblings God never gave us."

Mencius

It was spring of 1688. Two friends walked through the open field. The dark-red Helleborine, or English Iris flower, that would soon peak during June were already starting to meld with the other wildflowers. Lord Howard watched his wife as she laughed with young Ellen who desperately tried to keep up with Henry. He was already showing the stubborn side of his personality.

The elder Lord Henry Rockfort chuckled as he watched his son climb a rock fence and promptly tumble over the other side to land on his buttocks. Ellen ran to him. Of course he was fine. Lady Howard laughed as she held young Elizabeth, born just last September, now seven months old.

"You can't keep up with him Ellen," she cried as the younger woman grasped the boy's arm and lifted him over the rock fence.

"Beggin' the Lady's pardon," Ellen sputtered. "But you'll be doing the same in a short'!"

"They all do seem to get along well, don't you think," Lord Rockfort observed.

"They do indeed," Lord Howard, said to Lord Rockfort as he watched the ladies and children before him. "Ellen has done quite well since we made her the new Governess. This also gives me the opportunity to watch over young Henry in greater capacity! He can be hard to keep up with. He has his father's sense of recklessness and his temper."

"Will he be schooled then?" Lord Rockfort asked.

"Of course," Lord Howard replied, as he placed his arms behind his back and interlocked his fingers. "Remember my promise?"

"I do, old friend, and you have repaid me a thousand times over," Lord Rockfort said quietly. "It has been difficult since my eldest son passed away last year and my wife is simply not herself. The physician has already told us she will not bear any more children. I hope the time will come when Henry will be named my heir!"

"Then let us make certain your heir is the best nobleman a bastard can become," Lord Howard said as he placed a hand on his friend's shoulder. "In addition to mathematics, Latin, French, and of course the English language, he will thoroughly master the finer arts of the sword, musket, and pistol, as well as military theory and history."

"Are we making him a soldier then?" Lord Howard asked, noting young Henry had stopped to look at Elizabeth and gently tough her cheek. Although Henry had just turned four, Henry he had become Elizabeth's protector. Henry looked up at Sarah Howard and smiled.

"Together, we will make him a man's man and able to take whatever this world throws at him," Lord Howard said quietly as he observed the two children. "I do not believe his life will be an easy one."

Chapter 5

"You will never do anything in this world without courage. It is the greatest quality of the mind next to honor."

Aristotle

A little over five years passed. Henry and Elizabeth, christened Lizzie by Henry were almost inseparable. Henry was now nine and Lizzie seven. Lizzie had her Mother's dark features with dark reddish brown hair that fell down her shoulders and unusual brown eyes that seemed to snap at someone if she was angry. Henry had his father's stocky build and was beginning to grow stronger. With the help of Lord Howard's gamesman, a former ships captain and marksman in His Majesty's service, Henry had become an excellent shot with the Flintlock musket and the Flintlock pistol. Although the rifle would only shoot around one hundred fifty feet and the pistol less than that, both were dangerous weapons in the hands of a *musketeer*.

Learning to master the sword proved much more difficult. Although the old master used a round stick of an appropriate size for Henry's youth to practice, Henry was always bruised. He soon realized that if he were to win someday against his master, it would have to be of his own doing.

Henry remained Lizzie's constant protector and companion. When one of the male servant children pushed her to the ground over a confrontation with his hand carved horse toy, Henry promptly bloodied the lad's nose and strictly informed him if he chose to touch Lizzie again, that Henry would cut off his balls and throw them down the well. The boy believed him and the girls tittered. The lad never played close to Lizzie again.

Henry excelled in mathematics, geometry and military history. His French was passable, but would never have Lizzie's unique mastery of the language. Lizzie also excelled in playing the harpsichord, a trait Henry found admirable in her, but was not something he was interested in learning.

They were on holiday with Lord Howard and her Ladyship in London. Lizzie loved the theater and expressed a desire at her early age to become an actress, something her father quickly discouraged. Actresses were considered little more than common whores and looked down on by the more genteel public, once their show was completed.

British theatres were closed by Parliament in 1642, and did not officially reopen until King Charles II returned to the throne in 1660. Actresses were introduced to the public stage for the first time, and moveable scenery arranged in perspective. Audiences went to the new indoor theatres, initially in converted tennis courts, to meet their friends, show off their clothes, flirt and catch up on the latest gossip. For a few extra pennies they could even sit on the stage. The arts were returning to London!

Lord Howard gave the children a few pence for them to run down to a local merchant for a treat. Chocolate and coffee were discovered by the British in the 1600s, and were brought in from a Turkish merchant around 1650. Since then, adults and children alike enjoyed treats made from this new sweetened food, as well as desserts with a new chocolate twist.

As the children rushed to the merchant and turned the corner, Lizzie collided with one of two men that were leaving with some staple goods under their arm. The taller and better dressed of the two turned in an instant, expecting to see an assailant. Instead he saw a young girl. His comrade grabbed Lizzie by the arm.

"Here now! Best be watching where you are going little wench!" he said with a sneer. "I've got a good mind to take ye' behind this 'ere building and teach you some manners and maybe a good bit more!"

He pulled on Lizzie's arm and was immediately surprised as a well-placed fist from Henry plunged into the man's genitals causing immediate pain and anguish. He turned the girl loose, while Henry stepped in between her and the men.

Henry couldn't help but notice, the taller man was unusually dressed, but seemed to be well dressed for his profession. He was obviously a mariner, due to the stripes in his breeches. He also wore a tri-point hat with a long ostrich feather, a pure white linen shirt, and large jackboots. His jerkin actually had buttons for closure, another sign of wealth. He wore a large wide sword belt that hung from his right shoulder to his left hip that held the largest cutlass Henry had ever seen. He was certain the braid surrounding the sharkskin wrapped handle was gold. In the belt around his waist was a brace of new flintlock pistols. On his other side was a double brace of powder, one for filling the barrel and a much more fine powder for arming the frizzen pan of the weapons.

He laughed as his partner stepped forward to reach for young Henry. The man was surprised when his well-dressed companion produced a small dirk and pressed it at his comrade's throat.

"Nevel, have you forgotten what it was like to be young?" the man asked. "You are as usual, a perfect ass. Uh, pardon me young lady. We are a bit coarse, having just put in from the sea!"

Lord Howard had now stepped to his daughter's side.

"What is the meaning of this sir?" Lord Howard asked as he grasped Elizabeth and pulled her to him. He then gasped as he took in the man's persona. He knew who and what he was.

"Nothing sir," the man replied. "A mere misunderstanding. That's all! A childhood mistake!"

Two young soldiers appeared on the scene, rifles raised and bayonets ready.

"Is there trouble afoot?" the eldest asked.

"None sir," Lord Howard said. "I was just passing the day with an old friend of mine from my days in the military."

"Lord Howard," the soldier exclaimed. "A thousand pardons sir!"

And then to the youngest, "This is Lord Howard you idiot, not some common swill!"

Lord Howard shook hands with both men noting the mariner had removed his left hand from its threatening position on the butt of the right pistol.

"No harm done," Lord Howard said as he dismissed them.

The two made their exit quickly so as not to make their blunder even more noticeable.

"I am in your debt sir," the mariner stated as he swept off his hat and bowed to Lord Howard. "Not all of us from the sea are the devils we are depicted."

He then turned his attention to young Henry who was now wide eyed.

"Lad, you're a strong one and a brave one. You've got the

devils fight in ya, that's for sure," he said lowly. "But remember it takes great courage to kill a man. It often takes greater courage to be merciful and spare his life. If you ever need anything, go to the docks and tell them you are a friend o' Captain Jack Marsh. You will be well treated!"

Captain Marsh placed his hat back on his head.

"Well come on Nevel, you snivellin' shite! Bested by a young boy! The crew will sing of that for the next fortnight!"

Captain Marsh stopped, reached in his pocket, removed a coin and handed it to Henry.

"Do not spend it lad. Save it for the time whence ye' be needin' it! This be the calling card of Captain Jack Marsh and is known from the East Indies to the Americas!"

And with that, the two disappeared into the crowd, headed for the docks.

Henry opened his hand and looked at the coin. It was a silver Spanish *peso de ocho* or Spanish dollar, also known as a piece of eight. One slice of the piece of eight was missing, the calling card of Captain Jack Marsh. He held it tight as the heavens darkened for yet another storm. The clock of fate had once again ticked forward for Henry Jennings.

Chapter 6

"Sword and mind must be united. Technique by itself is insufficient, and spirit alone is not enough."

Yamada Jirokichi

"Dammit boy, parry, thrust, slide the foot and thrust again!" the old man said as he solidly whacked young Henry with the makeshift wooden training sword.

They had long since given up on simple sticks. They were now training with as close to a real sword in weight and size as they could without endangering Henry's life. A resounding whack across Henry's ribcage reminded him of the importance of parry and block.

"Dammit!" Henry exploded. "Mr. Simon, that was not fair!"

Simon Ludsthorp smiled and leaned forward on one end of his makeshift sword.

"Lord Howard wants me to teach ya' the proper British way of handlin' the Heavy English Calvary Sword," Simon said thoughtfully as he wiped the perspiration from his brow. "With your style, if it were me, I'd be teachin' ya another style. Your technique is not bad, but you lack the rhythm. Swordplay should flow, almost like a dance. How can ya' expect to be beatin' a man such as ye' and the young Miss Howard met in London. These men are trained and kill for the pure pleasure of killing. Lord Howard told me what he gave you. Do not ever think of using it lad. That piece of eight would be your ruination. What you be needin' is something to shoot for, a prize in the making. Come with me. I want to show you something."

"Where are we going?" Henry asked doubtfully.

"To my quarters at the back of the castle," Simon said. "I have not shared this with anyone before, except a few that did not live to talk about it!"

They walked to a small one-room cottage at the edge of the property next to a grove of trees. Simon opened the door.

"Well, come in!" Simon said coarsely. "No use standing outside!"

Henry stepped inside the small one room cottage. It was immaculate. Clothing was folded neatly and the few furnishings in the cottage were placed neatly and with purpose.

"Come on boy! We don't have all day!" Simon said again. "There we go. Now that's a good lad!"

He reached under the bed and removed a large wooden box that was about four feet long and 6 inches tall. The seal of England was burned into the center.

The older man sat on the bed, placed the box on his knees, gently caressed the seal of England on the top of the box and lifted the latch. Henry's breathed a sigh of disbelief. Inside was the most beautiful sword he had ever seen. The box lining was red velvet and under the sword was a black baldric with frogs to hold the scabbard. It was obvious the sword was to be used with the baldric over the right shoulder and down to the left waist.

"Go ahead lad," Simon whispered. "Ye can touch it."

Henry gently reached for the hilt of the sword and withdrew his hand.

"I said, reach for it. Remove it!" Simon insisted.

Henry complied and carefully removed the weapon from the box with both hands and then withdrew the sword from the sheath. The beautiful sword was made in the gothic style with a lion's head pommel and back strap. The solid bowl guard was pebbled to create the illusion of negative space, and in the center was a crown and fouled anchor. The sword knot slot in the guard had been rounded to allow the Navy cord knot to pass through. A very nice touch was the folding rear part of the guard, which latched into a stud on the gilt brass top piece of the scabbard. This latching system is requisite for a Naval officer side arm especially onboard during a gale. The white fish skin grip was wrapped with gilt wire to complete the gold (gilt) hilt.

"It is beautiful!" Henry exclaimed.

"Yes lad, she is a piece of work and the best balanced blade ever given," Simon said again. "It was a gift to me by His Majesty Charles II, when his brother James II was the *Lord High Admiral* during the Anglo-Dutch War. It was an honor for my bravery in battle. It was much better coming from His Majesty, than from his brother *James the shit!*"

Henry turned the shining thirty-one and one-half inch blade in his hand and said, "This would be something worth fighting for!"

"Learn your lessons well lad," Simon said. "And she will be yours some day. It is the sword of a Captain!"

"Perhaps someday, I may be a Captain!" Henry said.

"Lad, I can tell you that some day you will be all that and more," Simon replied.

"Then I need to practice," Henry said through pressed lips as he gently slid the sword back into its sheath and placed it into the box. "Show me how to parry again!"

Chapter 7

"Poetry spills from the cracks of a broken heart, but flows from one which is loved."

Christopher Paul Rubero

The spring of 1700 brought many changes. At sixteen, Henry was beginning to obtain much of his adult strength, height, and features. He kept his hair a little long as was the custom and often tied it up in the back with a piece of ribbon. Lizzie was beginning to show the features of adult womanhood as she approached her thirteenth birthday. Her hair had grown long and the promise of a young woman's beauty had begun to appear. Henry and Lizzie often took quiet walks on the grounds and to the fields and forests beyond. They remained inseparable.

Lord Howard watched these interludes with sadness, knowing it was a friendship that must never be allowed to grow beyond that which it was. Henry was in every way a gentleman and Lord Howard knew that as long as Lizzie was in Henry's company, no harm would come to her.

Still it would soon be time for Lord Howard to name Elizabeth's husband. As he had told Henry's father, so many years prior, it was their responsibility to marry well, to increase their lands and wealth. Lord Rockfort was not yet in a position to announce Henry's potential inheritance and might never be able to do so, if the political winds did not shift in England. As a bastard he would still never be welcome in polite society. The best he could hope for was the daughter of a well-to-do merchant. There was still time, but it was growing short. With the early death of Lord Rockfort's wife in 1698, the lack of an heir was plaguing him and it was beginning to appear as if the title, lands, property, and money would pass to his nephew upon his death.

Lord Howard had already begun to explore alternatives and

had settled on the son of the French Duke of Mortemart. The Rochechouart family was well known and furthering a liaison between France and Britain met with the wishes of the current monarch, King William III. His goal was to further strengthen the bond between the two countries in their mutual battle against the Dutch and the Dutch East India Company, who had mutilated the British fleet some thirty years prior. Certainly currying the favor of the King, while increasing the wealth of the family was doubly endearing. Although the son, Pierre Clovis Rochechouart, was seventeen years older than his daughter, and he had notoriety for frequenting gambling houses, as well as houses of soiled doves, he would still make an appropriate and politically correct husband for his daughter.

The two Dukes had been in contact by letter and Lord Howard had paid the Duke of Mortemart a visit at his home in the French border province of Corsica. The marriage arrangements were nearly solidified.

However on this beautiful day, neither Henry nor Lizzie knew of these arrangements as they walked hand-in-hand through the fields teeming with Cornflower, Foxglove, Wild Carrot, and Corn Chamomile. At one point, Henry stopped, picked some leaves of the Chamomile, crushed it between his fingers and handed it to Lizzie. She smelled them, first gingerly and then when a smile crossed her face she plucked a few leaves and placed them into her pocket to put in a cup in her room.

"Oh Henry!" she exclaimed. "You do know just about everything!"

Henry laughed swaggered, puffed up like a young peacock and plucked a purple flower to place it behind her right ear.

"You know in some cultures in the warmer islands, it is customary for a proper single girl to wear a flower behind her right ear," he teased.

"You are just making that up," Lizzie said, feigning indifference, but secretly delighted with the attention.

"No, it is true!" Henry insisted. "Mister Ludsthorp has told me stories of places he has seen and been as a young man, before he joined the Royal Navy! He says in the Polynesian Islands, there is a large island called Tahiti. The first European to arrive in Tahiti was Spanish explorer Juan Fernández in his expedition of 1577. He has been there and the women were beautiful, scantily dressed, and with long dark hair!"

"Oh, and I am sure the *scantily dressed* caught your attention, my dear Henry," Lizzie said again, this time feigning a little hurt, but at the same time wondering what Henry really thought when he heard the story.

For a moment, she felt just a tinge of what would have become jealousy, had she allowed it. She could tell Henry wasn't that interested and the feeling subsided.

"Oh, my dear Henry," she exclaimed. "Do tell me why I love you so!"

"Because I love you," Henry replied. "And I'll gladly beat the living shite, uh sorry, stuffing out of any lad that dares to take liberties with you!"

They had reached the tree line to the forest and she ran

behind a large Yew tree almost ten feet in girth, obviously quite old, perhaps a remainder of the last true Ice Age. Lizzie ran behind it.

"Bet you can't catch me!" she exclaimed.

"I bet I can," Henry replied as he ran first left, then right.

Lizzie shot from the tree back out into the open field with Henry right behind her. She had lifted her dress just a little, so as to not become entangled in it. It failed to work. Her shoe caught in the hem and down she went, landing on her side and then rolling onto her back. Henry was unable to stop and had to fall beside her to keep from stepping on top of her.

They both lay laughing in the tall grass. Lizzie's face had taken on a flushed look, with the laughter and excitement of the moment. Henry finally rolled onto his side, sat up on one elbow and stared down at her. For a moment, they both stopped laughing and became sober.

"Ah, Lizzie," Henry exclaimed. "If I could, I would give you the world!"

"I already have the world, my dear Henry," she said as she gently caressed the side of his face with one hand, feeling the stubble that had already began to creep into his face that afternoon.

"My darling Henry," Lizzie insisted. "My dearest friend and companion!"

She sat up on her elbow as well and with a quickness that belied her sex, her age, and her proper upbringing, kissed him quickly on the mouth. She jumped up, laughing again and ran in the direction of the castle, leaving a happy, dumfounded and surprised Henry who finally caught up with her a full half minute later.

Chapter 8

"One life is all we have and we live it as we believe in living it. But to sacrifice what you are and to live without belief, that is a fate more terrible than dying."

Joan of Arc

The summer of 1703 was indeed the turning point in the lives of Henry and Lizzie. The life they had known would never be the same again.

This particular evening, Lord Howard had consumed far too much port and was quite tipsy. He and his wife Sarah retired to the drawing room where Bernard continued with an additional glass.

Lady Howard had begun to chastise her husband.

"Why must Elizabeth marry this boor from France?" she exclaimed. "You know as well as I do, there is only one man that she has eyes for and I believe you know who it is!"

"You know that is quite impossible," Lord Howard harrumphed. "Even if my dear friend did declare Henry his rightful heir, he is still a bastard, and as such, unfit to wed our daughter!"

Lord Howard had long ago sworn his wife to secrecy and the secrets surrounding Henry's birth had been revealed to Lady Howard.

"Must all marriages be arranged?" Lady Howard replied.

"Dammit woman!" Lord Howard exclaimed. "It is done! Pierre Clovis Rochechouart will be Elizabeth's new husband. He arrives day after tomorrow for them to start becoming acquainted!"

"Very well," Sarah said icily. "But it will be a long time before you share my bed again!"

"My dear, it is the way of all things in our world," Lord Howard said. "In time, Henry will heal and forget. I plan to send his away shortly to finish his education. I anticipate France will give him the added outlook he needs to learn his place in this world and where he will fit in."

"You are creating a monster, my dear," Lady Howard replied. "If he cannot fit in here, or at his father's, he will be doomed to be an outcast; neither Lord nor commoner."

Lord Howard frowned. She was quite right. This was not the peace he had offered his old comrade. He turned toward the window.

"I will speak with his father," Lord Howard continued. "As a widower now, with no legal heir, he may be in a position to step outside the bounds of common decency and declare the boy his son and heir."

"Perhaps?" Lady Howard replied angrily. "You play with the lives of people as if they are nothing but puppets to satisfy you own foolish desires! Damn your decency sir!"

"Perhaps when he returns from France, I will purchase him a commission in Her Majesty's service," Lord Howard replied, ignoring his wife's outburst. "That may give him the station he deserves and an opportunity for a better life!"

"Perhaps," Sarah said sadly. "Or an early grave!"

Chapter 9

"As iron is eaten away by rust, so the envious are consumed by their own passion."

Antisthenes

At the age of eighteen, Henry had achieved his true adult height, weight, and strength. He had advanced past the skills of his master in rifle, pistol, and sword. Although not extremely tall, Henry had an air about him now. Like many young men, he tended to swagger a little. He could be quick tempered where matters of honor were concerned. He knew it was almost time for him to step out on his own. When he did so, he wanted Lizzie as his wife.

Dare he hope? Lord Howard had long since treated him as if he were his own son, despite what he perceived to be his lowly birth. He wanted to ask for Lizzie's hand, but in his heart of hearts he knew it would never be granted. However, like all young people, as long as there was life, there was hope and this was what he hoped for.

Today, he and Lizzie was horseback riding on the commons, an innocent enough outing. Lizzie packed a small picnic lunch for them and they rode to their Yew tree at the edge of the forest. Their intimacy had progressed slowly from Lizzie's quick, innocent kiss, to holding hands, gentle hugs and finally kisses of passion that stopped before their mutual desire got so far out of control that neither of them could stop it.

On every outing, they talked for hours, enjoying the simplicity of each other's company. Nobody was certain what he or she talked about. Some thought it was simply sharing the day. Other servants had seen them in tight embrace, but valued their position enough to know when to keep one's mouth closed.

On more than one occasion, Ellen tried to talk to Henry about Lizzie and the impossibility of their potential relationship, but

Henry refused to listen to the woman he believed was his mother. Ellen has been sick for a couple of weeks and was now improving. Henry attended to her whenever possible and bestowed on her all of the grace and love a son could offer a mother. Ellen continued to insist he was making a mistake and Henry refused to believe it.

Today was no different. Their horses were loosely tethered to the boughs of the large Yew tree from which sprang their first bout of physical intimacy.

Today Lizzie wore a simple light peach gown, sturdy enough for horseback riding, yet delicate and endearing. As usual she wore the latest style clothing.

Drawing inspiration from classic Greek and Roman statuary (all things ancient Greece were the rage at this time) the well to do allowed for column dresses with minimal flouncing. Where once layers of hoops and petticoats reined, now almost modern dress shape took over. Waists were raised to just under the bosom while skirts hung free. Modern underwear was yet to be invented. Under the dress, Lizzie wore only her chemise, with a ribbon tied under her bosom to provide enhancement, and nothing else.

Lizzie had a large checked tablecloth spread on the ground with a sumptuous bounty of roast beef, bread, and other items quietly retrieved from the kitchen when the servants were not looking.

Their fare was quite simply, a piece of beef between two slices of bread, a style becoming more and more prominent in the gambling houses of the day and one that would later be attributed as the "sandwich" by the Earl of Sandwich around 1729.

After eating, and consuming a small bottle of wine, Lizzie sat on the large tablecloth and Henry lay on the ground with his head in her lap.

"I think it's time to ask," Henry said, breaking the lighthearted mood of the moment.

"My dear Henry," Lizzie replied as she stroked the side of his face. "Nothing would please me more than to be your wife, but father will never allow it!"

"Perhaps not," Henry said. "But we will never know until we ask."

Henry sat up suddenly, and pulled her to her feet. He dropped to one knee and said, "If we are going to do this, then we will do it right!"

Henry pulled something from the pocket of his jerkin. It was a small ring, one that he had been saving his meager earnings to obtain for over two years.

Henry took her hand.

"Sarah Elizabeth Howard, would you do me the honor of becoming my wife?" Henry asked, his voice full of confidence.

Ah yes, what are the things that drive a woman to love? To be cherished and loved like to no other, to have someone listen to her when she needs someone to listen and not to fix. Most women want a man that is confident in themselves and the world around them. That combined with physical and financial security completed the package. Henry could and did meet all of these needs, except for currently the financial one, but that could easily be fixed with one word from her father. She knew she was not a possession. She was a cherished component of his life.

Had he not always been there for her? Any time there was need, or danger afoot, Henry her protector, saw to it she came to no harm. She still remembered falling through the ice on the large pond in front of their property when she was eight. Just as her tiny hands were freezing and she was slipping under the water, Henry's strong arms had pulled her from certain death, all the while screaming for help. Her father had responded, grappling Henry by the ankles to pull them both to safety. She was taken in to warm in the safety of the house and to be attended to by the servants. Poor Henry had to march soaked and freezing to Ellen who held him against her in front of the fire, while she silently cursed her lowly birth and the aristocratic society in which they lived.

All of these things ran through her mind with the speed of an eagle in flight. Yet she knew the answer immediately.

"Yes," she whispered. "A thousand times yes!"

Henry slipped the ring on her finger. It would be quite small compared to those of other women of her status. But it came complete with the gift of love and sacrifice.

"It is beautiful Henry," Lizzie whispered. "It must have cost you a lifetime of earnings."

"Money is nothing," Henry replied. "That is, unless you have none and then it can become horribly important."

"When do we tell father?" she asked.

"I will talk to him tonight!" Henry exclaimed.

"Wait, I will try to talk to Mother first. Perhaps she can influence over him," Lizzie insisted.

"Very well," Henry said.

Lizzie sat back onto the tablecloth.

"Sit with me, my husband to be!" she exclaimed.

Henry complied and soon she lay in his arms as a cooling wind caused the leaves of the Yew tree to dance back and forth.

"Do you remember when we were younger and used to come up here?" Henry asked.

"Of course I do," Lizzie replied. "This is our magic place. When I was a young girl, I used to believe that as long as we could reach our magic place, the rest of the world could never find us and we were the only two people to ever find it. It was a secret, one known only to us, and to no one else. Do you remember the night we slipped away and lay here under the stars?"

"Of course I do," Henry said quietly. "Lying here beside you with the stars above is the closest I have ever come to heaven."

"I felt the same way," Lizzie replied. "For a moment, it was as if we were at sea and the entire sky met the waves around us. I have never had such a tranquil feeling!"

Her words were another foreshadowing.

"Do you remember when you kissed me for the first time, not twenty yards from here?" Henry asked.

"Of course I do," Lizzie laughed. "I had wondered what it would be like, well you know, to kiss you for the first time. You were always so gentlemanly, so blasted honorable, that I knew if anyone were to initiate that first kiss, that it would have to be me."

"I am sorry," Henry replied. "I wanted to, so many times. But I was afraid that my social status and the humbleness of my birth would in the end, cause you pain. So I did not allow myself to indulge in that one sweet moment. But, I thought of it often, wondering, even then, what it would be like to kiss those full young lips. But you were younger then and I did not want you to feel as if I had taken advantage of you!"

"And now?" Lizzie asked.

"The same," Henry replied.

Lizzie lay on her back.

"Then show me, my husband to be," Lizzie whispered again.

At first, Henry gently stroked her hair, looked into her eyes and for a moment saw his own reflection therein. He leaned forward, stopped, and continued until his lips touched hers. At first, it was just a small kiss, almost chaste. It began to grow in intensity.

Henry kissed her neck, gently pulled down the top of her bodice and began to explore the golden valley between her ample breasts. Lizzie pulled him closer and felt his hard maleness against her. She moaned as Henry slid his hand under her dress and her chemise and gently touched a secret gilded place. There, he gently slid his finger up the lips thereof until it met a slightly hardened and blood enriched hood. He gently pressed and she moaned, reaching for him.

The moment for which they had awaited was upon them. Henry kissed her harder and she responded fervently, her young passion equaling his own.

The sound of approaching hoof beats coming from the far base of the hill interrupted them as they quickly adjusted their clothing and Lizzie tried to hide the flush that had crept up into her face. The visitor was none other than Henry's weapon instructor, Simon Ludsthorp.

"His Lordship has requested your presence at the castle mum," Simon said. "You are expecting a visitor tomorrow and he wishes to speak with you this evening."

"Now?" Lizzie asked, her face still flushed.

"Aye lass," Simon responded. "His' Lordship rarely asks for something other than now. We will clean up here. Henry, help her onto her horse. That's a good lad!"

"We'll be along directly," Simon said as he dismounted.

The two men watched as Lizzie disappeared into the distance.

"Lad, are ye a damn fool?" Simon blurted. "All of the work that has been put into 'ye, to see ye swinging at the gallows for the takin' of an English Noblewoman!"

"I'm not sure what you mean," Henry said as he turned his back on his old master and began to pitch the remainder of their bounty into the tablecloth.

Even Simon noticed the spot where Lizzie buttocks had been, remained moist and stained upon the cloth. He only hoped her dress wasn't as stained.

"Tell me you didn't lad," Simon insisted. "Tell me you stopped!"

"What do you want to hear?" Henry shouted back. "That we are in love and that I almost made love to my woman? We would have been successful too, if it weren't for your untimely arrival!"

"Then God was surely with us all," Simon insisted. "She is not your class boy! Forget her!"

"To hell with England and her damned classes," Henry exclaimed. "I'm as good as any man in this country or anywhere else!"

"You must forget her lad," Simon insisted. "Tomorrow or the next day, Miss Elizabeth meets French nobleman Pierre Clovis Rochechouart, destined to become the Duke of Norfolk Castle. He is her intended husband and there is nothing you can do about it!"

Chapter 10

"Anger is an acid that can do more harm to the vessel in which it is stored than to anything on which it is poured."

Mark Twain

"Mother, is there nothing you can do?" Lizzie cried.

Her tears of anguish through the heavy wooden doors caused the servants outside to find other duties rather than be found within earshot.

"I have tried daughter," Sarah Howard said gently as she stroked her daughter's hair. "Your father will not be swayed!"

"I met Pierre Clovis Rochechouart over three years ago!" Lizzie cried again. He is too old and an ass to boot. He will never be the man Henry is!"

"But the marriage will unite our families and more than double the riches of both," her mother replied. "It is our duty to our ancestors and our heirs! It will also strengthen England's alliance with France. The king is pleased!"

"I won't marry him!" Lizzie insisted. "I will kill myself first!"

This time, Sarah stood and grabbed her daughter by her arm.

"Listen to me, young woman! We are bound by our duty! Do you think I loved your father when we married? No, I did not love him and I had to learn to do so, as did he with me! But I did my duty and I will continue to do my duty! Yes, Rochechouart is an absolute ass! But he will make a husband that will be accepted by nobility, which is what you require. If you can't enjoy his evening advances, then spread your legs, close your eyes and pretend it is young Henry that is making love to you. In time, I guarantee he will take young mistresses and his advances toward you will lessen, especially once you give him an heir. When he arrives, you **will** greet him and be sociable as befitting a lady of your status. You will flirt, without appearing to be a common whore, and you will sit with him, titter at his jokes, pretend not to notice when he breaks wind at the table, and otherwise maintain yourself as a lady!"

The older woman finally breathed.

"Elizabeth, don't make this any harder than it has to be!"

While Lizzie poured her heart out to her Mother, Henry asked for an audience with Lord Howard and was greeted warmly as he entered the library, which had become Lord Howard's inner sanctum, a place of retreat from the world.

"May I speak frankly with you sir?" Henry said evenly.

"Of course lad. Please have a seat," Lord Howard said. "Would you like a glass of Cognac? I find Cognac to be a very calming liqueur, don't you?"

"I'm sorry sir," Henry replied. "I don't often have the opportunity, but with your kind permission, I will have a glass."

Lord Howard carefully poured two glasses of Cognac and motioned to a horsehair couch against the wall.

"What may I do for you Henry?" Lord Howard asked. "You haven't gotten one of the village girls pregnant have you?"

"No sir," Henry replied. "This is about Lizzie, I mean Elizabeth."

"Oh," Lord Howard said. "Is Elizabeth alright?"

"Yes sir," Henry replied again. "Sir, you know Elizabeth and I have known each other for a very long time."

"Since her birth," Lord Howard said. "You have been like brother and sister since the beginning!"

"I wouldn't say brother and sister," Henry replied.

"Well, as close as you can be since you are not related by blood," Lord Howard interrupted.

"That is exactly what I want to discuss with you sir," Henry said. The blood was beginning to rise in his neck and face. Lord Howard was being directly obtuse.

"Then damn it boy," Lord Howard exclaimed. "Spit it out. What do you want with my Elizabeth?"

"I want to ask you for her hand in marriage," Henry replied testily.

"Dear God!" Lord Howard exclaimed. "Is this how you repay my generosity, the money I have put into your education, saving you from your lowly birth to that little whore of a Mother of yours to where you are now? Is this how you repay me?"

Henry stood to his feet.

"Sir, don't you ever speak of my Mother like that again," Henry said. "If she was a whore, it was of your making!"

"Damn your eyes!" Lord Howard replied as he slowly rose from the couch to face Henry.

The two now stood face to face. For the first time, Henry began to see the age that was creeping into Lord Howard's face.

For once, Henry smiled and turned toward the window.

"My Mother told me a secret on my fifteenth birthday. Do you like secrets, Lord Howard?" Henry asked.

"Sometimes, what do you mean?" Lord Howard replied.

"Oh, you know, the ugly little secrets of the nobility. The ones the servants tell behind your back. Stories of how the Lord of the House sometimes slips into the servants quarters, finds a young, untouched woman, and shall we say forces himself on her?" Henry said with a touch of devious anger in his voice.

"What do you mean?" Lord Howard replied, although this time a little less self-assured.

"I mean the story of a Duke that forced his way into a young servant girls room, made her strip off her clothes, watching as she did so, and then raped her again and again. This same Duke continued to do so until the girl became pregnant and after that he left her alone!" Henry said angrily.

"Then one night, another servant calls for him to bring a midwife. The Duke refuses, and in the process the young woman loses her child, that could have been saved. Stricken with grief she almost takes her life. That is until . . ." Henry said, stopping to add emphasis to his next statement.

"Until what?" Lord Howard whispered, the memories of the past returning to him.

"Until the Duke brings her another child and asks her to wet nurse it," Henry adds. "She does so, but the Duke doesn't count on the one thing that nobody considered."

"And what is that, boy?" Lord Howard whispered again.

"That perhaps she really would accept that child as her own, and raise it, watching it grow under the Duke's watchful eye, all the while alluding that . . ."

"Alluding to what?" Lord Howard questioned, growing irritated.

In fact, his anger was becoming apparent.

"That there might be another secret," Henry replied, lost as if in thought.

"What?"

"That the child given to her might not be of a lowly birth after all. Perhaps the child might be of noble birth or perhaps just the bastard of a nearby farmer. Who knows? I am certain the Duke would not want this story to become public as it might have an impact on his place in polite society. I think he might be willing to allow a young man of lowly birth to marry his daughter and embrace him as perhaps his brother's child. It is not unusual for cousins to marry is it? Do you have any idea who that Duke might be?" Henry asked.

"Are you blackmailing me sir?" Lord Howard asked.

"Of course not!" Henry replied. "How could I blackmail you with something that could not possibly be true. A man of noble birth, like yourself would never resort to such tactics, would you?"

Lord Howard began to laugh.

"You are good boy," Lord Howard said. "But you are a little too late. Already your commission in Her Majesty's Army has been paid. You will report for training to prepare for the upcoming battle against Spain."

This time Lord Howard laughed.

"My boy, I will see to it you are on the front lines!" he said. "After I see that little whore Mother of yours stripped and horsewhipped in front of the castle! You will never see Elizabeth again after you leave. Enjoy the thought that a French nobleman will be the one to bed her again and again. Carry those thoughts with you into battle!"

This time it was Henry's turn to smile.

"We will see about the matter with Lizzie. As to my Mother, you are a little late, you precocious bastard," Henry replied. "I took the liberty of giving her some money, not much by your standards, but enough to keep her comfortable for the rest of her life if she is frugal. And she is some place where you can never touch her again."

"Get out," Lord Howard said. "Pack your bags. You leave in three days!"

"Oh, one more thing," Lord Howard said as he turned his back. "Be prepared to meet Pierre Clovis Rochechouart tomorrow morning. I understand his carriage is in town."

Henry tossed off the remainder of the Cognac and turned the glass upside down on the expensive teak table.

"I shall look forward to meeting the French peacock!" Henry said.

Chapter 11

"There are two kinds of pride, both good and bad. 'Good pride' represents our dignity and self-respect. 'Bad pride' is the deadly sin of superiority that reeks of conceit and arrogance."

John C. Maxwell

Pierre Clovis Rochechouart exited through the left side of the carriage. His friend and subordinate in the French Navy, Ambroise Francois' Cartier opened the right door of the carriage, took one look at the castle, rolled his eyes and walked around the it to stand with his friend.

"My dear Pierre," Ambroise said, his voice reeking of arrogance. "Really, how could you marry a girl from *this*?"

"You have not seen the girl!" Pierre said lewdly. "She will make a wonderful trophy on my spear!"

Ambroise laughed and said, "My dear Pierre. You think they all look good upon your cock! That little whore at the Blue Light Tavern looked good too, until you were no longer under the influence of the wine!"

At that moment, Lord and Lady Howard walked arm-in-arm down the steps to the carriage. Elizabeth followed behind them.

"Lord Howard, so good to see you again," Pierre said. "May I introduce my good friend and travelling companion Ambroise Francois' Cartier?"

Ambroise stepped forward and bowed.

"At your service," Ambroise said as he took Sarah Howard's hand and delicately kissed it.

"May I introduce my daughter, Sarah Elizabeth Howard. I believe you met her a few years ago," Lord Howard said as he stepped to one side as Lizzie stepped forward and made a polite curtsy.

"A beautiful day to greet a beautiful woman," Pierre said as his eyes lasciviously took in Elizabeth's shapely young figure. Even Sarah Howard was taken aback.

"Shall we retire inside?" Lady Howard asked. "You must be tired from your journey!"

At that moment Henry rounded the garden and appeared in the main courtyard.

"And who might this fine young gentleman be?" Ambroise asked.

"This is Elizabeth's cousin," Lord Howard said quickly. "He is leaving us for military service, to join England and France as they prepare for war against Spain."

"Ah," Pierre said as he quickly sized up Henry. "Well boy, keep your head down and your legs closed. Else those Spanish bastards will shoot your balls from a hundred yards. Stick with your officers and listen to them. They will make certain you come home safely to your tavern wench, whoever she may be!"

"You will find I can hold my own against any man with a sword, pistol, or rifle," Henry replied sternly. "I assume you must be Pierre Clovis Rochechouart."

"You are well informed," Pierre replied as he pulled a lace handkerchief from the sleeve of his lace jacket and placed it over his nose.

"Forgive me," Pierre replied, feigning laughter. "An unpleasant odor seems to have arisen. You must be young Elizabeth's enchanted friend, of whom I have heard. Some day I must thank you for properly saving her for me."

His meaning was clear.

Henry wrinkled his brow and said, "Rochechouart is a very uncommon name. Wasn't your father killed during the *War of the League of Augsburg*? I understand he was such a coward that King Louis XIV personally pissed on his grave!"

Pierre stepped forward, hand on sword, and drew it halfway from the scabbard.

"Be careful boy," Ambroise said. "Pierre's anger is legendary, as are his skills with the sword and dueling pistols."

"Ye' may be findin' young Henry's skill is of equal or better," said a voice from behind Henry.

It was Simon Ludsthorp. In his right hand, he carried an English fouling piece. In his left, were a couple of large rabbits. The fouling piece was pointed in the general direction of Pierre where it was not an immediate threat to anyone, but could be deployed in almost any manner.

"And how would you know that," Pierre replied as he hastily sheathed his weapon.

"Because, I taught Henry most of what he knows as to armament and military history," Simon said. "We shan't go into yer family history. I am perhaps better acquainted with it than most."

"And?" Pierre said as he once again held the lace handkerchief to his nose.

"I was there," Simon said with a smile. "Remember it was King Louis XIV that put William III on the British throne. Would ya' like to continue the conversation sir, or drop it where we are at the moment."

"Simon," Lord Howard exclaimed. "You forget yourself sir!

This man is a guest in our home and betrothed to the future Duchess. You will not use my home as one of your tavern fighting pits."

Simon nodded.

"My apologies my Lord," Simon said. "I was only replying to the question I was given."

"And mine as well Sir," Pierre said. "Such is youth. I suspect some time in the military will curb his impertinence. Shall we move past it?"

"Indeed," Ambroise replied.

Pierre turned his attention to Henry.

"Speaking of curbing," Pierre said. "You seem to be a strong backed, if not a weak minded individual. Get my bags from the boot of the carriage if you please."

"Get your own damn bags," Henry replied curtly. "Remember? I must prepare to go to war!"

"Oh my dear Pierre," Ambroise whispered. "You are right. She is a fetching little piece. I wouldn't mind having her on my own spear had the opportunity presented itself!"

"Perhaps you shall, " Pierre said. "When she gives me an heir, I shan't care what becomes of her!"

Henry walked past the two of them, stopped and looked at Pierre. He dropped his head slightly toward Pierre's left shoulder before walking past.

"Do what you will," Henry whispered. "Don't ever cause any harm to befall her or I will kill you."

Chapter 12

"Why are women... so much more interesting to men than men are to women?"

Virginia Woolf

Pierre took Elizabeth by the hand as the two walked through the beautiful gardens he had turned his nose up at earlier during his arrival. They stopped amidst the eight-foot hedges. There was a long, stone slab bench there, perfect for resting.

This afternoon, Elizabeth wore a pearl white gown. Twice she removed her hand from Pierre's. Twice he reached out to take it, the last time jerking her arm and clasping her hand so tightly that she exclaimed in pain.

"Listen to me, my young little lady," Pierre said testily. "You might as well get used to the feel of me. You are going to feel me a great deal after we are married!"

"I despise you!" Elizabeth exclaimed. "You are a filthy human being, despite all of your fancy clothing. Do you not know what a bath is?"

"Bathing is a requirement only to the English," Pierre said gaily. "You need to get used to my smell. You will come to love it, to beg for it."

"I hardly think so," Elizabeth said as she turned away.

Pierre grabbed her arm and pulled her to face him.

"Oh, you will learn to love it and every inch of me, you little English bitch," Pierre insisted.

Elizabeth struggled in his grip.

"Let go of me!" Elizabeth exclaimed.

"I have more in mind for you, you sassy little whore!" Pierre said as he laughed. "Here, give me your hand. Touch it. Just touch it!"

Vomit rose in Elizabeth's throat.

"No," she exclaimed. "You vile person. You have no idea how to treat a woman!"

"Oh yes, my dear!" Pierre said excitedly, as he forced his lips onto hers.

Elizabeth moved left and right to keep him from kissing her.

"Hold still!" Pierre exclaimed. "I don't think I will wait until our wedding night! I'm going to take your maidenhood right now, if that lout of a servant boy hasn't already done so!"

Elizabeth struggled to release herself. Pierre slipped his hand under her dress and between her legs. He covered her mouth as he forced her onto her back against the stone slab seat. Elizabeth did the only thing she could. She bit him. He exclaimed in pain and anger. Elizabeth screamed frantically over and over.

Later she would say it had all happened so fast. Suddenly Pierre was forcibly removed from her and thrown into the hedges. Her father had appeared, almost out of nowhere, as had Simon, who was now toting a large Dragoon flintlock pistol.

Henry pummeled Pierre in the gut again and again and then switched to his face, watching in satisfaction as the man's lip split and then his nose broke.

"What is the meaning of this outrage?" Lord Howard cried.

Nobody paid any attention to him.

Henry gave Pierre another shake as he continued to beat him.

"I told you what would happen if you hurt her," Henry said through gritted teeth. "Now you die!"

"I hardly think so," Ambroise said. He had moved in seemingly from nowhere. His hand also had a large pistol. He aimed it at Henry.

"Let me show you what happens to an English ruffian that dares to strike a French subject!" Ambroise said as he deliberately raised the pistol.

"Aye, and let me show ye', what we do to French swine that threatens the life of my student," Simon said nonchalantly as he cocked the large pistol and placed the end of the barrel at the base of Ambroise's skull.

Pierre slowly stumbled to his feet. He had taken a terrible beating at the hands of Henry.

"I demand satisfaction," Pierre said with an ugly tone. "You, Henry, I demand we meet on the *Field of Honor* tomorrow morning."

"I accept your invitation," Henry replied.

"Boy," Simon said quietly. "Are you sure you know what you are doing? This man is a dueling expert and you have never taken life."

"A dueling virgin," Pierre said laughing. "I may be merciful and simply shoot you in the cock!"

"May I remind you again that this is my home and my wife and daughter are present," Lord Howard said sternly.

"My apologies Lord Howard," Pierre said with a sneer. "However, if I am to be part of your family, you may wish to adjust to my little eccentricities!"

"Ambroise, would you do me the honor of being my second," Pierre said.

Ambroise feigned indifference.

"Of course my dear friend," Ambroise said. "Not that there will be need."

Simon lowered his pistol.

"Lad, I'll be your second," Simon whispered. "He may choose the method of his satisfaction."

"Yes, my dear Henry," Pierre said. "Since there are so many pistols present today, it shall be dueling pistols at dawn tomorrow on the Commons."

"I will be there," Henry replied as he went to stand beside Elizabeth.

"Are you alright?" Henry asked her, his voice lowered.

"For the moment," Lizzie replied. "Oh, Henry, if something happens to you, I don't know what I will do!"

"I know what I will do," Lord Howard said sternly. "This marriage is off!"

"Tut tut, my dear Lord Howard," Pierre said merrily. "Do not rob your virgin daughter the opportunity to lie with a real man, not some peasant boy!"

"You insolent swine," Lord Howard replied.

He started to step forward, but his wife, who had appeared just behind Lord Howard, pulled him back.

"You will leave Castle Norfolk after your satisfaction has been completed," Lord Howard said. "No one treats my Elizabeth in this fashion. Damn your eyes and damn your money sir! My daughter is not some tavern wench to be taken at will!"

Henry wondered at this last statement, especially since Lord Howard had treated women thusly in his own youth.

Lord Howard looked into Henry's eyes and saw the conflict that was arising within him.

"I will be on the Commons as well, " Lord Howard replied.

He turned to Henry and whispered, "God's speed and a straight aim for you tomorrow, Henry."

Henry nodded as Sarah took Elizabeth toward the house.

"Bring a change of clothing boy! You may need to change after the event, if Pierre allows you to live," Ambroise said gaily. "Pierre has never lost a duel."

"Perhaps," Simon replied. "Duels are just like any other fight. If you have always won, you have picked them. Ya' didn't take them the way they came!"

Chapter 13

"I thoroughly disapprove of duels. If a man should challenge me, I would take him kindly and forgiving by the hand and lead him to a quiet place and kill him."

Mark Twain

Dawn began to creep in upon the Commons, illuminating the fog that seemed to be everywhere. The sun was rising, but it cut a dark contrast to the dark clouds on the horizon, a foretelling or foreshadowing that something ominous was about to take place.

Henry and Simon were the first to arrive. Simon squinted through the fog. Should someone decide to take satisfaction before the duel, they were very large targets.

"Listen to me lad," Simon said. "We don't have much time. He's going to try to press ye' into making a shite shot, where he'll have the advantage. Expect no quarter from him. There won't be any. If ye' miss, he'll kill you for sure. If ye' kill 'em, you may still be damned for killing a French nobleman. Do ya' see what I be tellin' ye'?"

"I understand," Henry replied. "Either way, I'm damned."

"Aye," the older man replied. "And remember, if he shoots and misses, and there is time, and no other threat, ye' should fire your weapon into the ground and let him live."

"Why?" Henry said.

"Lad, if ye' both fire at the same time, there's no issue. But if ye' wait, and he fires and misses, your honor will suffer if ye' kill 'em, even if that's best for us all, and it will be murder!"

"Alright," Henry said. "If he misses, I'll let the bastard live!"

"Good," Simon replied. "My job is to make certain yer' weapon is properly loaded and to help ye' with a doctor if one is needed. I also have me own backup, just in case these French bastards decide they don't have to play by English rules!"

Simon pulled back both sides of his long coat. Nestled and crossed at his back was a brace of pistols.

"Oh, I can assure ye' lad they are quite loaded," Simon said. "And ready for French blood if needed."

"Simon, if this doesn't work out the way we want it to, I want to thank you for being my friend and teacher these many years," Henry said earnestly.

"Ah," Simon replied. "Ye were a good student! My very best and with more heart than most hardened soldiers or sailors I have met. Ye will be fine lad. Just remember what I've always told ye. Look at the front sight as you raise the pistol. That is where the ball will go. This isn't target shooting."

"I will," Henry replied.

A carriage rolled up to the grassy knoll. Pierre Clovis Rochechouart and Ambroise stepped from it. Their servants stood by their side. Ambroise carried a wooden box with a pair of dueling pistols.

"I have already loaded these," Ambroise said with a sniff.

"As his second, I'll be the judge of that," Simon replied.

At that moment, Lord Howard appeared on a large black stallion, accompanied by two servants with a horse drawn wagon.

"Lord Howard, would you like to invite the rest of the village?" Pierre complained.

"I'll invite whoever I damn well please," Lord Howard replied as he dismounted. He also carried a wooden box under his arm.

"If you don't mind, we will use these pistols," Lord Howard

said solemnly. "I can vouch for their accuracy and ability to fire. They were tested yesterday evening."

Ambroise appeared indifferent. He slipped his own box back into the carriage, fumbling with it for a moment and then closing the door of the carriage.

"You may load your own weapons," Lord Howard said as he presented the box, powder, patches, and ball.

"Ambroise, please take care of this for me as my second," Pierre said, as he again held the lace handkerchief to his nose.

"I'll take care of yours lad," Simon said. "You need to prepare yourself."

"Indeed," Pierre said. "You do need to prepare yourself."

"I'll thank ye' to be keepin' yer' mouth shut," Simon said. "Rules of honor apply. Ye' are not allowed to speak to each other."

"Lad, your weapon is ready," Simon said as he placed it back in the box, alongside Pierre's.

"The offended party is allowed to obtain his weapon first," Ambroise said.

Simon looked at Lord Howard who nodded.

Simon offered the wooden box to Pierre, carefully noting his keen observation as Pierre carefully picked a weapon.

Simon then presented the box to Henry, who picked his weapon up with his right hand and pointed it toward the sky.

"All right, gentlemen, to the center of the *Field of Honor*," Lord Howard said evenly. "It is time!"

"Gentlemen, please stand back to back," Lord Howard said. "Seconds prepare yourselves in the event cowardice is shown!

Gentlemen, you will walk a total of ten paces, turn on my order, and fire on my order and only on my order! Do you understand?"

"I do," Henry replied.

"Just start the count," Pierre said. "Let's get this over with. I must get on my way. My presence here is not wanted."

"Very well," Lord Howard replied. "One."

Each man advanced forward one full step. Lord Howard nodded his approval.

"Two, Three, Four, Five, Six, Seven, Eight, Nine, Ten!" Lord Howard counted.

Several times, Henry wanted to turn, aware that his enemy could show his cowardice at any moment and shoot him in the back.

Both men stopped. The air around them suddenly seemed to chill. Death was in these Commons today.

"Turn!" Lord Howard exclaimed.

Simon carefully noted Ambroise was feigning a sore back and had placed a hand there. Simon shifted his weight on his left foot, placed his front foot forward and placed a hand on the butt of one of the pistols at his back.

Both dueling combatants turned to face each other with their right side facing forward, pistols pointed to the sky at the ready.

"Aim," Lord Howard said.

Both men extended their forearms and took aim at their opponent.

"Fire!" Lord Howard exclaimed.

Henry stood his ground and waited. He would not be forced

into a quick shot that could prove his undoing. He saw the fog of smoke from the powder of Pierre's weapon before he heard the report of the weapon. It was obviously aimed a little to Henry's right.

"Damn!" Pierre exclaimed. "Ambroise, quickly, give me a weapon!"

"You will hold your ground sir!" Lord Howard bellowed. "Simon, make certain Ambroise does not provide him with a weapon!"

There was no answer.

Henry turned his head. Simon was on his knees, blood pouring from a bullet hole just under his solar plexus.

"You bastard!" Henry said angrily.

Pierre laughed.

"Oh well boy," Pierre said. "There are often other victims in duels!"

Henry turned and knelt beside his friend. The old man leaned on Henry. Henry's back was now turned toward Pierre and Ambroise.

"Watch them, lad," Simon said. "They are French cowards!"

Henry picked up Simon's pistol from the ground with his left hand and strode back to his position.

"My turn, you French prick," Henry said. "Steady, you French bastard. Or are you afraid of the servant boy?"

Pierre turned left and then right. There seemed to be no help.

Henry raised the weapon in his right hand.

"For Simon," he said.

Suddenly Ambroise tossed Pierre a pistol. He triumphantly caught it and leveled it at Henry. Ambroise produced a second pistol and also aimed it at Henry. Henry recognized them as the dueling pistols Ambroise had initially offered and taken back to the carriage. During the much to do in the early proceedings, he had hidden them on his person, waiting for the moment when they might be properly deployed.

Time seemed to move in slow motion. Ambroise raised his weapon. Henry fired the dueling pistol at his enemy. A small black hole appeared between Ambroise's eyes. He fell to the ground. Pierre raised his pistol immediately. Henry raised his left hand that held Simon's pistol. Both fired at the same instant.

Pierre's ball cut a swathe across Henry's forehead and just above his left eye. Henry's ball caught Pierre neatly in the stomach. He fell to the ground.

"My God!" Lord Howard exclaimed.

Henry ran to Simon's side. The old man's breathing was coming ragged now as blood filled the inside of his body.

"Listen to me lad," Simon whispered. "We've not much time. I'm dying."

"No," Henry replied and he cradled his friend's head in his arms and the tears flow from his eyes. "You're not dying. You will be fine."

"Husha' now," Simon gasped between breaths. "I'm dying. That's it. All warriors die. It is how they live that makes a difference. Take these pistols. Go to my cottage. Take the sword from under the bed and reach under the mattress. There is a bag of money there. Take it with you."

"Why do I need to leave?" Henry asked. "I have done nothing wrong!"

"Aye lad, ye have," Simon whispered as the blood began to run from his mouth. "Ye' have just killed two French nobleman and their servants are witnesses. There will be a price on your head by morning. Take Lord Howard's horse, pick up what I told ye'. Ride to London, to the ships there and take the first ship out that will take ye'. Go lad!"

"I won't leave you," Henry said.

"No lad," Simon replied as the light began to fade from his eyes. "It is I who be leavin' ye'. I never had any children. I would 'av been proud to call ye' my son."

He shuddered, his breathing rattled, and moaned for a moment. Henry's friend, confidant, and the closest man he had ever known as a father breathed his last.

"No," Henry screamed. It echoed across the Commons.

"Do as he told you," Lord Howard said. "Take this extra money. It is all I have on me. Go boy and do not come back!"

Chapter 14

"Shere Khan speaks this much truth. The cub must be shown to the Pack. Wilt thou still keep him, Mother? "Keep him!" she gasped. "He came naked, by night, alone and very hungry; yet he was not afraid! Look, he has pushed one of my babes to one side already. And that lame butcher would have killed him and would have run off to the Waingunga while the villagers here hunted through all our lairs in revenge! Keep him? Assuredly I will keep him. Lie still, little frog. O thou Mowgli --for Mowgli the Frog I will call thee--the time will come when thou wilt hunt Shere Khan as he has hunted thee."

The Jungle Book - Rudyard Kipling

Lizzie heard the report of the pistols across the open fields from the front steps of her home. She stood there, wondering, hoping for the best, and preparing for the worst. She listened for the sound of men and heard nothing, except for the birds as they began to add their sounds to those of the morning.

Suddenly, she heard the sound of hoof beats. She turned, hoping it was her father, or Henry, not one of those vile Frenchmen. Instead a small herd of large deer raced across the knoll, their hoofs pounding the ground as they race toward the open field and the ponds that lay within it. There was still no sign of any of the men.

Men! Why must they challenge each other constantly for the sake of honor? She had been duly rescued and her attacker beaten. Why did Henry have to accept Pierre's demands? Why? Why? Why? Why were men made the way they were? Still the thought of Henry coming to her rescue, beating her attacker repeatedly, made her breathless. In all honesty, it also made her a little weak. She wondered if all women felt this way when a man did something so gallant and used his *skills* in such a manner.

Still skills weren't worth a damn to anyone if the man died. And she feared for Henry. She knew that even if he won the duel, he might not come back the same man, as he was when he left.

Her father had once told her, in a moment of drunken stupor, that war was truly hell on earth and you never forgot the sound of your enemy as he died, or your comrades as you gave them comfort as the Reaper came to collect them at that one last sad moment.

Her thoughts were interrupted again with the sound of hoof

beats. Blasted deer, why were they so active this morning? But, it was not deer. It was Henry, atop her father's big black stallion. She watched him circle the castle and make for Simon's small cottage near the rear of the property. Heisting her dress, she began to run in that direction. It would take her a few minutes to get there.

Henry dismounted the large horse, which was rapidly blowing, the vapor from his nostrils illuminated by the morning dawn. Henry ran into Simon's cottage, retrieved the sword and box under the bed. Thinking a moment, he removed the sword and baldric from the box and put it on. The pistols were outside on the horse in the holsters on either wide of the saddle. He quickly retrieved the money under the mattress, selected an extra change of Simon's clothing and stuffed it into a worn sea bag hung on a peg at the end of the bed. He quickly retrieved a couple of extra powder flasks, ball, flint, and wadding. He had already charged the pistols before leaving the Commons. These other items he placed in the bag as well. That was it. A lifetime of achievement now hung on his left side, the bags of money placed about his person, and two pistols on the horse outside.

Henry quickly turned, noted the inkpot and quill on the table, as well as some parchment. He hastily scribbled out a letter, poured wax from the candle on it to seal it, and lacking no real seal, used the piece-of-eight, with the single slice of silver removed at the top to make it's impression. On the outside, he wrote simply, *Lizzie.*

As he turned with the letter in his hand, Lizzie stood in the doorway.

"My darling," Lizzie said as she searched his face. "What has happened?"

"The worst," Henry said as he tried to keep his voice from shaking. The very sight of her was breaking his heart. This was the woman he would never see again.

"What?" Lizzie demanded. "What have you done?"

"Pierre and Ambroise are both dead," Henry said flatly. "So is Simon. Pierre killed him to get to me, expecting me to forfeit the duel."

"How?" Lizzie struggled to say.

"What do you mean how?" Henry said testily. "I shot them both. They are dead. Don't you understand Lizzie? I have killed two French noblemen. The Crown will have a price on my head by tomorrow. The French will do the same. If I do not leave, I will face the gallows for sure!"

"Oh, Henry," Lizzie sobbed. "It was all because of me!"

Henry gathered Lizzie in his arms, savoring the sweet scent of her lavender soap and the soft feel of her hair.

"Look at me," Henry said softly. "I would have killed a thousand Pierre's if I had to, if they tried to hurt you."

"Please don't go," Lizzie cried. "If you leave, I will have no one!"

"Lizzie, I don't have much time," Henry said. "Listen to me. Pretend I died on that Common. I am already marked for death. If you wish, I will stay, and face the gallows. At least we will have a few more days of company before the soldiers come!"

"No," Lizzie cried. "I am too selfish. You must go! Just come back to me. When this is over, come back!"

"I can't love," Henry said softly as he gently kissed her lips. "I am afraid this is goodbye!"

"Wait!" Lizzie said, as she removed a locket from her neck. Inside was a painted likeness of her on one side and Henry on the other.

"I was going to give you this on our wedding night," Lizzie said. "Father gave it to me. He said to give it to you when we were older. It came with you the day you were brought here."

Henry smiled and closed the gold locket, and opened it again. On the front was a large red *R*.

"It is beautiful," Henry said. "But I cannot accept this."

"Henry, it is yours by birthright," Lizzie said. "I do not know what it means. Father said it was the key to the secret of your birth. I had the likenesses placed inside by a man in the village."

Henry nodded, placed the chain around his neck and inside his shirt, "Thank you love! Now, I must go!"

He handed Lizzie the letter, kissed her gently again, grasped his meager belongings and tied the sea bag to the back of the horse. As he mounted the large black stallion, the horse leapt with its front legs off the ground and pawed at the air.

"I love you Lizzie," Henry cried at the sky, with a few tears streaming from his eyes. "Forget me! Find another!"

The Black cut down the road, his shod hooves throwing sparks as Henry flipped the reins left and right over the withers, driving him on and forward.

Lizzie sobbed as she watched him gallop at full speed, down the road and out of her life.

Chapter 15

The Soul's Voice

The soul wishes to vies for a world of love, devoid of hatred, knowing full well the wish may not come true.
But it still wishes because it's the only thing it knows how to.
And the soul's wish, a soul's voice carries more power than this world is aware of.

Sobbing uncontrollably, Lizzie collapsed on the steps of the great house. Two servant girls came out to help, but when they saw her condition, one of them ran back into the house to Lady Howard.

"Beggin' the Lady's pardon mum," the girl stammered. "It's the young Lady Howard mum'. She's collapsed on the steps in front and refuses to come in. She jus' keeps cryin' and cryin'!"

Lady Howard dropped her stitchery and ran to the front of the house.

"Elizabeth darling," exclaimed Lady Howard. "Tell me what is wrong! Have they returned?"

Elizabeth fell into her mother's arms weeping.

"He's gone Mama," Elizabeth cried, her back rising and falling spasmodically. "He's gone and he'll never be back! My Henry! Mama, why should this ill befall him?"

Sarah now feared for her daughter's sanity. According to custom, she had not called her Mama, since she was four.

"Send for the doctor immediately," Lady Howard said. "Now!"

"At once mum," the younger servant girl cried as she ran to fetch a footman.

"No doctor Mother," Elizabeth cried. "He cannot fix this. My heart is broken!"

"Wait," Lady Howard whispered. "Stay the doctor!"

"Look, there is a wagon approaching," Lady Howard said. And your father is riding with the driver! Where is his horse?"

"Henry has it Mother," Elizabeth cried. "Father gave it to him. Henry is headed to London to the ports to board a ship for

God knows where. He says it is the gallows for him. Will they hang him Mother? Will they hang my Henry?"

"Hush child," Lady Howard replied. "Let me talk to your father. You are making no sense!"

"Will you still need me to take the mare and fetch the doctor, madam?" the footman said with a slightly nasal twang.

Everyone ignored him.

The wagon drew swiftly to the front of the house.

Lord Howard jumped from the wagon quickly and with agility, she had not seen in years. For a moment, she felt a twinge of something she had not felt in a long time.

"Where is he?" Lord Howard demanded.

"Who, my Lord?" the footman asked.

"Henry, damn you!" Lord Howard snapped back.

The footman tried to stammer a reply, but it was cut off when Lord Howard grasped him by the lapels of his coat and shook him the way a cat shakes a mouse.

"Damn your eyes!" Lord Howard exclaimed. "Where is the lad?"

"He's gone father," Elizabeth exclaimed. "He's gone and he's not coming back!"

"Damn, damn, damn!" Lord Howard exclaimed. "This is a real mayhem!"

He pointed to the footman.

"Open that dueling case on the wagon and charge both weapons!" Lord Howard said. "And get me a set of saddle holsters quickly!"

"Where are you going father?" Elizabeth sobbed.

"I ride to London!" Lord Howard exclaimed. "Pierre lives. The heir to the house of Rochechouart lives, at least for now. Ambroise Francois' Cartier is quite dead, in self-defense of course. We may be able to stop an international incident and possibly a war with France in the process, if we move quickly!"

"What does that mean Father?" Elizabeth asked, the sobbing subsided for now that there might be a glimmer of hope.

"It means Henry might miss the gallows yet, if I can catch up with him." Lord Howard exclaimed.

He took the reins to the horse, mounted her and threw the saddle holsters with their pistols across the front.

Elizabeth ran to her father as he sat on the horse. She hugged his leg.

"Thank you Father," Elizabeth whispered.

Lord Howard dropped his head toward his daughter and said, "Elizabeth, I have been so wrong, so damned wrong. I'm trying to correct the wrongs I have done. When I return, there is something that I must tell you!"

Lord Howard dug his heels into the mare, and bent low over her neck as she picked up speed.

Damn, he thought. Henry has the Black and several hours lead on me. I may not make it in time.

As Lady Howard and the servants returned inside, Lizzie became aware she was still holding Henry's letter. With the absence of a letter opener to remove the wax seal, she carefully pried it open. Inside, Henry's crisp, masculine writing was quite clear.

My dearest Lizzie,

By the time you read this, I will be gone. Today I took two lives and I must carry that weight forever. But the greatest weight that I carry now is that I can never be with you, touch your hair, feel the softness of your skin, or the rich fullness of your lips. I love you my dear, more than I have ever loved anyone in my entire existence. I never knew my father and I know the woman that proclaimed to be my mother was not my birth mother. She told me that much. She also loved me as only a mother possibly could. She is in Kent now, at The White Monastery of Our Lady, far from the reaches of English aristocracy. Please check on her once in a while, but do not let anyone else know where she is. Whatever secret she has, someone may try to kill her to extinguish it from her lips forever.

My dearest Lizzie, you have to know I will always remember the times we lay together and looked up at the stars in the night sky, our long and lazy picnics, and watching you walk through the fresh flowers in the field. Lizzie, you are like the wild Iris, tall and strong against all winds. You will overcome this. You have to know I will never forget you, but you must forget me. It is now done. We truly cannot be together and it breaks my heart more than you will ever know. If there were any way I could come home, I would do so. Find a man that will be good to you. My prayer for you is one that Simon taught me. May your days be full of love and your life full of happiness and may your children always live free!

You have my heart and I love you always,

Henry

Lizzie carefully folded the letter, placed it next to her heart, stood and looked toward the road. There could be no other for her, save her Henry. She would not have any man until Henry came back for her. And so, she began her wait.

All Out of Love

Air Supply

I'm lying alone with my head on the phone
Thinking of you till it hurts
I know you hurt too but what else can we do
Tormented and torn apart
I wish I could carry your smile and my heart
For times when my life seems so low
It would make me believe what tomorrow could bring
When today doesn't really know, doesn't really know

I'm all out of love, I'm so lost without you
I know you were right believing for so long
I'm all out of love, what am I without you
I can't be too late to say that I was so wrong

I want you to come back and carry me home
Away from this long lonely nights
I'm reaching for you, are you feeling it too
Does the feeling seem oh so right
And what would you say if I called on you now
And said that I can't hold on
There's no easy way, it gets harder each day
Please love me or I'll be gone, I'll be gone

I'm all out of love, I'm so lost without you
I know you were right believing for so long
I'm all out of love, what am I without you
I can't be too late to say that I was so wrong

Oh, what are you thinking of
What are you thinking of
What are you thinking of
What are you thinking of

I'm all out of love, I'm so lost without you
I know you were right believing for so long
I'm all out of love, what am I without you
I can't be too late I know I was so wrong

I'm all out of love, I'm so lost without you
I know you were right believing for so long
I'm all out of love, what am I without you
I can't be too late I know I was so wrong

I'm all out of love, I'm so lost without you
I know you were right believing for so long
I'm all out of love, what am I without you
I can't be too late to say that I was so wrong

Songwriters
RUSSELL, GRAHAM / DAVIS, CLIVE J.

Chapter 16

"Remember upon the conduct of each depends the fate of all."

Alexander the Great

Henry found the tavern he hoped for close to the docks. He carefully tied his horse outside *The Blue Dolphin*. As an afterthought, he moved the pistols to his belt and retrieved the sea bag from the saddle. After looking around the area, he felt he would be surprised if the horse were still there upon his return. In the corner, nearby was an old barrel with the top and bottom removed. Inside was a boy of about eight years old.

"Come here boy," Henry demanded.

The boy came forward.

"What can I be doin' for ye' my Lord?" the boy squinted.

"How much to watch my horse?" Henry inquired.

The boy appeared to think. It was obvious he was not new to this game and the barrel was his home.

"I keep my eye on it for ye' Lord for only a three pence!" the boy exclaimed.

"I'll give you a two pence," Henry replied. "One now, and one when I return. How's that?"

The boy smiled. Half of his teeth were missing.

"That will work sir! Would ya' be wantin' me to watch your duds and things?"

"No," Henry replied.

He fished in his spare pocket and retrieved one pence.

"Here, you get the other one when I come back," Henry said.

"Well see you come back within a couple of hours. Me price goes up after a couple of hours," the boy advised.

Henry couldn't help but smile. In his own way, this boy was providing very well for himself and for God knows whom else. He was street smart.

"If I'm not back before then, the beast is yours," Henry said.

"Aye sir," the boy replied back as he took another look at the animal and realized it was not an average horse. In the back of his mind, he was hoping Henry would not come back. An animal like this could feed himself and his little sister for a couple of years.

Henry turned toward the door of the tavern, opened the latch and stepped inside. Immediately, his nostrils were filled with a host of smells. The tavern smelled of sweat, spilled and soured beer, vomit, cooked fish, and oysters.

A tavern wench sashayed through the crowd, carrying a large tray of oysters and two tankards of beer. She was winking and nodding as she took the many buttocks and breast squeezes from the customers. Finally she sat the tray and beer in front of two seasoned mariners. One of her patrons followed her grasped her by the waist and pulled her to him. She promptly grasped the handle of an empty pewter tankard and brought it to the side of his head, knocking him down and into the table of two men next to him. Everyone laughed.

Henry quietly closed the door. He knew what he was looking for. These louts with their poor manners and loud ways were not the type of man he wanted to speak with. Rather, it was the quiet man that kept to himself that he wanted to find.

Finally Henry spotted him, sitting in a darkened corner with his back to the wall, facing the door. He sat under the inside walkway to the second floor where for a few pence, a weary sailor might find a few moments of heaven in the arms of a tavern wench.

For a guinea, he might be able to spend the night.

Henry carefully made his way past the rowdiest lot of men to the man in the corner. He was older than many of those present. His hair was grey, long and tied with a piece of navy cord behind. His clothing was worn, but clean and he had a single large earring in his left ear. A scarf was tied tightly around his head to keep the hair from his eyes. When he turned toward the light, Henry noticed his left eye was completely milky and a large cut ran three inches above it and three inches below it. It was obviously the mark of a well-placed cutlass.

"Sit," the man said after taking note of Henry's armaments and sea bag.

"What be your business with me?" the man said, feigning indifference.

"I'm looking for passage," Henry replied.

The man coughed.

"Boy, men listen better when their tankard is full of ale and their throats are not dry," the older sailor replied as he nodded to the nearest tavern wench.

"Refill me cup love and whatever my young friend wants, since he's payin'."

"How much for a bowl of meat and broth and a tankard?" Henry asked.

"A three pence sir for the meal, one pence for his tankard, and a three pence for me this evening," the wench said. She *was* young and pretty, despite the dirt that covered her hands and clothing.

She noticed Henry's appraisal and his clothing. She became ashamed of her own unkempt appearance and took note that Henry was taken aback.

"I'm sorry sir. I didn't mean ta' be so fo'ard ya' know," the girl said, obviously embarrassed. "Another three pence would get thee a bath upstairs before you travel again, and perhaps me as well?"

Henry couldn't help but note the pleading in her voice.

"Come see me in about an hour," Henry said. "After we have eaten."

"Me name's Alana," the girl said happily. "If you need *anything* just call!"

As she flounced off to get their fare, the sailor laughed.

"Alana is quite smitten with you lad, and she's picky. She won't lie with just anyone," the sailor said. "The name is Bill. Buccaneer Bill to my friends, which ye' ain't. So you can just call me Captain!"

"Alright Captain," Henry said. "How much for a decent berth to the colonies?"

"Ten pounds," Bill said.

"Ten, I heard the going rate was three," Henry replied.

"Yeah and all you get is a seat amongst the slaves and swim in a sea of puke and shit all day. If that is what ye' be wantin', I'll do it for five," the Captain replied gaily. "Other than that, good day to ye' and thank ye' for the ale."

Henry reached into his pocket and pulled forward his sacred coin.

"Have you ever seen one of these?" Henry asked as he opened his hand.

The piece of eight with the top sliver carefully removed and the nicks across the top gleamed. Captain Bill grabbed Henry's hand.

"Where did ye' get that boy?" he asked.

"I was told if I ever got into trouble, I should come to the docks and present this coin and anyone would help me. Captain Jack Marsh gave it to me himself," Henry said angrily.

Captain Bill released him and said, "Alright lad. Be on the dock tomorrow morning. We sail before daybreak. You'll have to work your way across in addition to your passage. I'm three men short this trip. Jack Marsh set sail to either Tortuga or Port Royal, Jamaica. Port Royal's our passage as well. Not much left in Tortuga now. Port Royal, now that's the place to be! One last thing! Do ye have a price on yer' head?"

Henry hesitated and said, "Yes I do."

"May I ask what for?" Captain Bill inquired.

"I killed two French nobles," Henry said.

"You'll do," Captain Bill said. "Be on the dock in the morning and be ready to go to work. Your sword and pistols, I keep in my cabin. Nobody goes armed on my ship until we take one."

"Take one what?" Henry asked.

"Why another ship lad," Bill said as he arose began to make his way toward the door. "What did ya' think we were? Priests? No lad, we take what plunder we find on the high seas!"

Henry watched Captain Bill leave the tavern. So was this

what he was reduced to? Once he was a man of honor, now he was a common criminal. It did not matter. Either way, the gallows waited for him. Thoughts of Lizzie flashed through his mind. That must remain in the past where it could not hurt him. Someday, he would be Captain of his own vessel! He would become Captain Henry Jennings and declare his own personal war against France and Spain!

Chapter 17

"He's mad that trusts in the tameness of a wolf, a horse's health, a boy's love, or a whore's oath."

William Shakespeare

Henry's concentration was broken by Alana's small voice.

"I get off in about an hour," Alana said quietly. "If you like, I can have that bath drawn for you. I have a clean coverlet on the bed."

Henry smiled at her.

"Sure." Henry said. There was a touch of hesitation in his voice.

Alana seemed elated.

"Do you have a girl back home?" Alana said. "You do don't you? What's her name?"

"Lizzie," Henry said as if he were in a trance.

"If you want, I can pretend to be her, if that will help," Alana said. "I can pretend to be a lady, at least for one night!"

"Have them draw the bath." Henry murmured.

An hour later, and more than a little full of rum, Henry made his way upstairs to Alana's room. To her credit, she had prepared a steaming tub.

There was a bar of home soap and a sponge nearby. It was obvious she had already bathed and added some sort of scent to the water.

"It was the last me mum gave me before I left home," Alana said from the darkness beyond the candle. "I been saving it for something special and you being a gentleman and all, I thought we could enjoy it."

"It's nice," Henry said as he began to disrobe.

"Here, let me help ya," Alana said as she stepped from the darkness.

She was nude and the light from the candle danced across her body, highlighting her small breasts and her buttocks. Henry was now nude as well and she helped him into the tub of steaming water. She took the sponge and began sponging his back.

"Do you like that?" Alana asked.

"Yeah, that's nice," Henry said.

"Like I told you," Alana said. "If you want, I can pretend to be her."

"No," Henry whispered. "There's only one her."

"I meant no disrespect," Alana said cautiously.

"None taken," Henry replied.

"You know, I don't do this often," Alana said.

"Nor I," Henry replied.

Alana handed him a towel to dry himself. He did so as she lay on the bed, the light from the candle dancing off her supine body. Henry lay beside her. She placed her hand on his chest.

"Could I ask somethin' of you sir?" she asked.

"You can if you will stop calling me sir," Henry laughed. "My name is Henry."

"I was wonderin' if you would mind, well, just holdin' me for a few minutes? I don't get treated the way you treat me. Sometimes a woman just likes to be held. I'll forget about the three pence," Alana whispered.

"No charge for the hug," Henry whispered back as he pulled her toward him and embraced her.

They lay together for a long time, two people with an uncertain future intertwined in each other's arms.

Finally Alana's playful hand aroused him. He gently rolled her over and entered her, enjoying the feel and the ripeness of her flesh as it received him. Her voice drove him on and on. Finally she achieved her climax. His came a moment later. This girl was much different than one of the young village girls with whom he had been before. She was much more ardent and knew how to please her lover.

Once it was over, they slept peacefully until the clock on the mantle struck four in the morning. Henry had slept poorly and images of Elizabeth danced through his mind most of the night.

Henry eased out of bed, dressed and gathered his belongings. The two bags of money, he combined into one and carefully counted out twenty-five pounds, a small fortune for a year in that time. This he placed on the nightstand, and as an afterthought added another five pounds.

Alana heard him and stirred.

"Are you leaving?" she asked.

"Yes," Henry said. "I must go to the docks."

"You left your money," she said.

"No, I left your money," Henry replied. "Where I'm going, I shan't need it for a while. There is thirty pounds sterling there. I want you to take five of it and buy some new clothes, as befitting a lady. Take the rest and leave this place and never look back!"

"I can't take your money," she protested.

"Yes, you can," Henry replied as he raised her chin and gently kissed her lips. "And if anyone tells you that you are not a lady, you tell them that Henry Jennings believes differently!"

"Thank you Henry," Alana said. "This will mean I can return home to my Mother and take care of her."

"Good," Henry replied as he tipped his hat. "Goodbye Lady Alana!"

Chapter 18

"A friend can betray you, but an enemy will always stay the same!"

Captain Jack Sparrow

The fog was heavy this morning. Even the ships at port were obscured as it rolled in. Henry carefully walked the length of the dock, watching the nooks and places that were hard to see, aware this was the perfect place to be robbed and beaten.

He saw a man holding a lantern close to one of the vessels. He was carefully checking some barrels that looked as if they were about to be loaded.

Henry approached the man, who became so startled he almost dropped the lantern.

"Need something lad?" the man asked.

"Yeah, I'm looking for Captain Bill's ship," Henry said.

The man's swarthy face paled immediately.

"Captain Buccaneer Bill?" the man asked.

"The same," Henry replied.

"That's his ship down at the end of the dock, *The Sea Devil,*" the man said. "Whatcha' be wantin' with him?"

"I've booked a working passage," Henry replied.

The man grinned and pointed.

"You've got a date with the Devil," the man said. "Don't keep him waitin' else you'll catch the end of a knotted rope atop yer' head."

Henry nodded and strode to the end of the dock. *The Sea Devil* was a large Galleon. These were the types of ships that pirates actively hunted because of their large cargo holds and expensive treasures. Spain relied heavily on galleons to transport goods around their colonies. The Spanish treasure fleet was made up almost exclusively of galleons. Although the rewards of capturing a galleon were high, taking a full broadside from one of these warships could be fatal. The previous owner of this one obviously no longer needed it.

Henry marched up the plank to the deck of the ship.

"Hello the ship!" Henry shouted.

"Who goes!" came the reply back.

"Henry Jennings, to see Captain Bill," Henry shouted.

"Come aboard, but keep yer' hands away from those weapons," came the reply. "Cap'n, there's a dudsy gentleman on deck to be seein' ye'."

Captain Bill marched down the steps from the rear of the Galleon deck or steerage section of the ship.

"Do you have my money?" he asked.

"Do you have my quarters?" Henry replied.

"Aye lad, we do and then some," Captain Bill replied. "But there's something here ye' have to sign or make yer' mark on. All what comes aboard this ship must follow the ship's articles. Here they be!"

A man unrolled a crude parchment before Henry while a crewmate held a lantern, grinning through rotted teeth.

It read:

I. *Every Man shall obey civil Command; the Captain shall have one full Share and a half of all Prizes; the Master, Carpenter, Boatswain and Gunner shall have one Share and quarter.*

II. *If any Man shall offer to run away, or keep any Secret from the Company, he shall be marooned with one Bottle of Powder, one Bottle of Water, one small Arm, and Shot.*

III. *If any Man shall steal any Thing in the Company, or game, to the Value of a Piece of Eight, he shall be marooned or shot.*

IV. *If any time we shall meet another Marooner that Man shall sign his Articles without the Consent of our Company, shall suffer such Punishment as the Captain and Company shall think fit.*

V. *That Man that shall strike another whilst these Articles are in force, shall receive Moses' Law (that is, 40 Stripes lacking one) on the bare Back.*

VI. *That Man that shall snap his Arms, or smoke Tobacco in the Hold, without a Cap to his Pipe, or carry a Candle lighted, shall suffer the same Punishment as in the former Article.*

VII. *That Man that shall not keep his Arms clean, fit for an Engagement, or neglect his Business, shall be cut off from his Share, and suffer such other Punishment as the Captain and the Company shall think fit.*

VIII. *If any Man shall lose a Joint in time of an Engagement, shall have 400 Pieces of Eight ; if a Limb, 800.*

IX. *If at any time you meet with a prudent Woman, that Man that offers to meddle with her, without her Consent, shall suffer present Death.*

"Do you have any problem signing or making your mark?" Captain Bill asked.

"None sir," Henry replied.

He signed the parchment as *Henry Jennings.*

"What now Captain?" Henry asked.

"Why it's a short nap fer' ya'!" Captain Bill exclaimed with a smile on his face.

A belaying pin struck Henry on the back of the head and he knew no more.

"Alright, ye' pukin' swine, draw the anchor and hoist the sails," Captain Bill exclaimed. "Let's be getting under way 'afore the sun rises!"

Then he said to two members of the crew, "Take his weapons and his money and put them in my quarters. And if any of ye' so much as scratch that pretty sword, I'll be feedin' yer' balls to the fishes!"

"What about him Cap'n?" one of the crew asked.

"Throw him down below and when he comes to, put him to work," Captain Bill responded. "If he don't work, overboard he goes!"

The two crewmen looked at each other. One finally shrugged.

"Ok, Muffy, pick his lordship's ass off the deck, else we will be joining him," one of them said and they both laughed.

"Raise all sail men!" Captain Bill shouted. "Mate Dasher, take her out. First man that sees a sail gets an extra share and an extra tankard of grog. I'll be in my cabin! Set sail for Port Royal, Jamaica!"

Chapter 19

"There is a tide in the affairs of men, which taken at the flood, leads on to fortune. Omitted, all the voyage of their life is bound in shallows and in miseries. On such a full sea are we now afloat. And we must take the current when it serves, or lose our ventures."

William Shakespeare

The first thing Henry was aware of was a deep throbbing sensation in his head. The second was a rather putrid smell. He could hear the sounds of the ship creaking around him and the sound of the ocean. He felt the heavy vessel rise and fall. Daylight came through various ports and crannies in the vessel. This was a large galleon, around twelve hundred tons. Henry had already identified her as a Spanish Galleon due to her high superstructure at the rear of the ship. That meant she was top heavy and could be sluggish in the water.

He opened his eyes. The first thing he saw was a man sitting atop an upside down bucket. He was squinting at Henry and finally grinned when he saw his eyes open.

"I was getting' worried about ye'," the man said. "Scurvy's the name. That damned Muffy put too much into that belaying pin. He's Second Mate and has his eye on First Mate, if he gets a chance."

"Where am I?" Henry asked.

"You are on the second deck in the forecastle," Scurvy said. "What do you know about sailing vessels?"

"Not a damn thing," Henry replied.

"I figured as much," Scurvy said. "This 'ere's an old Spanish Galleon. Captain Bill got her fair and square on the open sea. Let's just say the Spanish swine that was on her don't need her anymore. We got the ship and the plunder. She's old but she's sturdy. Most of these Galleons ride low in the water in the front. Can ye' feel it?"

"I do," Henry said. "I think I'm going to vomit."

"That will pass, as soon as you get your sea legs," Scurvy

observed. "And there's many that will still puke their daily ration on the right night, when the seas get rough! Here are you some new clothes. Put these on and get out of your other duds. You won't be needing them here."

"What are these?" Henry asked.

"They are clean and washed as best as we can," Scurvy observed. "The slops are a little wider where yer' balls sit and in the legs as well. The same is for the shirt. You need to be able to move around and not let your clothes bind you, when you are climbing up the rigging to raise and lower the sails."

Henry began to change clothes. The slops were comfortable and did allow free movement. As he started to don the pullover shirt, he was surprised to note a small slit around the abdomen as well as the remains of what appeared to be blood.

Scurvy noticed his surprise and laughed.

"Yeah, ye got the clothes of poor Louie," Scurvy noted. "We save almost everything. Louie was caught by a couple of the lads stealing more than his share and he got a dirk stuck in his belly."

"Damn," Henry replied. "How much did he steal?"

"I believe it was 4 pieces of eight," Scurvy said. He seemed nonplussed. "It don't really matter. Stealing is stealing!"

Henry began to wonder how pirates could put things into such black and white terms when they themselves were little more than thieves. Perhaps there was a code of honor amongst some of them that they had to follow, simply to stay alive.

"I'm supposed to be teachin' ye the ropes," Scurvy said. "Really, all of the ropes. Everything you need to know about this 'ere ship, I will teach ye'. That is exceptin' how to plot a course. That takes figures and I don't proclaim to know shite about figures or fancy writin'! Don't know shite about maps neither! The dumber you act, the less people expect of you and the less they worry about you takin' their place. That's one way a good Cap'n will control his crew. Without knowing where ye be goin' and how to get there, you're frankly dead!"

"I'm ready to learn," Henry said. "Where are my belongings?"

"First lesson," Scurvy said soberly. "The Capn's word is law. That's it. He took your stuff. He may decide to give it back after you've proven yourself. But don't cross him or the First Mate. And watch out for the Second Mate. He'll stick a knife in ye' fer' sure. Disobey an order and you'll get Moses's law across yer' back. That's forty lashes, less one, with a cat-o-nine-tails that will carve your back into shredded meat. Do you understand?"

Henry nodded his assent and watched in amazement as Scurvy lifted his shirt to reveal a back that was a tan as the rest of him. His back was covered with badly healed scar tissue.

"Aye," Scurvy said gaily. "That be what happens when ye' cross the Capn', if he don't drop you in the wake of the ship and feed ye' to the fishes. I got mine by me last Capn'. It was a British Man-O-War. I were new, like you and I didn't tie a rope well near the mizzen mast. Wind pulled it loose and ripped the sail."

"It was that bad?" Henry asked.

"This is part of what I'll teach ye'," Scurvy said. "Because it's so far astern, the sails rigged on this mast make a difference on the stern of the boat." You can often use the mizzen sail as a vane to push the stern around and the boat will come up with the bow into the wind. If the wind is coming from the beam, you can use the spanker in this way to push the stern off a dock without moving ahead or astern. You can also use it to turn the ship away from the wind."

"Sweet Jesus!" Henry exclaimed.

"There was two of us that screwed the fishes that day," Scurvy said. His face had taken a gray ashen look. "The British Capn', don't know his name, gave us both sixty lashes. Me mate died afore they were finished. Somehow I lived. The carpenter of the ship put axle grease on it every night fer me until Capn' Bill took his ship and his plunder. He asked me to sign on and I did. Didn't really have any choice, if ye know what I mean."

"Why?" Henry asked as he began to stand up. He was still a little dizzy, but the throbbing was beginning to ease.

"He killed all aboard and sunk the ship," Scurvy said quietly. "It was me first. The water was red with blood from the fishes feedin', but it cleared quickly when she sank."

"I have allot to learn," Henry said.

"Then let's get started," Scurvy replied. "One last word before we begin. Every lad on this 'ere boat has a hidin' place for his private things. If you find it, leave it alone. You don't have anything anymore, except 'fer this."

He handed Henry a dirk with a plain wooden handle inside a leather scabbard. A leather thong ran through the scabbard where the knife could be worn over the neck.

"Every lad has one," Scurvy said, "and this one is yours. You will need it to work certain parts of the ship anyway. Make sure ye don't find someone's knife in yer' belly same as poor Louie."

Henry nodded.

"One last thing," Scurvy noted. "Here's your calling card for Captain Jack Marsh."

"Why didn't he keep it?" Henry asked, as he quickly pocketed his long coveted treasure.

"Fer one, it would be bad luck, to take from another pirate," Scurvy observed. "Fer another, ifn' he were caught with it, his guts would be hanging from a yardarm. One thing ye' never do is cross Captain Jack Marsh!"

Chapter 20

"God moves in a mysterious way, His wonders to perform. He plants his footsteps in the sea, and rides upon the storm."

William Cowper

Lord Howard's horse thundered to the one place he could think of that Henry would go first. It was a place close to the docks, *The Blue Dolphin*.

It was just after noon and although the brief sun had burned off the morning fog, the sky was becoming overcast. Like Henry, he disliked the idea of leaving his horse unattended. He tied the horse to the hitching post and was immediately accosted by a young boy of about eight.

Watch yer' horse for ye' my Lord?" the boy asked.

"How much to watch my horse?" Lord Howard inquired.

The boy appeared to think. Even Lord Howard was impressed with his businesslike countenance.

"I keep my eye on it for ye' Lord for only a three pence!" the boy exclaimed.

"I'll give you a one pence," Lord Howard replied.

The boy appeared angry.

"Even the bloke that came in yesterday promised me a two pence and only gave me one. I didn't even get the second. But I got the bloody black stallion he rode. I'm trying to sell it now!" the boy observed.

"Describe the man," Lord Howard said quickly.

"Dressed good," the boy said. "Not as good as you, but real good for the docks. Good looking chap! Had a handsome sword and looked as if he knew how to use it."

"Where did he go?" Lord Howard asked. "Quickly boy! That was my horse!"

"I don't want to get in the middle with a horse thief," the

boy exclaimed. "He's in the alley. I can go get him!"

"Bring the animal and I'll give you 2 pounds," Lord Howard said. "Can you think of anyone that might know his whereabouts?"

"I heard Alana liked him," the boy said with a wrinkled brow. "Inside the tavern."

"Thank you," Lord Howard said. "Bring my horse and I'll pay you when I come out."

"*If* you come out," the boy whispered.

Lord Howard ignored him and opened the door. Today, the tavern was largely deserted, with only a few customers, most of which appeared to be more interested in food than drink. He walked to the main bar and rapped his cane on the plank boards.

The tavern keeper took note of Lord Howard's fine dress and the possibility of more money. He quickly moved to Lord Howard to be of service.

"Yes, my Lord?" the man asked. "Is it rum or food ye' be wantin, or somethin' else?"

"I am looking for a young man that came through here yesterday," Lord Howard sniffed. "He would have been comparatively well dressed, and might have seemed if he were in a hurry."

"I know who you are talkin' about," the man replied. "Alana really liked him. Maybe he told her."

"Alana, get your arse down ere'!" the tavern keep said with a surly tone. "You know that little whore is leaving me because of the man you speak of. He gave her a small fortune for leavin' this 'ere place. Not that she was much good except 'fer servin. She's damn pretty, but too picky!"

Alana trudged down the steps with a worn blanket that seemed to hold her meager possessions. She was dressed well, too well for a place such as this. For a moment, Lord Howard thought he might have the wrong girl.

"Now git yer' worthless arse outa' here!" the tavern owner screeched. "And don't ye' be coming back anymore! After all I done 'fer you and you just up and leave me high and dry!"

"Yes, you have done so much," Alana, said firmly. "You tried to have me spread my legs for every man that walked in here and took half me extras for sellin' yer grog and bad food. I'm leavin' now, cause I'm a lady. Henry said so!"

"Henry?" Lord Howard asked. "You know Henry?"

"Yes," Alana said, taken aback by Lord Howard's serious countenance. "If you be sayin' he done anything wrong, I won't believe it. Henry was a gentleman through and through. And he knows as how to treat a woman, something others could learn from!"

She gave the tavern owner a scathing look.

"Did he say where he was going?" Lord Howard asked.

"Yes," she said. "He was going to the docks afore morn to seek passage. I know he was going on Captain Bill's ship. Buccaneer Bill. Have you heard of him?"

Lord Howard nodded. Buccaneer Bill's name was famous amongst the English military and navy. He made no difference as to ships from any nation, be they English, Dutch, French, or Spanish.

"His girl is sure a lucky girl," Alana insisted quietly. Her eyes had a far away look in them. "He truly loves her!"

"What girl?" Lord Howard said. "Who is she? Out with it woman!"

"You can't talk to me that way, Sir," Alana said. "I'm a lady now and I'm leaving."

She started for the door.

"I'm sorry," Lord Howard apologized. "Would you tell me the lady's name?"

"Of course," Alana said quietly. "He said it many times in his sleep, over and over. I would give the rest of my life, just to feel special like that again and have someone dream of me. Her name is Lizzie!"

"Elizabeth," Lord Howard whispered quietly. "Of course. I knew the answer before I asked."

"Then I'll be taking my leave Sir," Alana said as she walked away and opened the door.

Lord Howard followed.

"Pardon me," he asked. "Where are you going?"

"To me home in Colchester," Alana replied. "And what business is it of yours?"

"I'd like the opportunity to demonstrate my apologies," Lord Howard said as he hailed the stage preparing to pull away from the tavern. "Colchester is six days by coach, if the roads aren't fouled."

"I need to go home and take care of me mother," Alana said. "Henry gave me enough money to last us for at least two years."

"That would be our Henry," Lord Howard said, as he

handed the fare and to the driver who touched the brim of his hat in thanks.

"What's the name of the ship?" Lord Howard asked as he helped her into the coach.

"It's the *Sea Devil,*" Alana said.

"Where's she berthed?" Lord Howard asked. "I must reach Henry before he leaves."

"I'm afraid you are too late, Sir," Alana said tearfully. "She left before the fog lifted this morning."

Chapter 21

"There is pleasure in the pathless woods, there is rapture in the lonely shore, there is society where none intrudes, by the deep sea, and music in its roar; I love not Man the less, but Nature more."

Lord Byron

Days led into weeks and weeks into months. Henry proved a quick study and mastered all that was put to him. He learned to scurry up and down the ships rigging, load and fire cannon, and even was allowed at the wheel a few times under the watchful eye of the Coxswain, that found Henry to be an apt pupil. More than once, he sought the compass and knew they were headed west and south. He was told they were headed for Port Royal, Jamaica, but felt Captain Bill had other plans.

After three months at sea, the vessel had become Henry's home. They weathered a couple of storms, but were able to outrun and steer around one severe storm. Although Captain Bill was a sour, sadistic individual, he proved to be a master with navigation and ship operations. As long as he was not crossed, everyone got his rum ration. On rare occasions, when Captain Bill had consumed more than his ration of rum, he would order an extra ration for the crew. Henry saw through his generosity, as it made him more popular at times when the crew grumbled about extra duties.

It was now four months since Henry's incarceration or "passage" began on *The Sea Devil*. Henry's life was about to take another severe and diverse change.

It was mid-morning when one of the crew in the crows-nest gave the resounding, "Sail ho! Starboard!" It only took a moment for Captain Bill to rush out on deck with his spyglass.

"She's English!" he exclaimed. "And a merchant ship headed home! She's riding low in the water, lads. And ye all know what that means!"

It was only too true. If an English ship was travelling

northwest, it meant she was coming back from the New World or the Americas loaded with many different types of plunder, ranging from tobacco to gold.

"Bring her about," Captain Bill ordered triumphantly. "Prepare the grappling hooks! Load the thirty pounders! Prepare the sixty pounders!"

"Cap'n, that's allot of powder and shot," the First Mate said cautiously, not wanting to enrage his superior.

"I said load 'em and I mean load 'em," Captain Bill ordered again. "She's riding in the gunnels, I tell ye' and we do not want to sink her. If we can, we'll take her as a prize and sell her when we gets to Port Royal. If not, we'll plunder her and send her to the bottom. Load the chain shot!"

Chain shot was most often used at close range to destroy the masts, lines, and rigging. This meant the Captain did not intend to use intimidation to win the ship. Often pirate ships gained close access to their intended target, using screams, howls and pistol discharges to frighten their intended prey into submissiveness. The harder they worked, the less apt they were to offer terms. Regardless, the Captain of the vessel was always killed as a reminder to the rest of the crew and passengers that resistance would be dealt with swiftly.

"Pick up speed and begin to get close to 'er," Captain Bill shouted. "Keep the cannon inside so they can't see 'em until its too late!"

The Sea Devil picked up speed and as they began to approach, Captain Bill gave the order to swing around.

"Bring the aft about and turn her," he shouted.

Finally with both ships running a parallel course and with their respective speeds matched, he hailed the ship. It was the *Providence* rebuilt and renamed after the original's wreck in the 1680s. She was definitely an English vessel.

"Hello the ship!" Captain Bill replied. "What news have ye' of the Americas?"

"She's teeming with milk and honey," the Captain of the *Providence* said. "We are heading home with a full hold!"

"Can you take some mail?" Captain Bill lied.

"Aye! Lads lower the sails. Drop speed!"

Captain Bill gave the same order.

"Fill this bag with powder, ball, and run a fuse into 'er", Captain Bill said. "Tie her tight!"

Then to the Coxswain, "When he lights and throws it, strike the colors and raise our own!"

The ships were now almost side-by-side with only a few feet between them.

"Watch the razors atop their yardarms!" the captain of the *Providence* advised.

"Here it comes, Cap'n," a crew of *The Sea Devil* cried as he lit the fuse and threw the bag.

At the same time, the English colors dropped on *The Sea Devil,* and the familiar skull and crossbones were raised.

"It's a trap!" screamed the Captain of *Providence*. "Pirates!"

His words were cut short by an explosion on his own deck and further silenced by a well-placed musket ball in his chest. He fell to the deck, blood spurting.

"Raise the sails," he whispered.

"Fire the aft thirty pounders," Captain Bill ordered.

The heavy cannon balls burst through the second deck of the *Providence* caving large holes in the ships side, but still above the water line.

"Fire the chains!" came the next order. The deck cannons added their echo to the din. The center mast on *Providence* split and fell, hanging from the deck, only by the rigging.

The grappling hooks were now deployed and the two vessels thudded against each other. The razor sharp tips of the yardarms on *the Sea Devil* were ripping rigging and sail alike.

"Board 'er!" Captain Bill screamed. "It's time to plunder! Take the crew hostage and check for passengers!"

The crew of *The Sea Devil* leapt from strategic positions on their ship to that of the crippled *Providence.* Sailors of merchant ships are often like sailors of many pirate ships. Not all are fighting men. Most crew of pirate ships would rather not fight, until they gain the necessary skills to do so. Unfortunately many of them did not make it, which created a constant shortage of crew, some of which could be obtained from a captured vessel.

In the case of *Providence* the men were poorly equipped to deal with a seasoned pirate crew. It didn't take long before the poor individuals were on deck assembled en masse, awaiting their death, or possibly a chance at life. There was still the possibility the pirates might let them live after they had taken what they wanted. Still, they were in the middle of the Atlantic Ocean. To remove their food and water meant death for all of them. It also meant life for the crew of *The Sea Devil.*

Captain Bill sauntered to the deck of *Providence*. First Mate had already given him a tally of the hold.

"Lads, we have got us a haul!" Captain Bill exclaimed. "Gold bars, sacks of vanilla beans and tobacco, make our haul. And there's plenty of fresh water, fruit, rum, salt pork, and dried beef! We'll be eatin' and drinkin' good tonight lads! Move the goods!"

It took almost ten hours to transfer the wealth of *Providence* to *The Sea Devil*, arrange it for the best buoyancy, and prepare for sea.

"That be it, Cap'n," First Mate said.

"David, how long 'av we been sailin' together?" Captain Bill asked the First Mate.

"A long time," David replied.

"Any regrets?" Captain Bill asked.

"None sir!" the First Mate replied. "And you sir?"

"Only that I can't trust my First Mate!" Captain Bill said as he pushed David against the bulwarks and fished in his pocket. His hand came out with a fistful of emeralds.

"I was going to give them to you," David replied. "I found them in the Captain's quarters aboard ship."

"I be disappointed in ye' David," Captain Bill said as he produced his knife and promptly slit the man's throat.

He released his First Mate and watched him fall to the deck gasping as the blood rushed out of him. His windpipe made a whistling sound.

"Muffy, where are ye, ye sniveling bastard," Captain Bill said.

"Here sir!" The Second Mate replied.

"Ye' just got promoted. You're now First Mate. See ye' don't end up like David here, poor soul!"

"Aye Captain!" Muffy replied with a leer. "What do ye want us to do with him?"

"Throw him overboard!" Captain Bill said gaily. "And the rest of ye' louts, this is what happens when ye' cross Buccaneer Bill! Henry, give him a hand!"

"Aye Cap'n," Henry replied as he grasped David's shoulders and Muffy grabbed his feet.

"Heave ho!" Muffy cried and laughed when David's body hit the water and disappeared.

"What do you want us to do with them?" Muffy asked as he pointed toward the crew of *Providence*.

"What do you think?" the Captain replied. "Feed 'em to the fishes and don't waste any more powder and shot. They'll go down soon enough!"

"Captain," Henry exclaimed. "We can't just kill them in cold blood. Can't we let them float, fix their craft, and find land?"

"Why," Captain Bill thundered. "So they can return home and tell them the crew of *The Sea Devil*'s what done this?"

"Sir, they are merchant sailors," Henry replied. "Can't we use a few of them on board our ship here?"

"Are you challenging me Henry, you slimy piece of fish gut?" Captain Bill exploded. "Bind him lads and take him to the brig. We'll show him later, what happens to those that question their Captain."

Henry was bound, kicked and pummeled to their makeshift brig, which was a small room composed of strong oak and iron mesh bars.

From there, he heard the screams of the men of *Providence* as they were thrown overboard. The sharks had already begun a feeding frenzy.

"Light the sixty pounder," Captain Bill shouted from the top deck. "Shoot her below the water line and let's get on with it!"

There was a thunderous noise and a strong vibration through the ship as the massive cannon fired. The crew's triumph was evident as their voices were raised and the massive merchant ship began its descent into the dark waters of the Atlantic. The *Providence* was no more. The sea and the devil had claimed their prize.

Chapter 22

"Her cheeks burned; a strange new life was in all her veins."
A Rose of a Hundred Leaves: A Love Story, 1891

Amelia E. Huddleston Barr

The night sky was illuminated by a full moon that cast its brilliance over the grounds. The trees added dancing shadows to the scenery, as if tiny imps were dancing under the leaves. The stars cast a blanket of light across the night sky.

Lizzie sat on the front steps of her large, ornate home, staring at the sky, remembering the night she and Henry had lain on the blanket at their secret place looking above and watching small meteors streak across the blanket of pin point lights.

Henry was a master in astronomy, as he was in mathematics. He could easily point out one light and then another, and name the constellations to her, all the while chewing on a mint stem to freshen his breath.

It was beginning to get cold outside and she put her hands between her knees to block the cold. A young servant girl noticed, put on a shawl, got one for Lizzie, and took it outside.

"Beggin' your pardon My Lady," the girl said. "I couldn't help but notice you out here all alone and it getting cold and all. Would you like a shawl?"

"Oh yes," Lizzie replied. "Thank you so much Cassie!"

Cassie wrapped the shawl around Lizzie's shoulders, curtsied, and said, "Well, if that will be all mum, I'll get to me duties."

"Why don't you sit Cassie?" Lizzie asked. "It would be nice to have some female company."

"Beggin' me Lady's pardon," Cassie said. "But I'm just a servant and I don't want anyone getting' any ideas that I'm tryin' to be more than I am!"

"It's ok," Lizzie said. "Sit next to me."

"Have you ever been in love?" Lizzie asked.

"Well, yes my Lady," Cassie replied. "There is a boy in the village that's a bit sweet on me and I have high hopes, but he won't be askin' the question until he feels he can support a family."

"Seems like a nice hearted young man," Lizzie said.

"Aye, he is and he's handsome enough," Cassie replied. "And I do love him so. We just has to wait a while, if I can keep him away that is. You know young men can be impatient for, well you know, certain things."

"I know what you mean," Lizzie said.

"And you, my Lady, we all know you were in love with that Mr. Henry. He was a nice looking man," Cassie said hesitantly. "I don't believe I have ever seen his Lordship so dejected as when he returned from London."

"I still am," Lizzie replied. "I will always love Henry!"

"Well, I best be getting my evening chores finished, "Cassie replied. "Is there anything I can get you?"

"No Cassie," Lizzie said quietly. "Thank you!"

Cassie stopped a moment at the top of the steps.

"You know me Lady," Cassie said. "In Ireland, we have an old tale that if you look at the North Star and your lover looks at it on the same night, that someday it will guide him back to you. Wish with me Lady, and I'll be prayin' for you."

"Thank you Cassie," Lizzie whispered. "What a lovely thought!"

Cassie curtsied and said, "Well good evening me Lady."

Cassie looked over her shoulder and smiled at her as she entered the house.

Lizzie searched the night sky. What was it Henry said? *Look for the Little Dipper. See Lizzie, there it is! The star at the end of the Little Dipper is the North Star. Look for it. It will always guide you home!*

She continued her scan. There it was! Glowing brightly at the end of the handle on the Little Dipper was their star. She watched it earnestly, hoping Henry could see the same star. If he did, perhaps he would come home to her and they could be together. She was no longer the same girl. She was now a woman and she yearned for the man she loved. *Come home Henry, she prayed.*

She was unaware that Henry was also watching through the small window in the brig of *The Sea Devil* and had found the same star.

She found herself humming an old Scottish love song and at the same time she watched the stars.

Oh Henry, she thought. Where are you? Can you see our star?

WHA WADNA BE IN LOVE

Bibliography of Bagpipe Music

1700 Scotland

Maggie Lauder

Wha wadna be in love
Wi' bonny Maggy Lawder
A piper met her gaun to Fife,
And spier'd what was't they ca'd her
Right scornfully she answer'd him
Begone, you hallanshaker;
Jog on your gate, you bladderskate
My name is Maggie Lawder.
Maggy, quoth he, and by my bags,
I'm fidging fain to see you [thee];
Sit down by me, my bonny bird,
In troth I winna steer thee:
For I'm a piper to my trade,
My name is Rob the Ranter;
The lasses loup as they were daft
When I blaw up my chanter.

Piper, quoth Meg, hae you your bags,
Or is your drone in order?
If you be Rob, I've heard of you,
Live you upo' the border?
The lasses a', baith far and near,
Have heard of Rob the Ranter;
I'll shak my foot wi' right good will,
Gif you'll blaw up your chanter.
Then to his bags he flew with speed,
About the drone he twisted,
Meg up, and wallop'd o'er the green,
For brawly cou'd she frisk it.
Weel done, quoth he; Play up, quoth she:
Weel bob'd, quoth Rob the Ranter;
'Tis worth my while to play indeed,
When I hae sic a dancer.
Weel hae you play'd your part, quoth Meg,
Your cheeks are like the crimson;
There's nane in Scotland plays sae weel,
Since we lost Habbie Simpson.

I've liv'd in Fife, baith maid and wife,
These ten years and a quarter;
Gin you should come to Enster fair,
Spier ye for Maggy Lawder.

Chapter 23

"To the solemn graves, near a lonely cemetery, my heart like a muffled drum is beating funeral marches."

Charles Baudelaire

They dragged Henry from the brig early the next morning. Captain Bill stood on deck holding a cat-o-nine-tails. Henry blinked as his eyes adjusted to the sun.

"Lash him to the mast," Captain Bill said sternly. "Lash him tight! Lads, this is what you will get if you disobey an order or question an order from your Cap'n!"

Henry was tied tightly to the mast, his chest pressing into the belaying pins that encircled it. Grinning, the First Mate grabbed Henry's shirt by the back of it's collar and ripped it down to his waist.

"Scurvy, ye snivelin' bastard," Captain Bill screeched. "Where be ye?"

"Here Captain!" Scurvy replied.

"Wasn't this 'ere man your responsibility?" Captain Bill sneered.

"Aye, Cap'n," Scurvy replied. "But I don't think he meant any harm. This was his first, that's all. We all get a little skittish on our first ship!"

"He's your responsibility," insisted Captain Bill as he handed the cat-o-nine-tails to Scurvy. "You give it to 'em!"

Scurvy hesitated.

"I said you give it to 'em and give it to 'em good or I'll have you tied up there next to 'em!" Captain Bill thundered.

The cat is made up of nine knotted thongs of cotton cord, about two and one-half feet long, designed to lacerate the skin and cause intense pain. It traditionally has nine thongs as a result of the manner in which rope is plaited. Thinner rope is made from three strands of yarn plaited together, and thicker rope from three strands of thinner rope plaited together. To make a cat o' nine tails, a rope is unravelled into three small ropes, each of which is unravelled again.

"Go ahead," Henry said. "If you don't, then you'll be next."

"I can't," Scurvy whispered to Henry.

"Come on, you bastard!" Henry shouted. "Come on! Give it to me!"

Scurvy took one more look at the Captain, who simply nodded and said. "Start with Moses law. Forty less one!"

"Alright, sorry lad," Scurvy said as he administered the first lash.

"Harder!" the Captain screamed. "I want to see his blood run on the deck planks!"

"Two," counted the First Mate who continued to grin.

By the time they got to thirty, Scurvy had to stop and rest for a moment hands on his knees. Henry hung by his arms on the ropes that encircled him, barely holding on to consciousness. Muffy grabbed Henry's hair and smashed his face into the mast.

"That's for disobeying the Captain's order," Muffy said as he looked to the Captain for approval and found it. He pulled Henry's hair and yanked his head back again. Blood ran from Henry's mouth where the blow had split his lip. Muffy sneered as he prepared another blow and then, without warning, Henry spat blood and mucous into Muffy's face.

"Screw you!" Henry said. "Someday you bitch, I will kill you."

"Stop, let Muffy finish him," the Captain ordered Scurvy.

"Let's see what he can do!"

"I can finish Cap'n," Scurvy cried.

"I know ye can," Captain Bill said gaily. "But so can Muffy! First Mate, take the Cat!"

"Gladly Cap'n!" Muffy replied.

"He gets nine more, unless you are feeling generous," Captain Bill said as he scoured the horizon.

"And 'ere they come!" Muffy cried.

The next nine lashes were with such enthusiasm that the flesh on Henry's back literally split as the braids did their work.

"There's the forty less one," Muffy cried. "And 'ere's a few more!"

Muffy continued to lash Henry. By now Henry had lost consciousness and the deck planks were indeed soaking Henry's blood into their cracks.

Muffy continued to lash him.

"Beggin' the Cap'n's pardon sir," the Coxswain said. "He's killin' him and we have no one to replace him."

"Alright," Captain Bill replied. "How many?"

"Seventy one lashes," Scurvy stammered. "He's taken seventy one. Never seen anyone take that many and live!"

"Then you best be taking good care of him and see that he doesn't die," Captain Bill replied. "I can't afford to lose any more men. Give him an extra ration of rum for the next three days. Scurvy, get some help and move him below!"

And then to two more crewmembers, "Ye swine, look at this blood on my deck. Get some seawater and clean it up! You would think we are running a slaughter shop 'ere!"

And with that, Henry was roughly untied and taken to the forecastle that would be his home for several days.

Chapter 24

"It is a revenge the devil sometimes takes upon the virtuous, that he entraps them by the force of the very passion they have suppressed and think themselves superior to."

George Santayana

It took Henry many weeks to return to full health after the massive beating at the hands of Muffy. Had it not been for Scurvy who had endured a similar tragedy, Henry would have surely died as several of the lacerations became infected from the salt water they used to treat the wounds and dry them up. Scurvy had slipped down to the third deck more than once to obtain tobacco leaves from which he made a poultice. The tobacco pulled out the poison and hastened the healing. The beating was a constant reminder what the cat-o-nine-tails could do.

Strangely enough, the Captain seemed to have totally forgotten the event and even greeted Henry civilly when he came out on deck. Henry disregarded the man as much as possible, stuck to his duties and stayed away from Muffy, who often tried to take out his sour disposition on Henry.

They took another vessel almost a month later. It was a small French ship headed on their same route. Captain Bill recognized it immediately for what it was. It was the *Adelaide*. This French frigate weighing four hundred tons left France from the port of Lorient in Brittany to pick up three hundred and sixty slaves in Guinea. After disembarking the slaves in Leogane, Haiti, fate caught up with them. Although they were listed as lost at sea and some of the ships remains ended up on the coast, they were actually another of Captain Bill's conquests.

"She's a slaver boys," Captain Bill said. "If'n we gets her, we can sell her plunder at the dock for the plantations around Port Royal, Jamaica and Nassau. Slaves mean money!"

They approached the ship slowly, noted her flag and ran up

the same Dutch flag. It didn't take long for the pirates to finish their conquest. The slavers were not fighting men and there were not that many of them on the smaller ship. It did not take long for the crew of *The Sea Devil* to subdue their opponents. Two of them asked to sign on as crew of the pirate ship. One of them, Captain Bill ran through with his cutlass and watched in cold fascination as the man fell to the deck and bled his last. The other, a large African male stood his ground and waited for his sentence. It was already a sentence of death.

"We have us a prize ship," Captain Bill said. "Henry, you and Scurvy take a look at what's in the hold and take a tally."

Henry and Scurvy carefully went below deck. There they found extremely cramped decks with low ceilings and the functional equivalent of bunk beds. Each bed held a naked chained African male, female, or child. The stench was terrible. Scurvy slipped on something on the deck and promptly pitched forward to land in another foul smell.

"Give us a light here," Scurvy said. "I'm covered in something, whatever the 'ell it is!"

Henry carefully lowered the lantern toward the deck and both men realized the foulness for what it was.

"I'm telling ya', it's shite," Scurvy exclaimed. "The whole deck is full of it. And this one is dead. So is that one!"

"Sweet Jesus," Henry exclaimed. "Look here! It's the Black Death, I'm telling you Scurvy. Get the hell out of here!"

Scurvy was the first one on deck, quickly found a barrel of water and washed the foulness from his person.

"I'm going to die!" he screeched.

"Well?" Captain Bill said. "What did ye' find?"

"Captain, we have to raise the *Yellow Jack*," Henry exclaimed. "It's the Death! Most of the people in the hold are already dead. The others are dying!"

The *Yellow Jack* was a sign there was sickness aboard the ship and for others to stay away.

"Alright," Captain Bill replied, scratching his head. "Scurvy, you and Henry take this 'ere ship and as many of what's below that you can turn into sailing men and follow behind us at a distance. As ye can, go into the hold and get them that's dead and give 'em a toss o'er the side."

The African male finally spoke. His English was fair, but it had a clipped sound as one that had learned it over time.

"Sir, the ship is doomed," the man said. "She must be sunk. She's a death ship now!"

"And you are lucky to still be alive," Captain Bill said as he dug the point of his cutlass into the man's stomach, just enough to watch it begin to bleed and then withdrew it.

"Better yet, black man," Captain Bill stated flatly. "You clean them out, one by one and bring the provisions up on deck so's my crew can put them on *The Sea Devil*."

"Captain," Henry asserted. "Their food is likely what killed them. It's the rats! We don't want anything off this ship!"

"I've had enough of you," Captain Bill sneered. "Time for you to go!"

"Duel!" screamed Scurvy. "Duel to lead! It's the law!"

"It's the law!" the rest of the crew shouted. "Duel!"

"I do so challenge you," Henry said sternly to Captain Bill.

"If you challenge, then you better do so with a blade in your hand!" Captain Bill cried as he slashed at Henry's face.

Henry recoiled and jumped backwards.

"Here!" Scurvy cried as he tossed Henry a cutlass.

Henry caught it, slashed it through the air and laughed.

"Come on, you son-of-a-bitch," Henry said angrily. "I've been waiting to give you your comeuppance for a while now."

"Then here it is," Captain Bill said as he slashed at Henry who expertly countered it, circled his opponent's blade and slashed back, striking the Captain's left arm.

"You bastard," Captain Bill screeched as he made slash after slash toward Henry who continued to parry and block as his old master had taught him.

Captain Bill picked up a belaying pin with his left hand, ignoring the blood that was spurting from the wounded forearm. He struck Henry with the pin, while hacking at him with the cutlass. Henry was tiring. Captain Bill was an excellent fighter. Soon this fight would be over and Henry would be dead.

Henry used his left hand to pull the dirk from the sheath attached to his neck. He was prepared to use it properly should the opportunity present itself. It did not.

Finally, Captain Bill made a backhanded slash with his cutlass toward Henry's neck. Had it connected, it would have severed Henry's head from his body. As his old master had taught him, Henry stepped into the blow, parried with his own cutlass and pushed back. The belaying pin was raised. If it connected, it would crush Henry's head. The two struggled.

"This is for me, and all those that went afore me," Henry said as he pushed the dirk directly into Captain Bill's throat and slashed left.

Captain Bill dropped both cutlass and belaying pin and dropped to his knees making strange gasping sounds. His hands tried to stem the blood that squirted from his right carotid artery. Finally he fell face first onto the deck.

"Is there anyone else as wants to challenge me as Captain of this ship?" Henry asked.

"I'll take some of that," Muffy, the First Mate exclaimed.

There was the sound of a pistol exploding and Muffy fell backwards, his blood mixing with that of Captain Bill.

"Guess that be that," Scurvy exclaimed as he put the pistol back into his belt.

"Alright," Henry exclaimed. "I'm Captain now, and my word is law. I'm appointing Scurvy here as my First Mate. If you disobey him, you'll get what these two got. I'm changing the rules too. We all share equally in any plunder. That makes it fair. Any questions?"

The crew looked at each other in amazement. This type of split amongst pirates was unheard of. They immediately pledged their lives, to a man, for their new Captain.

Henry turned to the large African.

"What do they call you?" Henry asked.

The man pounded his huge chest with one fist.

"I am called Gazini," the man said. "In your tongue, it means Blood!"

"Will you join us?" Henry asked.

"You mean to let me live among you, a slave on your ship?" Gazini said. "I do not have any choice!"

"No," Henry replied. "You join us as a free man, with your share of whatever we take."

"I will!" Gazini thundered.

"Then it's settled. And lads, we are still under the English flag. We will not attack an English ship. Do you understand?" Henry replied.

The men murmured their assent.

"What do we do with their ship, Captain?" Scurvy asked.

"I hate to do it," Henry replied. "But they are marked for death already. Use the sixty pounder and blow a hole under her water line. She will sink quickly. May God have mercy on their souls!"

Scurvy nodded.

"And throw these two to the fishes!" Henry said. "Let them go first."

"Alright lads, step lively!" Henry said. "Who's got some music? Let's celebrate. The dark days are behind us! Unfurl the sails! We got a strong wind. Unless I miss my guess, Port Royal, is less than two days away. With a fair wind, we will make it quickly!"

Henry took his place beside the helmsman.

"Let her go," Henry observed as he crossed his arms. "Wet the sails! Get her up and moving and there's an extra ration of rum for every man this evening. It has been a heavy day at sea and it's past us! Let's let the world know that Captain Henry Jennings is here!"

He was right. Captain Henry Jennings, the pirate of honor was born. The prophesy of his old master had been fulfilled.

Chapter 25

"We shall defend our island, whatever the cost may be, we shall fight on the beaches, we shall fight on the landing grounds, we shall fight in the fields and in the streets, we shall fight in the hills; we shall never surrender."

Winston Churchill

In March of 1717 tensions between the British Monarchy and France were becoming strained despite Britain having signed a preliminary alliance with France on November 28, 1716. The situation was exacerbated by the poor attempt by James Stuart to obtain the British crown and his subsequent exile in France. Once the treaty was signed, Stuart left France and sought refuge with Pope Clement XI. This tension bled over into the seas, where British and French ships fought for wealth amongst their hold, to feed the ever-needy war machines that were turning in Europe.

However, despite the issues at sea, the genteel amongst Britain's wealthy continued their lust for French cuisine, art and literature.

In 1715 the French greeted a new king for the first time in seventy-two years. Louis XV, a boy only five years old, succeeded his great-grandfather Louis XIV, the Sun King, who had made France the preeminent power in Europe. For the next eight years, the late king's nephew, the duc d'Orléans, governed as regent. His appetite for beauty and vivaciousness was well known, and he set aside the piety enforced by Louis XIV at Versailles. France turned away from imperial aspirations to focus on more personal—and pleasurable—pursuits. As political life and private morals relaxed, the change was mirrored by a new style in art, one that was intimate, decorative, and often erotic. This movement from imperialism and politics to art would be the beginning of the end of all that Louis XIV had fought for.

With France's attention turned inward, French ships began their movement toward the New World and the attainment of riches and plunder, far out of the reaches of the French Monarchy. With the death of England's Queen Anne in 1714, and the accession to the throne by King George I, the power of Britain's monarchy began to wane. It would eventually end with the power of the country falling to the Cabinet and the Prime Minister would eventually gain ultimate power.

George was active in directing British foreign policy during his early reign. In 1717 he contributed to the creation of the Triple Alliance, an anti-Spanish league composed of Great Britain, France and the United Provinces. In 1718 the Holy Roman Empire was added to the body, which became known as the Quadruple Alliance. The subsequent War of the Quadruple Alliance involved the same issue as the War of the Spanish Succession. The Treaty of Utrecht in 1713 recognized the grandson of King Louis XIV of France, Philip, as the King of Spain on the condition that he gave up his rights to succeed to the French throne. Upon the death of Louis XIV in 1715, however, Philip sought to overturn the treaty.

Spain supported a Jacobite-led invasion of Scotland in 1719 but stormy seas allowed only about three hundred Spanish troops to arrive in Scotland. A base was established on the west Scottish coast in April, only for it to be destroyed by British ships a month later. Attempts by the Jacobites to recruit Scottish clansmen yielded a fighting force of only about a thousand men. The Jacobites were poorly equipped, and were easily defeated by British artillery at the Battle of Glen Shiel. The clansmen dispersed into the Highlands, and the Spaniards surrendered. The invasion never posed any serious threat to George's government.

With the French this time fighting against him in the War, Philip's armies fared poorly. As a result, the Spanish and French thrones remained separate. This left the countries of Britain, France, and Spain open to plunder each other on the high seas with no survivors left on either side to lay claim to the deed. And so, the game of piracy continued!

Chapter 26

"The only rules that really matter are these: what a man can do and what a man can't do. For instance, you can accept that your father was a pirate and a good man or you can't. But pirate is in your blood, boy, so you'll have to square with that some day. And me, for example, I can let you drown, but I can't bring this ship into Port Royal, Jamaica all by me onesies, savvy? So, can you sail under the command of a pirate, or can you not?"

Captain Jack Sparrow
Pirate of the Caribbean: The Curse of the Black Pearl

"Land ho!" came the cry from the crow nest on the main mast.

Henry Jennings ran from his cabin, take the steps two at a time, a spyglass in his hand. He had never seen Port Royal, Jamaica, nor any place else in this new land and it excited and thrilled him. He handed the glass to Scurvy who viewed it and nodded.

"That be Port Royal, Captain!" Scurvy observed excitedly. "Beggin' the Captain's pardon, I'd like to speak freely."

"You may always speak freely," Henry said. "Go ahead!"

"Sir, if'n it was me, I'd only left half the lads go to shore at a time and let them cast lots to see who goes and stays," Scurvy said soberly. "This place is notorious for stealing ships and cargo."

During the "Golden Age of Piracy" in the late 17th and early 18th centuries, Port Royal, Jamaica stood as one of the most popular ports of call for thieves, prostitutes and pirates of every stripe. The small harbor's association with marauding began in the mid-1600s, when Jamaica's governors offered it up as a safe haven for pirates in exchange for protection from the Spanish. The buccaneers accepted the deal, and the town soon became a major staging ground for British and French privateers—ship captains commissioned by the Crown to disrupt Spanish shipping in the Caribbean and Atlantic. One of the most famous of these state-sanctioned pirates was Sir Henry Morgan, a Welsh captain who used Port Royal as a base of operations for raids on the Spanish strongholds at Portobello, Cartagena and Panama City.

Port Royal prospered on the back of its pirate economy, and by the 1660s its streets were lined with taverns and brothels eager to cater to the whims of young buccaneers flush with Spanish loot. The harbor was overrun with gambling, prostitution and drink, where hard-living mariners often squandered thousands of Spanish coins in a single night. Even after the age of privateering had ended, the so-called "wickedest city on Earth" continued to serve as a retreat for a new brand of lawless, freelance pirates.

"I believe you," Henry said. "Want to take care of that for me? I assume you and I will be among the first party to disembark. Rank does have its privileges!"

"Aye," Scurvy replied with a smile on his face. "The Royal's got some of the fanciest whores ye' ever laid eyes on. I'm going to buy me two!"

Henry laughed.

"Why two?" he asked.

"Because after enough rum, two starts to look like four and it's double the fun for half the price!" Scurvy insisted.

"Do you know the name of the ship belonging to Captain Jack Marsh?" Henry asked.

"Are ye still looking for him?" Scurvy requested with a slight frown on his face. "He's a hard 'un to get to."

"I still want to meet him," Henry insisted.

"Aye then," Scurvy said quietly. "His ship's name is *The Gallows* and I bet she is already in port. Captain, it's a rough town you're in. Please take Gazini with you if I ain't here!"

"Alright then," Henry replied. "Let's dock her and sell what we can, while I look for Captain Jack Marsh!"

Chapter 27

"We need to find God, and he cannot be found in noise and restlessness. God is the friend of silence. See how nature - trees, flowers, grass- grows in silence; see the stars, the moon and the sun, how they move in silence... We need silence to be able to touch souls."

Mother Teresa

While Henry was getting his first view of Port Royal in March of 1707, Elizabeth Howard and her handmaiden, Cassie, were finally becoming used to the creak of the ship and the sounds of men as they moved about. They were on a pilgrimage to Rome. As a devout Catholic, Lord Howard believed every member of their family should visit the Vatican at least once in their lifetime.

Elizabeth still recalled the terrible argument with her parents over the pilgrimage.

"Damn it girl," Lord Howard thundered. "I am your father and you will do as I say! You are going to Rome. I simply cannot stand to see you here pining away like some love struck teenager over someone that will never come home!"

"Henry will return for me," Elizabeth insisted.

"Henry might as well be dead," Lord Howard exclaimed. "If he is not dead, then he will be! You are going with Cassie and Lord Roche as chaperone!"

And that was that.

With the untimely disappearance of Henry and the strange circumstances following his quick exit from the county, Lord Howard believed the trip would put his daughter in better spirits. Of course a servant and an old friend of the family, who tried to make the trip once every four or five years, had to accompany her. Lord Roche was now in his early seventies. The women had a small, but well decorated cabin below that of the Captain. Lord Roche was immediately across the corridor. All proprieties had to be strictly observed. Generally the women stayed to themselves, except for a meek sailor who came down to exchange their dunny pots and bring them a meal. Sometimes they went on deck with Lord Roche, but never stayed long.

Their journey would take them past France, Spain and Portugal, through the Straits of Gibraltar and on to Rome. As land was usually in sight, thoughts that their trip would be interrupted were not anticipated.

This was the case one cold morning when both women were awakened by the sound of a cannon booming near the front of the ship.

"Quickly Cassie!" hissed Elizabeth. "Get dressed!"

"What is it mum?" Cassie asked.

"I'm not sure," Elizabeth replied. "Just get your clothes on!"

As the women finished dressing, there was a knock at the door.

Elizabeth opened it just a crack, saw that it was Lord Roche and opened it wider.

"What's wrong?" Elizabeth asked. "Why have we stopped and what was that explosion?"

"We have been intercepted by a French warship," Lord Roche exclaimed. "And we were so close to leaving French waters!"

"We have a truce with France," Elizabeth said. "Even if it is an uneasy one!"

"They are boarding us now," Lord Roche said. "All of us are to report to the upper deck. It is cold. You may want to don your shawls!"

He was correct. The winter air bit at them as it blew across the deck of the ship. Everyone aboard stood on the open deck.

"What cargo have you," a French sailor asked. "Do not lie, for we will search the ship!"

"We have nothing of value," the Captain of the English vessel replied. "We have only passengers on a pilgrimage to Rome!"

"Rome?" a familiar voice said. "Are you seeking God my good Captain, or is he seeking you?"

"I'm afraid I don't know what you mean," the Captain replied.

"Then you definitely need to meet your God!" the man replied.

Suddenly a French sword entered the Captain and the point protruded through his back. The sword wielder pushed it again and grunted in satisfaction as the blade pushed further into the Captain's gut. Blood spouted in all directions.

"There's your God," the sword wielder replied.

"Now see here!" Lord Roche said angrily. "This man was a British subject!"

"Quite so!" the man replied as he swiftly turned to face Lord Roche.

It was then Elizabeth saw his face.

"Monsieur Rochechouart!" she exclaimed.

"Why Miss Elizabeth Howard," the man said as an evil grin came across his face. "Yes, it is I, Pierre Clovis Rochechouart at your service! How strange it is to see you again."

"You have no right!" Elizabeth said angrily.

"Oh, but I have told you before," Pierre said. "I have every right by order of his Majesty to attack any ship that is not flying the

French flag and take from her what I will. Then I sell it either in the East Indies or in the New World for whoever will give me the highest price."

"You bastard!" Elizabeth said and some of the Frenchmen laughed.

"No, I was not the bastard," Pierre exclaimed. "Your dear Henry was the bastard as I understand it. Alphonse, move your gear to the Second Mate's cabin. You will bunk with him throughout the duration of this trip. Move the women to the First Mate's cabin."

"Where are you taking us?" Elizabeth demanded angrily.

"Well, since you didn't like me, or my smell, perhaps you will like that of your new gentleman friends. Where we are going, men will pay high for a beautiful, untouched woman. I assume you remain untouched? Perhaps I should see for myself!"

The men laughed as he made a pass toward Elizabeth's dress and she backed away.

"Don't think so well of yourself," Pierre said. "I wouldn't touch that little mound of flesh. But someone else will. Perhaps I will let the men share your servant. She's not much to look at, but since bringing women on board a ship is bad luck, it could be a good omen. What do you think?"

Cassie gasped, "Please Mum! No! Don't let them all take me!"

"Quiet Cassie," Elizabeth whispered. "He is trying to scare us. "

"And well I did!" Pierre said joyfully. "Men, prepare to set sail for Port Royal! We will take any ships we meet along the way!"

"What about them?" the First Mate said as he pointed toward the rest of the British ships crew.

"Kill them all and burn the ship," Pierre exclaimed. "And lock these two in the First Mate's cabin!"

"No!" Elizabeth exclaimed as she placed herself between Lord Rockfort and the French crew.

Something heavy struck her on the back of her head and Elizabeth knew no more.

Chapter 28

"If you prick us do we not bleed? If you tickle us do we not laugh? If you poison us do we not die? And if you wrong us shall we not revenge?"

William Shakespeare

Henry rummaged through the Captains quarters on *The Sea Devil.* He found many things of value, charts, navigation tools, and a series of circles drawn on a map that depicted something of interest to someone. As he reviewed the Captains log, he caught references to a series of wrecks from the Spanish Flotilla, a series of two Spanish convoys that left Spain twice a year for the Indies or the New World in search of gold and silver. Much of this came by way of the New World. There were many wrecks in and around Tortuga and Cuba. In fact, there appeared to be a line of these, which could lend credence to the fact this was indeed part of the lost Spanish Flotilla.

In an overhead storage bin, he found what he sought. His personal belongings, which included his sword and pistols, were neatly intact. These he carefully inspected and placed them on the bunk. He then furthered his search of the cabin and found his original clothing. This he also placed alongside his weapons.

Calling for a basin of water, he took what was commonly known as a "whore's bath", basically wiping his body with a cloth and the water available. Using the Captain's razor, he shaved, leaving the mustache to further define his new appearance.

He removed his clothing and cast the slops aside. He would not be wearing those again. He chose a clean white shirt from amongst the Captain's clothing and donned his own pants. He noticed a pair of nice Jackboots in the corner, and after careful examination decided they would be a fit. These he also transferred to his own person. A scarf around his head, his sword and brace of pistols completed the ensemble. He reviewed himself in the old mirror. It was a definite improvement.

He was finally ready.

He opened the door to the Captains cabin and tromped up the steps to the main deck. The first wave of hands that had cast lots for shore leave was ready to go as well. The remainder of the men gave them a sulky look.

"It's alright lads," Henry called, noting their sour disposition. "They'll just be warming up the Port Royal whores for you when you come ashore!"

All of the men laughed.

"Are you ready Captain?" Scurvy asked.

"Aye," Henry replied. "Let's be on our way. I want to see Port Royal."

Henry's future and his destiny with Captain Jack Marsh awaited, in the town the rest of the world knew as *the wickedest place on earth*, Port Royal.

Chapter 29

"True love is like ghosts, which everyone talks about and few have seen."

Francois de La Rochefoucauld

Elizabeth awoke, acutely aware of a throbbing headache and a large knot on the side of her head. Cassie was sitting next to the bunk. It was obvious she had been bathing Elizabeth's face with cool water, in an effort to bring her back to her senses.

"Praise the Saints and preserve us all!" Cassie stammered when she saw Elizabeth's eyes flutter. "You are alive!"

Elizabeth raised herself to one elbow. The movement brought agony and dizziness. She ignored it and sat up.

"Where are we?" Elizabeth asked.

"We are on board the French ship mum," Cassie said sadly. "Be glad you weren't awake to see it. It was terrible. Poor Lord Roche. He was so proper to the very end. One of the crew shot him in the head. I just thank God he went quickly. I can't say as much for many of the others. They left the dead and dying on the deck while they loaded the front of the ship with powder and set it off. It was horrible Miss Elizabeth, the men crying for mercy and all. The ship sank quickly!"

It was dark now. As their cabin was to the right of the Captain's, and starboard, Elizabeth could make out some lights in the night sky through their one small window. She stood gingerly, holding onto the sides of the room until she could see out of it clearly. She searched the various constellations in the night sky, praying it was early enough in the evening that she might see the Little Dipper. Suddenly she found it, and the bright star at the end of the handle. It was their North Star.

Oh Henry, she thought. Where are you? I need you so badly now. Have you forgotten me?

Chapter 30

"I like being in new places and seeing new sights."

Tom Welling

Henry and Scurvy walked from the docks at Port Royal toward the heart of the city itself, or what was left of it. Henry was amazed at how rich the town was, and the policies that all trade matters be settled in coin. Bartering was long since forgotten.

"Has it always been like this?" Henry asked Scurvy.

"No," Scurvy replied. "About 25 years ago she was hit by a big earthquake. Forts James and Carlisle sank into the sea and Fort Rupert became a large region of water."

"Did it destroy everything?" Henry asked. The town looked very rich and busy, certainly not like one that had suffered an earthquake.

"No,' Scurvy replied. "Although the earthquake hit the entire island of Jamaica, the citizens of Port Royal were at a greater risk of death due to falling buildings, and the tsunami that followed. And then there were the bodies. They tried without success to remove or sink all of the corpses from the water. Some simply got away from them, while others were trapped in places that ye' couldna' get to. People died Captain. There were over a thousand. Then the disease came in and killed over two thousand. It took a long time for it to become what ye' see today!"

"Where are we going?" Henry asked after nearly colliding with two swarthy men, one of whom reached for his pistol, but was pushed along by his mate, after noting Henry's steel gaze.

"I'm taking ye' to one of the better places here in town!" Scurvy said. "This one is clean and you won't be catching the *French Pox*!"

What Scurvy was referring to was syphilis. The disease

started with genital ulcers, progressed to a fever, general rash and joint and muscle pains, weeks or months later were followed by large, painful and foul-smelling abscesses and sores, or pocks, all over the body. Muscles and bones became painful, especially at night. The sores became ulcers that could eat into bones and destroy the nose, lips and eyes. They often extended into the mouth and throat, and early death occurred. It had a high mortality rate and spread quickly throughout Europe, Africa, and India.

The place they entered was clean enough. Clearly the clientele was slightly more upscale than the common sailor. Their brothels were closer to the docks.

An extremely attractive, young woman greeted them in her early twenties. She had thick tawny black hair and dark eyes. Her dress was a simple white cotton blouse, tucked into a red dress that stopped at her ankles. A wide belt around her waist offset the two and a very large pistol in the belt, completed the ensemble.

Scurvy made a mock bow to the woman. "This 'ere is Desiree'. She's the owner of this place and not some tavern whore!"

"It's a pleasure," Henry said as he gently took her right hand and laid the proper kiss on it.

"Why Scurvy," Desiree' said. "Where did you find this fine looking man with the manners of a gentleman? And you remembered this time that I was no common whore!"

Scurvy rubbed the back of his head and said, "I'm sorry mum. I was really drunk and well, you looked really good. I got me a handful Henry and she busted me with the butt of that pistol. Almost cracked my skull she did!"

"Scurvy," Desiree' said. "You didn't introduce him!"

"This here's Captain Henry Jennings," Scurvy said proudly. "He's the new Captain of *The Sea Devil*!"

"Really?" Desiree' said again as she gave Henry an appraising glance. "I guess that means Captain Bill is no longer living?"

"Aye!" Scurvy replied. "Henry beat him fair and square. Ran him through, he did!"

"Hmmmm," Desiree' said seductively. "Captain Bill was quite a swordsman."

"Aye," Scurvy replied.

"Drop by and see me a little later this evening," Desiree' whispered to Henry as she passed him. "I find you interesting."

"As you wish mam," Henry replied.

She turned her attention to a slender African female.

"Seiuse," she said loudly. "Give them a tankard on the house!"

"I will see you later Captain Jennings," Desiree' said.

It was not a question. She spoke it with confidence, nodded and walked toward the rear of the large tavern.

Scurvy grinned.

"I think Desiree' has her hat set for you," Scurvy said. "Don't know anyone that's ever been with her. She keeps things all business. That makes you purty special."

"Hmmm," Henry replied as he watched her buxom form across the room. "I like to feel special!"

Chapter 31

"The autumn wind is a pirate. Blustering in from sea with a rollicking song he sweeps along swaggering boisterously. His face is weather beaten, he wears a hooded sash with a silver hat about his head... The autumn wind is a Raider, pillaging just for fun."

Steve Sabol

While Scurvy set out to become very drunk, Henry assumed a position in the tavern with his back against the wall, a pistol on the table, and an eye on the front door. From here, he could see everyone as they entered and keep a close eye on the room.

Scurvy had already found his two mates for the evening who were helping to support him on his way up the steps to the rooms above. Scurvy gave Henry a wink as he passed, belched, almost fell and belched again. Desiree's eye remained on Henry as she watched her clientele, noting who came and went, both through the front door and up the steps. Her gaze was a little disconcerting, but secretly it exhilarated him after the long months at sea.

Suddenly the front door opened and a man stepped inside. The entire tavern became quiet for an instant. The man nodded to Desiree', people began to smile, and the music started again. He was obviously the mariner for whom Henry had long been seeking. He still wore a tri-point hat with a long ostrich feather, a pure white linen shirt, and large jackboots. His jerkin was clean and new. He wore the same large wide sword belt that hung from his right shoulder to his left hip with the handle of the cutlass wrapped in sharkskin. He no longer carried a brace of pistols, but a single flintlock pistol was carried inside his belt. It was Captain Jack Marsh. True enough, he was older, and his face bore a new, long badly healed scar, but it was the same man. He found a table to himself on the other side of the room, the side where the door was, in a darkened corner. Henry instantly saw the advantage. In the slightly darkened corner, he would not be seen until someone had already entered the room and it was too late to escape.

Henry stood, picked up his tankard, placed his pistol in his belt, and walked slowly to the man's table. When he got there, he noted Captain Jack Marsh had not placed his pistol on the table, but it no longer appeared in his belt.

Henry placed himself directly in front of Captain Jack Marsh, who feigned indifference, although he had already sized Henry up in terms of fighting ability and weapons.

"Is there something I can do for ye' lad," Captain Marsh said.

"I was wondering if I could buy you a drink?" Henry asked.

"I already have one," Captain Marsh replied, as he lifted his tankard, his eyes narrowing. "Have we met before lad?"

"Possibly."

"I don't play games," Captain Marsh said harshly. "Get the bloody hell out of here or I'll have to spank ye'."

Suddenly and without warning Henry flipped his long coveted piece-of-eight onto the table. It made a pinging sound as it landed, spun, and flipped over on its side. The missing triangle at the top of the coin gleamed in the light.

Captain Marsh grabbed Henry's right hand with his left.

"Where did you get this?" Captain Marsh demanded.

"You gave it to me," Henry said quietly.

"What? You are lying!" Captain Marsh said, his right hand moving beneath the table.

"No, do you remember when you were in London in the Spring of 1693?" Henry asked. "A young girl collided with you as you and Nevel were coming out of one of the stores."

"Aye!" Captain Marsh replied. "I do remember. Nevel was such an ass, but then he always was. He bought it in Tortuga a number of years ago. There was a boy with her, a high-spirited boy that busted Nevel's crusties. He bitched about it for three days."

"I remember," Henry said.

"How do you remember?" Captain Marsh replied, a little less scathing now.

"Because I am the boy," Henry said smiling.

"Damn my eyes!" Captain Marsh said unbelievingly. "After all these years and you did look for me!"

"Aye," Henry replied. "I killed a man in England and had to flee to escape the gallows. I missed you as I was hurriedly leaving. You told me to look for you if I ever needed you, so I did."

"How did you get 'ere?" Captain Marsh asked.

"I signed on Captain Bill's ship, *The Sea Devil,*" Henry replied.

"You don't look much like a common sailor," Captain Marsh said as he observed Henry's dress.

"I am now Captain Henry Jennings," Henry replied. "*The Sea Devil* is mine!"

"Well, well," Captain Marsh said. "How things change!"

"Aye," Henry replied. "And I have a plan that I need help with that could make us all wealthy beyond our wildest beliefs!"

"I can believe a lot Henry," Captain Marsh said. "Alright, here take your lucky piece-of-eight and meet me here at high noon tomorrow. By the look o' Desiree' you will need that time to recover from her womanly wiles!"

Henry laughed and said, "You could be right Captain. By the way, I bet that pistol in your right hand is getting heavy. If you are concerned about me, you can put it away."

Captain Marsh gave Henry a cruel and ruthless smile.

"I already had you sized up afore you made it to my table," Captain Marsh replied. "It's those two scum over again' the wall that I'm waiting for. They stole from me, and all they have left to show fer' it is their lives, which I intend to relieve them of tonight! Remember Captain. It be your skill and your reputation that keeps you alive. Make your own!"

Henry nodded and drank down the last of his ale.

"Until tomorrow, Captain Marsh," Henry said.

"Aye lad. Until tomorrow!"

Chapter 32

"He who gives away shall have real gain. He who subdues himself shall be free; he shall cease to be a slave of passions. The righteous man casts off evil, and by rooting out lust, bitterness, and illusion do we reach Nirvana."

Buddha

Desiree' wondered what Captain Jack Marsh found so interested in a newcomer like Captain Henry Jennings. True, Captain Jennings was young and nice to look at, but Captain Marsh had a reputation for being a fair, but sometimes-ruthless individual. He also had a history in the region as being a leader among pirates. Captain Jennings was new to her. Still, one didn't get many new and seemingly unspoiled men in her line of business. Henry exhilarated her, and brought feelings of lust she had not felt in a long time.

It was a little past eight o'clock in the evening when Desiree' walked to Henry's table and placed one foot in the chair beside him. Her long dress slid back to reveal a shapely leg, and for a moment, just a hint of something else.

"Are you finished, Captain Jennings?" Desiree' asked.

"I was just drinking the last of my ale," Henry replied.

Desiree' evaluated him again and leaned over so he could get a full view of her ample breasts beneath the neck of the clothing she wore.

"Good!" Desiree' said. "Wait ten minutes, go up the stairs and knock on the door at the end of the hall."

Henry nodded.

Ten minutes seemed like ten hours as he waited, noticing Desiree' went up the stairs immediately after she left him, stopping at the top of the landing and giving him a wink and a nod.

A few minutes later, Henry rose and nonchalantly walked up the stairs, passing by a number of doors until he came to the end of the hall. He paused for a moment and gently knocked.

"It's Henry," he said.

He heard Desiree's voice from the other side of the door.

"Come in Henry," she said.

He turned the knob and entered the bedroom. It was different than he expected. It was exceptionally neat and quite luxurious. The curtains were definitely oriental, as were the rugs on the floor. The bed was as large as any he had ever seen at any estate in London. Candles around the room cast shadows, but illuminated the finery.

"Do you like my private quarters?" Desiree' said from behind an oriental screen.

"Aye," Henry replied. "They are very nice!"

Desiree' stepped from behind the screen. She was quite nude and her body was accented by the candlelight. He tawny black hair fell down her back. She stretched, a move Henry was certain she performed to give him a better view of her body. She lay on the bed.

"Do, are you going to run me through with that fine sword, or something else?" Desiree' inquired and laughed.

Henry's face flushed as he removed his sword, pistols and belt. He then carefully removed the Jackboots, his breeches, and then finally his shirt. As he sat on the bed with his back to Desiree', she touched his back noting the badly healed scars.

"My God!" Desiree' whispered. "They sure put the *Cat* to you!"

"Aye," Henry said softly.

"Moses's law?" Desiree' asked.

"At first," Henry replied. "Them more! I took a total of

seventy-one."

"And you lived?" Desiree' said incredulously.

"Unless there is another bloke sitting on your bed with a hard cock," Henry replied.

Desiree' giggled and pulled him to her.

Henry relished in her embrace and the softness of her skin.

She rolled Henry on his back, straddled him and allowed his maleness to just touch the outside of her swollen and wet lips. She groaned as she pressed his maleness to the top of those lips, where a hardened mound of flesh had begun to throb. Desiree' lifted up her body and allowed the fullness of him to enter her. This time it was Henry who groaned as she lay over him using his body to her maximum benefit, while Henry grasped her buttocks.

Finally Desiree' arched her back as the spasms over took her and again as Henry's release came. Afterwards, they lay together. She placed her hand on Henry's midsection and absently caressed it.

"You are certainly full of surprises," Henry said laughingly.

"No, Captain Jennings," she said. "You are the one that is full of surprises."

"How so?"

"You come here, dressed like a wealthy mariner, bearing the stripes of seventy one on your back, looking for one of the most famous pirates the world has ever known, and you don't see how miraculous that is?" Desiree' questioned.

"So, what caused you to go to sea?" she asked. "Was it war, the search for riches, or a woman? What was it?"

Henry was silent.

"Oh," Desiree' said. "I should have known. It was a woman. It is always a woman! What was she, some little tavern girl, a village girl, or a rich bitch that simply liked your cock the way I do!"

"It's nothing," Henry said. "I don't want to talk about it. It seems like a long time ago and in another land far away. And I guess it was."

"It was a rich girl! And you loved her!"

"Change the subject," Henry said.

"Change it to what?" Desiree' responded seductively.

This time it was Henry who quickly flipped Desiree' onto her back.

"Oh my," she said. "What are you going to do with me?"

"Screw you until you can't walk tomorrow," Henry replied as he pulled her to the edge of the bed and cradled her legs. She was once again ready for him. In fact she still glistened from his semen that began to gently issue from her with this new angle of her body.

Henry entered her, thrusting down and into her body, using his pelvis against hers to drive her hard little mound of flesh again and again. She cried him on and on. She found her release, found it again, and then when Henry found his, she found another release with him.

That night, Henry slept with her arms wrapped around him, both of them wanting something from the other, though neither was certain what that was.

Desiree' was awakened in the middle of the night as Henry whispered quietly in his sleep. What was he saying? She strained closer to hear.

"Lizzie! Lizzie, where are you?" he whispered.

"Ah," she whispered back. "That is the name of the little rich bitch! Well guess what sweetheart? You are not here! And I have just given him what every man wants and needs! He will be mine!"

Chapter 33

"The great use of life is to spend it for something that will outlast it."

William James

"Mum, I just heard we are within seven to eight weeks from reaching Port Royal," Cassie said to Elizabeth excitedly.

"Wonderful news!" Elizabeth said as she clasped her hands together. "All I need to do is talk to a British mate or Captain. Once I tell them who we are, we will be able to obtain safe passage home!"

"That Pierre fellow has a foul mouth," Cassie observed. "He was talking about me privates, he was and in front of the rest of the crew. If'n we'd been at home, I would have smacked his face for it!"

"For God's sake Cassie, don't start anything with him or the crew. The fact he believes he has two virgins for sale is what is keeping them at bay!"

"Are ya miss? Well you know, a virgin?" Cassie asked.

"Of course I am," Elizabeth hissed.

"Well, it's just that me and everyone else know how you and Mister Henry felt about each other and I just sorta' figured. Well you know."

"No Cassie," Elizabeth replied. "We were almost lovers, but were interrupted. Knowing what I know now, I would give the rest of my life just to have him hold me and to hold him. And you?"

"Well, you know I've got that boy in the village back home, what's sweet on me, and well one thing kind of led to the other and next thing I know is that it's happened. I didn't like it much the first time. It hurt. And I think it hurt him too. I don't think he had experience with a virgin. He was too fast and didn't give me enough time to adjust. The second time was better and it kept getting better after that!"

"Cassie!" Elizabeth exclaimed. "I had no idea!"

"Well, don't be thinkin' me a trollop, cause I ain't mum. We will be getting married, good and proper just as soon as he gets the money."

"What kind of advice would you give Cassie?" Elizabeth asked, reddening a little.

"Why, I'd say mum to just relax, enjoy, and let nature take it's course. If I had a man like your Henry, I sure do me best to ruin 'im for some other woman. I can tell you that!"

"I can never give up hope," Elizabeth said firmly. "He is still alive. I can feel it!"

Chapter 34

"The greatness of a man is not in how much wealth he acquires, but in his integrity and his ability to affect those around him positively."

Bob Marley

On board *The Sea Devil* Henry and Captain Marsh peered at the maps Captain Bill had worked on so hard, night after night. A small journal accompanied them.

"Can you read it lad?" Captain Marsh said as he squinted at what appeared to him to be just a bunch of lines on a piece of paper.

"Sure, can't you?" Henry asked.

"No, I never had much use for letters. It was figures and navigation what done it for me!"

"Look at the line of circles," Henry said. "Unless I am very wrong, this was where the Spanish Treasure Fleet sank. Supposedly, according to his journal, the Spanish have set up a salvage operation these last two years on shore as they try to recover as much of the treasure as possible. Jack, if we had a crew of one hundred fifty to three hundred really good men, we could take what they've salvaged from under their very nose. But we would need at least two more ships, or maybe just one if I can count you in."

"Aye," Jack replied. "I'm in, and I know just the man to make up the next ship and he hates the bloody Spanish as much as we hate the French!"

"Do I know him?" asked Henry.

"Ye' know of him," Captain Marsh replied. "His name is Captain Black Sam Bellamy and he commands *The Whydah Gally*. I have a fourth ship I want you to look at Henry. She's a sweet one she is and one of the fastest in the Caribbean and she is all yours. Her name is *The Bathsheba* and like the original, she is a pretty little thing."

"Done!" Henry replied. "And here's my hand on it!"

"And mine," Captain Marsh replied. "You know lad, I been thinking that maybe this will be my last haul. I already have more riches than many kings and I have the largest working plantation in the Bahamas. I think it's time to furl the sail."

Henry grabbed two glasses, his best bottle of port and poured them full.

"Then here's to one last hurrah!" Henry exclaimed as they touched glasses and tossed it back.

"You know life sure is funny," mused Captain Marsh.

"How's that," Henry asked.

"I don't know," Captain Marsh said thoughtfully. "All of this because one silly little girl almost knocked me on my ditters and you found me with me callin' card. Ain't life funny?"

Chapter 35

"If you want to build a ship, don't drum up people to collect wood and don't assign them tasks and work, but rather teach them to long for the endless immensity of the sea."

Antoine de Saint-Exupery

The next morning Henry and Jack met at the docks to "shake down" as it were, the *Bathsheba.* Henry was expecting a tired old relic, much like *The Sea Witch,* but was very surprised.

Bathsheba was an eighty-ton sloop and heavily armed with cannon. She was designed for speed, surprise, and attack.

"She's got two masts," Henry remarked. "I thought a sloop only had one mast."

"That's because she is a *brig-sloop,*" Captain Marsh replied. It's part of what gives her the edge in the water. She's a little bigger than a standard sloop, which means she can take the deep water between here and England. And she's double fast cause you can add almost twice as much sail. And look, the superstructure at the rear has been cut down as well. There's still plenty of room for officer quarters, but not as much room for crew. About one hundred is all you can get on her and that's pushing it. So you have to make sure you got fighters and well as sailors."

"She's a beauty," Henry said as he admired the vessel. *The Sea Witch* was an overbearing boat anchor compared to *Bathsheba.*

"Well, she's yours. By the by, I sent word to Black Sam. He will meet us this afternoon at Desiree's tavern."

Henry nodded and then said thoughtfully, "This would really give us four ships if we count *The Sea Witch.*"

"Anyone as that ye would trust to be her Captain?" Marsh asked.

"Scurvy deserves it," Henry replied. "The men love him. Give him his own boat!"

"Done!" Marsh replied.

Chapter 36

"What I remember the most really was just running wild there. Barefooted, swimming in dirty lakes, selling fruit, picking mango trees, hoping not to get caught because they don't take kindly to thieves in Africa."

Akon

Captain Henry Jennings and Captain Jack Marsh met at the tavern of Desiree'. Captain Black Sam Bellamy had not yet arrived. Henry couldn't help but admire the thriving business Desiree' seemed to attract. True enough, almost all patrons were mariners and a bunch of bloody cut throats, but at least they were the upper crust of such and Desiree' maintained order through her own pistol and two young Jamaican men that also performed "other tasks" for certain patrons whose sexual fantasies were a little out of the norm. Even the name was different. Most of the patrons knew a little English, French, and Spanish. Her tavern was named *Le Palais de Delight* or The Palace of Delight.

Desiree' had strict rules. Each whore had to wash the genitals of her patron prior to intercourse. Patrons thought this was just part of the pleasure. It was, in reality, an opportunity for each prostitute to examine her customer for *The French Pox*. Syphilis was in full swing in The Old World. Although it could rarely be cured, it could be strongly abated through ingesting mercury. Unfortunately many died of mercury poisoning.

Desiree's girls were her livelihood and she took good care of them. Their efforts caused customers to buy so much alcohol that many were simply not up to the task (literally) of engaging in any additional pleasures. Those that did were well satisfied and came back for more. The tavern was always overcrowded and tumultuous.

Such was the case this evening when Black Sam Bellamy finally arrived with his small entourage of mariners, seeking their own pleasure for the evening.

Desiree' made it a point to walk to Henry and Jack's table to let them know their guest had arrived.

"He's here," she said. "Just came in."

"Aye love," Captain Marsh said as he placed his pistol under the table, this time in his left hand.

"Come to me tonight," Desiree' whispered to Henry as she contrived to press her bosom against his arm.

"Aye," Henry whispered back. "Just as soon as we are finished here!"

Captain Black Sam Bellamy strode to the table, took note of Desiree's desirable buttocks, grabbed one of them and laughed.

Henry instantly stood up and placed his pistol in Black Sam's face.

"Oh ho," Black Sam said playfully. "I didn't know this tavern wench had somebody's mark on her!"

"I don't have any man's mark on me," Desiree' snapped. "Henry, put that damn pistol down. And you, Mister Bellamy, touch me again and you will lose that hand."

"Aye," Henry assented.

"Aye, shite," Desiree' replied to Henry. "I'm perfectly able to take care of myself!"

And with that, she marched off, occasionally casting a hateful glance at Henry.

"What the bloody hell is wrong with her?" Henry whispered to Captain Marsh.

Marsh laughed.

"You're a gentleman for sure, Henry Jennings," Marsh

whispered to him so Black Sam could not hear. "But you have to understand. This is not England. This is her place. If she is going to run it her way, then she has to have the respect of the men. The only way to do that is to take care of herself and show no quarter."

Black Sam interrupted their quiet conversation.

"I didn't come here to have a pistol stuck in me face or take any shite from your second here," Sam said. "State yer business and let's get on with it."

"Well, for starters, this ain't me second," Jack said gaily. "This here's Captain Henry Jennings and we've got a plan to make us all bloody well rich!"

"Jennings?"

Black Sam was surprised.

"Is this the same Jennings what killed Captain Bill?" Sam asked.

"The one and the same," Marsh replied.

"So, I guess he got that old tub that Bill was so fukin' proud of," Bellamy laughed.

"I did," Henry said. "But, I am now the Captain of *Bathsheba*. My first mate is now Captain of *The Sea Witch*!"

Bellamy seemed to think.

"Alright then," Bellamy said. "What's the word?"

"Our young friend here has a plan to sail to La Florida and salvage the ships, right underneath the noses of the Spanish and the French who are stalking them," Marsh said soberly. "How many men have ye?"

"I'm down to about fifty," Bellamy replied. "But I can recruit some more."

"It would be good to have about four hundred men," Henry said quietly.

"And that's four hundred splits, if you catch my drift," Bellamy sneered. "Two hundred would be better."

"I'll split it with you," Henry replied. "Three hundred fighting men, not just sailors, will work. Not a man less."

"I don't need the sniveling likes of you to do this job," Bellamy sneered again. "I can do it meself!"

"You don't have the maps, the journal, or the wreckage locations," Henry said. "Jack, I thought you said he was the man for the job. He's a pompous ass! Forget him!"

"Not so fast," Bellamy said. "I didn't say I wouldn't do it. I was just testin' ya' that's all. I'm in."

"Alright." Henry replied. "We leave in a week. Have your ships prepared, plenty of shot, ball, powder, food and water. Won't be no stoppin' on the way!"

"Aye," Bellamy thundered. "We'll be ready. Let's go men. I've had about all I can of these fancy whores. I wants me some that will show you their tits and let you take 'em on the table! To bloody hell with the stairs!"

The men laughed gaily as the little crew made their way through *Le Palais de Delight* and out the door.

"Are you sure we can trust him?" Henry asked.

"He's a pompous weasel," Marsh replied. "But he'll do his part. Lad, how do you plan to salvage the wrecks in such a short period of time? It's next to impossible!"

"Huh?" Henry said. He was watching Desiree's buxom figure from across the room.

"Oh, sorry!" Henry replied. "We aren't going to salvage anything. I plan to attack the Spanish Salvage Yard on the mainland. We'll slip in, get our plunder, and slip out again. Fast and easy Jack!"

"I hope you've got this planned out well!" Jack said quietly. "There are English and French ships in those waters too! I have no desire to face a British Man-O-War or a French warship."

"Trust me Jack and we will be rich beyond our wildest dreams!" Henry said.

"I'm already rich beyond anyone's wildest dreams," Jack replied. "I'd just like to keep me head and me neck intact!"

Chapter 37

"We all have life storms, and when we get the rough times and we recover from them, we should celebrate that we got through it. No matter how bad it may seem, there's always something beautiful that you can find."

Mattie Stepanek

The storm grew in intensity. Sometimes the ocean waves came over the top of the window. Seawater often covered the top deck and flowed into the deck below, running under the door, while the two women sat on the bunk hugging each other and praying softly. At one point they heard a shout through the wind and the rain. They would later learn two of the sailors were lost at sea. The gale blew from the south, carrying them much further north than originally anticipated. Although they were still headed in a westerly fashion, they were now hundreds of miles off course. Exactly how much, no one knew. Navigation required stars and the stars were not yet visible.

When they finally came through the storm, the ship was a wreck. They had lost countless provisions and fresh water. Some of the gunpowder for the ships cannons was also lost, but there was still plenty for the coming battle.

Pierre was livid, and used a rope's end several times, whipping the men for moving too slowly, or sometimes for the sheer pleasure of it. Elizabeth was certain of one thing. Pierre Clovis Rochechouart was losing his mind. His decision-making became sloppy. He became even more sour and sadistic. The men murmured behind his back, but not one made a move against him. Pierre was an expert swordsman and on more than one occasion, he simply ran a man through for a small infraction of the rules, always watching in cold fascination as the life slowly faded from his eyes. He would then order the body to be thrown over the side of the ship. Killing was the only thing that seemed to put him in a better mood, so he did it frequently.

One evening, he paid Elizabeth and Cassie a visit. They were much surprised, as there was no knock at the door and Cassie was changing clothes. Both women had laundered their clothing as best as they could, using a lye soap, the only soap available to clean their clothing and remove the smell of the sea from it.

On this evening, Pierre opened the door to find Cassie bare to the waist. Elizabeth was, for the moment, on deck trying to determine their predicament.

"Why hello my pretty," Pierre crooned. "No, no, you don't have to cover those up. Those are nothing to be ashamed of. They are quite nice, actually. That's it. Now if you will just raise your dress and bare yourself, this will all be over too quickly!"

"No Sir. I mean please Sir," Cassie cried. "You don't want to do this. I'm betrothed, I am. Please?"

"That's it, beg a little more," Pierre said as he grasped one of her breasts and pushed her roughly down to the bunk. He had just dropped his hands to his belt when the door burst open. It was Elizabeth.

"Cassie, you little whore!" Elizabeth cried, when she fully took in what was happening before her.

"No mum, it's not what you think," Cassie said as she began to sob in earnest.

"Did you tell him? Did you?" Elizabeth demanded.

"Tell me what?" Pierre said, looking at Cassie and then at Elizabeth.

"I wanted to tell you sooner, but I was afraid you would throw us overboard," Elizabeth said.

"Tell me what? Damn your eyes woman! Out with it!" Pierre fumed.

"While we were on the English ship, two members of the crew took us against our will," Elizabeth lied, thinking fast.

"Well now, that's just a bitch, isn't it," Pierre said. "No virgin money for me. Well somebody will still pay something for you when we get to port."

"Maybe," Elizabeth said. "But there's one more thing you should know. They both gave us the *French Pox*. It is getting worse!"

Pierre began to laugh. He sat on the edge of the bunk and laughed more. Finally he stood and tightened his belt.

"There is a God after all," Pierre exclaimed. "If you ever do find your dear Henry, all you will be able to give him are sores. Maybe his cock will even fall off! This is far too rich for me! I still don't give a damn. I'll sell you both. And if you mention the *French Pox* to anyone, I'll kill you!"

Chapter 38

"The moment you realize that you can have everything you want in life. However, it takes timing, the right heart, the right actions, the right passion and a willingness to risk it all. If it is not yours, it is because you really didn't want it, need it or God prevented it."

Shannon Alder

Henry and Desiree' lay entwined together, with Henry's strong arms wrapped tightly around her and his chest against her back. This was the way every night ended, whenever Henry was in port, for the next several months.

Henry's plan to raid the Spanish Salvage Yard was a complete success and they split over one million four hundred thousand pesos or pieces-of-eight. Henry's share came to over six hundred and fifty thousand. Then on the way to Jamaica, he encountered another Spanish ship and captured another sixty thousand pieces-of-eight. Captain Marsh and Captain Black Sam Bellamy were pleased, although Black Sam became angry when Henry refused to share the sixty thousand pesos. Henry argued, and rightly so, that the ships had already split to go their separate ways and it was his action and his action alone that brought about the additional plunder.

To further cement the relationship, Henry agreed that he and Black Sam would work together to bring down new French ships as they began to appear ever more frequently in the warm waters of the Caribbean. They had already sacked two ships within the past month. Henry always spared all the lives that he could, even if they were French. Black Sam had no respect for merchant ships and so, often killed everyone aboard before sinking the vessel. It was a point of contention for them. Another point of contention was the fact Black Sam made no discretion between French and English ships and often treated English ships with the same degree of sadistic enthusiasm as he meted out to the French and Spanish.

Henry's fame and his wealth continued to increase. Henry

now owned tremendous land in Jamaica, as well as a huge plantation in Bermuda. The plantation in Bermuda was larger than any known at that time, anywhere in the New World. Henry decorated with the lavish style of his previous life, thereby making it as English as possible, many of the furnishings obtained from captured French ships that contained French furnishings, or furnishings from the British counterparts, whom they had already plundered. The plantation owned by Captain Jack Marsh paled in comparison to Henry's and they often argued as to which was the largest and most elaborate.

It was a good life. The one thing that continued to be missing from it was Elizabeth. Tonight, even with Desiree' sleeping in his arms, he still felt the emptiness. Earlier this evening, Desiree' caught him looking at the old locket, given to him by Elizabeth with both of their likenesses inside of it. He had been staring at it, unaware that she had crept up behind him to view the likenesses herself.

"You were a handsome lad," Desiree' said. "And you still are."

"Mmmmm," came Henry's reply as he hastened to close the locket and would have done so if Desiree' had not carefully placed her finger inside of it to point to Elizabeth.

"Is that her?" Desiree' asked, as she examined the likeness closer. "She is a beautiful young girl!"

"Yes," Henry replied. "That was she."

For a moment, Desiree' felt a pang of sorrow and then jealousy swept through her. She immediately began to compare herself to the young woman. True, the girl was younger than she and very beautiful. But did she know how to pleasure a man the way Desiree′ did? Desiree′ doubted it.

At least she now had a face and a name to put together. This was the demon she must conquer!

Chapter 39

"Dignity is the moment you realize that you were always the right person. Only ignorant people walk away from greatness."

Shannon Alder

It was late evening, October 15, 1710. Henry and Jack had finished counting out and dividing the latest plunder from a Spanish merchant ship. *Bathsheba* proved to be a significant advantage in the strike. The ship was so fast; their opponent's cannon often missed her entirely. The fact she could turn on a dime proved to be a huge advantage. Henry was growing increasingly fond of her.

This week, their work had netted over nine hundred thousand pieces of silver. Both men already had more riches than that of many small countries. They had shaken hands, embraced, and went their separate way for a few days. They would be out again by October 20, sailing north, up the coast toward La Florida, seeking more Spanish ships.

One of Henry's greatest finds was an Indian tomahawk, manufactured for their use by the Spaniards as a trade item. He practiced with it daily. Gazini proved to be an apt teacher as their tribe used something very similar and the British had used hand axes for many years in war, dating back to serfdom.

As usual, Henry slept with Desiree' when he was in port. To her credit, she took no other lovers, save him. He had not touched another woman since they met. The other mariners left her alone. Although all knew Desiree' did not belong to anyone, secretly, all knew she was the woman of Henry Jennings.

Tonight, a single candle was lit in the room. Henry was almost asleep, but awakened by Desiree's playful touch on the inside of his thigh. He raised himself to one elbow and allowed his eyes a moment to adjust to the light. She lay, reclining on the other side of the bed.

"I was hoping you would awaken," Desiree' said playfully.

"You definitely kept me from falling asleep," Henry assured her.

"Do you really love that little English twat?" Desiree' asked.

"I do. I mean I did at one time," Henry said, not wanting to hurt her feelings. "However, she is not, as you describe her simply an *English twat*!"

"What changed?" Desiree' asked.

"She is unattainable and you are here," Henry said.

"You know, Captain Jennings, I don't think I have ever heard you say that you love me."

"I am very fond of you," Henry replied. "Can't we leave it at that for now?"

Desiree' managed a slight pout.

"Only if you kiss me," she said.

Henry laughed and moved toward her, positioning his torso between her legs, enjoying the natural warmth and curve of her body.

"Kiss me, Henry. Make me yours!" Desiree' whispered.

Their lips met. Desiree' deliberately made her kiss, slow and deliberate, while she gently held the back of Henry's neck. Finally, Henry's tongue entered her mouth and she accepted it greedily, feeling the sensations growing within her.

Henry found her breasts and began to caress them, while gently teasing each nipple, whose centers were no longer sleeping. Desiree' moaned, as Henry kissed her stomach and her lower abdomen. He began to seek the top of the warm insides of her flesh while grasping each thigh. Desiree' moaned again and adjusted herself for this new experience. Henry continued to kiss the softness of her inner flesh, while focusing on the hard little mound at the top. Desiree' was now moaning in earnest as she began to let herself go, to relax in the splendor of the moment. She held the back of his head and pushed him in harder against her.

Finally her body began to convulse as she grasped the sheet left and right, her buttocks rising from the mattress. Instead of stopping, Henry continued faster, ignoring her pleas that *now* was the time to stop. Her body convulsed again and again until she was spent. Henry lay with his head on her stomach, also catching his breath until he began his slow ascent to gaze upon her face.

"Oh dear Lord, Henry," Desiree' said. "Where did you learn to do that?"

"Captains don't kiss and tell," Henry replied. "My turn!"

"Be easy," Desiree'said. "I'm a little sore now!"

"It will be so easy, I promise you it won't hurt at all," Henry replied as he gently entered the ripeness of her body. Her flesh glistened under the candlelight. Henry gently pulled almost all the way out of her and gently entered again and again until she had received the fullness of him. There he stopped and gently began to kiss her lips, her eyes, and her face. Desiree' grasped his buttocks in an attempt to pull him deeper inside her. Henry waited quietly, feeling his member increase in size, allowing his body to build, waiting for that final moment when his release would come. Tiny sensations came inside her, stimulating him as they did so. He convulsed as his body emptied its hot contents into hers, her release coming again.

Afterwards, Desiree' slept. But Henry could not. He thought of Elizabeth and for a moment felt a pang of shame, then jealousy. Was she enjoying herself in the arms of another as he was? The thought bothered him tremendously. It would be around two in the morning before he finally slept.

When the cock crowed morning, he donned his clothing and weapons and gently opened the door to Desiree's room to make his way down the steps and out to the docks. *Bathsheba* waited for him and the sea called him. Whatever secrets might make up his life, the sea was his haven to forget. He was at last, a mariner.

As he suspected, Gazini waited solemnly next to the door.

"Do you ever sleep, my friend?" Henry asked.

"Not while you do, Captain," Gazini replied. "Your woman makes much noise!"

"Gazini, I have to ask. What is your extreme loyalty to me?"

"You do not remember?" Gazini questioned. His countenance never changed.

"Remember what?"

"Mine was a sentence of death," Gazini said solemnly. "Not only did you release me from that sentence, you have treated me as an equal, as a Maasai warrior."

"Gazini, you are a great warrior," Henry said gently. "I'm not giving you anything you didn't already have or didn't earn!"

Gazini shook his head.

"The Maasai believe that each person is sent a guardian

spirit. They obtain this guardian during the birth ceremony. This guardian is sent to protect the person and ward off danger until the day the person dies. At the time of death, the guardians do one of two things with the people's spirits. If they were bad people during their time on earth, they are carried off to a desert, with no water and no cattle. If they were good people while on the earth, then they are carried off to a land with many cattle and plentiful pastures."

"Mine was a sentence of death," Gazini repeated. "I will not leave you until my oath has been fulfilled. You are my guardian spirit!"

"I've been called many things," Henry said. "Guardian spirit was not one of them."

"Captain, I wish to tell you something," Gazini insisted.

The man's eyes had narrowed.

"Sure," Henry replied.

"Watch Black Sam Bellamy. He does not look you in the eye. A man that does not look another man in the eye is either a liar or plots him ill will."

"True enough," Henry replied. "I'll be careful."

He noted Gazini's stance with his large black arms folded across his chest.

"Besides, with a Guardian like you," Henry insisted. "He would not stand a chance!"

Chapter 40

"Confidence... thrives on honesty, on honor, on the sacredness of obligations, on faithful protection and on unselfish performance. Without them it cannot live.

Franklin D. Roosevelt

The morning breeze picked up, offering the promise of fair winds north, and a good voyage. *Bathsheba* was well stocked with food, water, powder, cannon and men. Henry's men trained constantly and Gazini was an integral part of the training. Although the Maasai tribe settled primarily in Kenya and Tanzania, their travels often took them to South Africa where they learned the ancient art of South African Stick Fighting.

Nguni stick-fighting (also known as *donga*, or *dlala 'nduku*, which literally translates as 'playing sticks') is a martial art traditionally practiced by teenage Nguni herd boys in South Africa. Each combatant is armed with two long sticks, one of which is used for defense and the other for offense. Little armor is used. Although Nguni/Xhosa styles of fighting may use only two sticks, variations of Bantu/Nguni stick fighting throughout Southern Africa incorporate shields as part of the stick-fighting weaponry. Zulu stick fighting uses an *isiquili* or attacking stick, an *uboko* or defending stick and an *izolihauw* or defending shield.

Gazini was teaching the men how to use these methods to fight on a tightly confined ship and it was becoming very successful.

Today the sun was rising and it illuminated the water mixing the deep clear blue with colors of orange and yellow.

Scurvy and several of his men accompanied Captain Jennings on his northern voyage toward *La Florida* where they were to rendezvous with Captain Bellamy's ship to plunder a couple of Spanish frigates that were supposed to be in the area. This would mean another fine collection of wealth. As Henry already had more than enough for a hundred wealthy men, he had considered giving up this life of the sea. But there was nothing else for him. There was nothing to live for but the sea, and the sea itself.

The sea cared naught for the secrets of birth. It cared nothing for lost love. The sea covered the sins of man and the foulness of death. Henry knew nothing else. The sea took all a man's secrets and locked them within its deep dark waters. And there they stayed forever.

His relationship with Desiree' was largely a physical one. He liked her. He felt sorry for her and wanted to protect her. But Desiree' did not *need* Henry. In fact she did not need anyone. Henry sensed very strongly from their recent conversations that she was asking him for a commitment. Being an honest man, Henry knew he did not love Desiree', nor was he ever apt to do so. This was going to cause problems in their relationship, huge problems that would take him from her bed permanently if he did not commit.

Also, Henry ultimately wanted children. Desiree' did not, and according to her, could not, as she was barren. Still, he could not hold that against her. If it were meant for Henry to father a child, then he would father a child. If not, his legacy would die with him.

Henry shook himself from the morning fog and sipped on the hot coffee the cook had prepared that morning. Coffee was growing in abundance now in the colonies and there were huge coffee plantations on Jamaica and even in the Bahamas. Henry's own plantation home in the Bahamas, which he rarely saw, yielded a wealth of the coffee beans every season. Some he sold. Others he kept for his own personal pleasure.

"Scurvy, take her out, would you?" Henry asked. "I'll be in my quarters."

"Aye Captain!" Scurvy assented.

Henry smiled to himself as he descended to his quarters on the second deck at the back of the ship. Although they were not quite as large as *The Sea Devil*, they were more than sufficient for his purposes.

In his quarters, he once again opened the locket, given to him by Elizabeth. She said this locket belonged to him and was part of the secret to his birth. The likeness of the teenage girl stared at him from the locket and his likeness stared at him from the other side. He looked in the mirror, screwed to the cabin wall and compared the two. The man in the mirror was definitely older, weathered and seasoned. His rakish good looks were a little marred by a fine white scar that ran from the corner of his left eye, down the side of the same cheek toward his chin When he became angry, the scar seemed to glow with a life of its own.

Suddenly he dropped the locket onto the deck. Although it did not break, his likeness popped loose from inside of it. Henry hastened to pick it up and tried to put the parts back together. This, his weapons and his miraculous piece-of-eight were the few possessions that really meant anything to him. As he gently tried to insert his likeness inside the locket, he noticed some gold writing, somewhat diminished by time. It read simply, *To my darling Josephine, Love Henry Rockfort.*

Henry frowned. He knew Henry Rockfort, Duke of

Kensington. The man was a frequent visitor to Norfolk Castle, as Henry grew. Henry knew he was a good friend of Elizabeth's father and the two served together in the military. That was about all.

Still, there was no mistaking the name. Perhaps the woman he claimed as his mother thought him striking and named Henry after him. Or, perhaps it was just pure coincidence. Either way, it meant nothing. Henry reassembled the locket and placed it in the drawer of his small cabinet and securely fastened it. It was his one last link with Elizabeth.

Chapter 41

"I have learned to hate all traitors, and there is no disease that I spit on more than treachery."

Aeschylus

The *Whydah* nestled firmly in each ocean tough, the spray sometimes drifting up over the forecastle. They were hitting almost six knots, a good speed for the vessel. *Bathsheba* could easily run nine or ten knots with a good wind and her sails wet.

Captain Bellamy stared through the spyglass at the ship on the horizon.

"What is she Cap'n?" the First Mate asked, straining to see for himself without the benefit of a glass.

"Oh she's French all right," Bellamy sneered.

"Want to just float off from her until *Bathsheba* gets 'ere?" the Mate asked.

"No," Bellamy replied. "Fuk 'em! I'm tired of sharing with Jennings and his shite crew! Head toward her! Make ready the cannon. Prepare to hoist the colors on my order!"

"Aye Cap'n," the First Mate answered doubtfully.

"Move it! Now!" Bellamy fumed.

"You heard 'em lads! Hoist the mainsail! Water 'em down! You, Dukey! Go below and tell the lads to get the cannon ready. Ready the sixteen pounders. I want to blow that main mast in twain!"

"Aye," Dukey said sullenly. He wasn't looking forward to a fight where they might be outnumbered.

"That's it," Bellamy glowered. "We're gaining on her! Keep that French flag up until we gets close. Steady lads! Steady! We are almost there. Ready?"

Bellamy stood on the steering deck of the *Whydah* and waved to the Captain of the other vessel. He smiled and saved back, thinking there might be a good chance to parlay or trade provisions.

"Steady lads," Bellamy said lowly. "Steady. Strike the flag! Raise our colors!"

The moment the French flag went down and the skull and crossbones were raised; the Captain of the French vessel began shouting orders.

"Now!" Bellamy yelled triumphantly. "Give 'em the whole broadside!"

There was a series of massive explosions as the cannon ball and chains tore through the target vessel, tearing down rigging and creating great holes in the side of the French ship. She was already beginning to lisp.

"The French Captain is asking for terms," the First Mate shouted to Bellamy.

"Tell him to prepare to be boarded and we will discuss terms!" Bellamy cried over the din of gunshot volleys and still an occasional cannon.

The *Whydah* pulled alongside and the men deployed grappling hooks to pull the vessels together. The cannon of the *Whydah* had done the damage intended.

"See what's below!" Bellamy cried. "Line up her crew on deck!"

"Well?" Bellamy said as he massaged his beard.

"Ya' won't believe it Cap'n. There has to be at least four or five tons of treasure in her hold," the crewmember said.

"Aye," Bellamy replied. "Move it, and quickly."

"Aye Captain!"

"What about them?" the First Mate asked as he nodded his head toward the prisoners.

"Kill them!" Bellamy replied adamantly so the prisoners could hear. "Kill them all save one. Put him in a longboat with some food and water, compliments of Captain Henry Jennings and *Bathsheba*!"

The First Mate grinned.

"Oh, let him know our heading takes us south," Bellamy said defiantly.

And then quietly, Bellamy said, "And plot a new course north!"

"Aye Captain!" he said. "Captain Jennings gets the credit and we gets' the treasure!"

Chapter 42

"In a time of universal deceit - telling the truth is a revolutionary act."

George Orwell

Lord Rockfort greeted his friend Lord Howard as he entered the huge library. The library was a place Lord Rockfort also retreated, when he did not wish to be disturbed. The death of his wife brought him little pleasure. The death of his eldest son brought great emotional pain. He lived a dismal life, disconnected from the rest of British aristocracy.

"My good friend, come in. Sit!" Lord Rockfort said as he pointed to an expensive couch. "May I pour you a glass of port, or would you prefer something stronger?"

"Rum, if you have it Henry," Lord Howard said quietly.

The glass was offered to him. He tossed it back and held the glass for Henry to pour him another.

"Still no word about Elizabeth?" Lord Rockfort asked.

"Very little," Lord Howard replied. "All we know is that a French vessel attacked her ship en route to Rome. There was one survivor that was picked up by a British merchant ship a few days after the attack. He swears everyone was put to death, except for two women who were moved over to the French vessel. Where they went after that, he did not know."

"Then there is still hope," Lord Rockfort said. "Elizabeth is a resourceful young woman. If she can find a way to return, I am certain she will. We must hope."

"Yes," Lord Howard replied. "We must hope."

"If only I could get *some* word of Henry," Lord Rockfort said sadly. "He is the only close family I have left."

Lord Howard hesitated.

"I originally went to London to ask Parliament to solicit

King George to allocate resources to find Elizabeth," Lord Howard said quietly. "Of course there was little interest in spending thousands of pounds to find two women in a vast ocean. But while I was there, I received some news that I thought you would be interested in."

"Yes?" Lord Rockfort said absently.

"Henry lives, old friend," Lord Howard said quietly.

"How do you know?" Lord Rockfort demanded.

"The Governor of Jamaica has petitioned the King to declare one Captain Henry Jennings of stealing the King's portion of the plunder due him when the Governor made Henry Jennings a privateer. It would seem Henry is now a pirate on the open sea!"

"Henry? A pirate? The entire idea is preposterous!" Lord Rockfort seethed.

"I don't think so, old friend," Lord Howard said. "His fame is spreading from Port Royal to England, France, Spain, and even to the colonies in the New World. He is known for leniency when it comes to prisoners and will spare the lives of the crew, if possible, once he relieves them of the burden of whatever treasure they may be carrying. The Spanish have had a price on his head for over a year now. The only reason England has turned their head is that he refuses to attack an English ship."

"Are you sure it is him?" Lord Rockfort asked.

"They are as sure as they can be, without laying eyes on him. They say he keeps company with several other villains, one Captain Jack Marsh and a Captain Bellamy. Bellamy is a brute and attacks any ship that crosses his path. Marsh is much more selective and seems to have some personal vendetta against the French and the Spanish."

"So my son is a pirate and a scallywag," Lord Rockfort said sadly.

"Henry had very little choice after the misadventure of the duel, and while defending Elizabeth's honor," Lord Howard replied. "Part of this is my fault. If I had not been so damned blind as to how close the two of them had become, I would have been able to stop this."

"What do you mean?" Lord Rockfort asked.

"I mean Henry and Elizabeth are in love," Lord Howard replied. "I denied him her hand in marriage due to his status and my desire to increase our family's wealth. Surely you see that old boy!"

"Status? My son was not good enough for Elizabeth?" Lord Rockfort thundered.

"Henry, show some clear thinking. He is, after all a bastard!"

"He was not just a bastard," Lord Rockfort thundered again. "He is my heir. He is Henry Rockfort, Ninth Duke of Kensington and my son! This is how you repay me? You set the stage for my son to become a wanted man, with a noose waiting for him? If you had allowed Henry and Elizabeth their wishes, Elizabeth would still be here! Get out of my house Bernard. Get out and don't ever come back. If you do, I will kill you!"

"Now see here!" Lord Howard exclaimed.

"No, you see here," Lord Rockfort exclaimed as he opened a drawer beside the opposing couch, removed a pistol, and cocked it.

"Very well," Lord Howard said as he stood and walked to the door. Once he got there he paused.

"Henry, all of this makes little difference," Lord Howard said quietly as he tipped his hat to leave. "By week's end, your son will be declared a traitor to the crown and a pirate. His Majesty will have no choice but to send British warships in search of him."

Lord Howard stopped.

"And when they find him, they will hang him from the yardarm!"

Chapter 43

"Christianity is, I believe, about expanded life, heightened consciousness and achieving a new humanity. It is not about closed minds, supernatural interventions, a fallen creation, guilt, original sin or divine rescue."

John Shelby Spong

"Man ho!" came the cry from the crow's nest aboard Pierre Clovis Rochechouart's ship, *King Louis Revenge.*

It was unusual to come across an individual still alive out in the open ocean. The combination of the sun, lack of drinkable water, and food quickly takes its toll on the human body. Almost everyone finally begins to drink the seawater. The end result is dehydration, nausea, delirium and finally death.

"Bring him aboard!" Pierre shouted. "And be quick about it. Perhaps he can tell us exactly where we are, since we are so off course!"

The poor man was pulled aboard. He was delirious, but reacted well to an influx of fresh water and some bread.

"Who are you?" Pierre asked.

It was obvious he cared naught for the man pulled from the sea, but only for his selfish and narcissistic desires.

"Andre'," the man said breathing heavily. "I was mate aboard the French Frigate *Rapière.* Pirates overtook us two days ago. They killed everyone aboard, except me and set me free in a longboat!"

"Who were they?" Pierre snarled. "Who dares to attack a ship of France?"

"I heard it was Captain Henry Jennings," Andre replied. "He has set sail south."

"And where are we?" Pierre asked.

"Hard to say for certain, but I would say you are about one hundred miles west and fifty miles north of *La Florida,*" Andre said smartly.

"Great. Very good!" Pierre said.

Pierre was deep in thought.

Henry Jennings. After all this time and you are indeed alive, and flourishing. Oh that I had killed you that day on the commons.

"Wet the sails!" Pierre screeched. "Plot a course due South, and watch for Spanish sails. First man that sees any sail gets an extra ration of rum!"

"Do you want us to take Andre' below?" one of the deck hands asked.

"No, too much trouble," Pierre, replied. "Throw his worthless *cul* overboard! First ship we come to that is headed south to Jamaica, we tell them Captain Henry Jennings is now attacking French vessels, an act of war!"

Chapter 44

"Tragedy in life normally comes with betrayal and compromise, and trading on your integrity and not having dignity in life. That's really where failure comes."

Tom Cochrane

Henry verified their location again. *Bathsheba* had slowed to a speed of about two knots. It was just enough to keep underway, but slow enough to focus on their location for the *Whydah.*

"I don't understand," Scurvy said. "They had at least a day's lead on us. She should be here."

"I know," Henry said thoughtfully. "Hell, Bellamy may be drunk in the hold, too drunk to plot a decent course."

Gazini shook his big head.

"Something is not right. I feel it," the big man said evenly.

Henry did not doubt him. Gazini had been right too many times about too many things. How he knew, Henry did not want to know. But the fact that he was right most of the time had proven invaluable on many voyages.

Suddenly one of the men in the forecastle cried out.

"It's wreckage, Captain!"

Henry ran forward. Gazini stayed on his heel. For a moment, Henry was irritable. Hell, if he had to piss, it seemed Gazini had to be there to make certain the stream went the right way.

"It is wreckage Captain," Gazini cried. "Look, she was French!"

A keg floated past *Bathsheba*. The writing on the keg was unmistakable. It was definitely French.

"Do you think Bellamy did this?" Scurvy asked.

"Aye," Henry replied. "I would almost bet on it. But he knows it's the Spanish ships we are looking for. England has an uneasy truce with France. I have no desire to start an all out war!"

"Shite," Henry exclaimed. "This is what is left of that French frigate that's been taking some of our Spanish vessels the past few months. Yes, this is Bellamy's work!"

"What do you mean," Scurvy said.

"I mean the bastard hit the French ship *after* it had plundered the Spanish Galleon that was our original mark. He culled us men. He double crossed us!"

"What are you going to do?" Scurvy asked, noting the scar at the side of Henry's eye and cheek had taken on a crimson color.

"I'm going to find him and kill him!" Henry said evenly.

"Captain, revenge will only eat at the one taking revenge," Gazini said quietly.

"And one of the first lessons Captain Jack Marsh taught me is that if people think you are soft and that you won't retaliate, it will cost you your plunder, perhaps your ship and maybe your life. My reputation is at stake!"

"What is your wish Captain?" Scurvy asked.

Henry looked up at the sun. It appeared to be about one o'clock in the afternoon.

"This came from the north," Henry said. "Plot a course due north. Let's find the *Whydah*."

Chapter 45

"Betrayal is the only truth that sticks."

Arthur Miller

Aboard *King Louis Revenge*, Pierre stayed on deck, one foot on the boatswain's box and the other on the worn decking, watching the horizon for signs of a sail. None came. He had almost decided they had passed Henry's ship, when a member of the crew on the starboard side of the ship announced his visual.

"Sail ho!" he cried.

Pierre took a long look through his spyglass, carefully measuring each inch of the ship and trying to count guns. *Bathsheba* was now equipped with about thirty guns on the gun deck, fifteen on each side. What he did not know was that Henry had added another four sixty pounders on the upper deck where he kept them concealed. Two were located on the forecastle and two more were counter opposed near the front sides of the ship. It gave *Bathsheba* a great advantage if she needed to pass her quarry and take a massive shot at her below the water line.

"She's running the British flag, alright," Pierre said. "Set a course dead for her. Load the guns. I want everything aboard this ship loaded and ready. Prepare the side arms and the grappling hooks. Pass out the cutlasses! I want this ship, do you hear me. And the Captain is mine!"

"We are on course to cross her bow Captain," the First Mate, Bastian noted.

"Steady," Pierre cried. "If we must ram her to have her, then we shall!"

On board *Bathsheba* the crew had already noted the slightly larger French ship bearing down on them.

"Captain, I think she means to ram us!" Scurvy exclaimed.

"Shall we pour on the sail and outrun her?"

"No," Henry said firmly. "Let her come to us. Pass out the small arms, cutlasses, and gaffs. She's flying a French flag and she likely thinks we are the ones responsible for the demise of the frigate we found earlier. We have no choice. Gazini, quickly assemble as many men as we can toward the front of the ship. We don't have long."

After the men were assembled, they looked at their Captain for guidance and reassurance. Henry was going to be able to give them very little.

"Men, we've all been through a great deal together. We've fought, taken our plunder, and celebrated. Today's fight is different. We aren't fighting for gold or wealth. We are fighting for our very survival. That is a French warship. That means her crew are as seasoned as we are, if not more so. We must stand our ground and fight. We can't outrun her forever. Some of you will die. Stand by each other and I'll stand by you. Let's show these bastards what the crew of *Bathsheba* is capable of. Do not ask for any quarter for none will be offered. Do you understand?"

The men nodded their assent.

"Alright then," Henry said. "To your stations, man the cannon. Arm the sixty pounders. I want to blow this bitch out of the water!"

King Louis Revenge drew closer. Pierre could now see the swarthy faces of the men on the other ship. He had expected something less, something soft. In his arrogant French aristocrat mind, he could not fathom that a common man could compete with the skill and training of one whom was better bred.

On *Bathsheba*, Henry was formulating his plan.

"Alright men, on my mark I want to turn our starboard just a little, just enough to bypass a direct hit, scrape past her, and as we do, fire the cannon in sequence, starting with the front and ending with the rear. When we get center mast, Gazini I want you to fire the sixty pounder, toward her middle mast. Let's bring her down. Get ready lads, here she comes!"

Pierre was formulating his own plan.

"Prepare the forward cannon!" Pierre called. "Before we collide, I want you to give her everything we have in front. Ready?'

"Ok," Henry called to his crew on *Bathsheba*. "Make ready, steady, steady, now! Turn!"

True to her design, *Bathsheba* quickly slipped to the left so that her starboard side now faced the other vessel. However, they were not parallel.

"Hold! Hold! Hold! Prepare to take their fire," Henry ordered.

"Damn them!" screeched Pierre. "Fire! Fire everything on the port side!"

King Louis Revenge emptied her guns into *Bathsheba's* starboard side. Due to their position, many of the cannon balls struck the forecastle of the craft at an angle, diverting much of their energy. Other balls simply emptied into the sea. Some rigging fell. Two of the cannon balls blasted through the thinner wood of the upper forecastle of Bathsheba. A portion of the structure broke free and fell into the sea. Still, it was high above the water line. *Bathsheba* was in no danger of sinking.

The massive firing of all port cannon on *King Louis Revenge* caused the vessel to unbalance for a moment, driving the starboard side closer to the water and revealing some of the port hull that was normally under the water line. It was what Henry had waited for.

"Fire!" Henry screamed as he pointed his sword toward the enemy vessel.

The thirty-pounder front deck cannon spoke first, then each one in sequence as *Bathsheba* parallel to *King Louis Revenge.*

"Take out the center mast with the sixty pounders," Henry cried.

There was a massive explosion as the large cannon on *Bathsheba's* upper deck spoke. The center mast of *King Louis Revenge* splintered, tipped, and would have fallen to the deck, had a portion of the remaining rigging not prevented it from doing so. The other cannon balls broke through portions of *King Louis Revenge,* taking out their cannon. One ball punched through the side deck planking, dangerously close to the water line.

"Steady!" Henry shouted. "Prepare the grappling hooks! Board her! Take your prize!"

The crew of *Bathsheba* boarded the unfortunate *King Louis Revenge.* Fighting ensued. Henry grasped a rope from the broken rigging on *Bathsheba* and swung to the deck of *King Louis Revenge.* A member of the French crew with a cutlass met him. Henry parried the thrust of his sword and quickly dispatched him. As Henry fought his way to the rear of the ship, he began to notice very few of his men were writhing on the deck. In fact, most of the dying and wounded appeared to be French, a fact that pleased him greatly. His men had trained well. He saw the figure of a ships officer close to the helm or ships wheel. The amount of gold braid told him it was likely the Captain. From the back, this one looked familiar. The height and slender build, combined with the additional lace around the wrists that extended below the jacket, told him the man was not a common officer. His skill with the sword was remarkable. He quickly dispatched one of *Bathsheba's* seasoned fighters and stood waiting for another opponent. It was then he turned and Henry saw his face. It was Pierre Clovis Rochechouart. Recognition came across Pierre's face and he smiled.

Henry's simply could not believe what he saw. His thoughts became jumbled. *How could this be Pierre? Pierre should be dead. Henry had killed him on the Commons several years ago. But nonetheless, here he was. This new life he had chosen, or that had been chosen for him was based on a lie. His life was a lie! He recalled his parting words to Lizzie. "I love you Lizzie! Forget me! Find another!"*

He was still trying to come to terms with his past, when Pierre moved to attack!

Chapter 46

"Certainly, in taking revenge, a man is but even with his enemy, but in passing it over, he is superior; for it is a prince's part to pardon."

Francis Bacon

Henry leapt from his position and fought his way to Pierre. The two men stood before each other.

"You live!" Henry stated flatly. "It was all a lie!"

"Not all of it," Pierre stated merrily. "Now look at you, my dear Henry. Aren't you a sight? I knew when I met you that you were meant to become nothing more than a common hoodlum. You have exceeded my expectations! Your dear Elizabeth will be thrilled to hear of the man you have become. Perhaps I will show her your dead body. That is to say, before I feed you to the fishes!"

"Elizabeth? Tell me news of my Lizzie, you bastard!" Henry exclaimed.

"Kill me and you can ask her yourself," Pierre stated as he removed a handkerchief from the wrist of his right sleeve, covered his nose for a moment and then stuffed it back from whence it came.

"She is here?" Henry asked.

"Oh yes," Pierre said smoothly. "She is below deck. I pulled her from a British vessel just a few months ago, on their way to Rome. I'm selling her and her handmaiden to a brothel, when we berth at Port Royal."

"Defend yourself!" Henry declared as he raised his sword vertically, with the sword grip 6 inches in front of his neck, and then lowered the sword to the right side, pointing to the ground at a 45-degree angle.

"Vous êtes un homme mort," Pierre said flatly, as he slid toward Henry.

"No, you are a dead man!" Henry exclaimed as he made a motion to run Pierre through with his sword.

He would have done so, if Pierre had not expertly stepped back, diverted Henry's sword down and slashed toward Henry's torso. Henry jumped back and swung his sword in a downward arc toward Pierre's face. Pierre laughed, dodged the strike and slashed again. Henry parried, and managed to inflict a wound in Pierre's left side.

"You are the first in a long time to ever pierce this flesh," Pierre cried in agony. "Now taste my steel!"

Pierre struck at Henry again and again. Henry was growing tired. The sword had never been his best weapon and Pierre was a very accomplished swordsman. The sounds around them became silent. The Frenchmen that remained had been rounded up and were now in the ships brig. There were only a few of them left. Henry was aware that his men were surrounding them, watching in anticipation for their Captain to kill this French dog.

Henry finally saw an opening to remove Pierre's head from his body and took it, swinging his sword from right to left. Pierre dodged the blow and Henry's sword bit deeply into the mizzenmast and hung there. He tried to break it free. It held.

Scurvy quickly jumped toward Henry, to either take the blow or offer him a weapon. Gazini picked Scurvy up and pinned his arms.

"Let me go!" Scurvy cried.

"No," boomed Gazini's voice. "This is a blood duel. What the Gods have ordained, they have ordained!"

Henry finally retrieved his weapon, unaware of the faint hairline crack that had begun mid blade. He slashed at Pierre, who parried the blow and screamed in triumph as Henry's faithful sword broke. Pierre's strike continued downward and sliced into Henry's leg. Henry fell onto the deck.

"Now," Pierre said as he seized the butt of his sword with both hands, preparing to impale Henry palms down through his torso and into the deck. "Now, we will finally see who is a noble, and who is just a bastard!"

He raised his sword and brought it straight down. Henry caught the blade, pushing it away. The sharp steel blade sliced his hand, causing the blood to pour forth from it. Henry ignored the pain in his left hand, reached behind his right side, and retrieved his one remaining weapon. It was the Indian tomahawk he had taken in La Florida.

Henry screamed, a long war like scream and using the tomahawk slashed deeply into Pierre's side. The blow was true, but too late. Pierre's sword had already penetrated Henry's chest. Blood ran from him in earnest, but it was not heart's blood. Henry screamed again, in anger and pulled the sword from his body while hooking Pierre's boots and pulling his feet out from under him. Pierre toppled to the deck.

Ignoring the intense pain in his chest, Henry straddled his opponent, raised the tomahawk, and stopped. What he saw in Pierre's eyes was fear, intense fear. He knew he was going to die. For the first time, since the duel on the Commons, a struggle began to take place within Henry. The words of Captain Jack Marsh came back to him from his youth. *Lad, you're a strong one and a brave one. You've got the devils fight in ya, that's for sure. But remember it takes great courage to kill a man. It often takes greater courage to be merciful and spare his life.*

Henry raised the tomahawk again and watched Pierre turn his face toward the deck, knowing the end was near. Dare he grant mercy to this pitiful human before him? Life was running out of Henry. He had to decide. Finally Henry stood, staggered, and righted himself with his bleeding left hand. He shoved the tomahawk into his belt.

"You lose!" Henry whispered, as he pointed to Pierre.

Gazini nodded and released Scurvy.

"The lion within him has been fed," Gazini noted. "It is finished."

Suddenly, Pierre saw his final opportunity and snatched at the pistol in his belt. Everything moved so slowly. Henry saw the muzzle begin to rise. He was too weak to respond. He heard Gazini's roar of anger and felt the tomahawk ripped from his belt. In a blur, he saw the 'hawk turn end to end toward Pierre, before burying itself between Pierre's eyes. Pierre fell back to the deck, emptying his bowels. His eyes began to glaze. He was dead.

Henry slumped and would have fallen, had Gazini not caught him.

"My blood oath to you is redeemed, my friend," Gazini whispered.

Henry nodded weakly.

"Take me to my cabin," Henry whispered.

"What do we do with the rest of the crew?" Scurvy asked.

"There are two women below. Treat them with respect and

dignity. Move them to a Mate's cabin aboard the *Bathsheba*. I do not want the women to see me. Keep them below deck. Provide them with clean clothing from the plunder we took last week."

"And the rest?" Scurvy asked.

Henry looked upward at Gazini, who still held him.

"Feed the lion," Henry said softly. "Cut their shittin' throats and sink the ship!"

Chapter 47

"I speak not for myself but for those without voice... those who have fought for their rights... their right to live in peace, their right to be treated with dignity, their right to equality of opportunity, their right to be educated."

Malala Yousafzai

Elizabeth and Cassie were very frightened in the move to their new quarters aboard *Bathsheba*. They knew naught what awaited them and the large African male that coordinated their move seemed solemn and unfeeling. Their new quarters was much cleaner that that which they occupied on *King Louis Revenge*. They were concerned when the Second Mate vacated the small room, but he seemed quite genteel, as if they were honored guests, rather than prisoners. Elizabeth was genuinely shocked as to how well they were treated, and even more so when a knock resounded on their door on their second day at sea.

Elizabeth gingerly answered the door. Outside was a man, she knew only as *Scurvy*. She sensed he and Gazini were very close to the Captain, whom she had never seen.

"Begging the lady's pardon," Scurvy said. "We worked most of the morning for ye' with a tub and some hot water. If'n you would allow us, may we bring it in?"

"Of course," Elizabeth said excitedly. "Please!"

Scurvy nodded and two swarthy members of the crew carried in a fair sized tub, not one of a tavern variety, but certainly large enough to take a decent bath in, even if it was a cramped one. Several members of the crew carried in buckets of steaming hot water and poured it into the tub until it was about halfway full.

"Pardon me again," Scurvy said. "Beggin' the lady's pardon. These are compliments of the Captain. If they don't fit, let us know. We've got a decent sail maker on board. He can shore them up for you, he can. And this 'ere's some smell good oil from India, also compliments of the Captain."

"I would like to thank the Captain later," Elizabeth said gently.

"I'll tell him, mum," Scurvy said. "Our Captain ain't much of a socializer, if you know what I mean. But ye' are invited to the Captain's table at eighteen bells for dinner."

"That will be wonderful," Elizabeth said as she cast a sideways glance at Cassie. "Tell him, we accept his gracious offer!"

"I'll tell him my lady," Scurvy said as he backed out and carefully closed the door.

Then from the other side Scurvy continued, "Mum, there's a bolt on the door. If you slide the latch pin ye' won't be bothered accidentally!"

"Thank you," Elizabeth said through the door.

"Mum, can you believe this?" Cassie said. "Have you seen these clothes? These are new and some of the finest silks I have seen in many a year. The fragrance is Jasmine!"

"I know Cassie," Elizabeth said. "Let's enjoy our good luck for a change. A bath and fresh clothes are most welcome after all we have been through. I want to make it in time for dinner. I want to personally thank the Captain for his good will and gentlemanly manners."

The two women bathed, relishing in the steaming hot water and fresh clothing. Elizabeth added a little of the Jasmine oil to her wrists and behind her ears. She and Cassie did each other's hair, trying to make themselves as presentable as possible for this potential first meeting with the Captain and his most trusted crew. After they finished dressing, Elizabeth took the small mirror from the wall of the cabin and looked carefully at her appearance.

Something had changed. She could not definitely ascertain what it was. The image of the young girl was still there. However the mirror revealed a young woman, formed by life's experiences, with an inner core forged by circumstance. She was finally a woman, bold and courageous. She was now Sarah Elizabeth Howard, destined to become the Duchess of Norfolk.

Chapter 48

"Every man must do two things alone; he must do his own believing and his own dying."

Martin Luther

The meal at the Captain's table proved to be a slightly better fare than that of the average mariner. Their dining partners included Scurvy, Gazini, the Second Mate, and a couple of other individuals she did not recognize. The Captain was not present. It was obvious the men tried their best to clean up with what they had available. It was also obvious their manners were not in sync with their portrayal of the dinner. On one occasion, the Second Mate raised his right leg, squinted and promptly broke wind. Scurvy backhanded the man across the face and knocked him backward, spilling part of his food on the plank table.

"Damn ye," Scurvy said. "This 'ere's a lady. Act like a mate what's got some manners!"

The Second Mate murmured his apologies, sat up, and promptly spilled some of the fresh stew down the front of his shirt. This time it was Gazini that bellowed his displeasure. The mate would have taken another backhand, if Elizabeth had not gently touched the big man's arm.

"It is alright," she said. "We are not at a ball, back in England. It is we that must adjust to your style of living."

The mate, once again murmured his apologies.

"See, I've spilled some on myself. Silly me!" Elizabeth said as she deliberately dropped a few drops of broth on her bodice and quickly began to dab at it with a cloth and some water.

Gazini said nothing, but cast an approving glance at Elizabeth and Cassie as they tried to genuinely cheer up the conversation. The men finally began to be more at ease, although they were much more careful to act as it they had manners whether they had them or not.

Toward the end of the meal, Elizabeth heard moaning from the hallway. The sounds seemed to be coming from the cabin at the very rear of the ship and adjacent to theirs. Gazini nodded to Scurvy, who excused himself and proceeded to the cabin. As he opened the door, Elizabeth saw the figure of a man lying on the bunk with his back to the door. The image came quickly as Scurvy rapidly closed the door. A few minutes later, he emerged with a handful of bloody rags. He shook his head back and forth to Gazini, whose flat facial expression changed for a moment.

"I am sorry ladies," Gazini said gently. "I must escort you back to your cabin. You are not prisoners, but the deck of a ship is no place for one who has no knowledge of the art. And the water is getting a little rough. We are pulling out to sea, away from the coast in an effort to move behind the upcoming storm."

"Of course," Elizabeth said. "Cassie, we've overextended the generosity of our host. Let's go back to our cabin. Thank you Mr. Gazini!"

"His name's just Gazini," Scurvy observed. "Nigras get only one name!"

"I have many names," Gazini boomed. "None of which you could say or have the honor of such."

The women retired to their cabin under Gazini's watchful eye. Elizabeth cracked the door just a little a few minutes later as she overheard the conversation between Gazini and Scurvy as they whispered outside.

"The wound is very near the heart," Scurvy said quietly.

"This is out of my doctorin'!"

"He must not die!" Gazini whispered back. "He has fed the wrong lion. It is important he feed the other one before he leaves this world!"

"You check on him then," Scurvy whispered back. "I swear to you, the fever is rising. He is out of his head! If it continues, we will have to tie him to his bunk!"

Gazini nodded, gently open the door to Captain Jennings cabin and positioned his big frame inside. The figure on the bed bore little resemblance to the cocky young man whom Gazini had learned to love and serve. Blood covered a good portion of his upper torso and continued to ebb from the wound Pierre's sword had inflicted on him. Although not deep, it was indeed very close to the heart, but had not ruptured the sack around it. It was the loss of blood and the infection that seemed to be taking their toll. Without some intervention, the Captain of *Bathsheba* would die.

The ship took a sudden lisp starboard and Gazini would have fallen had he not grabbed at the captain's small cupboard, dislodging a drawer and knocking it to the floor. He promptly picked it up, inserted it into place and began to replace the items, ignoring the moans from the figure on the bed.

One of the items was a locket, more than a little feminine for a man of the Captain's position. He picked it up from the floor, noting the fall had caused it to open.

Inside was a likeness of a younger Henry Jennings. Gazini carefully compared the picture against the one of the man that lay before him. It was the same man, from a more gentle time. The other likeness was that of a girl, obviously several years younger than Henry. Gazini blinked and moved the locket closer to the candle. Yes, she was younger, but the likeness was that of the woman in the cabin next door. This secret was finally revealed. The girl had something to do with the lion, which the Captain was feeding.

Gazini's blank face looked from the locket to Henry and back again. Somewhere, his Guardian told him the answer. This was the birthplace of the evil lion, which Henry now fed. Holding the locket, he opened the door to the cabin, entered the hallway and gently closed the Captain's door. He stood for a moment outside the door to the women's cabin, pressed his lips together, and knocked.

It was Cassie that answered the door.

"I wish to see Miss Elizabeth," Gazini said sternly.

"She is preparing for bed," Cassie replied testily. "Can this not wait?"

"No," Gazini replied.

"It's alright," Elizabeth said. "Gazini, what is it?"

"Here," the big man said as he pushed the locket toward her. "Do you know this man?"

"Where did you get this?" Elizabeth exploded. "This belongs to my Henry. Did someone steal it from him? Where is he?"

Gazini's gaze never changed.

"You say you know this man?" Gazini boomed again, as he reached to take the locket from Elizabeth who refused to give it to him and placed it behind her back.

"This is Henry's birthright. This is part of his past that only a few people know!" Elizabeth said. "I gave this to him. He asked me to marry him and Father refused."

Gazini's gaze never faltered.

"Keep the locket," he said. "Come with me!"

"Prepare yourself," Gazini whispered as they moved into the small hallway between the cabins.

The moans of the man inside were plainly audible.

Gazini cracked the door. Elizabeth pushed through it and past him. She noted the blood stained bedding. Turning the man over, the candle revealed the answer to the secret of all secrets. It revealed the ashen and feverish face of Henry Jennings.

Elizabeth sank to the floor sobbing, as she pulled him toward her. Her tears fell on his face.

"Oh my God," Elizabeth said over and over as she carefully and continually caressed his face. "Where have you been? My darling Henry! At last!"

Chapter 49

"True love is eternal, infinite, and always like itself. It is equal and pure, without violent demonstrations: it is seen with white hairs and is always young in the heart."

Honore de Balzac

"Begging the Lord's pardon sir," the footman said.

Lord Rockfort looked up from his glass of sherry. It was almost evening. He couldn't recall how many glasses had been tossed back, before this one. Neither did he care.

"Yes," Lord Rockfort said absently.

"A rider sir, bearing a letter from the Duke of Norfolk," the footman said. "He brings a letter."

"Throw it into the fire," Lord Rockfort replied. "I want no tidings from a traitor!"

"Sir, the rider was most insistent you must read this," the footman replied as he pushed the silver plate holding the letter closer to his Lordship.

"Place it on the table," Lord Rockfort replied drunkenly. "And leave me."

"Yes sir!" the footman replied as he carefully placed the tray holding the letter in close proximity to his Lordship, gave a short bow and removed himself from Lord Rockfort's presence.

Lord Rockfort considered the letter and became angry. He stood suddenly, knocking the bottle of sherry on its side. Very little stained the expensive Oriental rug. There was not much left within the bottle. Ignoring the bottle, Lord Rockfort staggered a little, tossed off the sherry that remained in his glass and threw it into the roaring fireplace.

He approached the letter, gave it a disdainful look and instead of opening the letter, he opened the door to the liquor cabinet and poured himself a glass of rum. He tossed it back, feeling it as it warmed his stomach. He turned to the letter, noting the wax seal was indeed that of the Duke of Norfolk. He half walked, half staggered to his desk, picked up his letter opener and carefully slid it under the wax seal. He opened the letter.

The style was simple and he recognized the handwriting immediately. It was that of Lord Norfolk. His hand trembled in anger as he began to read and then his breathing calmed through the fog created by the alcohol he had consumed in such quantity this day. He squinted under the lamp. It read:

My dear friend,

Please forgive me for the wrongs I have committed in the name of the aristocracy, which we live under. I thought, perhaps, I was doing the best for both of them. Henry would have never been accepted in our world and although Elizabeth loves him deeply, she would have never given up on her goal to make him accepted. I was wrong. I thought the marriage of Elizabeth to Pierre Clovis Rochechouart would strengthen our families and our relationship with France. I was wrong on all accounts.

I have word from London. It is not pleasant. I have heard the Governor of Jamaica has indeed declared our Henry an outlaw, a pirate, and has placed a price of 500 pounds for the return of his head as proof of his demise.

I understand King George has accepted the Governor's recommendation and formally declared Henry a traitor to the throne and is demanding his life as payment.

I have sent word to King George and asked for leniency, but have received no correspondence in return and doubt that I shall.

I felt like you needed to know, so as to prepare yourself when the word comes.

I remain your faithful servant.

Bernard

Lord Rockfort jumped to his feet, the drunkenness of the evening washing from him as cleanly as a wave washes the sand.

"Stanley," he screeched to the footman.

The man appeared in the doorway.

"Tell my valet to prepare me a small trunk, with my best clothing, and make ready my carriage!"

"For the morning sir?" the footman asked.

"Morning?" Lord Rockfort exclaimed. "Hell no, a thousand times no! We are going to London! Tonight! Send a rider ahead with word we request an audience with the King! Tell him to take my stallion!"

"The King?" the footman said, astonished.

"Yes, the King! Move it, damn your eyes! Now!"

The footman ran toward the stables, shouting orders to the valet as he went. Something terrible was amiss. He had not seen his Lordship this animated and with purpose in many years!

Chapter 50

"The death clock is ticking slowly in our breast, and each drop of blood measures its time, and our life is a lingering fever."

Georg Buchner

The man on the bunk moaned deeply. The perspiration dripped from his body. Elizabeth did the only thing she knew, which was to bathe his face with cool water. Gazini stood at her side, his arms folded.

"I am afraid he will not live," Gazini observed.

"I don't want to hear anything about death spoken in this room ever again," Elizabeth said flatly. "He will live. He must live!"

"As you wish," Gazini replied.

Gazini continued his stare across the room. Dare he tell his Master's woman that he felt the presence of Enkai Na-nyokie, the evil Maasai red god, in this very room? He could be here for no other purpose than to take the soul of Henry Jennings.

The Maasai believe in a single but dualistic god. The Maasai god has two opposing identities, the generous black god (Enkai Na-rok). He is the good, generous and benevolent god personified by wind and rain. There is also the vindictive red god (Enkai Na-nyokie). He is the bad or revenging god, the master of life and death and personified by thunder and lightning. It is the benevolent Narok that has declared the Maasai tribe the rightful owners of all the world's cattle, much to the unease of their neighbors. So when Enk-ai Na-nyokie strikes and there is death in a Maasai family, the entire community is affected. Death is really dreaded among the Maasai community and its occurrence brings along a sorrowful dark cloud that envelops all those who hear of it. There are no elaborate mortuary practices among the Maasai. The Maasai people believe that once life has come out of the body, the body has no use anymore and that's why they do not bury the dead but rather throw them away in the forest to be devoured by wild animals. If his Master died, Gazini would see to it that his body was dropped into the ocean to return to the earth from whence it came.

Scurvy entered the room.

"How is he?" Scurvy asked.

"I cannot stop this bleeding," Elizabeth exclaimed. "Every time I get close, it starts again with every beat of his heart!"

"It is his spirit that yearns to be free," Gazini observed.

Elizabeth shot the big man another look. It was not a kind look.

"Mate, I think you need to go up on deck and get some fresh air," Scurvy said to Gazini.

Gazini gave them both a look of disgust, opened the door, walked down the short hall and took the steps to the upper deck. It was a cool night and the sea glowed with a light of it's own as it reflected the light of the full moon.

These white people did not understand that death was a simple part of life and the manner in which one died was as important as the manner in which they lived. Henry Jennings was dying like the warrior he had always been, fierce and proud. Did they not understand this was as it should be? Still, despite the fulfilling of his blood oath to Henry Jennings, Gazini still felt a sense of kinship, and loyalty to the man. Henry had always treated Gazini as an equal, and not only as an equal, but also as an advisor. There was only one remaining route Gazini could take.

The Maasai believed if you were a male that one life could be given as a sacrifice for another. This was a birthright only available to the male population. This was the last thing Gazini could do for his warrior friend.

There was little activity on the upper deck. Gazini strode to the forward deck. There was no one present. The ship was facing the moon in the night sky. Gazini removed his knife. It was one of the few precious belongings that he rescued from the ship on which he had been imprisoned. Made in his native land, the sheath was of dried animal hide, stitched together. The knife blade was of steel, likely the broken end of a sword or long dagger. The handle was made of wood and covered with the same thin animal hide. Once assembled, the knife was placed in the sheath, soaked in water and dried over a smoking campfire until the skin became rigid and taunt.

Gazini grasped both sides of his shirt and ripped it open. The moonlight danced on the taunt muscular chest. Muttering a prayer to Enkai Na-rok, the good black god, Gazini closed his eyes. Using the knife from his homeland, he made a single slash above the left side of the heart on the left side of his chest downward and across his right breast. Blood trickled down his abdomen. Using his left index finger, he dipped it in the blood and made a single smear down the left side and right side of his face. It was finished. Gazini's life would now be shortened, but his friend's life would be spared. At least this action guaranteed Gazini would die a good death, a warrior's death for his sacrifice, and a place of greatness in the afterlife. He had traded one life for another.

Sheathing the knife, Gazini pulled the remnants of his shirt together and returned to the lower deck to find another. The moon and Enkai Na-rok watched as the night wore on.

Chapter 51

"Love is composed is a single soul inhabiting two bodies."

Aristotle

"No!" the man on the bunk screamed as he thrashed from side to side.

"I will kill you!" he said in a more cunning voice.

Elizabeth quickly raised herself from the pallet she had made on the floor and tried to quiet Henry. She was surprised to find him so strong that he almost knocked her down in his efforts to fight this unseen enemy.

She finally shushed him as a mother does to a young babe and Henry returned to the darkness that seemed to surround his mind. He was still bleeding and the infection was growing worse, as evidenced by his ranting.

Having calmed him, she lay on her pallet, still unable to sleep as she listened to the sounds of his breathing.

Quietly, he whispered something in his sleep. She strained to hear him, hoping silently that it was her name that breeched his lips. Sometimes she was afraid of what she might hear. Henry had been missing for several years. She was certain he might find solace in the arms of another. The thought was agonizing to her. Yet, there was a part of her that *hoped* he had some pleasure in these years of hell on the high seas. Yes, there it was, a mumbling of something from his lips.

"I do not love you," he whispered.

Tears crept into her eyes and one gently slid down her right cheek. Did he know she was there? Was it she to whom these words were spoken? For her, at this moment, there could be no other reason. Then, he whispered a woman's name.

"Desiree'," Henry whispered.

Elizabeth heard. There it was. Was this the name of Henry's lover? She did not wonder at the pronunciation of another woman's name. Henry's last words came to her as he left her father's estate on his large black stallion. *I love you Lizzie! Forget me! Find another!*

As much as he wanted her to do so, Elizabeth simply could not envision giving herself to another. She had chosen to wait and wait she would.

Suddenly, Henry arched his back and screamed.

"Elizabeth! Elizabeth! Where are you!"

Then in a low, cunning voice, Henry whispered, *"Lizzie, I have killed for you!"*

This was the answer for which she had long awaited. More tears flowed from her eyes and fell onto Henry's face as he settled back into his bunk, sweat flowing from him in earnest.

But who was this Desiree' and what did she mean to Henry? Was this the woman he loved? Or was this just an acquaintance from one of his many ports? How could she know? Right now it made no difference. If she did not do something quickly, the boy she remembered, and the man that lay before her would die.

Elizabeth opened the door to Henry's small cabin and almost collided with Gazini whose stolid figure stood outside the cabin with crossed arms.

"What are you doing here?" Elizabeth hissed.

"I guard my friend from Enkai Na-nyokie," Gazini replied.

"Who?" Elizabeth asked.

"The evil one that comes in the night to take great warriors," Gazini said. "He will not take this one, without taking my life first!"

Elizabeth had no answer. If Gazini believed his presence would help Henry, then his presence was welcome.

"If we do not do something quickly, Henry will die," Elizabeth said.

Gazini nodded.

"I know," he said simply.

"Gather Scurvy and anyone else that has any experience with serious wounds," Elizabeth said. "It is time to discuss our alternatives. His life changed for the worse because of me. He is dying. I will not let him die!"

Chapter 52

"Honesty is the first chapter in the book of wisdom."

Thomas Jefferson

"No, Lord Rockfort," the well-dressed servant to King George stated. "The King is very busy attending to matters of state. He simply cannot see you now."

"I sent word ahead," Lord Rockfort stated flatly, wanting to get his point across, but not wanting to anger this man that *could* influence his position with the King of England.

"I know," the gentleman said to Lord Rockfort. "He sends his regrets."

Lord Rockfort reached in his pocket and gently pulled a piece of parchment from it. He handed it to the servant, who first began to read it with an aura of detachment and then interest.

"Are you telling me the infamous Henry Jennings is *your* bastard son and heir?"

Lord Rockfort nodded his assent.

"I have kept this secret all these long years," Lord Rockfort stated. "If his life is taken on the gallows, or by an executioners sword, the King will end the life of an English nobleman. The man the Crown, and the Governor of Jamaica calls an outlaw, is really Henry Rockfort, the Ninth Duke of Kensington!"

"Can you provide proof?"

"Yes, Lord Howard, the Seventh Duke of Norfolk was with me the night he was born, when I bestowed his birthright upon him," Lord Rockfort retorted.

"I will show this to the King. I do recall Lord Howard asking for amnesty for Henry Jennings, but this information was never given."

"Then, please sir. Give it to him now. Let him know I served the Crown at the Battle of Sole Bay and my wounds still disturb me. Please let him know that I serve the Crown still and all I ask is this single boon, after these many long years," Lord Rockfort said quickly.

"Very well," the servant stated. "Please make yourself comfortable. I shall return shortly."

Lord Rockfort waited for hours, each moment dragging by and it seemed to be an eternity. Finally, almost three hours later, the attendant returned.

"His Majesty did not say no," he stated flatly. "But neither did he say yes. He asks that you give him time to consider the matter and to verify the veracity of the information you have placed before him. It is a most extraordinary situation. Word has reached us of the death of a French nobleman at his hands, and the sinking of a French vessel. While we are not at war with France, our truce is an uneasy one. This places the King in a precarious position. Do you understand?"

Lord Rockfort nodded, made a short bow, and said, "I do understand. Tell his Highness I appreciate his consideration. I will return to my home and await his reply."

Lord Rockfort turned to leave and stopped for a moment.

"May I ask the name of the ship and the French nobleman?" Lord Rockfort asked.

"Certainly," the King's representative stated. "It was *King Louis Revenge* captained by Pierre Clovis Rochechouart."

Lord Rockfort's explosive reply was heard through several corridors of the palace, as he remembered Lord Howard's correspondence.

"Dear God!" he exclaimed.

Chapter 53

"Death is nothing, but to live defeated and inglorious is to die daily."

Napoleon Bonaparte

The three gathered in the small cabin around Henry. He no longer struggled with the fever, which continued to grow at a maddening rate. Instead, a calm seemed to have come over him. Perhaps his body was now in acceptance of that which was about to occur. Perhaps instead, his spirit was now in control as it carefully negotiated its way to the land of the dead.

Elizabeth continued to bathe his face and chest with cool water in an attempt to reduce the fever. Gazini stood toward the rear, his face as impassive as ever.

Scurvy gently removed the rags from the top of the wound. The bleeding had not subsided, but it still ebbed and flowed. He put his ear to Henry's chest to listen for the sound of his beating heart. He found it, still strong and vibrant.

"I have an idea," Scurvy said thoughtfully. "I've done it in the past with gunshot wounds, although never with a sword wound."

"Name it," Gazini said quickly. His patience was running thin at this lack of action on the part of these white people. Did they not know the pain of the spirit trapped in a dying body?

"Sometimes, we have made a poultice of flour and tobacco leaves to pull out the poison and stop the bleeding, much the same as I did on Henry's back when Captain Bill had the cat laid on him. He took it more times than anyone I ever saw and lived," Scurvy said thoughtfully. "That's after you stop the bleeding. It's the bleeding and poison that's killing him."

"How can we stop it?" Elizabeth asked. "I've put pressure on it. It won't clot!"

"We burn it," Scurvy said quietly. "Aye missy, and you won't like my answer. You burn the wound so that a scab causes it to clot. Because the wound is so deep, the inside of the wound will have to be burned and then a larger burn over the top of the wound itself to finish closing it. It's going to take someone with small hands to do the job right."

"You mean me," Elizabeth said boldly.

"Aye, lass," Scurvy replied.

"Then let's get on with it," Elizabeth said firmly.

Gazini nodded to Scurvy who disappeared for almost twenty minutes. When he returned, he had a large pan of red-hot coals, a large knife and a smaller kitchen knife. Both handles were wrapped with cloth and cord to hold it in place. He also carried a small bottle of rum.

"Keep them in the coals until they become red hot," Scurvy said. "You will have to use them quickly as they will cool quickly. It won't take much. Push the smaller knife into the wound and move it around so that it burns the flesh. That will stop the bleedin' inside. Then after he calms down close the hole with the big one. Jest' lay it flat o'er it and hold it there. That will do the job!"

"Got it," Elizabeth said.

"One more thing," Scurvy said, just a little tenderly. "The left side of the wound is close to the heart. Hold it too long and you will kill him. Don't hold it long enough and he will bleed inside."

Elizabeth nodded.

"Are you ready?" Gazini asked.

Scurvy and Elizabeth both nodded. Gazini gently pried

Henry's mouth open and poured as much rum as he could inside. Although unconscious, Henry choked and almost spewed it, but managed to keep most of it down. Gazini did this several times until Henry's breathing became smooth.

"Now," he said.

Scurvy nodded to Elizabeth who picked up the smaller knife, noting the point was glowing as red as the coals from whence it came. Scurvy quickly removed the bandage while Elizabeth inserted the smaller knife into the wound, moving it left and right. Henry's back arched in pain as Elizabeth cauterized the inside of the wound. She removed the smaller knife and placed it back in the fire, in case it was needed again.

Henry moaned.

"It is working woman," Gazini boomed. "Look, the blood is stopping!"

"Gazini, hold him down," Elizabeth said. "This one is going to hurt much worse!"

Scurvy grasped Henry's shoulders, while Gazini laid his body full across Henry's lower torso and midriff.

"Now!" Gazini cried.

Elizabeth picked up the large knife with the glowing blade.

"Forgive me, my love!" she said. "Hold him!"

Elizabeth placed the flat of the blade across the open wound and pressed down. The stench of burning flesh was sickening. Henry tried to arch his back again, screamed in pain and thankfully passed out. Elizabeth held the knife against the wound until the burn closed the bleeding flesh. It did not take long.

"Now we wait," Scurvy said emphatically.

"Gazini, Scurvy, thank you!" Elizabeth said as she cast a sideways glance at Henry. "You know he would thank you as well!"

Gazini's granite face revealed no emotion.

"Warrior for warrior and brother for brother," Gazini said and left the room.

"Thank you Scurvy," Elizabeth said as she gave him a small peck on the cheek.

Scurvy reddened. He was embarrassed.

"We take care of each other out here mam," Scurvy said. "Out here, we are all we have!"

He turned to leave.

"Scurvy, I don't even know your real name," Elizabeth said gently.

Scurvy grunted.

"You know it's been so long since anyone said it, I doubt I would turn if they did," Scurvy replied. "My real name is William Tanner."

"Good night William," Elizabeth said gently.

"Too early to turn in yet," Scurvy sputtered. "I promised Miss Cassie I would let her steer the ship this evening."

"Really?" Elizabeth said.

"Aye, well she seems interested that's all," Scurvy replied quickly. "As long as it is alright with you, of course."

"Cassie is her own woman," Elizabeth replied.

"Aye," Scurvy said dreamily. "She is that!"

"It's not good to keep a lady waiting!"

"Aye mum," Scurvy replied. "If there is any change or you need me, just let one of the men on deck know and they will find me."

Elizabeth watched him exit the small cabin and lay on her pallet for yet again another long night as she listened to her man's breathing from above.

Chapter 54

"There is a place you can touch a woman that will drive her crazy. Her heart."

Melanie Griffith

Four days after the bleeding stopped, Henry Jennings opened his eyes. At first they fluttered and the bright light that came through the window struck him directly in the face.

He moaned and said, "Am I dead?"

Elizabeth turned from her position at the window.

"Henry!" she cried. "I'm here!"

For a moment there was no recognition. Elizabeth's face was blurred. Finally Henry's view began to stabilize. Although still blurry, he recognized her.

"I am dead," he croaked as he raised his head and then dropped it back onto the bunk.

"No, you are very much alive!" Elizabeth whispered. "Do you know me?"

"How could I not know you, my darling Lizzie?" Henry whispered back. "I have dreamed of nothing but you these long years."

He tried to hold her, but had to satisfy himself with gently taking her hand.

"Is there anything to drink?" Henry said. "I am very thirsty!"

It was a good sign.

Lizzie poured some water into a tin cup, held the back of Henry's head and helped him as he greedily drank the water.

"Easy," Lizzie said gently. "Not too fast. You will be sick!"

Henry relaxed his grip on the cup and Lizzie gently helped him lay his head down.

"I did not want you to see me like this," Henry said. "I do

not want you to know the man I have become, the things I have done and the life I have come to lead!"

"You did all of these things and more, because of me!" Lizzie retorted, her eyes flashing a moment of anger.

"I made my choices long ago," Henry said simply.

"And I made mine," Lizzie responded. "Now that I have found you Henry Jennings, you shall not escape from me so quickly again!"

The door burst open at the sound of their voices. Gazini's huge form filled it, combined with Scurvy's smaller form behind.

"He lives!" Gazini boomed. "Enkai Na-nyokie, the red god is gone!"

"Ya' son bitch," Scurvy said. "You gave us a scare! I thought you would be feedin' the fishes fer' sure!"

"My thanks to all of you," Henry said weakly. "One man is lucky to have so many friends! Is there anything to eat? I think I could eat half a whale's arse right now!"

"Cookie just finished some fish stew," Scurvy said. "I'll get you some straight away."

Henry nodded his thanks.

For the first time, Gazini actually smiled and grasped Henry by his shoulder.

"I am glad you live, my brother," Gazini said.

Henry cast another weak look at Gazini and smiled.

"I now owe *you* my life, and am in your debt my friend," Henry said. "All of you!"

"Get well," Scurvy boasted. "Miss Cassie wants to see how

we bring 'er about and it's almost time to move further southwest, away from the coast. I'm guessin' about three weeks to port."

"Let's get her there," Henry ordered. "Any word of Black Sam?"

"None Captain," Scurvy replied.

"I'll find him!"

"Have you not fed the lion of hatred enough?" Gazini whispered quietly from the corner of the room. "It has almost cost you your life twice. Is that not enough?"

"The last time I fed the lion of forgiveness, it almost cost me my life," Henry said with an ugly tone in his voice. "I won't let it happen again."

"Then in your language, you are a damn fool," Gazini said testily. "You have your life, the woman you love, your ship, and more money than many kings. You have learned nothing."

"The first thing Captain Jack Marsh taught me is to never be taken advantage of. It shows weakness!"

Gazini snorted, "The weakness is within!"

He slammed the door as he left the cabin.

Scurvy laughed.

"It's all good Cap'n," he said. "He'll be alright in a few."

"Ok," Henry said. "Do you think you could get one of the crew to bring me some warm water, at least so I can take a whore's bath? I'm sure I stink like three day old fish guts."

"You don't," Elizabeth said hastily. "I've kept you clean and bathed."

She reddened.

Scurvy laughed again.

"Don't you be saying a shite word, Scurvy," Henry said. "Don't you have business on deck?"

"Aye Captain!" Scurvy replied.

He opened the door, winked at Lizzie, and then proceeded to sing part of an old tavern song that he knew Henry would hear as he left.

"I went to see me old whore Sally. She gave me some and washed my tally," he sang as he rushed down the hall.

"I'm going to cut your balls off and feed them to the fishes," Henry screamed and then he laughed.

"I'm sorry," he said to Lizzie. "At sea, we have to find things to laugh about. The life is rough and without a good laugh, it gets rougher."

"I've heard much worse, Henry Jennings," Elizabeth said. "Don't think that because I grew up in a life of luxury that I didn't hear the servants talking or my mother and father in the room down the hall. And since my incarceration on *King Louis Revenge*, I've heard much worse. I'm not a child, Henry!"

"No, you are not a child, or even the young girl I left behind," Henry said. "You are a grown beautiful woman. There is still a touch of the girl in your eyes and I can still see her in your face. But you are a grown woman and I'll stake my life on that. We have many things to discuss."

"Let's focus on getting you well. Then we can talk!"

"Shadows Of the Night"

Performed by Pat Benatar

Written by D.L. Byron

(Reprinted by permission)

We're running with the shadows of the night
So baby take my hand, it'll be all right
Surrender all your dreams to me tonight
They'll come true in the end

You said, oh girl, it's a cold world
When you keep it all to yourself
I said, you can't hide on the inside
All the pain you've ever felt
Ransom my heart, but baby don't look back
'Cause we got nobody else

We're running with the shadows of the night
So baby take my hand, it'll be all right
Surrender all your dreams to me tonight
They'll come true in the end

You know that sometimes, it feels like
It's all moving way too fast
Use every alibi and words you deny
That love ain't meant to last
You can cry tough, baby
It's all right
You can let me down easy
But not tonight

We're running with the shadows of the night
So baby take my hand, it'll be all right
Surrender all your dreams to me tonight
They'll come true in the end

We're running with the shadows of the night
So baby take my hand, it'll be all right
Surrender all your dreams to me tonight
They'll come true in the end

And now the hands of time are standin' still
Midnight angel, won't you say you will

We're running with the shadows of the night
So baby take my hand, it'll be all right
Surrender all your dreams to me tonight
They'll come true in the end

We're running with the shadows of the night
So baby take my hand, it'll be all right
Surrender all your dreams to me tonight
They'll come true in the end

We're running with the shadows of the night
So baby take my hand, it'll be all right
Surrender all your dreams to me tonight
They'll come true in the end

Chapter 55

"We're running with the shadows of the night. So baby, take my hand, it'll be all right. Surrender all your dreams to me tonight. They'll come true in the end."

Pat Benatar

Days and weeks followed. Henry's strength grew and thanks to the axle grease and tobacco leaves, Scurvy insisted he apply over the huge scab, the wound continued to heal. One day, as Henry was bathing his upper torso, the large scab just slid off, leaving an ugly red scar in it's place. Although the color would diminish over time, Henry would carry the scar with him the rest of his life. The scars on his body were not nearly as bad as those on his soul.

There were several days when he ventured on deck to be met by members of the crew. To a man, they dropped their eyes as he passed, mumbled a greeting to both he and Lizzie, and turned back to their duties.

"Morning Cap'n," they would say.

"Morning me Lady," they would offer to Lizzie.

There was none of the sour, sadistic attitude that existed on *King Louis Revenge*. Although Henry was definitely in charge, these men did their duties as *if* they chose to do so.

Early one morning just before sunset, Lizzie and Henry were taking a stroll about the ship. Henry, ever mindful of his ship and his crew, quickly studied portion of the upper deck as they walked past it. It was small things, things that most would have let pass, yet Henry knew small issues led to large accidents and he would take no chances with lives of the men that served under him.

"Henry, why do the men treat you with such deference?" Lizzie asked as Henry checked another rope on their way forward toward the bow.

"Because they work this ship as free men," Henry replied.

"They take an equal share in all plunder, unheard of in the world in which we live. They know my word, as Captain, is law. However, any man is free to leave whenever he wants."

"It was not that way on *King Louis Revenge*," Elizabeth said. "The men were afraid of their Captain."

"Lizzie, there are two types of leaders," Henry replied. "There are sour, sadistic leaders who rule by imparting fear into the hearts of those that serve under them. Then, there are leaders that *inspire* their men by setting the example, encouragement, and firm yet fair discipline. The true art of being a good leader is making people *want* to step forward and do a good job under terrible circumstances."

"Are you a good leader?" Lizzie asked teasingly.

"I think so," Henry. "History will tell. Come here. I want to show you something. The sun has yet to set. We are sailing west now."

"Okay," Lizzie replied.

"Do you trust me?" Henry asked.

"Of course," Lizzie replied.

"Okay then, close your eyes and take a step forward," Henry said mindful of the setting sun.

"Keep them closed," Henry said as he watched the sun begin to slip below the horizon. Henry was waiting for that one brilliant moment of sunset that may last for only a second or two. Only mariners have seen it and only a few have looked for it. Henry has seen this brilliance many times and it always reminded him this great light as the earth went to sleep, could only come from God.

Henry put both arms around Lizzie's small waist.

"Okay, when I tell you, open your eyes quickly," Henry said.

"I will," Lizzie replied, with a little suspicion. "Are you getting even with me for dropping that frog in your tea, when we were children?"

"No, my dear," Henry replied. "Get ready to see one of the greatest sights on the high seas!"

"Okay," Lizzie replied, less confidently.

The sun had begun to set and the light from the setting sun was casting its brilliance upon the waters. It was as if the water was on fire.

"Now Lizzie!" Henry exclaimed.

Lizzie opened her eyes. She quickly took in the ball of red as it continued to slip below the horizon. Just before the sun changed from red to orange, there was a brilliant green flash that lasted for almost two seconds, and then was gone. She gasped. She didn't know the flash was viewable because refraction bends the light of the sun and the atmosphere acts as a weak prism, which separates the light into a rainbow of colors. But its beauty was unmistakable.

"Henry, I've never seen anything like that," Lizzie said as she leaned backwards into his supporting arms.

"And you never will, unless the sea shows it to you," Henry said softly. "She has her own secrets."

Lizzie turned to face him, his strong arms still surrounding her. The light from the setting sun accented the red hues in her brown hair and the wind from the ship's speed caused it to blow about her face. Her brown eyes seemed to gleam.

Henry lowered his face toward her, paused a moment, his lips just the distance of a blade of grass from hers. Her eyes closed, as did his a moment later. He was so close he could feel the warmth of her face.

Henry gently placed his lips against hers and kissed her. It was a long gentle kiss of love and passion, denied between the two of them for years. Lizzie fell deeper into his arms and placed her arms around him. Henry moved one hand to the back of her neck, relishing in the softness of her hair.

Finally, she opened her mouth and accepted his tongue. A little frightened by her own boldness he greedily accepted hers, his body and hers responding to this final moment that life had denied these two would-be lovers.

The sun had now set and darkness was falling. The shadows of the night danced around them. She bowed her head into his chest and heard the sound of his heart as it beat faster. Henry took her hand and together they walked to the steps to take them below deck. Henry stopped her, touched her chin with his index finger and gently tipped her face up so that her gaze met his.

"Do you remember the day I asked you to marry me?" Henry asked.

"Of course," Lizzie replied softly. "I will always remember that moment."

"I would still want that," Henry replied. "If our circumstances were different."

"Why do they have to be different?" Lizzie whispered back.

"I am here. You are here. The future is uncertain for both of us."

Lizzie placed her hand on the nape of Henry's neck and pulled his mouth down to hers.

"I have waited a long time for this moment," Lizzie whispered. "Surrender all your dreams to me tonight, Henry Jennings."

Their lips met in a hot, passionate kiss that immediately turned up the heat between them. Henry laughed, scooped her up, and carried her down the steps to his cabin. Once below, he kicked the door to his cabin open. Placing Elizabeth on the bunk, he closed the door and set the latch.

The moonlight streamed through the open window as the salt air added a clean smell to the small cabin. Elizabeth lifted herself from the bunk before Henry, pulled the thong of the garment at her neck and allowed the dress to fall to the floor. She stood before him in her shift or chemise. This she also removed and watched it drop to the floor. Elizabeth was now completely nude, the moonlight from the window, accenting the contours of her body.

Henry removed his jackboots, breeches, and shirt. He was now as naked as she. She placed her hand on the center of his chest, feeling the gentle softness of the hair on his chest, as well as the ugly remains of the scar, which she had helped to create in order to save his life.

Henry pulled her young body close, relishing in the softness of her skin. Starting at her shoulders, he ran his hands gently down the contours of her shoulders and back, until they ended on her hips. There, he paused for a moment, and gently proceeded lower, as he felt the contours of her buttocks. He cupped them and pulled her close, his stiffening member brushing the hair on her pubis. She felt the touch and moaned.

Elizabeth also began her exploration of Henry's body as she slowly caressed his back, feeling the ugly scars left by Captain Bill's flogging. Henry allowed it, but was ashamed at how his scarred body might appear to her.

"Do they still hurt?" Elizabeth asked.

"No," Henry replied. "They are just a part of my past, like so many other things."

"Henry, I want you to make love to me," Elizabeth said, her voice shaking just a little. "I have waited a long time for this moment, to know what it is to hold you and to feel you inside me."

"I have waited for this moment as well," Henry said. "I believe sometimes it was the thought of seeing you again that kept me going, kept me alive, and made me believe in myself, because I knew that somewhere you were out there."

"Be gentle," Elizabeth whispered. "I have never held another."

Instead of answering, Henry gently placed his finger on her lips and then kissed her. The moonlight spilled over them both, illuminating their bodies which had almost become one. The kiss grew in intensity. Her body was now ready to receive him.

Henry picked her up, placed her gently on the bunk, and lay beside her. He continued his caresses, taking great care for this one special moment. He gently fondled and kissed her breasts, the centers of her nipples no longer sleeping. She moaned again as Henry slid between her outstretched legs and poised above her. Then he gently entered her, the swollen lips of her body greedily hunting his flesh. He stopped as he encountered the expected resistance, kissed her deeply again and gently completed his penetration.

There was a flash of pain as the taboo secret was finally revealed to Lizzie. She cried out for a moment and tried to relax as they gently made love. Afterwards they lay together in each other's arms. Elizabeth could see through the open window. And lo, there was the Dipper and their star. She felt this was somehow a mark of destiny and their interlude was somehow sanctified in some deity's eyes as the proper way of things. Henry apologized.

"I'm sorry," he said. "It was over too quickly. I wanted this to be special."

"It was very special and painful," Lizzie said as she stroked his face. "And isn't that the way the first time is supposed to be?"

The continued to lie there, bathed in moonlight until a wicked, womanly laugh aroused Henry. They made love again. This time, she was urging him on and on, with an ardor that surprised even her. Finally, she arched her back as the sensations overtook her, grasping the sides of the bunk as wave after wave added to her release. His release came a moment later. This time, it had been perfect.

Chapter 56

"Man rarely places a proper valuation upon his womankind, at least not until deprived of them. He has no conception of the subtle atmosphere exhaled by the sex feminine, so long as he bathes in it; but let it be withdrawn, and an ever-growing void begins to manifest itself in his existence, and he becomes hungry, in a vague sort of way, for a something so indefinite that he cannot characterize it. If his comrades have no more experience than himself, they will shake their heads dubiously and dose him with strong physic. But the hunger will continue and become stronger; he will lose interest in the things of his everyday life and wax morbid; and one day, when the emptiness has become unbearable, a revelation will dawn upon him."

The Son of the Wolf - Jack London

Henry was awakened by a cry taken up by the upper deck from the crow's nest.

"Port Ho!" the voice cried.

Henry gently moved his arm where it had encircled Lizzie's form during the night. He donned his clothing, careful to add to it a brace of pistols. He reached for his trusty sword, but grimaced when he saw the broken blade. He quietly rummaged until he found Pierre's sword and sheath hanging from he nail. He shook his head at the dried blood on the end of the blade and realized it was his. The blade had gone much deeper than even he had realized. He donned the weapon, quietly opened the door and moved to the upper deck.

There was a crisp wind blowing this morning, a mariners wind as it was often called. It tossed his hair about his face, He relished in it. For the first time in many years, he was fulfilled. His ladylove lay in the cabin below and they had slept in each other's arms all night. The enemy that had set him forth on this unusual change in life direction was now dead. He was wealthy beyond anyone's wildest dreams and had proven himself a man to be reckoned with.

Yet in the midst of all of this success, there was a part of him that deeply dreaded the conversation that must take place this morning. Desiree' had to know the truth. And yet while telling her the truth, he was going to ask her to take responsibility for the one thing that mattered most to him. Lizzie. He knew a little of women, and frankly most rarely surprised him. Of the women he had known in his life, Lizzie and Desiree' made him a little uneasy where his confidence was a little shaken. Both could be unpredictable. There was one major difference. Henry loved Elizabeth with all his heart and soul. He simply did not love Desiree', nor would he ever be able to. Yet, after all the men he had killed in his young life, he still could not bring himself to deliberately hurt an innocent. But he knew he would have to do so.

His thoughts were interrupted as a member of the crew jostled his elbow.

"Will the Cap'n be going ashore?" he asked.

"Aye, Parker," Henry said quietly. "I'll be going by myself. Ask Gazini to look after the women and tell Scurvy to move over to *The Sea Devil* and get her ready to sail."

"Aye Cap'n!" the man said.

The men knew their work and within thirty minutes of dock at Port Royal, Henry was off and walking the main street toward Desiree's place of business. As he entered, he noted there were only a handful of customers. This was to be expected at this time of the morning. The girls upstairs were finally getting some much needed sleep and what men were here were likely getting ready to ship out in a few hours. One of the men squinted at Henry. His eyes widened and he almost knocked Henry down in his hurry to quickly exit the establishment, mumbling apologies in the process. Several others simply looked away.

As Henry suspected, Desiree' was already moving behind the makeshift bar. She was preparing items for the lunch crowd, from whence her business would slowly build until late evening when there would be no room left inside the building. Her back was facing Henry as he sauntered to the plank bar.

"Tankard of ale mum?" Henry said.

Desiree' turned in surprise.

"Quickly, back here," she said pointing toward the storeroom.

Henry followed her and was surprised as she ardently encircled her arms around him and tried to kiss his mouth. He turned away so the kiss fell onto his cheek instead. She was surprised again. Henry pretended not to notice.

"What are you doing here?" she said as she placed her hand on his chest. There she could feel the rough edges of the wound.

"Are you hurt?" she asked as she tugged his shirt open.

"Oh God Henry, that is a terrible wound! Are you alright?"

"I'm fine," Henry replied as he gently pushed down her hand.

"You are lying to me," Desiree' said. "Something is different. Something is wrong!"

"Some things have changed," Henry said quietly.

"You are damn right some things have changed!" Desiree' said pointedly. "You have been declared a common pirate and a price has been placed on your head by the King of England. Of course, our dear Governor, Archibald Hamilton, planned it. Henry I heard you almost started a war between England and France, and over what, a bloody French war ship? You must leave Port Royal as soon as possible! There is a prize that goes to the first man that sends your head to the King!"

"I hadn't heard," Henry said. "We just put in from the sea

this morning. I'm loading provisions and headed north again, in search of Black Sam. That bastard double-crossed me on our deal, took our part of the plunder and left me to face the devil. I'll have his head hanging from a yardarm!"

"Then go," Desiree' said. "At least until things calm down!"

"Aye," Henry said quietly.

"What is it?" Desiree' asked. "Something is wrong."

"You won't like it," Henry advised.

"Well?" Desiree' said, her eyes flashing.

"She is here," Henry replied.

"Who?" Desiree' demanded.

"Elizabeth," Henry replied. "She is on board my ship at this moment."

"Damn you Henry Jennings!" Desiree' exploded. "And what am I to do? Jump up and down for joy? I'm sure you have already explored that little muff of hers by now! How in the hell did you find her?"

"She was on board *King Louis Revenge* as a prisoner," Henry explained. "When we took the ship the Captain and I, old enemies, fought to the death. He almost killed me. She and two members of my crew saved my life."

"Too bad your opponent didn't end yours," Desiree' retorted, although this time a little less vehemently. "What do you intend to do?"

"I have to leave her someplace safe, with someone I can trust," Henry said quietly, not wanting to meet her eyes. "At least until I can hunt down and kill Black Sam Bellamy for double crossing me and leaving me as bait for the French Navy."

"And I guess you want me to look o'er her while you seek your revenge," Desiree' replied.

"I was hoping you would do so," Henry said. "She's not the same aristocratic girl that I grew up with. She too has changed. She's a woman now and one to be reckoned with. I've seen strength in her that equals your own!"

"Where does this leave us?" Desiree' demanded.

"The most honest answer I can give is that I do not know," Henry replied.

"Why?"

"Because after I finish with Black Sam, I am taking her home to England," Henry said simply. "Her family doesn't know where she is or if she is even alive. Her father may be an ass, but he saw to it I was treated well, educated, and I lived a good life while I was under his roof. I owe him that much."

"Damn you! Damn you! Damn you!" Desiree' exploded. "If you go to England, they will hang you for certain. Is that how you want to end your life, swinging from the gallows at the docks of London?"

"No, I'll be fine," insisted Henry.

"Alright, bring her here. I'll see to it she is fed and has a decent bed to sleep in," Desiree' said icily. "But when you return, or if you return, from your liaison with Black Sam, I expect an answer."

Henry nodded.

"Agreed," he said.

A few hours later an enraged Elizabeth arrived.

"What exactly is the meaning of this?" she sputtered.

"Shhhh," Henry replied. "I have one more thing to do. I'll only be gone a few weeks. I'm just sailing up the coast of the Americas. It will be an easy trip."

"You are lying," Elizabeth said. "Gazini already told me what you intend to do. You plan to hunt down Black Sam Bellamy and kill him."

"I do what I must," Henry retorted. "A man in my position must never show fear or allow others to take lead over him."

"And I'm supposed to stay here with this, this Desiree'?" Elizabeth asked.

"Just for a short time," Henry crooned.

"I know who she is. You spoke her name when you were with the fever," Elizabeth retorted. "I also know *what* she is!"

"Don't be too quick to judge Lizzie," Henry said sternly. "Life out here is not the same as in your drawing room in England."

Elizabeth dropped her head.

"Will you promise to come back to me?" Elizabeth said. "A woman will only wait so long and I have waited longer than any I know."

Henry folded her in his arms.

"My darling Lizzie," he whispered. "I have thought of you every day, since we were children. There will not be a day that goes by that I will not think of you. I will come home to you. And when I come home, I won't leave you at sea again."

Lizzie missed the two special words, *at sea.*

Henry tipped her chin up and kissed her gently and slowly. It was almost a chaste kiss, yet it was a kiss of promise. Desiree' couldn't help but notice the way Henry looked at her and she at him.

"Damn you, Henry Jennings," she whispered. "You have already made up your mind and although it is my loss, I am glad for both of you. I waited forever to see you look at me that way, just one time, and it will never happen! Damn you!"

Total Eclipse Of The Heart

Performed by Bonnie Tyler

(Turn around)
Every now and then
I get a little bit lonely
And you're never coming round

(Turn around)
Every now and then
I get a little bit tired
Of listening to the sound of my tears

(Turn around)
Every now and then
I get a little bit nervous
That the best of all the years have gone by

(Turn around)
Every now and then I get a little bit terrified
And then I see the look in your eyes
(Turn Around, bright eyes)
Every now and then I fall apart
(Turn Around, bright eyes)
Every now and then
I fall apart

(Turn around)
Every now and then
I get a little bit restless
And I dream of something wild
(Turn around)
Every now and then
I get a little bit helpless
And I'm lying like a child in your arms
(Turn around)
Every now and then
I get a little bit angry
And I know I've got to get out and cry
(Turn around)
Every now and then
I get a little bit terrified
But then I see the look in your eyes
(Turn Around, bright eyes)
Every now and then
I fall apart
Turn around, bright eyes
Every now and then
I fall apart

And I need you now tonight
And I need you more than ever
And if you only hold me tight
We'll be holding on forever
And we'll only be making it right
'Cause we'll never be wrong
Together we can take it to the end of the line
Your love is like a shadow on me all of the time
(All of the time)
I don't know what to do and I'm always in the dark
We're living in a powder keg and giving off sparks
I really need you tonight
Forever's gonna start tonight
(Forever's gonna start tonight)

Once upon a time
I was falling in love
But now I'm only falling apart
There's nothing I can do
A total eclipse of the heart

Once upon a time there was light in my life
But now there's only love in the dark
Nothing I can say
A total eclipse of the heart

[Instrumental Interlude]

(Turn Around, bright eyes)
(Turn Around, bright eyes)

(Turn around)
Every now and then
I know you'll never be the boy
You always wanted to be
(Turn around)
But every now and then
I know you'll always be the only boy
Who wanted me the way that I am
(Turn around)
Every now and then
I know there's no one in the universe
As magical and wondrous as you
(Turn around)
Every now and then
I know there's nothing any better
There's nothing that I just wouldn't do
(Turn Around, bright eyes)
Every now and then I fall apart
(Turn Around, bright eyes)
Every now and then I fall apart

And I need you now tonight
And I need you more than ever
And if you only hold me tight
We'll be holding on forever
And we'll only be making it right
'Cause we'll never be wrong
Together we can take it to the end of the line
Your love is like a shadow on me all of the time
(All of the time)
I don't know what to do
I'm always in the dark
Living in a powder keg and giving off sparks
I really need you tonight
Forever's gonna start tonight
(Forever's gonna start tonight)

Once upon a time I was
I was falling in love
But now I'm only falling apart
There's nothing I can do
A total eclipse of the heart

Once upon a time there was light in my life
But now there's only love in the dark
Nothing I can say
A total eclipse of the heart

A total eclipse of the heart
A total eclipse of the heart
(Turn Around, bright eyes)
(Turn Around, bright eyes)
(Turn around)

Desiree's Song

Chapter 57

"Shere Khan speaks this much truth. The cub must be shown to the Pack. Wilt thou still keep him, Mother?"

"Keep him!" she gasped. "He came naked, by night, alone and very hungry; yet he was not afraid! Look, he has pushed one of my babes to one side already. And that lame butcher would have killed him and would have run off to the Waingunga while the villagers here hunted through all our lairs in revenge! Keep him? Assuredly I will keep him. Lie still, little frog. O thou Mowgli --for Mowgli the Frog I will call thee--the time will come when thou wilt hunt Shere Khan as he has hunted thee."

The Jungle Book – Rudyard Kipling

The *Bathsheba* set sail north, toward the American colonies with a strong wind at her back, plenty of provisions, and a load of powder and ball. The hunt was on! As Black Sam had cowardly made others hunt for Captain Henry Jennings, it was now Black Sam that was the hunted.

Henry stood in the forecastle, one boot on the footboard, lazily cutting a ripe pineapple and lobbing slices of it into his mouth. His concentration was interrupted by the sound of Scurvy's voice.

"Been lookin' fer ya Cap'n," Scurvy said solemnly.

"I've been here most of the morning," Henry said absently.

"Are we really going after Black Sam," Scurvy asked.

"Aye," Henry replied.

"Cap'n, we are outmanned and outgunned," Scurvy said tersely. "This is madness!"

"Sam's overconfidence in his men and his guns will be his undoing," Henry replied.

"Henry," Scurvy said as he clapped a hand on his old friend's shoulder. "This is a death wish. You have the woman, you have money, and you have lands. All you don't have is a title and you can buy one, as wealthy as you are, if that is what you want. Take the money and the woman and go. This sounds like a good plan to me."

"You are right on all counts," Henry grinned as he cut another slice of pineapple and handed it to Scurvy who took it gratefully.

"Well, shall we turn about?"

"No, keep our course north," Henry replied.

"I do not understand!"

"I plan to hunt down Black Sam, kill him, plunder his ship if we can. If we can't it's of no consequence. Once Sam is dead, I will turn *Bathsheba* to Port Royal, pick up Lizzie, and set sail for England where I plan to return her to her family and ask the Crown for full pardon."

"Have ye lost the last little bit of mind that ye were born with Henry?" sputtered Scurvy. "They will hang ye the minute ye set foot on the dock!"

Henry turned, placed both his hands on his friend's shoulders, and managed a weak smile.

"You have been my friend since I set out on this journey and you know me better than anyone, except for Lizzie. Or Gazini. Sometimes I wonder about him. Frankly, there are times he makes chills run up my back! Either way old friend, I am tired of running. I am still honor bound to return Elizabeth home, safe and unharmed. This is a matter of honor and I will fulfill it."

Scurvy nodded and scratched his head.

"Alright Cap'n," he said. "I would say this trip and the next are your arse, but mine is beside the mizzen with ye. Where ye go, I go. Even if it is to the death!"

"Let's hope it does not come to that," Henry replied as he turned to face the wind and the spray from the sea as Bathsheba plowed through it.

Finally he frowned.

"Scurvy, don't alarm the men. But I want you to take

Bathsheba inland a bit," Henry said. "There is a storm brewing and we are now halfway up the coast of the Americas. This one is going to be a bad one. Keep her clear of the rocks. If the waves begin to trough too large, take her back out and let's try to ride through it. Black Sam is no fool, but I bet he's riding low with all of that treasure on board. One good shot at the bow line and we'll sink the bastard!"

"Aye Cap'n," Scurvy replied as he immediately beset about his business and began giving orders.

Henry frowned again and turned his attention to the sea and the wind that continued to climb in ferocity. The sea has many secrets. Not the least of them are buried in her depths.

Chapter 58

" Pah! Singed jungle cat--go now! But remember when next I come to the Council Rock, as a man should come, it will be with Shere Khan's hide on my head."

The Jungle Book - Rudyard Kipling

The storm gathered in intensity. The crew of *Bathsheba* fought bitterly to keep her into the wind, to reduce the possibility of taking a wave, broadside and causing another unfortunate turn of events that would topple their vessel under the waters of the sea.

The lantern aft had long since been extinguished, partially from the rolling seas and partially from the Captain's order. There was to be no lights on *Bathsheba* at night, certainly not this close to the coast of the Americas.

It was April 26 and the storm off the New England coast was one of the worst yet. *Bathsheba* was kept from capsizing only by the Captain's good wisdom and the steady hand of the helmsman. Henry was almost ready to give up the search when a call came from the bow.

"Light ho!" a member of the crew cried triumphantly.

"Keep your voices down," Henry shouted back into the wind, "No more loud noises. This could be the *Whydah* and we are coming in dark and silent!"

Then to the helmsman, "Plot a course dead for her!"

"I don't know if I can hold her Captain," the man cried, his Scottish brogue coming through. "The rudder is sluggish as it is and too much may cause her to break!"

"Damn your eyes," Henry cursed. "Turn her, or I'll do it myself!"

"Aye Captain," the man replied nervously. "Here she goes!"

Bathsheba turned a little out of the wind in the direction of the light. The effect on the ship was immediate. *Bathsheba* began to list to the starboard.

"Jam the mizzen," Henry cried.

The change in sail brought *Bathsheba* around, her list adjusted.

"Drive toward her!" Henry shouted.

"The sails won't hold," Gazini shouted back. "They are going to rip!"

"Hold!" Henry commanded. "We are coming up on her. The sails are down! Prepare the main cannon and cover her! We'll be lucky to get one shot!"

"It is the *Whydah*!" Gazini exclaimed. "And she's too close to shore! Captain, we are as well!"

"Steady dammit!" Henry cursed into the wind. "Set a course to ram her!"

"Are you out of your mind?" Scurvy exclaimed.

"There! On deck!" Henry said excitedly. "It's Black Sam himself! Gazini, she's riding low as I suspected. He's making for the coast! You, on the cannon, keep it covered. Tom, help him. On my mark, drop the sailcloth and let her have it!"

"Aye Captain!" the crew in the forecastle called.

Henry steadied himself. This was going to be close indeed. They had to get close enough to catch the *Whydah* on the crest of a wave while *Bathsheba* was in a trough. The storm was getting worse, making this single shot their only opportunity.

Finally, the *Whydah* lifted high on wave and *Bathsheba* dipped low in a trough.

"Make ready!" Henry screamed above the roar of the storm.

"Everything is too wet Captain!" Gazini cried. "She may not even light!"

"Then we will ride her to hell!" Henry exclaimed. "Here we go! The bow is coming up! Sailcloth off! FIRE!"

One member of the crew ripped the sailcloth off the cannon. Tom touched the touchhole with a carefully guarded igniter. It sputtered. For a moment, all seemed lost. Then it caught. As *Bathsheba*'s bow finished her slow ascent from the rough, *Whydah* dipped and listed to her starboard, revealing the much-coveted shot below her waterline. The heavy ball shot directly through the wooden planking and exploded inside. With the beat of the water, part of her bow gave in.

"Hard to port," Henry cried. "Move it boys, or we will join her! Watch the wind for we are about to be cross her. Move your arse or die!"

Bathsheba turned quickly despite the strong wind and waves.

"Head out to sea!" Henry cried. "Get out of this shite!"

"She's breaking apart Cap'n," Scurvy cried. "She just broke in two. She's going down with all hands!"

"To hell with them!" Henry cried. "This is what you get when you cross Captain Henry Jennings!"

"Aye," Gazini said sorrowfully.

"I'm going below," Henry said. "We are already outrunning the storm as we head out to sea. Once we get past it, set a course for Port Royal."

"Aye Capn," Scurvy replied.

And then, "Ye heard the Cap'n. Move your arses. I don't

want to be sitting in Hell with the crew of the *Whydah* this evening!"

In his small cabin, Henry sat on the edge of his bunk. For the first time in years, he felt tired, old, and somehow sad. He had allowed his hatred for Black Sam to ruin better judgment and almost get his crew killed, something he had never done before. He knew there was no way Sam could have survived the wreckage of the *Whydah,* yet there was no gloating, no real feeling of excitement or joy at his death, just as there had been none for Pierre. So, he sat there with his head between his hands until there was a knock at his door.

"Come," Henry said.

"It's me Captain," Gazini replied. He carried two metal cups and a bottle of rum.

"Your timing is good," Henry said as Gazini poured them both a generous drink.

They both tossed it off and Gazini poured them another.

"Gazini," Henry said. "I feel like I have come to the end of something. Is this the end of my life? What is wrong with me?"

"No, I do not believe this is the end of your life," Gazini said solemnly. "In fact, I see this as the beginning."

"What do you mean?" Henry asked.

"There are many times I have watched the battle of the lions since I have known you. Each time, I think the lion of evil has been fed and you will change. Then something else happens that changes your good fortune. It is my belief the lion of evil within you has finally been fed," Gazini replied. "You have reached a place of new beginning."

Chapter 59

"Ye choose and ye do not choose! What talk is this of choosing? By the bull that I killed, am I to stand nosing into your dog's den for my fair dues? It is I, Shere Khan, who speak!"

The tiger's roar filled the cave with thunder. Mother Wolf shook herself clear of the cubs and sprang forward, her eyes, like two green moons in the darkness, facing the blazing eyes of Shere Khan.

"And it is I, Raksha [The Demon], who answers. The man's cub is mine, Lungri--mine to me! He shall not be killed. He shall live to run with the Pack and to hunt with the Pack; and in the end, look you, hunter of little naked cubs--frog-eater-- fish-killer--he shall hunt thee! Now get hence, or by the Sambhur that I killed (I eat no starved cattle), back thou goest to thy mother, burned beast of the jungle, lamer than ever thou camest into the world! Go!"

Father Wolf looked on amazed. He had almost forgotten the days when he won Mother Wolf in fair fight from five other wolves, when she ran in the Pack and was not called The Demon for compliment's sake. Shere Khan might have faced Father Wolf, but he could not stand up against Mother Wolf, for he knew that where he was she had all the advantage of the ground, and would fight to the death.

The Jungle Book - Rudyard Kipling

While Henry carried out his plan of vengeance upon Black Sam, Elizabeth tried to find *her place* within *The Pleasure Palace.* Desiree' was initially a sour individual and ordered Elizabeth as she would any other servant. Her attempts to push Elizabeth into an enraged temper never occurred. Elizabeth took her duties seriously and fulfilled them to the best of her ability. Finally, after scrubbing the floor on her hands and knees, even Desiree' gave Elizabeth a grudging nod and acknowledged her work.

More than once, Elizabeth noticed a very pretty young girl, Desiree' kept in a small room in the back of the establishment. The fact she was kept out of sight, well away from the patrons, meant she was special. The young girl was about ten years old, beautiful, with a slight golden color to her skin, and large blue eyes. Elizabeth noted an elderly man tutored the girl and on more than one occasion, she caught the sound of her speaking in French, Spanish, and Greek.

She once made the mistake of asking Desiree' who she was. Desiree's eyes smoldered with anger and Elizabeth was told to mind her own business.

Elizabeth served the patrons within the establishment, and learned to handle a large platter laden with bowls of meat and tankards of ale. She also learned how to dodge the patrons who tried to grasp her from behind. More than once she simply poured a tankard of ale over the top of an unsuspecting patron's head, much to the amusement of those around him.

Desiree' watched, secretly hoping one of the men would bend her over the table and take her, but then feeling remorse and shame, as she watched Elizabeth gently earn the respect of these seasoned mariners.

One night, two new individuals walked into the establishment. They were already drunk and had to take a table in the back of the room, close to the storage rooms. Desiree' nodded Elizabeth off and served them herself. She was used to this business and could smell trouble before it came.

"Evening gents," Desiree' said loudly. "What's your pleasure?"

"A couple of pints of ale for me and me friend," one of them sneered. "And may a bit o' what be under that skirt of yours!"

"Sorry," Desiree' replied. "The ale is for sale, but I am not. Any one of these other girls might interest you though!"

Just then, the curtains to the back room parted and the young girl peeked through them. One of the men saw, smiled, and elbowed his friend.

"We'll take some o' that instead," he said as he nodded his head toward the curtains.

Elizabeth couldn't help but note the way Desiree' turned cold and stiffened as she saw the parted curtains.

"No," Desiree said. "You men will be wanting a fine, grown up woman for this evening. Sherrie' come over here and drink with these fine men!"

"Oh, we know what we want," one of the men said as he stood up and his mate followed.

He pushed Desiree' through the curtains, knocking the young girl to the floor. She cried as one of the men began to tear at

Desiree's clothing.

"You're a sassy little bitch, aren't you?" he said as he revealed a breast. "Pete, you take the little one and when you are done, we'll swap 'em around."

Elizabeth saw the men push Desiree' into the back room. As a woman, she knew exactly what was about to happen. She looked for help amongst the men that kept order in the establishment. They were otherwise engaged. One was dragging a male out the front door. She knew if there was to be any help, it had to come from her.

Elizabeth reached under the bar and pulled out a large Dragoon flintlock pistol. It was so heavy she had to lift it with both hands. Desiree' had once shown her how to cock it, which she did the only way she knew how. She placed the weapon between her knees and using both hands, pulled at the hammer until it locked into position. Thinking quickly, she picked up a knife from the bar and inserted it into the sash at her waist. She then hurried toward the curtains.

When Elizabeth pushed the curtains aside, it took her a brief moment to take everything in. Desiree' lay across the top of two kegs, her upper clothing torn. Her captor was so drunk he was struggling with the long skirt, trying to position it so he would have access to Desiree's hips.

The little girl was crying. Her assailant had picked her up to place her on a table and proceeded to drop his pants to the floor while holding her in place with one hand. The child was still clothed.

Fury came over Elizabeth in a way she had not know since

Pierre tried to rape her so many years ago. She leveled the pistol at the child's assailant and then at Desiree's.

"Let them go!" she commanded.

The men were surprised. Pete was amused.

"Why lookey here! We done got us a third one. Come on missy, give me that hand cannon! There's a good lass!"

"You want this pistol, you take it," Elizabeth warned.

"Aye, I'll do just that," he said as he cast a cunning eye toward his friend who had stopped fumbling with Desiree's dress.

Both men were now moving in Elizabeth's direction.

"Shoot him," Desiree' cried.

But shoot which one? Both were a threat. Elizabeth moved the pistol back and forth between them.

"Stop," Elizabeth warned. "Or I'll shoot!"

"You only got one ball," Pete warned. "And I bet you will miss with that one!"

"You only got one ball too," Elizabeth said pointedly as he pistol lowered toward the man's genitals. "If you want to keep what you have, clear out of here!"

It all happened so fast! Desiree's attacker narrowed the distance between he and Elizabeth in a moment as Elizabeth swung the heavy pistol around. There was a deafening sound in the small room as the weapon resounded. The ball caught Desiree's attacker in the center of his chest. He clutched at the wound and fell to his knees before pitching forward onto the floor.

Desiree' tore the knife from Elizabeth's sash and began to stab the child's attacker as Elizabeth reversed the pistol and used the butt against Pete's head, again and again until he lay motionless on the floor.

Crouching above him, Desiree' issued the final end to his life.

"This is what happens when you attack a mother's child you worthless piece of shite!" Desiree' said through gritted teeth as she expertly slit his throat.

Chapter 60

"What is it? What is it?" he said. "I do not wish to leave the jungle, and I do not know what this is. Am I dying, Bagheera?"
"No, Little Brother. That is only tears such as men use," said Bagheera. "Now I know thou art a man, and a man's cub no longer. The jungle is shut indeed to thee henceforward. Let them fall, Mowgli. They are only tears." So Mowgli sat and cried as though his heart would break; and he had never cried in all his life before.

The Jungle Book - Rudyard Kipling

Night was leaving. The customers had already left. None were allowed to stay and sleep in the arms of their sweet concubines this evening. Elizabeth and Desiree' sat at a nearby table, with two cups and a bottle of rum between them. The young girl was curled up across another chair with her head in Desiree's lap. Desiree' stroked her dark black hair absently.

"I should say thank you," Desiree' said to Elizabeth. "You saved her from a terrible calamity. I do not know what I would do if I ever allowed anything to happen to her."

"Who is she?" Elizabeth asked, although she already knew the answer.

"This is my daughter, Anastasia," Desiree' said quietly.

"I thought so," Elizabeth replied. "Hence the private teacher and the secrecy that she is hidden in the back room."

"So true," Desiree replied. "You don't miss much!"

And then she added, "For an aristocrat!"

"Perhaps I should turn in," Elizabeth said testily as she began to stand.

She was startled as Desiree gently placed her hand over Elizabeth's.

"Please stay," Desiree said gently. "Please? Do you know how long it has been since I had another woman to talk to?"

Elizabeth eased slowly back into her chair.

"I thought you hated me!" she said.

"Yes, I did," Desiree' replied. "And there are times I am sure I will not be very fond of you. But at least for now, can we declare a truce of sorts?"

"I will try, if you will," Elizabeth replied. "Where is the girl's father?"

"He is dead," Desiree' replied. "Or at least I have been told as much. His ship was sunk at sea somewhere in the Atlantic. He was returning home to gather his family fortune and return here to me."

"I am sorry," Elizabeth said quietly.

"Evangelos was a good man. He wanted a different life for both of us. Before he left, he gave me all the money that he had after provisioning his ship. It wasn't a fortune, but it was enough, at least for a few years. I survived the earthquake and the tsunami. Then I waited for two years, patiently awaiting his return until I ran into a member of his crew in the street. He was sailing on a different ship and he gave me the news of Evangelos."

"How did you get here, of all places?" Elizabeth asked.

"I came as an indentured servant to an older man who saved me from being sent to the Australian colonies. You see, my dear Elizabeth, I killed a man while I was making a living for myself in a tavern. Oh you don't have to look that way! If you haven't figured out by now I used to be nothing more than a tavern whore, then you are not as smart as I believe you to be!"

"It is not up to me to judge," Elizabeth said quietly.

"Oh, but you did judge, and quite endlessly, if I recall," Desiree' replied. "The day Henry left, you asked not to be left with the likes of *her*."

"I'm sorry," Elizabeth apologized. "I was wrong."

"That's alright," Desiree' said arrogantly. "I judged you as well. I thought you were nothing more than a rich bitch that wouldn't be able to clean a cup, let alone a floor. I was wrong on both counts."

They both laughed.

"At any rate, I had a customer that had unusual tastes in pleasure. I told him no. He tried to force himself on me. I protected myself the only way I knew how and that was with a dirk. It was the only thing my mother left me. She told me to marry well and I would never need it. Well, I was too young to understand about marrying well. I thought sex and love was the same thing. I never understood that sex was a part of love; a way to bring couples closer together. That is, until I met Evangelos, and he changed all of that. Then I met Henry."

Elizabeth dropped her head. This part of the conversation was too real and too close as it challenged her emotions. She knew how *she* felt about Henry. But it was disconcerting to hear another woman expressing her view of sex with the man Elizabeth had always loved. Frankly, it hurt. What hurt worse was the knowledge Henry had not fully disclosed his relationship with Desiree', which was another cause for alarm.

Desiree' ignored her, staring off into space, as she remembered bits of her own past.

"Anyway, I was caught and I stood trial. You know in England, a tavern whore isn't given much in the way of a defense. So, because I was a young woman, I was to be sent to the penal colonies in Australia. Instead, this old man, who wanted to come to the New World, bought me. He tried to rape me night after night.

Let's say he only consummated our relationship twice. The rest of the time it was like having a limp noodle between your legs with no place to go. Do you know what I mean?"

Elizabeth shook her head no, her face flushing.

"No, I don't guess you do," Desiree' said as an afterthought. "Be glad you don't. Be glad you haven't seen what I have seen. A woman must often do many things, in order to survive. Anyway, when Evangelos did not return, I took the money I had left and put it all into the only type of life I had ever known. The difference is that I was the owner and this port is crawling with money. I was determined I would never again have to depend on a man to survive."

"And her?" Elizabeth nodded toward Anastasia.

"Nothing is too good for my little girl," Desiree' said. "I am trying to save enough money so we can go to the home of Evangelos in southern Greece. His family is wealthy. Evangelos always said Greek families are everlasting."

"Aren't you wealthy already?" Elizabeth said pointedly.

"I do well for myself," Desiree' replied. "But everything here costs ten times what it should. Most of it has to be shipped in, or we buy it from a buccaneer that has just plundered another ship. I am saving everything I can, but it will still cost another thousand pounds to get us there safely and with money to tide us over if we have to take a ship back. It will be a hard journey, but from what Henry has told me, you already know what it is like to cross the Atlantic."

"I do," Elizabeth replied. "It is a hard and difficult journey, especially during the stormy months."

"It would be worth it for me not to have to raise my daughter in a place like this," Desiree' said boldly.

"It would indeed," Elizabeth noted as she watched the sleeping child.

"Elizabeth, it is time for us to be honest with ourselves. We both love the same man. My love for Henry is not the same as it was for Evangelos, but Evangelos is dead."

Elizabeth nodded, and this time it was she who reached for the hand of Desiree', offering comfort to another woman as only a woman can.

Desiree' sighed and continued.

"I have known for a long time of Henry's love for you," Desiree' said. "I caught him looking at that little locket of his, one night and I fooled myself into believing that I could use sex as a way to keep him and to force your memory away. I see now that I was wrong. I have seen the two of you together. I have seen the way you look at each other. He loves you, not me. That is something I must get used to."

A tear slid down Elizabeth's cheek.

Desiree' continued.

"Henry is like a wild animal. To cage him or force him into something he does only out of honor would force the person that loves him to watch him die a little each day, until there is nothing left. All that would remain is the shell of the man that once existed. I see now that you and he belong together. I am just a part of Henry's past that is in the way. And so, my dear girl, I will release him from my clutches with only one promise."

"And what is that?" Elizabeth asked as Desiree stood unsteadily on her feet and picked up her daughter, who mumbled and returned to sleep.

"You've seen my work first hand," Desiree' said as tears began to slide down her cheeks. "Promise me you will spend the rest of your life making him happy. If you hurt him, I will kill you."

Chapter 61

"There are no secrets that time does not reveal."

Jean Racine

Bathsheba slid quietly into Port Royal under the darkness of night. The full moon added iridescence to the clear blue water. Henry was eagerly waiting an opportunity to see Lizzie, but was dreading the possibility of another confrontation with Desiree'. He was really dreading seeing both women together, if they had made it during his absence.

Scurvy met him as he prepared to disembark.

"I don't need to be reminding ye, there's a price on yer' head," Scurvy said solemnly. "Don't ye want myself or Gazini to go with ye'?"

"I think that I will go by myself," Henry insisted. "The less people, the less apt to attract attention."

Scurvy nodded.

"At least take these," Scurvy said as he handed Henry two new pistols.

The weapons were smaller than the normal Dragoon pistols they were used to carrying, yet appeared extremely sturdy.

"What is this?" Henry asked. "I have not seen the likes of these!"

"It's called the Queen Anne Pistol," Scurvy explained. "The barrel unscrews which let ye' load the ball tighter. It hits the mark well and harder than anything I have seen! I pulled them off a dead Frenchman, last plunder! It is said Blackbeard himself carries a pair of these!"

"Thanks," Henry exclaimed as he exchanged his pistols for the smaller, more concealable ones.

"Then, there's the matter o' yer' blade," Scurvy insisted.

"That one 'ye' be carryin' ain't the blade of a Cap'n."

"I'll get another," Henry exclaimed. "I have more to worry about now, than a new sword."

"Maybe ye' won't have to." Scurvy said slyly, as he reached behind the bulwark of the ship and pulled out a sword.

He soberly handed it to Henry. It was *his* sword, given to him by his old friend and teacher, Simon. Henry gave Scurvy a surprised look, expecting to remove the sword from the sheath and reveal a broken blade.

"Go ahead, Cap'n." Scurvy said. "Draw her out!"

Henry did as he was asked and the gleaming blade slid out of the scabbard, revealing an extremely sharp edge. The blade had a slightly different feel. It was a little lighter, but the blade was far superior to the original.

"How did you do this?" Henry asked. "We've not even been to port!"

"After the storm, I asked the armorer to work on it." Scurvy said. "You know he was stranded somewhere on the islands of a place called *Okinawa* for a while. While he was there, he learned an ancient art of sword making. The sword has an iron core with a steel exterior. It makes it strong, light, and exceedingly sharp. It's the same way of sword making, but its done in a different way. They cool their swords so quickly it makes the blade turn up slightly so that as you slice through your opponent, the curve of the blade allows you to continue to cut deeper. You won't break this one!"

"She is a beauty," Henry exclaimed. "How can I ever repay

you?"

"Ye can start by giving this to Cassie," Scurvy said as he looked down and shuffled his feet.

It was a letter, carefully folded and wax sealed.

"For Cassie?" Henry said with a smile on his face.

"Aye, and don't be giv'n me no shite about it," Scurvy grumbled. "And don't ye be readin' it. It's fer' her, not fer' you."

"You have my word as a gentleman," Henry replied.

"Gentleman's arse," Scurvy grumbled again. "You'll read it first chance ye' get."

"No," Henry replied. "Its for her, not me."

Henry turned away for a moment and then turned back as he cast a sideways glance at Scurvy.

"Where in the hell did you learn to read and write?" Henry said.

"I have me own secrets," Scurvy replied. "You ain't the only one that come from a decent upbringing. I wasn't always this sea bird you see before ye'."

Scurvy turned away and began to sing.

"I went to see me old whore Sally. She gave me some and washed my tally!"

Henry laughed and disembarked, not knowing what lay before him.

Chapter 62

"There was a certain man from Zorah, of the clan of the Danites,
whose name was Manoah.
His wife was barren and had borne no children.
An angel of the LORD appeared to the woman and said to her,
"Though you are barren and have had no children,
yet you will conceive and bear a son.
Now, then, be careful to take no wine or strong drink
and to eat nothing unclean.
As for the son you will conceive and bear,
no razor shall touch his head,
for this boy is to be consecrated to God from the womb.
It is he who will begin the deliverance of Israel
from the power of the Philistines." ...."

JGS 13:2-7, 24-25A

Daily Readings
December 19, 2015

St. Peter Claver Catholic Church
Archdiocese of Kingston
Kingston, Jamaica

As Henry took the long walk toward Desiree's establishment, he passed a small Catholic chapel. He had passed this way many times during the last few years and never given it a second thought. But today, something was different. He had not given confession, nor taken the holy sacrament since his youth. Today, he looked at the small chapel as if it were something new and different.

The old building contrasted only a little with the rest of the city. It was brick, something unusual, and had survived the earthquake and subsequent tidal waves that hammered the port. The dead in the cemetery were given up to the sea when it overtook that part of the island, but still the church remained and a few patrons repaired it to the best of their ability. One could not say the church *flourished*. However, one could say the church survived and continued to be a beacon when a wayside traveller chose to make things right with God.

Henry stopped, took note of the building, and started to walk past it. Something tugged at him. Perhaps it was the memories of his youth. Perhaps it was something unseen. Either way, he felt an overwhelming need to go inside.

Henry gingerly opened one of the double doors, and stepped into the dimly lit chapel. He stood there for a moment, allowing his eyes to adjust to the light. A few torch sconces dotted the wall, but only a few. The holy cross was at the end of the church, along with a single stained glass window of the Virgin Mary holding the infant Jesus. Satisfied there was no adversary in the dimly lit corridors, he gingerly dipped his fingers into the holy water, made the sign of the cross and walked to the front. This was his first visit inside a church in many years.

There were only a couple of candles lit before the cross. The light from the candles danced off the symbol of life and resurrection, giving it an unnatural glow.

Henry picked up a match stem and held it in the fire of a candle lighting it. He used it to light another candle, thinking of the woman he had known as his mother and blew out the stem. There were no other patrons, certainly at this time of the night. Henry looked again to make certain nobody could see him and fell to his knees before the cross.

He sucked in his breath, closed his eyes and began to pray.

"Ok, Lord. It's me. Henry Jennings. Yeah I know it's been a while. I know I ain't been the best I could have been. I let my temper and thirst for honor get the better of me. But is that so bad? I mean, most of the things I have done, I did to protect someone else."

He sighed and thought of Elizabeth. He also thought of several other things he had done. It wasn't good to lie to God. He knew the truth anyway.

"Well, many of the things I did to protect someone else. The French and Spanish ships, they had it coming to them. They would have killed us had we not killed them. Guess we don't need to talk about Black Sam. I reckon that *was* wrong, even if the bastard, uh sorry, rascal double-crossed me. I've done many things. I've killed a lot of men, but they weren't good men, at least I don't think they were. Well, maybe some of them were. I don't know. Maybe they were just doing *their* job or their duty."

Henry paused again and looked around, unaware that the old priest was now standing in the shadows listening.

"I guess it's all about over now. I'm going to do what I think is the right thing. I'm going to take Lizzie home and turn myself in. It'll likely be a short rope and a keg for Captain Henry Jennings, but maybe that's best. I know Lizzie and me could never really be together. I love her too much! Wouldn't that be a fine thing, putting her through a life of misery, always on the run, watching for the first lucky son-of-a-bitch, oh sorry. I mean lucky rascal that can put a ball in me and claim my head. I think my time is coming to an end. Not just for me, but also for me, and my kind. I'm tired! Guess that's about it. I mean if you *want* to forgive me for what I done, and what I likely will do before I get Lizzie home, then I thank ye' for it. If not, I reckon there's not much I can do about that either. Amen!"

Henry stood and felt the touch of a hand on his shoulder. He immediately turned, drawing a pistol and held it in the man's stomach. It was the priest.

"I'm sorry Father," Henry sputtered as he put the weapon back into place.

"I was not eaves dropping, my son," the old man said quietly. "But I don't think I have ever heard a prayer like yours, since I came here."

"First time I been in here," Henry replied. He was more than a little disconcerted that someone had actually heard his innermost feelings.

"Are you Henry Jennings?" the old man asked.

"Aye, Father," Henry replied. "Are you going to try to collect my head as well?"

The old priest smiled.

"No, it is your soul I am most worried about," he said.

"Well, I have made up my mind," Henry replied. "I'm going to do what's right. That's my final hooray here. Then they can do with me what they wish!"

"Would you like me to go ahead and give you absolution?" the priest said. "It is all I can do."

"Well, if that will help," Henry said somewhat reluctantly.

"Please return to your knees," the old man replied.

Henry did so.

The priest dipped his fingers in holy water and made the sign of the cross.

"Bow your head," he said.

Again, Henry obliged. The priest placed his left hand on Henry's head and raised his right hand open, toward the heaven.

Then with a voice of strength the belied his age, he said, "God the Father of mercies, through the death and resurrection of your son, you have reconciled the world to yourself and sent the Holy Spirit among us for the forgiveness of sins. Through the ministry of the church, may God grant you pardon and peace. Captain Henry Jennings I absolve you of your sins, in the name of the Father, and of the Son and of the Holy Spirit. Amen."

He removed his hand from Henry's head.

"You may arise my son," he said.

Henry smiled.

"I feel better than I have in years," Henry said. "If I had known it was that easy, I would have stepped in long before now."

"The key is to go and sin no more," the old priest chastised.

"I'll do my best to remember that," Henry replied.

He dipped his hand to his belt and open one of the two pouches that hung there. He removed a bag of silver and handed it to the priest, who took it slack jawed.

"That's for you and for fixing the church," Henry said. "It looks like offerings have been a bit scarce."

"God will bless you my son," the old man said with a priests love for a member of his flock.

"Hope so, but I doubt it." Henry replied. "Though where I am going, I will need it."

As an afterthought, Henry reached into his pocket and removed an item. He took the old man's hand, placed it in his palm and closed his fingers around it.

"Reckon I won't be needin' this anymore," Henry said. "So, take it. Don't be spending it now. Save it for a time when you need it most. It is famous from here to the East Indies, to the British Isles, and to the Americas beyond. If you are ever accosted, all you have to do is show that coin and you will be spared. Goodbye Father. I won't be back."

Henry walked out the door whistling as he returned to his walk toward his original destination.

The old man watched Henry leave and opened his hand. In it lay a single piece-of-eight, with one sliver missing at the top. It was the calling card of Captain Jack Marsh. Even he recognized it for what it was.

He clutched the coin.

"God go with you, my son," he whispered.

Chapter 63

" No price is too high for a parent to redeem his child. No energy too great. No effort too demanding. A parent will go to any length to find his or her own."

Max Lucado

Half a world away, Lord Rockfort, Eighth Duke of Kensington poured another glass of sherry and stared into the fireplace. His constant writing to King George appeared to fall on deaf ears. He had not received any correspondence in months. The last letter, which bore the King's seal, informed him the situation had been taken under advisement. If Henry performed some deed worthy of exonerating him, then a pardon would be considered.

He did not mind losing the estate upon his death. Money, power, luxury, and holdings no longer meant anything to him. Nor had they for many years. He had seen the corruption that could so easily come to man when he had the gift of plenty, that it sickened him.

In fact, he recently gave his workers at the old weapons foundry a forty percent increase in pay after an explosion injured several and sent one of the men home. It cost the man the use of his leg, his job, and had put his family on the edge of starvation.

When Lord Rockfort heard his circumstances and his heroism in trying to save others, he visited the man at his small shack on the edge of the village. That cold morning the fog rolled throughout the British countryside and the wind beat a cold drum against the buildings. Lord Rockfort's carriage made an incongruous appearance against the homemade wagons, straw, and animals that ran throughout the small neighborhood. Pig shite covered the muddy ground. Lord Rockfort's servants attempted to cover the ground to the man's shack with a couple of blankets made for that purpose. He shoved them to one side, paying no attention to the pig manure that oozed under his boot.

Lord Rockfort rapped on the plank door with his cane. A woman answered the door. She had obviously been handsome as a young girl, but time, hard work, children, and fate had stolen much of her youth and young beauty. Her mouth made a perfect *O*, when she recognized him and managed a curtsy.

"Me Lord," she said awkwardly. "What brings you to our humble door this morning?"

"I came to see John," Lord Rockfort said as he tried to maintain the dignity of the upper class. "May I come in?"

"Of course, me Lord," the woman said. "Please excuse our home. I am sure it is not the finery to what you be used to."

"Woman, I came to see your husband and inquire as to his health, not to see your home," Lord Rockfort retorted and then was ashamed at how quickly he dropped back to the sense of arrogance and privilege, so common to his kind.

She opened the door wider and allowed him to enter. There was a small fire in the fireplace and against one of the broken stones of the fireplace a few more pieces of the precious wood. Two small, frightened children peered at him behind an old wooden rocker, the only piece of real furniture in the one room shack. A plank table and hand hewn backless benches completed the ensemble of the room. In the corner, a man lay upon a straw bed, moaning. Despite his pain, he managed to sit up on one elbow.

"Good day to ye' Laird," he croaked. "I guess I'm of no good to anyone with this busted up laig'. So I be supposing ye' are here to relieve me of my duties permanently at the foundry?"

Instead of replying, Lord Rockfort continued his visual

auditing of the one room. There literally were no personal possessions, other than a few clothes stacked neatly in the corner, a pair of brass candlesticks and the large pot that hung in a crook next to the fireplace.

Ah, the fireplace. Nestled above the mantle on hand made hooks was an old Swedish musket. It was obviously for decoration only, as there was a split down the side of the barrel. Early muskets were prone to fouling due to the black powder. It was quite possible that a misfire could cause so much pressure inside the barrel that it literally split.

"May I sir?" Lord Rockfort asked as he moved toward the rifle.

"Be me guest," the ailing man replied. "It's all that I have left of me time in the King's service."

"John, what was your unit?" Lord Rockfort asked.

It was the second time Lord Rockfort had spoken his name since entering the poor hovel.

"Laird, my father was a member of the Coldstream Guards." John replied. "They distinguished themselves many times in battle. He was killed as part of the ground troops on the coast at the Battle of Sole Bay."

"Coldstream Guards?" Lord Rockfort questioned. "George Monck's private regiment, sanctioned by Oliver Cromwell himself?"

"Aye," John replied. "The same. Do ye' know of them?"

"I have personal knowledge of many of these soldiers." Lord Rockfort said quietly. "They were some of the bravest men I have ever known or fought alongside. But then they were largely made up of Scots. Never cross a Scot, John. Else you may learn to savor the moment just before the dirk cuts your throat."

"I miss him," John said sadly. "I was young when he was killed. I wish you could have known him. He was a brave man!"

"I might have known him John." Lord Rockfort said. "I was at the Battle of Sole Bay. But, let's put ancient history aside for a moment. What are your plans for the future?"

"Future Laird?" the man replied as he squinted. "Not much future for me as a one legged man. That's what the village quack be sayin'."

"Let me see your leg," Lord Rockfort said as he gingerly lifted the lower end of the tattered blanket to reveal a swollen purple mass of flesh. A piece of bone protruded through the lower calf muscle.

"Why did they bloody well not set your leg?" Lord Rockfort demanded.

"The village witch bitch said me leg was going to have to come off anyway, so there was no need to put me through the agony."

"That's shite," Lord Rockfort said. "I've seen worse on the battlefield."

"Well, we can't afford no real doctorin'," John said. "Hell, I can't even be putting food on me table for me young ones."

"He tried Lord!" His wife said bursting into tears. "He wrapped cord and rags around his laig' and chopped wood for half a day, until he passed out and the men brought him home. He tried.

He has tried so hard!"

Once again, Lord Rockfort ignored the comments, instead, paying attention to the little voice inside of him that nagged for an explanation.

"John, how did the accident happen?" Lord Rockfort asked solemnly.

"Well, I don't want to be talkin' out 'o school," John said. "But I reckon it don't make no difference now."

"John, no!" his wife interrupted as she chimed into the conversation.

Lord Rockfort held his right hand in the air, elbow bent.

"Enough!" he bellowed.

She bowed her head and curtsied again.

"I'm sorry my Lord," she said. "I'm afeard you won't like what you hear and we'll be the worse for it."

"The truth never hurt anyone," Lord Rockfort replied, thinking about the small babe he had given up to be raised without knowing whom his father really was.

"Perhaps that is not always so," he said again. "I'm sorry."

"Oh, no need to apologize. I am sure you were quite right!" John's wife replied again, this time a little more friendly.

Lord Rockfort gently shook his head back and forth. God, what he would give for a drink right now!

"John?" he said.

The question hung in the air for a couple of moments. John finally took a deep breath and began.

"It was Harry, Laird. We told him over and over, not to put

the acid solvent too close to the casting furnace. He insisted it needed to be there to be applied the moment the rifle barrels came out of the fire. You know to put a finish on em'. Well, an ember from one of the rifle barrels fell into the acid and the room went up like an inferno from hell. Thank God most of the lads had taken a water break. I was blown backward from the furnace and one of the castings landed on me leg."

"Harry has been told about this more than once," Lord Rockfort said. "I have warned him twice in the last three months. It's cutting corners that cost money and lives. I understand despite your leg, you dragged two of the other lads out of the burning wreckage, including Harry."

"Aye, I hope he is quite alright," John replied. "He was a decent lad, but a little light between the ears if ye' know what I mean."

"He's better than all of us," Lord Rockfort said amicably. "He is quite dead!"

"I'm sorry," John reluctantly replied, his voice dropping. "I really am. Dying is bad business."

"Forgive me John. How long have you worked for me?"

"Nigh on five years, Laird. And I've never missed a day."

"Do you know the business of making rifle barrels well?" Lord Rockfort inquired.

"Well sure," John said. "It's all about melting the right amount of steel, pouring it into the mold right, breaking it out of the mold and then applying the acid. If'n it was me though, I would do it different."

"How's that?"

"Well, I'd use the way swords are made. Instead of letting it cool into a finished barrel, I would drop it in water, like a smithy does, heat it, cool it again, and then heat it well one last time and let it cool natural like. Then you smooth it down, eliminate the burrs and apply the acid."

"You think this will work?" Lord Rockfort asked.

"Aye," John relied. "And you'll have stronger musket barrels with more temper in the steel. I already know the acid that keeps the barrel doesn't care if the metal is hot or cold. It acts the same."

"Do you have animals?" Lord Rockfort said, as an afterthought. He hadn't considered the possibility of animals when he formulated the plan for this visit over last night's bottle of rum.

"I had me one," one of the children, a young boy of about six spoke. "It was me piglet. I called him James, after James the Shite. Uh oh, I'm sorry. I'm not supposed to talk. Mum says I talk too much."

"He really does you know," his sister said. "He talks way too much."

She appeared to be about eight.

Lord Rockfort knelt before them.

"Did you like this pig?" he asked gently.

"We did," the boy cried. "He was the bestest pig in the whole world!"

"We had to eat him," his sister cried, tears streaming down her face. "We didn't have no choice. We wuz hungry. I have to say he was a good pig. He was a *tasty* pig."

Her brother punched her.

"Don't be talking no shite about James!" he bellowed. "He was a good pig and he fed your empty gullet. He was just such a little pig, he didn't make more than two meals."

"I see," Lord Rockfort said as he handed the girl his lace handkerchief.

She wiped her eyes with it, blew her nose and promptly tried to hand it back to Lord Rockfort.

"Uh, no," he replied. "You keep it."

"Oh, she can't my Lord," her mother replied. "That's an expensive gift."

"I insist," Lord Rockfort said as he stood hastily.

The girl clutched the handkerchief to her chest, not paying any attention to the mucous that dripped from it.

"Thank you sir!" she said.

"Mmmm, you are welcome," Lord Rockfort replied. "Well, I've made up my mind."

"Mind about what me Laird?" John asked.

"You and your family, of course," Lord Rockfort said. "Gather anything you want to keep and be prepared to clear out of this disgusting hovel."

The woman fell to her knees before him and grasped his legs.

"Please don't throw us out into the cold," she cried. "This ain't much, but its all poor folks like us can afford. We'll find work somehow. John's a clever man, even if he ends up with one leg.

He'll find something."

"That is *not* what I am doing," Lord Rockfort replied. "Please woman, stand to your feet. You are embarrassing me!"

"Carpenter," Lord Rockfort called. "Get you blinkin' arse in here!"

"You called sir!"

"Yes, there is a nice cottage close inside the wall at Kensington Castle. You know the one I speak of?"

"Yes sir," Carpenter said smartly. "You mean the one that was remodeled and boarded up for almost twenty five years now?"

"Yes, that is the one," Henry Rockfort thought as he remembered a cold winter day and a tremendous ice storm. It was a day that had haunted him his entire life.

"John, I want you to manage my foundry," Lord Rockfort said. "No, I won't take no for an answer. You know the business, the men, and ways to build a better weapon. In order for you to be successful, we have to change your living conditions. I am not asking you to move out into the cold. I am asking you to move onto the grounds of Kensington Castle. I have several cottages on the grounds. The one I am thinking of is nicer than the others and has a large bedroom and a small bedroom. It is already furnished, so I doubt you will need much of what is here."

"Carpenter?"

"Yes, Lord Rockfort?"

"I want you to send for my doctor. Tell him to waste no time. This man will not lose his leg. Get some clean clothing and fresh food in the cottage as well. Also, we need plenty of wood for the fireplace."

Lord Rockfort knelt down beside the two children.

"What are your names?" he asked.

"I'm Catherine and that's my brother Luke. Mum's real name is Natalie, but we call her Mum." Catherine replied.

"I am very sorry about your pig," Lord Rockfort said gently. "But children your age *do* need a pet. How would you like a puppy?"

"A real puppy?" Luke shrieked. "One that barks?"

"Unfortunately, incessantly for the first few weeks," Lord Rockfort said. "Carpenter, when they arrive, take the children down to my hunting Spaniel. Her puppies should be around eight weeks old now. Give them pick of the litter."

"You ain't kickin' us out after all," Natalie asked dubiously.

"No, of course not." Lord Rockfort said. "I'm having you taken to a cottage on my estate. Your children will have free run, of course with a few exceptions. Your husband will become my new foreman with a monthly pay of 10 pounds a month."

"Ten pounds?" John asked. He couldn't believe his good luck.

"Well, alright then," Lord Rockfort replied. "Fifteen pounds, and there's no rent. You are also welcome to eat with the servants at their table. The men will answer to you and you will answer to me. Together, we will make muskets the world has never seen! Carpenter will send a wagon for you, so we can get you to your new home. The doctor should be there when you arrive."

"I don't know how to thankee sir!" John whispered. "This is

like a miracle from the Holy Mother herself!"

"I'm far from a miracle," Lord Rockfort said softly. "But, I knew another young man that chose to give up a life of ease for a world of danger and still kept his honor. Perhaps by following his example I will keep some of mine."

Natalie threw herself at Lord Rockfort's feet again.

"Thankee Lord, thankee! But what have we done to have so much charity shown to us?"

The figure on the bed looked down. He had heard the word. *Charity*.

"Charity be damned woman!" Lord Rockfort retorted. "Your husband almost lost his life and perhaps his leg in service to me. This is the least I can do!"

Thinking of Henry, he said, "I know of another than has given much more!"

He turned to leave.

"John, one more thing. As God is my witness, you will not lose that leg. It will be saved!"

Chapter 64

" It's always wonderful to get to know women, with the mystery and the joy and the depth. If you can make a woman laugh, you're seeing the most beautiful thing on God's Earth."

Keanu Reeves

It was still early night when Henry arrived at Le *Palais de Delight.* He was in much better spirits than he had been, prior to his visit at the chapel just a few minutes before. He entered the front door of the building. As usual it was quite full, and he was narrowly able to step aside as a large black Jamaican male literally threw a patron through the open door and out into the street. This action brought great laughter among the patrons that remained inside the building, many of them unaware they would suffer the same fate before the night was out.

As usual, Desiree' worked behind the bar, with a weather eye on the front door, lest one of the patrons decide to leave without paying. He spied Lizzie's small form as she stood with one hand on her hip and another holding a tray. The position seemed incongruous for one of such breeding. Yet, it pleased him she was able to adapt so quickly to her new environment.

Deciding to surprise her, Henry slipped behind her and encircled her small waist in his arms and rested his face against the side of her head.

"Miss me?" he whispered huskily.

"Did you miss this?" Lizzie said angrily as she turned and broke the wooden tray over the top of Henry's head.

The blow knocked him to the floor, much to the entertainment of those around him. For a moment the room appeared milky. He rose to one elbow and was surprised to find a large Dragoon pistol aimed directly in his face. The person wielding the large pistol was Desiree'.

"Henry," Lizzy screeched as she knelt to the floor.

"Aye," Henry replied. "It's me."

"Get your arse off the floor," Desiree' said with an air of indifference as she eased the hammer forward on the pistol. "Lizzy, take him in back."

Then Desiree yelled loudly and laughed.

"I told ye' not to mess with this one. She may be small, but she's got the fight in her for sure!"

The men laughed and returned to their drinks, the incident now simply one more case for amusement before the night's end.

Once they were safely behind the curtains that separated the storage room from the rest of the business, Henry grabbed Lizzie and pulled her close to him.

"I have missed you love," Henry insisted.

"Oh Henry, and I have missed you," Lizzie replied. "I was afraid you might not come for me and leave me here in this place."

"I told you I would return," Henry stated quietly.

"And?"

"Sam Bellamy is dead," Henry said flatly. "I get no joy out of the event. I've changed Lizzie. I'm tired."

"Then we leave. You have lands in the Bahamas and even a large plantation! We can go there and never look back! We don't need this life!"

"Lizzie, is this what you want? Do you want to be on the run for the rest of our life, looking over our shoulder, wondering who will be the lucky man to claim the head of Captain Henry Jennings?"

"It's better than me watching you swing at the end of a

hangman's noose!" Lizzie retorted.

At that moment, the curtains swung open and Desiree's head slid through.

"I hate to break up this little family reunion, but you can be heard above the shite outside!" Desiree' cautioned. "Elizabeth, take him up to your room and get him out of sight!"

"Room?" Henry questioned. "You have a real room? What in the bloody hell has happened since I been gone. I thought you would be killing each other by now!"

Both women laughed.

"He really doesn't know women as well as I thought he did," Elizabeth noted.

"Most men don't," Desiree' said. "Get him the hell upstairs. I still have a long night."

Chapter 65

" I love my husband very much. I knew it was real true love because I felt like I could be myself around that person. Your true, true innermost authentic self, the stuff you don't let anyone else see, if you can be that way with that person, I think that that's real love."

Idina Menzel

Elizabeth pulled Henry into her room. Henry had expected to see a small, slovenly, whores room. Instead, it was a decent bedroom for the island, complete with a fireplace if needed, which was seldom, whale oil lamps instead of candles and a decent sized bed with a coverlet.

She began to help him remove his sword and carefully placed the pistols on the nightstand.

"Come on then," Elizabeth said excitedly.

She was already removing her clothing. With one final deliberate act, she pulled the string her top and watched it fall to the floor.

Henry sat on the bed and removed his jackboots.

"Hurry," Elizabeth insisted.

"I am," Henry hissed.

"Oh bloody hell!" Elizabeth exclaimed as she grasped at Henry's trousers and pulled them off straightaway. Henry removed his linen shirt as well.

The moonlight from the open window, combined with the sounds of the sea bathed them both. Elizabeth moved between Henry's legs so he could feel the ripeness of her. She brushed against his maleness, relishing in the fact *she* had made it stiffen.

"Ah Lizzie," Henry whispered. "I have missed you so much!"

"I have missed you too," Elizabeth said. "Now scoot back on the bed!"

Elizabeth straddled Henry relishing the fact that his stiffened maleness was now directly in front of her and she was the one responsible for it.

"Where did you learn all of this?" Henry asked dubiously.

"Oh, I took every male patron that came in," Elizabeth laughed. "Where do you think? Desiree' gave me some pointers."

Henry's maleness began to wither.

"What?" he stammered.

"Oh, we can't have that," Elizabeth said as she gently grasped his testicles in one hand and ran her tongue the length of him.

Henry quickly reasserted himself.

Elizabeth assumed her original position, except this time she hovered above him for a moment and gently pushed the little mound of flesh down on him. She forced his entry slowly until she finally had all of him. She first began to rock back and forth and then as he became even more engorged, she used her thighs to slide up and down the length of him.

"Take them," she said as she offered her breasts to him.

Henry grasped each, using the palm of his hand to gently squeeze and press upward. Her nipples stiffened, the centers no longer sleeping.

"I love you Henry Jennings," Elizabeth said as she made one more hard push that caused the lips of her flesh to greedily gobble all of him, relishing as she felt the hot spurt of his man juices that mixed with those of her own. She panted and fell on top of him, holding his shoulders as her own spasms shook her.

Afterwards, they lay in each other's arms, with only the thin coverlet pulled to their thighs. Henrys arm encircled her and held her tight, while he absently stroked her right breast. She snuggled closer into him, feeling his juices drying between her legs.

There was a knock at their door.

"Come in," Elizabeth said as she pulled the coverlet over her upper torso.

It was Desiree'. A small face with dark curly hair and large dark eyes peered at them from behind her skirt.

"Need anything?" she inquired.

Then after seeing their condition and Elizabeth's smile, she muttered, "I guess not. I want you both out of here by morning."

The door closed.

Henry was dumfounded.

"Just like that?" he demanded. "Here today and bloody well gone by tomorrow?"

"What did you want to do?" Elizabeth barked back. "Invite her in for a midnight spin with both of us?"

"Not hardly," Henry replied. "She's a damn fighter. I just figured she would do *something* really ugly, like throw us out in the mud with you in your shift."

"There was a time when she would have done that," Elizabeth retorted. "But Desiree' and I have become friends. Good friends."

"Now how in the hell can *that* be," Henry demanded. "I mean, well I've told you of our past history."

"That's the point," Elizabeth said. "It's ancient history!"

"If I live to be a hundred," Henry said. "I don't think I will ever truly understand women."

"That's it," Elizabeth said. "Women are supposed to be mysterious. In our own way, we are as mysterious as the sea itself."

"I believe that," Henry replied.

"I want to ask you a boon," Elizabeth said quietly.

"Anything, my love!" Henry replied. "If I can give it to you, I will."

Elizabeth quietly reiterated the story of Desiree' and Anastasia's attempted rape and the events that followed. Henry was wide eyed when he heard how this little aristocratic girl, now a grown woman, had come to their aid with such bravery. He knew of the strength that lay within her, but sometimes society and breeding could stifle that strength. He was glad she was able to call on it when needed. It made her even more mysterious.

Elizabeth told Henry the story of Evangelos and Anastasia and the goal Desiree' had set to return to Greece to be with his family. She felt certain they would be accepted and Anastasia would grow up around a real family, instead of a bunch of drunken louts.

"Is your intention still to return to England?" Elizabeth asked.

"It is the only way we will ever be free," Henry insisted. "I have done nothing against the Crown, other than kill a few French, well a lot of French, and Spanish. If I can offer the King something in return, like additional wealth, I may stand the chance of a pardon. Once that is done, we can go wherever we wish. We can stay in England or return to my plantation in the Bahamas or go back and forth as we please."

"I have no desire to go back and forth. Truly I have no desire to return to England at all, at least not permanently," Elizabeth said. "But as much as I don't like the risk of losing you, what you say makes sense. I wouldn't want our children to grow up knowing their father has a price on his head."

"Children?" Henry asked. "What children? Lizzie, are you?" He stopped.

"Well, I don't know that I am and I don't know that I'm not," Lizzie replied with a smile. "But, if I know you, you won't stop. I'm going to end up big and fat with lots of stretch marks, and a cush with no strength in it. Although Desiree' has told me how to solve that one too, when the time comes."

Henry laughed.

"Well aren't the two of you quite the little pair?"

"Seriously Henry," Elizabeth insisted. "I want to take Desiree' and Anastasia with us. From England they could easily get a ship to Greece. His family is from city of Kalamata on the Peloponnese peninsula in southern Greece. They are very close to the African continent."

"I have heard of this Kalamata," Henry said. "The country has been plagued by war and invaded by the Turks. That was until the *Venetion War*. I could get her safe passage on a trade ship headed for Greece and the Middle East and provide her with enough money to survive if she cannot find this Evangelos' family immediately."

"Will you give me this as a wedding gift?" Elizabeth asked.

"Aye, I will," Henry replied as he grabbed her by her

buttocks and flipped her over onto her back.

"And what should I give you in return," she said teasing.

"A bit more o' you," Henry said slyly. "You know pirates rut longer and better for sure! Or I am a fool!"

"Then kiss me, fool. Make good thy claim!" Elizabeth said, remembering their childhood day attending the theater.

Henry kissed her, igniting the flames of passion deep within her.. She spread herself, giving him easy access to the place of their mutual desire. He entered her a little roughly. But it did not matter. Her body was already ripe for him from their previous encounter and he glided into her tightly. She urged him on with a passion that surprised even her and finally that one moment came over both of them and she clasped his back with an ardor and the sound of passion that caused her to clap her hand over her mouth as they both giggled like two naughty school children.

Henry fell back to the bed. They were both exhausted. Elizabeth giggled as she clutched for him again. He was just again becoming aroused when there was a knock at their door and Desiree's voice came through quite loudly.

"Can't you at least keep your fukin' to yourselves? You are waking the whole bloody house!"

They could hear the sound of her stomping back to her room. They laughed again and slept quietly intertwined until daylight's rosy fingers began to creep through the morning window.

Holding Out for a Hero

Performed by Bonnie Tyler
Written by Jim Steinman and Dean Pitchford

Where have all the good men gone
and where are all the gods?
Where's the streetwise Hercules to fight the rising odds?
Isn't there a white knight upon a fiery steed?
Late at night I toss
and I turn
and I dream of what I need.
I need a hero. I'm holding out for a hero 'til the end of the night.
He's gotta be strong
and he's gotta be fast

And he's gotta be fresh from the fight.
I need a hero. I'm holding out for a hero 'til the morning light.
He's gotta be sure
and it's gotta be soon

And he's gotta be larger than life!
larger than life.
Somewhere after midnight
in my wildest fantasy

Somewhere just beyond my reach
there's someone reaching back for me.
Racing on the thunder and rising with the heat

It's gonna take a superman to sweep me off my feet.
I need a hero. I'm holding out for a hero 'til the end of the night.
He's gotta be strong
and he's gotta be fast

And he's gotta be fresh from the fight.
I need a hero. I'm holding out for a hero 'til the morning light.
He's gotta be sure
and it's gotta be soon

And he's gotta be larger than life.
I need a hero. I'm holding out for a hero 'til the end of the night.
Up where the mountains meet the heavens above

Out where the lightning splits the sea

I could swear there is someone
somewhere
watching me.
Through the wind
and the chill
and the rain

And the storm
and the flood

I can feel his approach like a fire in my blood.
I need a hero. I'm holding out for a hero 'til the end of the night.
He's gotta be strong and he's gotta be fast

And he's gotta be fresh from the fight.
I need a hero. I'm holding out for a hero 'til the morning light.
He's gotta be sure
and it's gotta be soon

And he's gotta be larger than life.
I need a hero. I'm hoXding out for a hero 'til the end of the night.

Elizabeth's Song
Reprinted By Permission

Chapter 66

" My husband has quite simply been my strength and stay all these years, and I owe him a debt greater than he would ever claim."

Queen Elizabeth II

Elizabeth awoke the next morning as the sunlight from the window penetrated the bedroom. She stretched, recalled the night before and turned toward Henry who lay peacefully asleep. She smiled, remembering the moments that had overtaken both of them, several times during the night. She had never dreamed the intimate act itself could make one feel so good. Yet is also seemed to draw she and Henry closer, if that were possible. She didn't fully understand it, but really didn't feel the need to. The fact that it was true was enough.

She propped herself up on one elbow and stared at Henry's face. Here, asleep, all his problems seemed to have dropped from him. His face was a little different, older, and bore a few scars from various fighting. The worst was the one above his left eye. It was unusual in shape and a little darker than the rest. When she quizzed him about it, he quietly told her it was from the duel with Pierre, when they were younger. It made her quite sick to her stomach to think Henry could have died that day. It made her sicker to think it was because he was defending her honor.

As she gazed upon his peaceful face, she realized the boy she had known was still there. She could see him quite clearly. One simply had to look through the face of the man to find it.

Finally Henry's eyes fluttered and opened.

"Good morning!" Elizabeth said happily.

"Morning," Henry repeated quietly. The fog of sleep had not yet completely left him.

Finally he sat up in the bed, rubbing his eyes, allowing the coverlet to fall from his shoulders to his waist.

"I've got to have *Bathsheba* outfitted for a long sail." Henry observed. "Hurricane season is almost over. If we leave now, we have a good chance of making it to England in record time."

"And Desiree'?" Elizabeth inquired

"She and the little girl comes as well," Henry said. "I'll find her passage on a ship headed to the Mediterranean Sea, as soon as we arrive in England."

"When do we leave?"

"Tomorrow morning," Henry replied. "That should give us enough time to stock the ship. I'll be going for speed, rather than fighting, so I'll lose a couple of cannon and ball in exchange for more provisions."

"Sounds good!" Desiree' said. "I'll talk to Desiree'. There isn't much time."

"Yeah, I've return to the ship. Can you have Cassie prepare to travel as well? I have two small cabins that should suffice. Well, hell you know my ship as well as I do now."

"I had enough time to learn it," Elizabeth said gleefully. "And I had a really good teacher."

Henry slipped out of his side of the bed and began to dress. Elizabeth did the same, taking her time to allow Henry a moment to savor her young and strikingly beautiful body.

"If you don't get some clothes on, we aren't going to get much done today," Henry insisted.

"Oh, I should think the thought of seeing me again this evening would be enough to keep you motivated during the day," Elizabeth insisted as she turned to face him and cupped her breasts.

"Do you think my breasts are too small? They are quite firm!"

"I think your breasts are perfect," Henry replied as he faced her and playfully pulled her to him.

"You keep your hands right where they are Captain," Elizabeth insisted again. "You mistake my intentions!"

They both laughed as Elizabeth gently pushed him away.

"I almost forgot," Henry said. "Would you give this to Cassie for me?"

"What is it?" Elizabeth said as she turned the carefully folded and sealed parchment from Scurvy over and over in her small hands.

"I don't know," Henry replied. "Scurvy gave me strict instructions to have it delivered and not to read it."

"It's a letter of love, silly," Elizabeth said as she carefully placed the parchment on the dresser. "I'll see she gets it. I wonder how she would do, being the wife of a mariner?"

"Wife?" Henry responded. "Scurvy a husband? Do you know how many wres he's bedded since I have known him?"

"Men change," Elizabeth replied. "Sometimes for the better. Sometimes for the worse! By the way, how many of those unfortunate women you label as *whores* have you bedded since you left England?"

"None," Henry said soberly. "I've been as virtuous as a monk!"

"Liar," Elizabeth whispered. "But you better be the rest of your life!"

Henry took her small face in his hands and gently kissed her lips, savoring the softness thereof.

"Ah Lizzie," Henry whispered. "Why do I love you so?"

Chapter 67

"Victorious warriors win first and then go to war, while defeated warriors go to war first and then seek to win."

Sun Tzu

When Henry reached *Bathsheba,* he found Scurvy was already having her outfitted and supplies were being brought aboard. The vessel was clean and had been checked from bow to stern and judged sea worthy.

"She is a thing of beauty isn't she?" Henry asked Scurvy who was checking his list of supplies, including a couple of extra yardarms, rope, an anchor, powder and shot.

"Aye, she is," Scurvy said dreamily, thinking of Cassie.

Henry glanced sideways at Scurvy and frowned.

"What are you thinking of? I am talking about *Bathsheba.*"

Scurvy cleared his throat.

"Aye, and so am I," he sputtered.

"Whale shite!" Henry retorted. "Would you find Gazini? I'll be waiting for both of you in my cabin."

"Aye," Scurvy said. "Is everything alright Henry, I mean Cap'n?"

To avoid the appearance of favoritism Scurvy and Gazini both thought it better to address Henry by the more formal title accustomed by someone in his position, rather than by his name.

"Yes, I have a few things I want to discuss with you," Henry replied as he disappeared down the steps toward his small cabin at the rear of the ship.

Once inside, he gently loosened a plank floorboard at the edge of his bunk. Inside was a small tin box, only large enough to hold folded paper materials and a few trinkets.

There was a knock at the door and Scurvy's voice announced their arrival.

"Come!" Henry said as he continued to sift through the box.

"Captain, it is good to see you again," Gazini boomed as a broad smile spread over his face.

"And you, my friend," Henry replied as he grasped the big man's shoulder. "Come in."

"I may be making my last trip under sail," Henry told them. "I have decided to return to England to take Elizabeth home and to turn myself in to the King's soldiers and ask for pardon for myself and all of you."

"You can't do that Captain," Gazini said pointedly. "It will be your death!"

"Then it will be a death of honor," Henry replied. "The world knows little of my crew. I want you to anchor off shore. I'll take a longboat, Lizzie, Cassie, and two others with me. I'll put in at the docks. There I can find them a coach home. I'll then turn myself in to King George's men. Hopefully, I'll be able to get close enough to his castle before getting picked up by the British troops. You don't have to go. I can put you off here. Scurvy, you still have your ship and the second crew. You can return to the sea or sell her. You are both wealthy by Jamaican standards. You could make a good life for yourselves here."

"No Henry," Scurvy replied. "I'll be going with you."

"I will also," Gazini said quietly.

"Very well," Henry replied. "If I don't return to the ship by the evening of the fifth day, I want you to draw anchor and head toward a place where you won't be found. Just make sure that Lizzie gets these."

He showed them a large key and several documents in the tin box and then inserted it into hiding and replaced the plank.

"What are they Henry?" Scurvy asked.

"These are documents that attest all my riches go to Lizzie. This includes my plantation and most of my wealth, which is hidden in the old well at the back of the plantation. The key is to the front door of the plantation house. Supposedly the servants there are keeping the house, grounds, and crops in good standing."

Henry paused for a moment.

"We are taking Desiree' and her daughter on board this trip. She desires to return to the homeland of her daughter's father. Evidently they are very wealthy. It will give her daughter a chance for a better life. We will make arrangements for their transportation to southern Greece when we arrive in England."

"Greece?" Gazini asked.

"Aye," Henry replied. "Greece."

"I have heard of this Greece," Gazini said quietly, staring at the wall. "My land, Kanya, is far southeast from there, but the great land is just across the small sea. Even as a boy, I remember Greek traders that traveled to Kanya with Egyptians to trade for animals and goods with the Maasai. This is a way for me to return to my home."

"So, you would be willing to travel with Desiree', make certain she arrived safely, and then obtain passage around the coast?" Henry asked. "If so, I can make the necessary payment arrangements."

"I do not need your money, Henry Jennings, " Gazini

retorted. "I have money enough, most of which I will give to Miz' Desiree' upon safe arrival. I just need enough to buy two days passage across the small sea. Once we land, I need enough money to buy a horse and a few supplies. From there I will get to my home."

"You don't want money?" Henry asked.

"Money is good only to people who do not understand the land." Gazini said steadfast. "What good is silver coin? You cannot eat it. You cannot make it into a weapon. All you can do is buy something in the white man's world. We don't need money in my country."

"As you wish," Henry replied. "I was hoping you would come to my home outside of Nassau. There are many plantations a man of wealth can purchase."

"My warrior friend," Gazini said gently. "We are a nomadic people and move frequently. Your ways are not my ways."

Henry nodded and said, "It's done then."

He looked at Scurvy.

"What about you?"

"I dunno yet," Scurvy replied. "That's all I can say honestly."

"Alright," Henry said. "Will you both swear you will see to it that my last wishes are carried out?"

Both men grimly nodded.

"Gazini, would you bring the women and the little girl here just before sunset? I am afraid if I go into town again, I may stir up suspicion."

"Yes Henry," Gazini replied.

Henry managed a weak smile.

"Alright lads. Prepare to set sail for England."

Chapter 68

"Aside from what it teaches you, there is simply the indescribable degree of peace that can be achieved on a sailing vessel at sea. I guess a combination of hard work and the seemingly infinite expanse of the sea - the profound solitude - that does it for me."

Billy Campbell

They had been at sea for two months. If the winds prevailed and good luck followed, they would still reach England on schedule.

During this time, Lizzie and Henry spent every moment possible together. He taught her every aspect of sailing and navigation possible, thinking she would find it interesting. Actually she thought the entire affair was the most *boring* thing she had ever been instructed in and the mathematical equations to plot direction and navigate the ship were far above her. However, she did not dare to tell Henry who actually swaggered a little when he told her of the art of sailing. It reminded her again of the boy that he once was and why she was attracted to him.

One night, after a long night of making love, she asked him a question many people often ask of a warrior. She was still trying to come to terms with the man she had killed in Desiree's tavern. It was a sobering thought process that shook the threads of her Christian upbringing. She kept reliving the incident and the sounds of the man that lay dying at her hand. So, she asked Henry the question most real warriors never wish to hear.

"How many men have you killed Henry?"

The question hung there in the darkness, with only the sounds of the sea coming through the open window.

"Too many," Henry replied.

"Like three or four?" Lizzie asked.

"Why do you want to know?" Henry questioned.

"I'm just curious," Lizzie replied. "I'm having trouble putting the face of that dying man behind me. I had just pulled the trigger. First he seemed surprised, then in agony, and finally fear."

"I have seen that look many times," Henry said quietly. "But understand, they were very bad men. If you did not have that weapon, they would have raped Desiree' and little Anastasia. They would have turned on you, had you been in their way. They would have raped and killed all of you! Would that have been justice? I think their screams of anguish and pain would have been harder to live with. Because you were able to obtain access to a pistol, you were able to make a difference. Do you understand?"

Lizzie nodded and said, "You are saying my taking of life was justified."

"Aye," Henry replied. "Sometimes one must use a weapon to take life in defense of ones self or others."

"And you?" Lizzie asked again. "How many have you taken?"

"Lizzie, you took one life. I had taken one before I was nineteen. Since then, I have lost count. I've sent entire ships to the bottom with fifty to a hundred men on board. I assume most of them died. I've killed many in hand-to-hand combat. It was the only life left open to me."

Henry sighed, "It doesn't matter. We are almost halfway through our journey home. I'll be facing my accusers soon."

"I am so sorry," Elizabeth said solemnly. "I've hurt you."

"No problem love," Henry replied quietly. "I did what I did because I had to. Yet there's not a day that goes by that I don't ask God for forgiveness!"

"He understands," Lizzie replied soberly.

"Does he?" Henry whispered as the demons of the past rose up to greet him. "I really hope he does, for I am guilty, many times over!"

Chapter 69

"There can be no keener revelation of a society's soul than the way in which it treats its children."

Nelson Mandela
Former President of South Africa

They had now been at sea for several months. They looked and felt it. There was little time for bathing and very little water that could be spared. While seawater could be boiled, one was never quite able to remove the salt from it. While it might be acceptable for men, it was not as acceptable for the women.

Desiree' had turned the first deck upside down searching for Anastasia, literally, much to the grumbling of some of the men she had awakened in her search that would take care of their ship during the night. She finally solicited Lizzie in their search and together they combed the vessel. Finally it was Lizzie that spied the little girl's curly black hair in the bow of the ship. Henry knelt beside her. Whatever he was saying, she was obviously taking it in quite intently as her head bobbed up and down and she occasionally pointed at something just off the starboard side of the ship.

As the two women approached, they could hear her laughter and finally she literally jumped up and down, clapping her hands. It was Desiree' that reached her first.

"Where have you been, young lady?" Desiree' scolded as she grabbed the girl's arm.

"Shhhh," Henry exclaimed quietly. "You will scare him away."

"Henry Jennings, she can't simply go anywhere she wants on this ship, not without us, Gazini, or Scurvy. You know that!" Lizzie said, scolding Henry vigorously.

"She was with me the entire time," Henry said. "Now be quiet and watch one of the greatest sights the sea has to offer. If you don't be quiet, he'll run. His hearing is better than ours and he knows we are here, because we attract curious fish. Watch now! Here he comes!"

Suddenly a massive form breached the sea, rising out of the water, spewing a massive spray into the air, arching it's back, while a huge finned tail slapped the water as it submerged again.

"What is that?" Desiree' asked, as she clutched Anastasia to her.

"Don't be afraid Mommy," Anastasia said, grasping Desiree's hand. "These are Blue Whales! Captain Jennings says they are the largest creatures in the ocean. Isn't it beautiful?"

"I saw him just before she peeked out on deck," Henry said. "This guy is a big boy! He's easily a hundred feet long and I bet he weighs around two hundred tons!"

"Isn't he dangerous?" Lizzie asked. "Won't he run into the ship?"

"No, they are too smart!" Henry said. "He may follow us for a while. Sometimes I think they are as curious about us as we are about them. Other times, I think they follow us because we attract larger fish when we dump our shite and offal overboard. In short, we attract food for them. We will see how long he decides to stay with us."

"Lizzie, would you mind taking Anastasia to the cabin and brush her hair?" Desiree' said. "I'd like to speak to Henry for a moment."

"Certainly," Lizzie said, but you could tell she didn't like it as tiny fingers of jealousy began to creep up her spine.

Henry knew what she was thinking and put his arm around her.

"It will be alright," he said.

Lizzie nodded.

"Come with me Anastasia," Lizzie said, taking her hand.

Henry and Desiree' watched them leave. Henry leaned on the ship's rail and faced the sea.

"I'm sorry," Henry said. "I had no idea taking her to the forecastle would cause such a stir. It won't happen again."

"Thank you Henry," Desiree' said. "But that is not why I want to talk to you. I was the one that over reacted. She adores you and she wants a Da' so bad. I was kinda' hoping you would be the one for the job, but that was not meant to be."

"Desiree', I never meant to hurt you and knew nothing of Anastasia. I also had no idea Lizzie would ever come back into my life. I never lied to you."

"Whatever," Desiree' said. "Ancient history now. I just wanted to thank you for doing this for us, especially since I am not your woman any longer."

Henry nodded.

"Desiree', Lizzie and I are glad to be able to help you, especially if it gives you and Anastasia a better life. And I don't think you could ever belong to anyone or be anyone's woman. You are much like the sea, wild and untamed, somewhat like me. You will always be so."

"I will take that as a compliment. However, I would like to know something," Desiree' said seriously. "Did I ever mean anything to you?"

Henry thought for a moment, carefully considering his next response. It was one that could either hurt forever, or give comfort. Finally he decided the truth was the best answer.

"Desiree' you always did and you always will. You were there for me when nobody else was and I will always be grateful. You wanted me to give you something I had given to a young girl a long time ago. It was impossible for me to ever change. I am what I am."

"Fair answer," Desiree' replied. "You are a good man. You reminded me of my Evangelos. Not in looks, but in mannerisms. You knew how to treat a whore like a lady. We don't get that very often."

Henry gently kissed her on the forehead, the last kiss he would ever deliver to her.

"That is because you were never a whore," Henry said. "And you were always a lady!"

Desiree's laughter was cut short by a cry from the Crow's Nest.

"Land Ho!"

It was the English shoreline.

Chapter 70

"I can control my destiny, but not my fate. Destiny means there are opportunities to turn right or left, but fate is a one-way street. I believe we all have the choice as to whether we fulfill our destiny, but our fate is sealed."

Paulo Coelho

Bathsheba silent crept up the River Thames toward the port of London. As Henry ordered, she anchored offshore, not altogether uncommon for those who had little to deliver or supplies to retrieve. The ships watch was doubled and arms were distributed among the men.

They waited until early evening. The longboat was prepared. Elizabeth, Henry, Gazini, Desiree' and Anastasia were waiting as it was lowered into the gentle water of the Thames. Henry dressed is his best mariners clothing, to mimic that of the man that had helped decide his destiny so many years ago. The women were also dressed in an appropriate manner for the genteel wealthy of London's population.

Elizabeth kept watching for Cassie and finally after fifteen minutes, went below to find her. She was not there. She returned to the little company gathered at the longboat and shook her head at Henry.

"Scurvy," Henry called. "Would you please find Miss Cassie and tell her we are ready to go!"

"I'm here," Cassie replied as she stepped out from behind Scurvy. "I'm sorry Lady Elizabeth, but I'm not going."

"What do you mean you aren't going," Henry insisted. "The boat's seaworthy. All will be well!"

"I mean I ain't goin', Cap'n Henry," Cassie replied as she grasped Scurvy's hand. "I'll be stayin' here with William. I'm sorry my Lady, but I know my own heart and my heart is with William."

"Are you serious?" Henry said dubiously.

Elizabeth gently touched Henry's elbow.

"Cassie, are you sure?" she asked.

Cassie looked up into Scurvy's face, saw the answer she wanted, and nodded.

"I'm sure, Lady Elizabeth," she said as she left Scurvy's side to embrace Elizabeth.

"This may be goodbye then," Elizabeth said as a tear slid down first one cheek and then another.

"Ah hushamon then," Cassie said as she gently wiped one tear from Elizabeth's face and then a couple from her own. "I ain't much on goodbye!"

"Be happy!" Elizabeth whispered. "Always be happy!"

"I will," Cassie whispered back. "He makes me happy!"

"Then live well," Elizabeth said as she hugged her again. "I must go!"

"God be with ya' all!" Cassie cried as the longboat was lowered. "He will be!"

Four members of Henry's crew rowed the long boat to a small stretch of land adjacent to the docks. There, they beached the craft for a moment to allow the landing party time to get off.

"Thank you lads," Henry said. "Don't come back until I send word." If you don't hear from me, don't come back or it's a short rope and a round keg for ye'. Do you understand?"

They nodded. One young crewmember stood for a moment.

"I'll come with ye' Cap'n!" he cried. "I'll come! You saved me from a beating and me head being caved in back in Po' Royal! I'll die with ye'!"

For a moment, Henry's features softened. How old was the

boy? Eighteen? Twenty? He looked back toward the docks of London. For a moment, he felt as if he had passed his own shadow on the pier above him. Was he ever *that* young? Was he ever *that* naïve? The answer came back to him in the affirmative. So young, ready for action, ready for the unknown, and yet so unaware how quickly youth could be sucked out of him as quickly as one pulls the juice from an orange. Youth was removed with the first squeeze of a trigger. What was the boy's name? For a moment, he didn't remember. And this boy was willing to die for him, Captain Henry Jennings! Finally the name came to him.

"No, Ned," Henry said firmly. "The men on ship will be needing another strong and able bodied warrior, just in case things go badly. I'm the worse for having to let you go, because I can always use a good man like you at my side. But *Bathsheba* needs you more!"

The young man nodded; satisfied his place within the group and his honor was sanctioned.

"Listen to me," Henry said. "Tell the others to watch for boarding parties. I have no idea what will befall us here. If you hear word I am dead, leave as quickly as you can!"

The men looked at him soberly. One looked at the bottom of the boat. Henry continued.

"And, if after it's all said and done, and you are on your back watching the night sky, then you must be either French or Spanish!"

"Why us that Captain?" Ned asked.

"Why lad, then that means you are dead!" Henry joked.

The men laughed and Henry pushed the longboat off shore.

Henry carefully helped the women up the small rise as easily as possible until they could reach the dock itself. Henry noted little had changed in the time since he had left. The docks still smelled sour and rats were in abundance. Unsavory characters still sneered their lascivious looks at the women and one boldly asked Henry how much for a half hour with the little one.

Henry drew his sword and used the knuckle guard to break the man's nose. There were no further mishaps on the dock.

The *Blue Dolphin* was still in business after these many years. Henry opened the door and ushered the women inside. Gazini followed, unabashed by the stares that followed them. He stood behind those he was destined to protect, for at least a while longer. Henry continued to feed the good Lion, regardless of where the end of this rope would take him. At long as he followed to this end, Gazini would keep his word.

The innkeeper looked up from his makeshift bar and his eyes narrowed. This stranger looked somewhat familiar, but he didn't quite know why.

"Excuse me," Henry said. "We'd like some bread, beef and broth, and some ale. Wine for the ladies."

"And I suppose you can pay?" the innkeeper said inquisitively. He was used to being taken.

"Of course," Henry replied as he laid some coin on the counter. It quickly disappeared.

"I also want rooms for these women, the child, and the big man behind them." Henry said quietly so the rest of the clientele could not hear.

"The women and the child are no problem," the innkeeper said. "But we don't serve his kind here."

Henry looked coolly at Gazini who stood with his arms crossed.

"He's a savage," the innkeeper said with an ugly undertone to his breath.

"Aye, sometimes he is," Henry said. "But I can assure you at the moment he is quite harmless."

"He can eat shite," the innkeeper replied. "And sleep with the pigs!"

Henry grabbed the man by the back of the head, and at the same moment swept the tomahawk from his belt. He buried it beside the man's face, grazing his nose and then pulled it free, holding it above the back of the man's neck. The nose began to bleed in earnest.

"Do you wish to keep your head?" Henry said with gritted teeth.

"Henry, we are in London now," Elizabeth whispered. "Not some whore's nest in Port Royal. You must act accordingly!"

"Henry?" the innkeeper said, staring at the wall at the end of the counter. "Oh Lord, sir, I didn't mean to offend ye'. Of course he can stay and anywhere he wishes. He can have my room!"

"A regular room will be all that is necessary," Henry said. "When does the coach arrive?"

"Tomorrow morning at six bells," the innkeeper replied from his lowered position.

"Wake us in time for me to put this woman on it," Henry said as he gestured toward Elizabeth. But he still held the man's head.

"Any ships leaving for Italy and Greece?" Henry asked.

"Aye sir! *Windsong* leaves for the holy land in a few days."

"Then I'll need rooms for my other guests until then," Henry said. "Help them book passage."

"Aye sir," the innkeeper replied with his head still on the counter. His nose had begun to clot. He continued to stare past Henry toward the wall.

Henry released his hold on the back of the man's neck.

"Good God man!" Henry said. "What in the bloody hell are you looking at?"

"I'm sorry Captain Jennings!" the man said, craving favor.

Henry grabbed him by his lapel.

"How do you know who I am?"

The innkeeper gulped and pointed. The wall held a wanted poster. There was a likeness of Henry in the middle. It read, *"WANTED for PIRACY and LOOTING – Captain Henry Jennings – A bounty of twenty thousand pieces of eight will be paid to the person responsible for his Capture or Death. Exchange with the local magistrate for payment from Lord Archibald Hamilton, Governor of Jamaica."*

"Well, don't be trying to collect that debt," Henry said as he placed the tomahawk back in his belt and some more coin on the counter. "Or I'll show you how my friends in *La Florida* use this little tool."

"Aye, you can count on me!" the innkeeper replied. "If it's

any consolation to ye' Captain, I knew who ye' were the minute they put it up."

"How?" Henry asked.

"Oh, I've seen many people come and go and mariners not a few. I remember faces, not names. But I remember you talking with Captain Bill that night many years ago and you showed him the calling card o' Captain Jack Marsh. I've a good memory for faces Captain Jennings. You left here a boy and came back a legend ye' did. The lads come here from all over the Caribbean and the New World and tell tales of ye'. Some say you are ten feet tall. Others say there is no one faster with a pistol or sword. Some say you would rather gut a bloody Frenchman as to look at him. Your legend has proceeded ye'."

"What?" Henry said.

"I mean you are famous, Captain Henry Jennings! You are the Gentleman Pirate!"

Chapter 71

"True love is eternal, infinite, and always like itself. It is equal and pure, without violent demonstrations: it is seen with white hairs and is always young in the heart."

Honore de Balzac

Henry heard the cock crow the first of his morning alarm at four bells. He quietly slipped out of bed and dressed. While adjusting his weapons he watched Elizabeth's sleeping face. There had been no lovemaking last night, at least not in the sense of intense sexual arousal. Instead they held each other tightly, relishing in the closeness, the feel of each other's skin, and the beating of two hearts.

Each knew the events that would unwind within the next several days, would permanently affect them for the rest of their lives. Henry tried to portray an optimistic front, but deep down he knew either a noose or an executioners' axe awaited him. He simply did not wish his Lizzie to be there to witness his execution and death.

Elizabeth stirred.

"It is time my love," Henry said. "The coach will be here soon."

Elizabeth stretched and donned her clothing.

Together they walked downstairs to find Gazini already waiting for them.

"You still have this in your heart," the big man said quietly.

"Aye," Henry replied as he grasped his shoulders. "I would like to thank you for your friendship and your service, these past several years. You have saved my life many times."

"As you have saved mine," Gazini said pointedly. "Remember the slaver you took me from. You gave me my life back and treated me as an equal."

"You took your life back," Henry replied quietly. "Even I

could see there was something special in you."

Henry turned to Elizabeth and took her in his arms.

"It is time for me to go now," Henry said.

Elizabeth began to cry. She buried her face in Henry's chest.

"Must you go," she asked. "We can go back to port and wave the torch for *Bathsheba* to send a boat for us. I don't have to go home. I don't want to go home. I hate my father for what he did to you!"

"Lizzie, hate will eat you up. Your father is a good man. He was watching for your best interests," Henry lied, thinking the man's best interest lay in lining his pockets. Nonetheless, he owed the man a debt of gratitude. He had seen to it Henry had a good education and taken care of him when nobody else would.

"I'm leaving," Henry said. "Gazini will stay with you until the coach comes and then he has a few days until he leaves with Desiree' and Anastasia."

He gently kissed Lizzie's lips, likely for the last time, savoring the softness and the fullness thereof.

"When this is over, I'll come for you," Henry promised. "Goodbye my love!"

With that, Henry turned on his heel, nodded at Gazini and strode though the door to find the magistrate.

Lizzie watched in desperation as the man she loved walked out of her life, again. This time it seemed like the final time.

She and Gazini sat at the nearest table. She was weeping silently, clutching her small handbag.

"Tea," Gazini boomed to the owner, who had just walked

into the main room of the tavern, rubbing the sleep from his eyes.

He started to make a scathing reply, but noting Elizabeth's sorrowed condition, nodded and proceeded to make the English breakfast tea, that would eventually be known the world over.

Gazini did not know how to comfort her. He had only comforted one woman in his lifetime and that was his sister when their mother died. Death is dreaded among the *Maa* community and its occurrence brings along a sorrowful dark cloud that envelops all those who hear of it. There are no elaborate mortuary practices among the *Maasai*. Known as *En-keeya* in *Maasai* language, death is one thing no *Maasai* wanted to encounter. When a person dies at their home, or *enkang'* the *Maasai* would vacate the *enkaji* and move to another one. After death there is *En-jung'ore* or *En-ju*ng'*go*. This is their inheritance.

Gazini did not totally believe in the ways of his people. It is one thing to believe it when *someone else* dies. It is entirely a different matter to believe it when one of your own passes away. For his sister, the belief was a never-ending internal battle that the woman whose paps had suckled her, was now gone forever.

The owner approached their table with a small tray. On it were two steaming cups of tea, a small amount of precious sugar, and two flat pieces of hot homemade bread that smelled like apples.

"Husha now lass," the man said. "Here's what you be needin'! Good hot tea and some o' me wife's hot apple bread, just out o' the oven."

Even Gazini was surprised by the man's sudden empathy and generosity. He eyed him suspiciously.

The tavern owner saw the expression and said, "Well a man can change the way he thinks, can't he? If you are a friend of Captain Henry Jennings, then you are a friend o' mine. It will all work out lass. He's a man of the sea. You can't expect him to settle down like King George!"

"He goes to surrender himself and ask for pardon," Gazini said quietly.

"Ah shite!" the owner whispered as he leaned down to Gazini's ear. "He won't be a findin' none o' that here. They just hung twenty or so pirates at Execution Dock, not far from here, and left them there to rot until the tide had washed over their heads three times. Why ole' Cap'n Kidd himself was hung there and the rope broke and then they hanged him again! I think that was a little while back in 1701. My new savage friend, please do not let the young woman see. It is truly a gruesome sight!"

Gazini nodded. He had no idea of English executions, but knew it would be one that ripped a man's honor and dignity from him in those last fateful moments before death.

Elizabeth calling his name interrupted his thoughts. She held Henry's locket in her hand. It was still quite beautiful and still bore the red *R* crest on the front of it. She had it open. Inside were the worn likenesses of she and Henry. It brought back memories of youth, of a much happier time, before fate had cast them an evil blow.

"Is it possible we were ever so young?" she said.

"Youth is the beginning of life," Gazini said noncommittally. "We were all young."

"Just look," she said as she tried to handle him the locket.

Suddenly and without warning, she dropped the locket onto the oiled oak plank floor. Henry's likeness popped out of it, and onto the planks.

"I've broken it," Elizabeth exclaimed. "I've broken Henry's birthright!"

Gazini carefully picked it up and started to replace the likeness back into the gold backing.

"Miss Elizabeth," Gazini said soberly. "There are your markings here that speak!"

"Markings that speak?" Elizabeth asked. "What are you talking about?"

"It is nothing," Gazini replied. "I do not hear them saying anything."

"Let me see," Elizabeth asked dubiously as she retrieved the pieces of the locket from Gazini's large hands.

Yes, there was writing inside the locket. It was a little worn with time, but still very legible. It read, *To my darling Josephine, Love Henry Rockfort*. Elizabeth frowned. She knew Henry Rockfort, Duke of Kensington. The man was a dear friend of her father's and on his visits spent a great deal of time with Henry. Suddenly, it all began to come together. Henry Jennings, Henry Rockfort. Her father raised Henry. Josephine must have been Henry's birth mother. And Lord Henry Rockfort, the Eighth Duke of Kensington, was in love with her.

There had always been this secret surrounding Henry's birth. It was a secret nobody dared to speak of. It was one her mother had partially whispered to her that *perhaps* there was more to Henry Jennings than anyone knew.

Suddenly everything fell into place. Why had her father taken in a baby with no father, even if it were one of his servant girls that bore the child? It was rumored that perhaps Henry was indeed her father's bastard. She had always known in her heart of hearts it was not true. The locket was part of the secret to Henry's birth and it was here Lord Rockfort professed his love for a woman she had never heard of or seen. With the insight, possessed only by women, the answers came. Josephine was Henry Jennings birth mother and Lord Rockfort was Henry's father. Henry was not only Captain Henry Jennings. He was also Lord Henry Rockfort, the Ninth Duke of Kensington!

"Gazini," she whispered as she reassembled the locket. "I need one last boon from you. It may save Henry's life."

"Yes, Miss Elizabeth," Gazini said, leaning forward. "What can I do?"

"Can you ride a horse?" Elizabeth asked as she gently wrapped the locket in a lace handkerchief.

"Of course," Gazini replied as he frowned. "We are a nomadic people, and all of the world's cattle belong to us. We have no horses, but I have learned to ride the white man's horse."

"I must take the stage to reach my father. He can help, if he will," Elizabeth whispered. "I want you to take this locket to Lord Henry Rockfort at Kensington Castle. He is the Eighth Duke of Kensington and Henry's father. Henry is, in reality, Henry Rockfort, Ninth Duke of Kensington. He is English nobility."

Gazini nodded.

"So he is a chief?"

"Yes Gazini," Elizabeth said quietly. "He is a chief, and so is our Henry. It is possible this may save his life. Ride to Lord Rockfort! Take this locket as proof!"

"I need a quill, ink and paper," Elizabeth cried to the owner.

He brought them, with much greater speed than which he had shown to date. The young woman was extremely excited.

Elizabeth hastily scribbled a note, folded it, and folded it again, sealing it with wax from the candle at their table.

"Give him this as well!" Elizabeth said hastily. "Show it to no one else."

"More of the talking signs?" Gazini asked.

"Yes," Elizabeth replied.

Then to everyone's surprise, the young, proper English woman hugged the savage and whispered, "If you have ever loved our Henry as your friend, ride like the wind. We will not have long!"

Chapter 72

"Take him away," he said to Father Wolf, "and train him as befits one of the Free People. "

"But why--but why should any wish to kill me?" said Mowgli.

"Look at me," said Bagheera. And Mowgli looked at him steadily between the eyes. The big panther turned his head away in half a minute.

"That is why," he said, shifting his paw on the leaves. "Not even I can look thee between the eyes, and I was born among men, and I love thee, Little Brother. The others they hate thee because their eyes cannot meet thine; because thou art wise; because thou hast pulled out thorns from their feet--because thou art a man."

"I did not know these things," said Mowgli sullenly, and he frowned under his heavy black eyebrows.

"What is the Law of the Jungle? Strike first and then give tongue. By thy very carelessness they know that thou art a man. But be wise. It is in my heart that when Akela misses his next kill--and at each hunt it costs him more to pin the buck--the Pack will turn against him and against thee. They will hold a jungle Council at the Rock, and then--and then--I have it!" said Bagheera, leaping up. "Go thou down quickly to the men's huts in the valley, and take some of the Red Flower which they grow there, so that when the time comes thou mayest have even a stronger friend than I or Baloo or those of the Pack that love thee. Get the Red Flower."

"I wish that horse," Gazini told the man at the stables.

"Sir, the animal is not fully broken and under the wrong man could kill him," the owner said. "He is wild."

"Wild is good," Gazini said as he carefully walked toward the tall black stallion.

The animal dropped its head, raised it, and leaped onto its back legs, its front hooves pawing the air.

"Hóo taá (well done)," Gazini crooned in Maa, the language of his people.

The horse dropped to all four legs and nervously pawed the ground.

"You are a strong warrior," Gazini continued. "I need to borrow your strength. You are like me. You yearn to be free! You yearn to feel the l-wuaó (wind) in your face!"

The horse pawed the ground and once again returned to his rear legs, feet pawing at the empty air. However, this time, the gesture was less menacing.

"I will not have us áa-ibaro, or come to hate each other." Gazini continued. "Áátásáyia tɛnákatá (I am beseeching you right now) to allow me the honor to ride you."

The horse seemed to listen, twitched its ears, pushed them forward and finally walked to Gazini and nuzzled him with his head.

"Hóo taá", Gazini whispered. "It is good this has happened."

He handed the man some coin, which took the pieces of eight gratefully.

"This is too much money," the man said. "This is twice what the animal is worth. At least let me get you a saddle and a riding bit."

Gazini thought for a moment.

"The saddle and bit, you are to keep for a friend that may need it soon," he said, as he grasped the horse's mane and threw himself onto his back. "I will not ride this horse as an Englishman."

"Yes sir," the stable owner said. He would not argue with this savage that could practice witchcraft on an animal and make it bend to his wishes.

"Which way to this place you call Kensington," Gazini asked.

"What business do ye' have at Kensington?" the stable owner said slyly. "What would a savage be doing there? I'll call the soldiers and let them ask!"

Gazini produced a pistol and pointed it at the man's chest from atop the horse.

"I go there to ask a boon for a friend that will face certain death," Gazini said sternly. "What is it to you *where* I go?"

"Oh none sir," he said warily as the end of the pistol now looked like a small cannon before his eyes. "Lord Rockfort does a bit of business with me now and again. I was just looking out for his best interest."

Gazini's pistol disappeared.

"In my country, we do not pry into another man's life as it should be nothing to him," Gazini boomed. "If you see this Lord Rockfort, tell him death is coming to his Henry and Lord Howard's daughter is safe."

"Yes sir," the stable owner said solemnly. "Just ride north. When the road splits take the left split. It will lead you to Kensington. It's a good day and a half ride."

Gazini nodded and bent down low over the horse's neck an gratefully slid his hand across the upper muscles. The horse shook nervously at the unusual touch and bobbed his head.

"We shall make it in one. Come my brave friend. Let us light this English countryside with the fire of your hooves!"

The horse bobbed his head. The pair made an interesting appearance throughout the streets of London. It was not often one saw a large African savage, riding low over an extremely fast horse, whose hooves threw sparks off the cobblestone streets. It was as if the two of they had ridden straight from hell itself.

Chapter 73

Akela raised his old head wearily:-- "Free People, and ye too, jackals of Shere Khan, for twelve seasons I have led ye to and from the kill, and in all that time not one has been trapped or maimed. Now I have missed my kill. Ye know how that plot was made. Ye know how ye brought me up to an untried buck to make my weakness known. It was cleverly done. Your right is to kill me here on the Council Rock, now. Therefore, I ask, who comes to make an end of the Lone Wolf? For it is my right, by the Law of the Jungle, that ye come one by one."

There was a long hush, for no single wolf cared to fight Akela to the death. Then Shere Khan roared: "Bah! What have we to do with this toothless fool? He is doomed to die! It is the man-cub who has lived too long. Free People, he was my meat from the first. Give him to me. I am weary of this man-wolf folly. He has troubled the jungle for ten seasons. Give me the man-cub, or I will hunt here always, and not give you one bone. He is a man, a man's child, and from the marrow of my bones I hate him!"

Then more than half the Pack yelled: "A man! A man! What has a man to do with us? Let him go to his own place."

"And turn all the people of the villages against us?" clamored Shere Khan. "No, give him to me. He is a man, and none of us can look him between the eyes."

Akela lifted his head again and said, "He has eaten our food. He has slept with us. He has driven game for us. He has broken no word of the Law of the Jungle."

"Also, I paid for him with a bull when he was accepted. The worth of a bull is little, but Bagheera's honor is something that he will perhaps fight for," said Bagheera in his gentlest voice.

"Rudyard Kipling"
The Jungle Book

Henry arrived at the magistrate's office just after daybreak. Two British soldiers stood at attention in front of the small building. Both glanced at him as he entered. But neither offered any resistance. Henry was unarmed. At the last moment he had given his weapons to Gazini. Not even the most cowardly of London's population would dare to attack Henry unarmed. He would have been taken into custody and delivered to the magistrate anyway, which was his final wish.

Once he entered the large room, two more British soldiers met him.

"State your business here," one of them said as he barred Henry's advance with his musket.

"I'm here on business of the Crown," Henry said.

"He looks like another piece of fish tripe, fresh off the docks," the other soldier noted.

"Looks can be deceiving," Henry said jovially. "I would like to speak with the magistrate directly. It is a matter of great urgency."

The two soldiers looked at each other. Finally one of them said, "Just a moment."

He left the room. The other stayed behind.

"Ain't I see ya' somewhere?" he asked.

"I don't think we have ever met," Henry replied. "You might remember if we had."

"I don't likely forget a face," the soldier replied.

"Lucky you," Henry quipped, needling him.

The magistrate finally appeared. His wig was askew and

you could tell he had dressed quickly.

"I am Magistrate Wilkinson," he said angrily. "Now what the devil is this about?"

Henry bowed courteously and said, "I am here to turn myself in and beg His Majesty's forgiveness for any reproach I have brought to England."

The soldiers began to laugh. Finally even Magistrate Wilkinson was amused.

"And what is your crime," the Magistrate asked. "Too much whoring, too much gambling, stealing a loaf of bread? What is it lad? I don't have all day!"

"No," Henry replied quietly. "I am a man of the sea. I placed His Highness and England in a tumultuous political position with France. I'm here to ask for pardon."

The magistrate was laughing in earnest now.

"And what did ye' do lad," he said as tears of laughter slid down his face? Did ye' screw the Queen of France or just one of her rat dogs?"

Henry knew he was talking about the *Bichon Frise*, the little dog that was soon doomed to die almost to the point of extinction, as part of the French Revolution, yet to come. It was the gypsies, abhorred by the public that would snatch the animals out of extinction and train them to work in pairs to pick pockets of the genteel rich. Bichons are natural thieves and the gypsies would put them to good use.

"No, I am a pirate," Henry explained.

They were all laughing in earnest now. Even the soldiers

allowed themselves a good laugh at Henry's expense.

"That's a good one son," the Magistrate said. "Next you will be telling me you are Captain Jack Marsh, or Blackbeard, or perhaps Black Sam Bellamy! Now go, before I have my soldiers spank you!"

"When I last left Port Royal, Captain Marsh was thinking of retiring. I'm not sure of Blackbeard. But you can remove Black Sam Bellamy from your list. I killed him and his ship in a storm off the coast of New England."

"I've had about all the laugh I can have for one day," the Magistrate said. "What is your name?"

"I am Captain Henry Jennings," Henry said, as he stood tall. "I am here to request an audience with His Majesty or his appointee to discuss a potential pardon myself and my crew. I am quite wealthy. I can pay!"

The magistrate was taken aback. He motioned to one of the soldiers who brought him a poster. The likeness was quite similar. Henry wondered who had given it.

"Well, saints preserve us," Magistrate Wilkinson said quietly. "You are the famous Captain Henry Jennings. I applaud you for turning yourself into us. You have saved the Crown many months of tracking you down."

"When may I speak with His Highness or his appointee?" Henry asked again.

"Oh, I'm sorry lad," the magistrate said. "You have already had a fair trial. The King has asked for your head and your head he shall have!"

"No!" Henry replied. "I must see the King."

"Take his worthless arse!" the magistrate shouted. The two guards from the front door burst through to help. Three soldiers now held Henry. A fourth stood before him.

The Magistrate stood.

"Henry Jennings, by the power given to me by His Majesty King George, I do hereby find you guilty of the crimes of piracy, murder, looting, and sedition. I sentence you to hang by the neck until you are dead. Your execution will take place five days hence at Execution Dock during low tide. Your body will hang until the tide has washed over your head thrice. Such is the justice for pirates. May Almighty God have mercy on your soul!"

"No!" Henry cried as he pressed forward. "I demand a trial!"

A rifle butt connected with the back of his head and Henry knew no more.

"Brave lad, for a pirate," the Magistrate said quietly. "Take him to Marshalsea Prison until the day of his execution. Put him in chains. He is to see no one!"

Chapter 74

"He is our brother in all but blood," Akela went on, "and ye would kill him here! In truth, I have lived too long. Some of ye are eaters of cattle, and of others I have heard that, under Shere Khan's teaching, ye go by dark night and snatch children from the villager's doorstep. Therefore I know ye to be cowards, and it is to cowards I speak. It is certain that I must die, and my life is of no worth, or I would offer that in the man-cub's place. But for the sake of the Honor of the Pack,--a little matter that by being without a leader ye have forgotten,--I promise that if ye let the man-cub go to his own place, I will not, when my time comes to die, bare one tooth against ye. I will die without fighting. That will at least save the Pack three lives. More I cannot do; but if ye will, I can save ye the shame that comes of killing a brother against whom there is no fault--a brother spoken for and bought into the Pack according to the Law of the Jungle."

"He is a man--a man--a man!" snarled the Pack. And most of the wolves began to gather round Shere Khan, whose tail was beginning to switch.

"Now the business is in thy hands," said Bagheera to Mowgli. "We can do no more except fight."

"Rudyard Kipling"
The Jungle Book

Lord Rockfort looked up from his business ledger. Business was improving, thanks to one of his first generous acts of bringing John and his family to Kensington Castle. John had a way with men and was extremely good at new design, something England was in desperate need for. He even brought Lord Rockfort a drawing of a different type of musket that he wanted to try to make.

"See the lines, My Lord," John said as he moved around the table. "It is a little different than what we use now. But, the ball will travel much further and because we use a more refined powder for the frizzen pan, it ignites quicker so it is more accurate."

Lord Rockfort held the newly designed musket in his hands. It was lighter, stronger, and certainly felt better in the hands than any rifle he had held before.

"Why the brown color?" he asked John.

"I'm testing a different kind of acid to cure the barrel. It turns the metal brown, but makes it almost impossible to rust and you have less fouling. I use it inside the barrel as well."

"Good work John!" Lord Rockfort said enthusiastically. "Let's make fifty of them and we'll ask the King's Guard to test them!"

"Yes sir," John replied as he moved away. His gait still held a very slight limp, but as Lord Rockfort had promised, he kept his leg.

"Do we have a name for this?" Lord Rockfort asked.

John hesitated.

Finally he said, "Well me Lord, I was kinda thinking o' naming if after me mother. Her name was Bess."

"Bess?" Lord Rockfort asked.

"Aye, she was like this musket," John replied. "Quiet until need be and then all hell would break loose!"

"Bess," Lord Rockfort murmured. "I like it and I like the color. Let's call it *The Brown Bess*!"

"*Brown Bess* it is," John replied, beaming. "If that's all, I must return to the foundry. I need to inspect the musket barrels before we ship them."

"Very well," Lord Rockfort replied. "That is all."

John brushed past the Downstairs Footman who seemed quite pale and breathing heavily. Lord Rockfort sat down, automatically poured himself a glass of sherry and after thinking a moment, poured it back into the bottle. He had long since decided he was drinking far too much and something had to give. It was either the alcohol or his life.

"Excuse me sir," the butler said to Lord Rockfort. Usually his voice was nasal and had the air of someone that was also an aristocrat, an opportunity given to him by serving someone that was. At this moment his voice quivered.

"You have a visitor sir." he said.

"Unannounced? Mid-morning? Send him away. Tell him to come back tomorrow."

"He refuses to leave sir," the butler replied.

"Tell him I am indisposed."

"Begging your pardon my Lord, I don't think he will understand what that means," the butler said.

"Peter, can you not handle this simple matter yourself?"

Lord Rockfort demanded. "Get some help from the staff, the kitchen staff even, if you have too."

"He refuses to leave. Sir, he is a large savage!" the butler said. He was almost crying.

"Good Lord! Are you afraid of this man?" Lord Rockfort demanded.

"Yes, My Lord, I am," he replied. "I've never met a real savage before and this one is very big. He says if you don't come out and see him right now, he will cut me crusties off and feed them to the fishes!"

"We'll see about that," Lord Rockfort said as he reached above the mantle and took down his military sword.

"He also said to give you this," Peter said as he handed Lord Rockfort a small leather bag.

Lord Rockfort opened it. Inside was an old locket with a red *R* crest on it. For a moment Lord Rockfort faltered. He pushed the release and opened it. Inside was the likeness of Elizabeth and Henry, both young. He touched the face of each and then flipped out the right hand likeness of Henry. Inside was his inscription. It took him back many years to a time when he was happy, drank very little and he and Josephine would slip off for a quiet interlude. They both knew it was wrong. To her credit, Josephine tried to break it off more than once. But their love for each other remained strong. Lord Rockfort's love for her still did.

He was removed from his moment of nostalgia by his butler's voice.

"He also said to give you this," he said as he handed Lord

Rockfort a wax sealed folded paper.

"Show him in," Lord Rockfort said intently as he gingerly took the folded paper.

Ignoring his own advice earlier, he poured another glass of sherry, which he gulped down and then poured another. His hands were shaking as he carefully loosened the clumsy wax seal and gently unfolded the letter. It was a woman's handwriting and had obviously been scrawled hurriedly. He recognized the signature and the name as that of Lady Elizabeth Howard. It read:

My dearest Lord Rockfort,
It has been so long since the days of my youth and your visits to Norfolk Castle. I am well. Our ship, bound for Rome was hijacked and sunk by Pierre Clovis Rochechouart under the flag of the French Navy. Only Cassie and I survived. The ship who saved us was the Bathsheba, captained by someone you and I know very well. Yes, Lord Rockfort, it was Captain Henry Jennings. Or should I say Henry Rockfort, the Ninth Duke of Kensington? Is his birth mother indeed Miss Josephine, whom you profess your love for in the inscription behind Henry's likeness? Even now, our Henry has turned himself over to the magistrate near Execution Dock in London. His hope is to obtain a pardon and prove his innocence in that he never attacked an English ship and on more than once has saved English ships from certain calamity. I know Henry to be your son and I ask you upon your honor to hasten to London to help save him. I have sent one of Henry's true and trusted friends to you with the locket as proof of what I say. I am on my way by carriage to my father's home and I will

await word of your success. The life of the man I love is in your hands sir. I ask you to do what must be done for the sake of Henry, me, and your unborn grandchild. The child must be kept secret until after Henry's release. I must be the one to tell him. If he is told now, he will come to regret his honorable decision and if he is executed, I do not want him to go to his grave knowing that be abandoned his child, as he was abandoned. I tell you, because other than Henry, you have no living heirs. I thought you would like to know the Tenth Duke of Kensington grows within my belly.

Best wishes,
Elizabeth Howard

Lord Rockfort stared at Gazini's face.

"It is true then?" he asked.

"I do not know what the markings on the paper spoke to you," Gazini said. "But my friend needs us and I will die before I see him hung like the son of a jackal!"

"Peter," Lord Rockfort screeched. "Saddle my horse and fetch my pistols!"

"You will come?" Gazini said.

It was a question.

"I would be honored to die with you, friend of my son," Lord Rockfort said matter-of-factly.

"We ride for London and His Majesty," Lord Rockfort said.

"Who is a Majesty?" Gazini asked.

"He runs our country," Lord Rockfort replied as he stamped

on his boots.

"Mmmmm," Gazini replied. "Your chief does not know his people. He has lost touch with his tribe. This is a sad thing that we should mourn if there were time. We must go. Now!"

The two mounted their horses. Lord Rockfort's horse bore the typical English saddle. Gazini had none.

"No saddle?" Lord Rockfort inquired.

For the first time Gazini smiled.

"My people are in touch with their animals and nature," he said. "We are not soft in what ye' English call your arse!"

"Then keep up," Lord Rockfort exclaimed as he kicked his horse into a full gallop. "My son's life quite literally hangs in the balance!"

Gazini smiled as he also kicked his horse into a gallop. He liked this man. It was easy to see where Henry got his core and his strength.

Chapter 75

Mowgli stood upright--the fire pot in his hands. Then he stretched out his arms, and yawned in the face of the Council; but he was furious with rage and sorrow, for, wolflike, the wolves had never told him how they hated him. "Listen you!" he cried. "There is no need for this dog's jabber. Ye have told me so often tonight that I am a man (and indeed I would have been a wolf with you to my life's end) that I feel your words are true. So I do not call ye my brothers any more, but sag [dogs], as a man should. What ye will do, and what ye will not do, is not yours to say. That matter is with me; and that we may see the matter more plainly, I, the man, have brought here a little of the Red Flower which ye, dogs, fear."

"Rudyard Kipling"
The Jungle Book

When Henry began to awaken, he found his senses severely conflicted. He was frightened at first as he could not see and he thought they had taken his eyes, a common practice for a prisoner being tortured for a confession, or sometimes even for the condemned. In his case, he found he could not see because his eyes were crusted shut with blood from the blow to his head, or some other misfortune. As he hurt badly on all fronts, he was certain he had taken a severe beating at the hands of his captors while he was unconscious.

Finally he managed to force first one eye, and then the other open. His surroundings were indeed dismal. He had expected to be poorly treated, but not initially as a man condemned to death. He was wrong. Henry hung from a rack of chains that gave him just enough room to pull his feet back underneath him in order to stand. No further movement would be allowed. The manacles around his wrists had already cut through the skin from carrying his unconscious weight. He stood, and almost fell again. Damn, he hurt all over. They certainly had a grand time with him while he was on the floor. He suspected the arresting soldiers must have kicked him severely, showing they were indeed afraid of him. The view around told him he was in a dungeon somewhere. The rock walls and floor were wet and the stench was overpowering. One could easily detect the pungent smell of sour urine, vomit, and the even more undesirable aroma of feces and pus.

He raised his head. The only light came from a barred window almost ten feet above him. It allowed the only light available to enter the cell and served as a gate to allow some fresh air to enter to disrupt the ripe smells around him.

A voice behind him broke his attention to his physical details.

"I was wonderin' when ye' would wake up, or if ye' would at all," the voice said.

It was the voice of an old man.

Henry turned so he could see through the barred wall next to him. The man was not shackled so he at least had some freedom of movement. He was indeed older and wore the robes of a priest. Although disheveled, he still had some of the dignity in his voice that afforded his position.

"They brought you in this morning," the man said to Henry. "They beat the living God out of you before you got here. One of them told me you are the famous pirate, Captain Henry Jennings. Is that true?"

Henry managed a weak smile and then groaned. Even a smile hurt.

"Aye, they told you right," Henry replied.

"You don't look like a bad person, or even a pirate," the man commented. "And you don't look like how they depict you."

"And how is that?" Henry asked slowly as he began to raise himself to a comfortable height that put less strain on his mangled wrists.

"Lad, they say you are twelve feet tall, with teeth like a wolf," the man began. "And they also say you swing a sword the size of an executioner's axe with one hand. We are told you eat children for your meals and keep company with barbarous savages from the African continent. I have even heard that ye' shite on the faces of priests and commit fornication with them before you slice their throats!"

"You hear a great deal," Henry said weakly. "How much of it do you think is true?"

"Well, after seein' ye', I think most of it was a lie!" the priest muttered. "I did think ye' would be bigger."

"I'm glad you see it as a lie," Henry replied. "I thought for a priest you might be holier!"

The man laughed.

"Father O'Donnell at your service, Captain Henry Jennings!" the priest said. "I can even deliver your last rites before they take ye' away."

"Already done," Henry replied. "What was your crime?"

"I gave the Lord's grace to a poor soul that demanded it," Father O'Donnell replied.

"Lord's grace?"

"Yes, a poor tormented soul was about to force himself on a child of the street and I cut his snivellin' throat."

"I see," Henry replied. "You murdered him. That's odd for a priest!"

"I did not murder him," Father O'Donnell insisted. "I gave him the Lord's grace and as he lay dying, I gave him his Last Rites. That is how I came to be here."

"I guess that's one way to look at it," Henry replied. "Where is here?"

"You are at Marshalsea Prison," Father O'Donnell said

sadly. "And the only way out of here is the executioner's axe or Execution Dock. I was told you would go to the dock four days hence!"

Chapter 76

"Family isn't always blood. It's the people in your life who want you in theirs. The ones you accept you for who you are. The ones who would do anything to see you smile, and who love you you no matter what."

Author Unknown

Lord Rockfort was an unusual sight this day, standing in the small room off the main waiting hall, outside the King's reception area. He was not well dressed and wore no coat or usual finery of a gentleman. He was tired and smelled of horse, sweat, and tobacco. He did not smell of alcohol and in fact had declined a polite glass of sherry while he waited. Alcohol no longer held any magic for him.

Lord Rockfort knew the British monarchy was approaching the end of its glorious history. Within another hundred years, he suspected the monarchy and the governing powers of Britain would bear little resemblance to their present condition. With the implementation of Parliament, King George continued to lose more and more power to the new governing body. King George himself would not remain King for long as he would pass away in a few years on a trip to his native Hanover.

Power had begun to lie with Robert Walpole, the First Earl of Oxford. As the first Prime Minister, and a Whig from the gentry class, he was first elected to Parliament in 1701. He was a country squire and looked to country gentlemen for his political base. His leadership in Parliament reflected his reasonable and persuasive oratory, his ability to move the emotions as well as the minds of men, and, above all, his extraordinary self-confidence. His policies sought moderation: he worked for peace, lower taxes, growing exports, and allowed a little more tolerance for Protestant Dissenters. He avoided controversy and high-intensity disputes, as his middle way attracted moderates from both the Whig and Tory camps. Walpole was one of the greatest politicians in British history. He played a significant role in sustaining the Whig party, safeguarding the Hanoverian succession, and defending the principles of the *Glorious Revolution*. He established a stable political supremacy for the Whig party and taught succeeding ministers how best to establish an effective working relationship between Crown and Parliament.

It was he with whom Lord Rockfort sought audience as the balance of power had already begun to tilt. As a country squire, he had fewer notions of aristocratic nonsense than some of his counterparts in the House of Lords.

Lord Rockfort stood and was aghast when the Prime Minister himself entered the small room and sat down behind the desk. His visual surveillance of Lord Rockfort brought a smile to his face at the sight of this dishevelled nobleman.

"Lord Rockfort, please take a seat sir," Robert Walpole said as he indicated a comfortable chair before the desk. "I understand you have paid several visits to His Majesty regarding a .....let me see, oh yes. A certain Henry Jennings."

"Yes," Lord Rockfort responded. "I have and my requests seem to fall on deaf ears. Captain Jennings is being held a prisoner somewhere within the city and I am certain will be hanged, if he is not already!"

"No, he has not," the Prime Minister, said as he looked through some parchment. "It appears he surrendered to the magistrate at the docks and is scheduled to be hanged at noon tomorrow."

"Then we have time," Lord Rockfort said. "We can do *something*."

"Perhaps," the Prime Minister noted. "Our situation in the Caribbean grows worse. We have our own issues, but France and Spain continue to plague the arrival and departure of our ships to the region. They plunder our ships, kill His Majesty's crews, and in short make a mockery of this country. War with France is eminent, Lord Rockfort, and it was almost kindled before Parliament was prepared to declare war, thanks to this young Captain Jennings exploits with a number of French ships. The question bodes, why would an English nobleman give two shites about a pirate and a murderer? Do you know this man personally?"

"He is my son," Lord Rockfort replied simply. "Bastard son, nonetheless, but my blood courses through his veins."

"Ah, then that explains the mysterious bond," the Prime Minister said thoughtfully.

"He is my son, and I will do anything to save him," Lord Rockfort replied. "He is the last of my blood line."

"Which you cannot of course claim," the Prime Minister said as he once again looked thoughtfully at the ceiling. "I tell you Lord Rockfort, the days of British aristocracy are numbered. It will take years. But it will come. I believe there will always be a Royal family, as Britain does love her traditions. But, the day is coming when the people shall have the power to govern themselves and every day, Parliament grows stronger to represent both the well to do and even the genteel poor. That is what the House of Lords and the House of Commons was established to do. And we are concerned as to our interests in the New World and the threats against it. And with the upcoming war against France, which will be unavoidable, the crown will need money and much of it to build ships and pay our military."

"Yes, I understand," Lord Rockfort replied. "What has this to do with me?"

"I am sure you are familiar with Kensington Palace, not to be confused of course with Kensington Castle. Your cousin, the Earl of Nottingham sold the property in London for roughly £20,000. The royal court took residence in the palace shortly before Christmas 1689, and Kensington Palace was the favoured residence of British monarchs, since 1700. Queen Mary extended of her apartments by building the Queen's Gallery, and after the fire in 1691, the King's Staircase was rebuilt in marble and a Guard Chamber was constructed, facing the foot of the stairs. William built the Kings' Gallery, where he hung many works from his picture collection. Remember Mary II died of smallpox in the palace in 1694, and in 1702 William died from pneumonia after suffering a fall from a horse and was brought to Kensington Palace."

"What is your point sir?" Lord Rockfort asked.

"Suppose I were to ask His Majesty to quickly sign an order, releasing your son and pardoning non only him, but all other pirates that have taken up sword against England, providing of course they would accept the terms. Under these guidelines, they would become privateers for His Majesty, providing an even one third of all plunders to the British crown to help fight the upcoming war with France. The rest they would split amongst themselves. They would normally fly the flag of England. They would agree not to attack English ships and fly the Jolly Roger when they attacked

France or Spain, so as to not implicate the Crown. Their base of operations would extend out of the Bahamas, where I believe your son has great wealth and a large plantation. As part of this agreement, your son would become the Governor and the head of all privateers for England."

"And what do you want in return?" Lord Rockfort inquired.

"As you have no living *legitimate heirs*, your properties would be forever assigned to the Crown. As you know a bastard cannot inherit his father's properties. However, he can inherit his father's business operations, which I assume you would leave to young Henry anyway."

"And if I seek other means to free him?"

"You will not have time. Your son will die tomorrow."

"My lands become forfeit and my business operations go to my son? You are certain?"

"You would have my word, and that of His Majesty," the Prime Minister exclaimed.

"Very well," Lord Rockfort said solidly. "When do I have documents?"

"Now," Robert Walpole said as he unrolled two pieces of parchment. "If you will sign here, noting our individual agreement concerning the property, which of course takes place at your death, and here, noting the transfer of all business enterprises to Henry Jennings at the same time, unless you decide to transfer them to him sooner. And here is the document with His Majesty's signature, and that of my own, which will be served tomorrow before the execution. I will have two senior members of the King's Guard accompany you to Execution Dock with another document demanding his immediate release. Of course all other monies and wealth continue to belong to you. What the bloody hell! I may go myself!"

"Very well," Lord Rockfort replied as he signed the necessary parchment.

"Good job! I'll have Charles make certain you and your friend can tidy up for the night and bring you clothing as more befits a man of your status. Welcome to the new world, Lord Rockfort, where Lord and Commoner come together as one."

"By the way, I forgot to tell you, this transaction comes with another twist as well, " the Prime Minister said. "I want you to take a vacant seat we have on the House of Lords. I could use a good man like you on the side of all men."

"I would be honoured sir, despite feeling a little fleeced at the moment. However, it does take a great worry off me, knowing what will happen to Kensington at my death. I would like to know what changed the mind of His Majesty."

"It would seem Lord Hamilton may be using the pirates for his own personal gain and he has thus fallen out of favour with His Majesty. Plans are being made for him to return to England. It seems he declared our young Henry a pirate, only after Hamilton didn't get the cut of treasure he demanded."

Lord Rockfort nodded.

"Besides, the only man a pirate may trust is another pirate," the Prime Minister noted. "And, I have heard your son is an honourable man, and an honourable pirate!"

Chapter 77

"Respect your parents. What they tell you is true. Hard work, dedication and faith will get you anything. Imagination will drive itself. You can get anything you want, but you have to have faith behind all your ideas. Stick to your goals and have an undying faith."

Russell Simmons

"Lady Howard, the coach is pulling in front," the Butler announced. "Shall I greet your guests?"

"Were you expecting someone?" Lady Howard said to her husband.

"Not at all," Lord Howard replied as he looked upward above the top of the *London Gazette*. "It is early afternoon. Who would be calling on us this day? Likely a tired traveller."

Although it was already several days old, it brought them the latest news and gossip from London. Printed in pamphlet style, instead of what would later become the standard newspaper style of printing, it was easy to manipulate over one's morning cup of coffee or breakfast tea. Coffee was beginning to become the rage. However, Lord Howard still preferred hot tea during the day. Coffee was his new drink of the morning.

"Oh well my dear. I suppose I should look my best to greet them." Lord Howard said as he started to reach for his coat, which was immediately picked up by the Downstairs Footman who held it for him and quickly whisked it with a small brush once Lord Howard had donned it.

"Very well Hoover," Lord Howard said. "You may announce them when they are ready."

He sat down once again to resume reading his newspaper.

A few moments later the door to the study burst open. Lord Howard raised his head angrily at the sound, expecting it to be that of Hoover with some unexpected and inappropriate behavior. He was, after all, a *newly* promoted butler and newly promoted butlers were prone to mistakes.

"Mama! Papa!" a familiar voice screeched as one of the study's double doors slammed against the wall.

"What the bloody hell!" Lord Howard exclaimed as he stood.

"Oh, Mother Mary," Sarah Howard exclaimed as she broke into tears and rushed to embrace her daughter. "Elizabeth is that really you. Am I hallucinating? Oh, my darling girl!"

Forgetting his proper manners, the status of his birth, and all that was sacred in this English century, Bernard Howard rushed forward to embrace them both. He held them in a tight embrace, as it fate might possibly take one of them away from him forever. He buried his face in Elizabeth's hair and laughed incessantly to keep from crying. Sarah was already crying in earnest as she held her arms around her daughter's midriff, noting there was something slightly different in that touch. It was perhaps something only another woman might recognize. Bernard was a typical man. The thought never crossed his mind.

"We thought the worst," he exclaimed. "When your ship was taken by the bloody French, we thought you had been sold into the prostitute trade in the Middle East, or perhaps worse. Are you quite alright my dear?"

"I was not ill treated," Elizabeth said, wiping the tears from her own eyes. She was overjoyed to see her parents, but thoughts of Henry and what he might be facing this day permeated her mind.

"Oh, Pierre tried," Elizabeth, said. "But he was going to sell me in Port Royal as a fresh woman, rather than take me himself."

"Pierre!" Lord Howard exclaimed. "His ship was sunk and

he was killed as a result. His Majesty had to work desperately to avoid an immediate war with France. And you were taken hostage by the pirate ship that sank *King Louis Revenge*. Perhaps there is some honor amongst these savages after all! Who am I indebted to for saving your life?"

"Henry," Elizabeth whispered. "Henry saved me, brought me home and may now be facing the gallows again, as he is asking the magistrate for pardon."

"Oh, my dear," Lord Howard said sadly. "I have already been down this path to London several times to beg for his pardon and his life. He already was declared a traitor to the Crown. That is the only trial he will ever get. Henry will be hanged and there is nothing we can do about it!"

Chapter 78

"They were being driven to a prison, through no fault of their own, in all probability for life. In comparison, how much easier it would be to walk to the gallows than to this tomb of living horrors!"

Nellie Bly

"Well good day sir!" one of the four regimental guards said to Henry as he hung from his shackles. "It's a bloody good day to die! The birds are singing! The sky is blue! And that's to be the color of ye' face shortly!"

Two guards carefully unshackled Henry and tied his hands tightly behind his back.

"Ye' don't look so bloody big now," one of them said as he gave Henry a show, knocking him to the floor.

"Damn you," Henry retorted. "So much for justice in this country I left!"

"Oh you are going to get your justice," one of the other guards said as he broke wind and they all laughed. "You'll get your justice at the end of a rope, chokin' for all those Englishmen you have killed!"

"I didn't kill Englishmen," Henry retorted. "We preyed on France and Spain and a few others."

"Well ye' won't be preyin' on nobody, now will ye?" the first guard retorted. "Hey lads, whatta ya' say? Should he hang from the gallows *en castratum?"*

"No time for that Spence," the lead of the group, whom Henry identified as a Lieutenant, replied. "They want him now. His cart is in front."

"Aye, and we be having a little parade, jest for you," Spence said jokingly as they ushered him outside.

"Tie him up there on the cross arm," the Lieutenant said sternly. "And make certain his bonds are tight. We want no chance of him getting' loose. The crowd is expectin' this one and there will be hell to pay if they don't get 'em!"

Although Henry struggled, this time trying to escape, as he knew this was his last chance before certain death, he was quickly subdued with pistol butts and fists. This was to be the only mercy he would achieve.

"Here's what be happening lad," the Lieutenant said solemnly. "You as the condemned will be paraded across London Bridge past the Tower of London. The High Court Marshal will be on horseback with a silver oar that represents the authority of the Admiralty. You may have a chaplain or priest for confession. You will get the short rope. Sorry for that mate. It means yer' neck won't break, but your own body weight will choke 'ye to death. There will be many to watch ye' do the Marshall's dance 'cause as ye' choke your arms and legs will do a little jig for everyone's amusement. Ye will be hung there until the tide has washed over yer' head three times. Maybe they will tar ye. Maybe they won't. Either way this is a way to show those that take the road to piracy that death ends at Execution Dock!"

"Fine," Henry replied solemnly as he looked the man in the eyes. "I am not afraid of you. I died many years ago as a young lad that left this country because of a duel with the damn French. You can't kill what is already dead!"

The Lieutenant nodded.

"You'll have a chance for your last say as they put the rope on yer' neck," he said solemnly. "Save it for then."

"I want the priest to hear my confession," Henry said.

"You mean the blighter we have locked up with ye'?"

Spence asked.

"The same," Henry replied.

"Well, I dunno. Can we do that Lieutenant? Are they going to condemn a holy man to death anyway?"

"Perhaps," the Lieutenant said. "It's either death or life in prison. Either way, it's death. Get him out, tie his hands and tie him to the cart with a rope. He can bloody well walk!"

The priest was brought forward; his hand bound tightly and told of his commission for the day.

"I be thankin' ye' Captain Henry Jennings," Father O'Donnell said. "This may be the last time I see the real light of a glorious day, which our Lord has made. I'll hear your confession and give you God's grace and pardon for them!"

"Sure," Henry replied," And thank you!"

Henry was thinking of God's grace that had been given to the child molester. Perhaps that would have been a better grace than he was about to receive.

"Let's go then!" the Lieutenant cried.

Henry was on his knees in the small cart with his back, arms, and wrists tied tightly to a cross shaped structure in the center. There were few people until they crossed the London Bridge and then the crowds became denser. Jeers and laughter accompanied his passing through. Finally members of the crowd began to throw things at him. A raw, spoiled egg hit the side of the cart, splattering him. A large piece of rotten cabbage struck him in the face. A small boy picked up a horse turd from the side of the road and expertly struck Henry in the face with it.

All manner of rotten garbage and waste were thrown at the poor prisoner until the cart finally stopped and two of the soldiers who were inadvertently struck with some of the waste intended for Henry began to chastise the crowd. Finally it was the priest who stepped forward and spoke.

"Have you no remorse for the condemned? Have you no empathy? This man did not choose his life! It was chosen for him! You there! Joseph! Have I not heard *your* confession? Would you like me to share it here with yer' wife and children? Let he who is without sin, cast the first stone!"

"Here's your bloody stone," a woman cried as she struck the priest in the temple with a roadside rock.

Father O'Donnell slumped to the ground, blood streaming down his face.

"Oh now, ye' went and done him, ye' have," the woman's husband chastised. "You've struck a bloody priest. We'll be cursed now for the rest of our lives! You stupid bitch!"

"He's a priest what's a prisoner," she exclaimed. "He's little more than a thief, he is!"

"They are all thieves," the man retorted as he slapped her full across her face. "But they are still men of God!"

He tried to move forward to help the priest from the ground.

"Take a watch there!" the Lieutenant exclaimed as he pushed the man back. "None o' ye' come near the prisoners, or it will be the end for ye'!"

He nodded to move the group forward.

"If these come too close, shoot them," the Lieutenant

observed.

The finally reached Execution Dock. There were already three unfortunates hanging from long ropes. They had been given the opportunity for a quick death, which Henry would not have.

"Let's be on with it then," Henry said. "I'm ready!"

"Untie him," the Lieutenant said quietly. "Let's do our job lads and be done with it."

Henry was untied, dismounted the wagon and after making certain his wrists was still well bound, was escorted to the steps leading up to the hangman's platform. He placed one boot on the bottom step and stopped. Fate had caught up with him at last.

Chapter 79

"But in the moments before the fight, if you were a smart man, you'd figure out a way to convince yourself that it didn't matter to you if you lived or died. If you're safe in your house, with your children running around underfoot and with fields that need to be worked, it's an impossible way of thinking, unless you are sick in the head. Of course it mattered if you lived or died. But if you went into battle caring what happened to you, you wouldn't be able to fight, even though you were as likely ot die as the next man whether you cared or not. There wasn't any logic as to who got killed and who didn't, and it was better that your final thoughts not be of cowardice and regret. It was better not to care, and to let yourself be swept up in the rush of the men beside you, to drive forward into the smoke and fire with the knowledge that you had already cheated death. When you let yourself go like that, you could fight on."

Sergeant Zachariah Cashwell, 24th Arkansas

"Papa, there must be something we can do," Elizabeth cried. "Go to the King. Ask him for pardon!"

"Elizabeth, I have already done so, more than once," Lord Howard replied.

"Please father," Elizabeth whispered. "I will do anything!"

"This is not about you," Lord Howard said quietly. "We have run out of time. This time you must face it. Our Henry is about to be lost to us forever. And oh, I rue the day, he made an offer of marriage for you, and I turned him down. Much of this fault I must accept as my own stupid pride! But now, at this moment, I believe my decision was the right one. A man of lower birth should not marry a woman of higher birth. It is simply not respectable."

Elizabeth lifted her head high, and retreated up the stairs to her room. It had not changed. Her parents had kept it just as she had left it. She reached inside a special slit in the mattress. Yes, the folded piece of paper was still there. She gently opened it. The ink was a little faded with time, but it was still quite legible. It read:

My dearest Lizzie,

By the time you read this, I will be gone. Today I took two lives and I must carry that weight forever. But the greatest weight that I carry now is that I can never be with you, touch your hair, feel the softness of your skin, or the rich fullness of your lips. I love you my dear, more than I have ever loved anyone in my entire existence. I never knew my father and I know the woman that proclaimed to be my mother was not my birth mother. She told me that much. She also loved me as only a mother possibly could. She is in Kent now, at The White Monastery of Our Lady, far from the reaches of English aristocracy. Please check on her once in a while, but do not let anyone else know where she is. Whatever secret she has, someone may try to kill her to extinguish it from her lips forever.

My dearest Lizzie, you have to know I will always remember the times we lay together and looked up at the stars in the night sky, our long and lazy picnics, and watching you walk through the fresh flowers in the field. Lizzie, you are like the wild Iris, tall and strong against all winds. You will overcome this. You have to know I will never forget you, but you must forget about me. It is now done. We truly cannot be together and it breaks my heart more than you will ever know. If there were any way I could come home, I would do so. Find a man that will be good to you.

My prayer for you is one that Simon taught me. May your days be full of love and your life full of happiness and may your children always live free!

You have my heart and I love you always,
Henry

Once again, she held the letter close to her heart and lay on the bed crying, knowing the life inside her would also someday weep when he or she learned of their brave, honourable father.

Sarah Howard heard her daughter, gently opened Elizabeth's bedroom door and closed it. She sat on the bed with Elizabeth and held her as a woman would a small child. Elizabeth buried her face in her mother's bosom and cried as if her heart would break. Finally Sarah placed her hand on Elizabeth's lower stomach.

"How far along?" she asked.

"What are you talking about?" Elizabeth said through the tears.

"Oh, my dear, I think you know very well what I am talking

about. "Were you taken against your will? There is no shame!"

"No," Elizabeth replied. "Why do people always suspect when a young woman gives herself to someone, they are raped?"

Sarah paled at the forbidden word.

"So you gave yourself willingly?" she asked her daughter.

"Yes, I did," Elizabeth sad flatly. "And not just once. I did so over and over again, so many times that even I have lost count."

"And who is the father?" Sarah Howard asked her daughter gently.

"I think you know very well who the father is," Elizabeth said. "There was a woman in Port Royal that ran a tavern and a brothel. She told me that women might have sex with more than one man during the course of her life, but that she would only truly give herself to one special man. That man is my love and my lover, Henry Jennings!"

Sarah Howard picked up the letter from the coverlet upon which it had fallen and quickly read it. Just for a moment, tears welled in eyes.

"Do you know how special our Henry is?" she asked Elizabeth as she gently pulled her closer.

"I do!" Elizabeth replied.

"I hope you do," Sarah whispered. "Our Henry loved you so much, that he was prepared to unselfishly give you up, rather than put you through a life of heartache. This letter had nothing to do with his fear of the gallows, as it still does not. He returned you home. He is not afraid of the executioner and never has been. He is afraid you will be hurt either physically or emotionally, and for that, he is willing to give his life to protect you!"

Chapter 80

"Now," he said, "I will go to men. But first I must say farewell to my mother." And he went to the cave where she lived with Father Wolf, and he cried on her coat, while the four cubs howled miserably.

"Ye will not forget me?" said Mowgli.

"Never while we can follow a trail," said the cubs. "Come to the foot of the hill when thou art a man, and we will talk to thee; and we will come into the croplands to play with thee by night."

"Come soon!" said Father Wolf. "Oh, wise little frog, come again soon; for we be old, thy mother and I."

"Come soon," said Mother Wolf, "little naked son of mine. For, listen, child of man, I loved thee more than ever I loved my cubs."

"I will surely come," said Mowgli. "And when I come it will be to lay out Sher Khan's hide upon the Council Rock. Do not forget me! Tell them in the jungle never to forget me!"

Henry smiled at Father O'Donnell.

"Don't look so glum Father," he said. "It's just a bloody hanging, even if it is mine. Just think in the years that follow, you can say you gave Captain Henry Jennings his last rights!"

"Aye lad, do you want them now?" Father O'Donnell said solemnly.

"Na," Henry replied. "I've already had them from a priest in Port Royal. I'm as good as gold. Hell, I'm better than gold. How many men can say they have so much wealth that their children's children couldn't spend it all? Cheer up and watch me dance. I'll give these bastards a bloody show!"

Henry slowly ascended each step, his boots making a solid *thunk* sound on the wooden steps.

"These look a little worn," he said the hooded executioner. "Used them a lot?"

"Aye Captain, we have lately," the man said. "Captain, I want ye' to know I do not like what I am going to have to do. Do you forgive me Captain?"

"Aye, you are forgiven my brother, for you do nothing more than your job. Let me have my say, and let's be on with it," Henry said. "Not every man can say they hung the notorious Captain Henry Jennings!"

"Thank you, Captain Jennings," the executioner replied.

Henry raised his head erect.

The executioner nodded, placed the noose around Henry's neck, helped him atop the keg and tied the other end off. It was going to be a short rope for Captain Henry Jennings.

Henry thought he would feel fear. Instead, he felt anger and resentment. His young life had been ripped away from him as quickly as one rips the petal from a rose. He had retreated to the only opportunity the seemed open to him to escape the gallows. Perhaps one cannot escape destiny after all.

"Does the condemned have anything to say?" the executioner cried as he positioned his foot against the keg for a proper kick.

"Aye, I do," Henry said. "You people of England that never would have come to help me as a boy need to look well to yourselves and your children. Life can change in the twinkling of an eye. It is how you live your life that defines you. Damn these aristocratic peacocks! All men die! Let England know that Captain Henry Jennings really lived and was game through to the bitter end! I protect those whom I love!"

The crowd who had once called for his death began to shuffle their feet and talk amongst themselves. Finally one woman called out.

"Me husband was taken and gutted like a fish for poaching the Lord's deer. We were hungry, we were, and our little ones were starving. He did all a man could do, and lost his life for it. Mercy! Mercy for Captain Henry Jennings!"

"Aye, mercy!" a man shouted above the roar of the crowd, which was beginning to grow. "Me wife was sick and the Duke himself had the power to send for a doctor. He would not and simply said it was one less mouth to feed in the village!"

"Alright then," Henry shouted. "Stay the course! Make them

hear you! You have a voice in Parliament now. Use it!"

The crowd applauded and began to nod their heads. Some shook their hands viciously at the Executioner.

"Do not hold my death against this man!" Henry exclaimed over the din. "He does his job and has no choice in it any more than you do!"

"Alright mate," Henry said quietly. "Do your work!"

The executioner shook his head sadly and nodded to the drummers who began their quick cadence. When it was over, the keg would be kicked out from under Henry and he would begin the process of his slow, agonizing death.

The military drummers began their cadence. Suddenly the crowd began to part. An ornate carriage with two horses tied to the back quickly sped through the crowd. A footman on the back was rapidly blowing a trumpet, the sound that preceded the arrival of an important member of the King's court. The carriage pulled as close as possible to the hangman's platform. Two men jumped from the carriage. One held a rolled parchment.

"Stop!" he cried.

"Who dares to stop an execution directed by the King?" the Lieutenant said as he drew his sword.

The other, older, man, drew a pistol and levelled it at the Lieutenant.

"I do," the man with the parchment, replied smartly after handing the document to the Lieutenant. "I am Robert Walpole, the first Earl of Oxford and Prime Minister of Parliament. I come on behalf of His Majesty King George I, King of England, Scotland,

Ireland, and Wales. I have in my hand a letter of pardon for Captain Henry Jennings, his crew, and all other pirates willing to devote themselves to becoming privateers for the Crown. This order also grants Caption Henry Jennings the status of Governor of the Bahamas out of New Providence and makes him the leader of a new Navy of privateers in the name of His Majesty!"

The Lieutenant read the document.

"Release the prisoner!" he demanded.

"And who are you?" he asked Lord Rockfort.

"I am Lord Henry Rockfort, the Eighth Duke of Kensington and father of Captain Henry Jennings, the Ninth Duke of Kensington. I do publically declare Henry Jennings to be my blood and my sole remaining heir."

The older man faltered.

"And I ask his humble forgiveness for the wrong I have done him these many years. Damn England and damn her ways!"

The executioner removed the rope from Henry's neck and helped him from the keg. The priest smiled.

"See my son, prayers are answered," he said.

"Indeed," Henry replied. "Release the priest. He is a member of my crew."

"This is ridiculous!" the Lieutenant cried. "Are we now to release every vagrant that is declared to be a member of this ruffian's crew?"

"Only the ones that matter," Henry said. "Release him!"

"Release the man and note his pardon," the Lieutenant said.

Then to the crowd he ordered, "Everyone can go home now!

There will be no more executions today!"

There were mutterings of disappointment, but the crowd dispersed, having no wish to take Henry's place at the gallows themselves.

"Let me look at you boy," Lord Rockfort said. "It is the look of your mother you have about you. She was a wonderful woman. I wish you had known her."

"What happened to her?" Henry asked quietly.

"She gave her life brining you into this world," Lord Rockfort replied. "It broke my heart."

"The lion is now fully fed Captain," a voice boomed as he stepped out of the carriage.

"Gazini!" Henry cried as he grabbed his friend by his shoulders. "You did this!"

"I rode the horse. As usual there was the work of a woman involved. It was Miss Elizabeth that put the pieces together like a blanket and sent me on my travel to visit your father."

"How can I ever repay you?" Henry asked.

"You can repay me by letting me go," Gazini said quietly. "I still have time to meet Miss Desiree' and Miss Anastasia on the ship that takes them to Greece and then to mine own homeland. That is all I can ask of my friend."

"I will hate to see you go," Henry replied.

Gazini smiled and said, " You know the Maasai own all of the cattle in the world. When you and Miss Elizabeth look into the night sky to see *your* star, look well, for the sign of the bull is also there. It watches over the Maasai and their friends."

"Goodbye Gazini!" Henry said quietly. "You have been a good friend. You are released. But then you never needed release. You are and always have been your own man. You stayed because you wanted to do so. And for that, I am grateful. Perhaps we will meet again."

"*Ole seri*," Gazini noted. "But in our language goodbye is only for a time. Heed my words, my friend. Do not feed the lion of anger any longer. It almost destroyed you."

And with that he seemed to simply disappear into the crowd.

"Rather endearing chap, for a savage," the Prime Minister observed. "I would have liked to know him better."

"You know almost as much about him as I do," Henry replied. "He is a very private person."

"It is the silent ones that scare the shite out of me," Walpole noted. "They cut your throat quietly in the night and you never hear them coming. Lord Rockfort, all's well that ends well or some blighter like that. My carriage will return you to your estate, after I return to His Majesty. He desires to know how we faired today."

"That is most kind," Lord Rockfort replied. "I shall accept your gracious offer!"

Lord Rockfort turned to his son and gave him a large hug.

"My boy," he whispered. "Promise to see me before you leave!"

"I will father," Henry whispered back. "I have so many questions."

I will do my best to answer them," the older man said.

"However, for now I know where you wish to go. I brought you a few clean clothes so you can go to her as a gentleman!"

Henry quickly changed clothes outside the carriage, while two women from one of the local taverns looked on in great interest.

"You look a little better," Lord Rockfort said.

Henry handed his father a letter.

"Can you see this is delivered to *Bathsheba* before this evening?"

"I will see the letter is delivered and the documents needed for your authorization in the Bahamas are given to your father so you will have them once your journey is completed to Nassau," the Prime Minister said. "Lad, you are lucky. A few moments delay and, well, things could have been different."

"Gazini said to take the black. He said that the black is like you, wild and untamed and with the spirit of a lion!" Lord Rockfort suggested.

He grasped at his chest.

"Are you quite alright?" the Prime Minister asked.

"Nothing a younger age and tankard of ale wouldn't cure," Lord Rockfort replied

He handed the horse's reins to Henry.

The pain in his chest lessened.

"Ride my son," he said. "Ride like the wind. I am sure she believes you to be dead."

Chapter 81

"True love is eternal, infinite, and always like itself. It is equal and pure, without violent demonstrations: it is seen with white hairs and is always young in the heart."

Honore de Balzac

The large black stallion raced through the country roads toward Norfolk Castle. As Gazini had promised, the horse was a little wild and untamed and snorted profusely as Henry bent down low over his back, as Gazini had and urged him on. Despite that which fate had dealt to Henry, he remained very much like the horse. He was still wild and untamed and would likely remain so most of his life.

The countryside had changed very little during the time he had been gone. An occasional farmer or peasant would raise their hand to him as he sped by, aghast that a proud member of the upper class would dare to be in such a hurry. It was quite unusual.

Henry knew he was close when he hit the fields and forest of the commons. There was the Yew tree where he and Lizzie had spent so much of their early years together. He dismounted, savouring the smell of the wild Iris in the field. From here, he could see where he and Lizzie had shared their first kiss, their picnic lunches, and that one intimate moment that had almost been theirs, but once again fate had other plans.

He relished in that moment for an instance and took comfort in their youth and innocence. For a moment he yearned for the past, for innocence lost, something that could never be replaced, once it was taken. He yearned for the life they had lived and he thought of Simon's teaching in the art of sword and pistol. The man that started Henry toward this loss of innocence was dead. Still Henry could take little satisfaction from that moment. He mounted the large stallion and began to race across the commons where he could see Norfolk castle in the background.

Chapter 82

"Forgiving does not erase the bitter past. A healed memory is not a deleted memory. Instead, forgiving what we cannot forget creates a new way to remember. We change the memory of our past into a hope for our future."

Lewis B. Smedes

Life aboard *The Windsong* was a little different than other ships and because they had sailed south and through the straits between Spain and Morocco, the sea was less violent and rough. In fact the Mediterranean Sea was quite welcoming as it was surrounded almost completely by land.

As promised, Gazini was able to make this final trip with Desiree' and Anastasia. To prevent problems, he insisted Desiree' refer to him as her slave. For his good intentions, the females were issued a small cabin and he slept in steerage in a hammock with the rest of the slaves. It was small price to pay to complete his last honorable deed for these people and to allow him opportunity to return home.

Gazini knew when they began to sail a little south that the Tyrrhenian Sea and Rome was now north of them. They were getting closer and closer to their final destination. After about three days, they arrived at a port on the Peloponnese peninsula of Greece.

Once they disembarked, Gazini bade them wait until he found an older man he perceived to be an honest individual. Frankly, he had spent so much time with dishonest people for the last several years; it was extremely easy to identify them. These unsavory people he avoided until he met his mark.

"May I speak with you?" Gazini asked the old man.

"Yes, what is it that you wish?" the old man asked.

"I am Gazini of the Maasai tribe of Kanya. I am for the moment in the service of that woman and her daughter. I seek someone to help them to their family's home."

"Where is this home?" the old man asked.

"I understand it is close by," Gazini replied. "It is in the city of Kalamata on this very peninsula."

"You are within two hours by wagon," the old man said. "You could get them there."

"I would prefer someone with knowledge of the people and the city," Gazini replied. "I can pay!"

"There is no need, other than to rent a wagon," the man said. "My name is Pelias. What house do you seek?"

"I understand it is a rich man's house," Gazini replied. "The house is the House of the Palamara family. The son was a brave mariner. His name was Evangelos."

"Ah, I have heard of this family and I know of their house," Pelias replied. "One gold coin will provide for the wagon and a little for my family this next several days. Can you afford that black man?"

"I will give you ten gold coins," Gazini offered, thinking more money meant more protection.

"No, I said one gold coin, and that is what I meant. One gold coin." Pelias said.

"Here it is," Gazini said as he handed it to him and motioned for Desiree' and Anastasia to come forward.

"You are sure you can take care of them?" Gazini said.

"I am certain," Pelias said. "The wars are over for now. You are in Greece, the center of learning for the world!"

He waved for a wagon, whose driver had been watching the exchange of coin and came speedily to them.

"This is where we separate," Gazini said to Desiree'. "Pelias knows where the House of Palamara lies and will see you there. I go now to my own home."

Little Anastasia threw her arms around Gazini's legs.

"Please don't go, Mr. Gazini! Can't you stay with us forever?"

Gazini dropped to one knee. Very few times did he smile, but at this moment he smiled very broadly, revealing a mouth of straight white teeth.

"Little one, where you go, I cannot," he said simply. "You and your Mother have your lives. I have my own. I also have a woman and two children in Kanya that I desire to return home to."

Anastasia nodded.

"I understand. I wish I had my Da' to go home to, but he's with God now."

Gazini nodded and patted her head as he arose from his knee.

"Very well done," Desiree' said.

She could swear Gazini blushed under his dark black skin.

"Maasai warriors are also fathers," he stated flatly.

"And good ones," Desiree' said. "We will miss you greatly as we already miss Henry and Elizabeth. At least Henry was spared, so there is hope for them! Scurvy will marry Cassie and become one of Henry's great Captains for the Crown. Balance has been restored."

"Enkai Na-rok is good!" Gazini boomed. "*Ole seri,* may Enkai Na-rok always be with you!"

He turned and within an instant was gone.

The wagon ride proved uneventful and eventually they pulled in front of a large, ornate house, the outside of which was planted with luscious greenery. Grape fields could be seen in the distance. Desiree' guessed this may have been from whence came part of their wealth.

The wagon driver and Pelias unloaded the small travelling case, which was all Desiree brought with them.

"Would you like us to stay, just to make sure you are received?" Pelias asked.

"Are you sure this is the House of Palamara?" Desiree asked.

Both men nodded.

"The family is know from here to Turkey and North Africa," Pelias said. "This is their home."

Desiree nodded, took Anastasia's hand and knocked on the large door. She was a little taken aback by the luxury and waited until an elderly woman opened the door.

"Χαίρετε?" she asked.

It took Desiree' a moment to translate Greek to English.

"Oh, yes," Desiree' said. "I am a friend of Evangelos'. May we come in?"

"I hear English," an older male voice said inside. "Show them in!"

An older man appeared. He was simply, but well dressed with a pleasant smile.

"May I help you?" he asked. "What can the House of Palamara offer to two such charming guests?"

At first Desiree's guard went up. For a moment he reminded her of the charming gentleman that had once been her benefactor and rapist. Sensing her guardedness, the older man smiled again.

"Delia, please ask my wife Agape to accompany us. Tell her we have guests."

The old woman mumbled something that did not sound very nice and received a sharp look from her employer. However, it was obvious she often spoke her opinion and had likely been with the family for many long years.

A woman of approximately the same age as the man joined them. She was quite beautiful for her age, and her skin tone was that of a woman twenty years younger. She smiled and looked at Desiree and Anastasia left and right.

"Hello," she said. "My English is not too poor. I don't have nearly as much time to exercise it as I used to. You are both quite beautiful!"

"And so are you," Desiree' said. "The description Evangelos depicted was very exact. You skin tone is amazing!"

"It comes from the olive oil. We grow grapes and olives, among other business interests. I use the oil on my skin," she replied. "You know our Evangelos?"

"I know him very well," Desiree' replied.

"Then he must see you," Agape replied.

Desiree' started to reply. *He is dead! He is not here! He is not alive! Do not torment me!*

And then quite loudly, she cried, "Evangelos, my son, we have guests! Evangelos!"

Then softly to Desiree', "He doesn't hear as well now. Too much cannon fire, I am afraid. Oh, we were all young once, weren't we? But then you still are! Evangelos!!!!"

"Coming!" a voice said from the rear of the house.

Desiree' heard the sound of a man's boots on the wooden floors. One was the usual hard thump. The other sounded as if the foot were sliding. Could this be happening? This had to be the wrong house or the wrong Evangelos. Perhaps a son of some other woman he had married. Perhaps he had been married the entire time he was with Desiree'. She had been lied to before.

"Who is visiting Mother?" a familiar voice said.

He entered the room. It was as if time had reversed instead of moving forward. True, he was a little older and there was a touch of gray in his short beard now. But here before her was her Evangelos.

For a moment, she was taken aback and began to swoon. His father started to rush to her side. But Evangelos beat him to her.

"Oh my darling Desiree'! You do not know how often I have begged and prayed to see you again. I thought you were dead. When I returned to Port Royal, the entire island was a graveyard from the tsunami. There were dead bodies everywhere. I looked for weeks, but could not find you. Finally I gave up all hope and left. The Spanish sunk my ship just off the coast, entering the Mediterranean. I was taken prisoner. I escaped twice. The first time, they cut my Achilles tendon to keep me from escaping again. But finally I did mange to escape and return home. Oh, my darling there has never been a day when I have not prayed for your return, some how, some way!"

Desiree' clung to him, hoping this was all not some evil dream to pay her back for her own twisted past. But this time, she would not let him go.

"You don't know the things I have done to survive," Desiree' whispered to Evangelos. "And if I were to tell you . . ."

Evangelos finished softly for her.

"And if you were to tell me, they would not mean anything between us, as long as you are well," he said. "The past is the past. Let's live for now and for our future!"

Desiree' nodded. She was scarcely able to believe her good fortune. There was a God after all!

"So, Desiree' would you do me the honor of being my wife?" Evangelos asked, dropping to one knee, blocking out the pain the movement caused him. "I will not lose you again!"

"Yes," Desiree' replied. "If you will accept me as I am. I am not completely the same woman you knew."

"Again, ancient history my love!"

"If you will have me as I am, I am yours and the answer is yes," Desiree replied hurriedly.

"A marriage ceremony and a marriage party to follow," his father exclaimed. "We have gained a daughter! Let the entire house know the love my son lost is returned to him. This is a day of celebration!"

Evangelos knelt down in front of Anastasia who taken aback and could not completely comprehend what had just happened.

"Hello little one!" Evangelos said as he touched her black

curls and looked into her dark eyes.

"Mommy, who is *this* man?" Anastasia asked.

Desiree' gently placed both hands on Anastasia's shoulders to comfort her.

"It is alright darling," she whispered to the little girl. "Anastasia, I want you to meet Evangelos Palamara, your father!"

Chapter 83

"Home is not far away when you are alive."

Maasai Proverb

The trip south of the Peloponnese peninsula of Greece to Alexandria, Egypt took several days. Gazini's normal patience had finally flattened. He could take no more. He could smell his native continent, and even in Egypt, the caravans brought back memories of trading with the Egyptians when he was a boy.

Once he travelled to Egypt, he took passage on a small boat that took him most of the distance down the Red Sea to Massawa, close to Ethiopia. This was his last sea excursion. The land called to him. He knew his homeland of Kanya (or what would become modern day Kenya) lay just on the other side of Ethiopia. The Ethiopian people were good people, extremely intelligent and schooled in many curing arts, as well as religious doctrine.

Once on the ground, he paid his host well, and began various stretching exercises. The Maasai, and in short all of Kanya were renowned the world over for their ability to run long distances in a day's time. *Hakuna matata* loosely translates to *no worries.* The Maasai keep stress to a minimum by embracing hakuna matata in their everyday lives. It's important to leave stress behind to allow your body to perform at its best, and sometimes the best way to relieve stress is to run.

Over the course of the next several weeks, Gazini lived as his people lived. He killed for food, and for food alone. He made a spear point out of a long sharp piece of flint, which he attached to a wooden shaft and sharpened the spear head to an almost razor sharp edge using other pieces of flint and special bark known to his people for that purpose.

As his people were a nomadic people, it might take him a

while to find them, but find them he would. He stayed clear of most of the large cats that could quickly turn him into an evening meal and feasted on smaller animals, always hanging the carcass high in a tree, so as to not attract them to his trail.

Once, he came upon a group of Maa people, only to find it was not his tribe. He quizzed an old man as to their possible location. All he could do was point south, which meant they could have moved into modern day Tanzania.

Gazini was growing weary. But now, thanks to the generosity of the tribe he had just met, looked and felt like a Maasai warrior. The clothing of the white man was gone and in its place was the typical Maa body covering. His knife, he kept, along with his hand made spear, which even the old man expressed an appreciation for, as he "liked its feel and weight".

So Gazini kept moving south. That is until he came upon the herd of lions feeding on the remains of a zebra. One male in particular raised his head and sniffed the air. Gazini noted with dismay he was downwind from the animal. All he could do was to run or fight. He decided to run.

The lion saw him and became curious. When game begins to run, it is an instant attraction. Moving food that presented a challenge was always better than one that simply stands there, waiting to be eaten.

Finally the animal caught up with him, knocked him down and began to circle him as Gazini stood with his spear, preparing for the fight. The two circled each other and for a moment Gazini felt the old presence again, that of Enkai Na-nyokie, the evil Maasai red god. He was here at this moment in the flesh of this lion.

"Great one, you are a fierce warrior," Gazini boomed to the lion. "I am also a fierce warrior! Do not let Enkai Na-nyokie force this battle! One of us will surely die!"

The lion roared and began to circle Gazini again. Feeling the scars on his chest, he recalled the sacrifice he had offered to the Gods if Henry Jennings were to live. Enkai Na-nyokie had come to reclaim his debt. He would have it, but not without a fight.

The lion roared again and Gazini screamed back at him. Two primordial devils fought on the African plain that day. The trusty spear skewered the lion and broke, leaving Gazini with only his knife. As the lion rushed and pounced on him, Gazini continued to stab the beast as the lion's sharp teeth bit through flesh and sinew, literally ripping one arm from his body. The next day, the tribe would find Gazini and his attacker. The dead lion covered the great warrior with his body. Gazini kept his honor. Enkai Na-nyokie was cheated. It was a good death.

Chapter 84

"Winning a woman's heart doesn't make someone a man.
Learning to treasure that heart after its won is what makes someone a real man!"

Author Unknown

The black pounded the cobblestone drive to the front of Norfolk Castle. The Downstairs Butler heard the commotion as the animal pawed the air, whinnied viciously and shook it's head. The rider was equally unkempt. His hair ribbon was long since gone and his hair fluttered about his face. He kept pushing it back as the horse pawed the air. The scar that ran from his eye down the side of his face was a brilliant red hue.

"May I help you Sir?" the Butler asked.

"Yes, you may tell Lady Elizabeth that I have arrived and Lord Howard that I have come to take what is mine!" Henry replied in an ugly fashion, as his eyes widened and an animalistic smile began to spread across his face.

"I will return word sir, but he may be indisposed."

"You tell his *Lordship* to either get his arse out here, or I'll ride my horse through the front door and into the vestibule of his home." Henry said, the ugly tone still creeping into his voice.

"And who may I say is calling?"

Henry had to admire the man. He had likely shite in his trousers, but somehow managed to be professional as a person in his station was required.

"Tell him Captain Henry Jennings Rockfort, the Ninth Duke of Kensington and the Governor of His Majesty's holdings in the Bahamas is at his door."

The butler visibly paled and reentered the house. Henry rode back and forth across the drive until Lord Howard appeared.

"Now see here," he began. "This is not the behavior of a gentleman! Remove yourself from my property this instant or you will feel my wrath!"

"Your wrath?" Henry began. "Your wrath? I don't give a good damn about your wrath sir. You may take your wrath and go to hell with it. I have come for what is mine and this time, I shan't be disappointed."

At that moment, Sarah and Elizabeth Howard appeared at the open door.

"Henry!" Elizabeth shouted joyously and would have made it to him, had her father not grabbed her roughly by her arm.

"My original decision stands," Lord Howard, said steadily. "She will not marry a ruffian or a commoner."

Henry pulled a pistol from one of his saddle holsters and leveled it at Lord Bernard Howard.

"I am neither," Henry replied. "My father has come forward and named me. I am the son of Lord Rockfort and as such I am the Ninth Duke of Kensington. I, and all who swear allegiance, to become privateers for King George has a pardon. I am now the new Governor for the Bahamas and the head of the new Privateer Navy. I am also a savage!"

"Can this be true?" Lord Howard asked incredulously.

"It is true," Henry declared. "And if you hurt her like that again, I will be forced to come off my horse and give you a thrashing you won't soon forget. Again, I have come to claim what is mine, if she is indeed mine!"

"I am!" Elizabeth cried as she broke free of her parents and rushed to the horse.

Henry offered her the stirrup and gently lifted her to the

front of the saddle where his arms could encircle her to keep her from falling.

"Elizabeth, now see here!" her father began.

"No, you see here!" Elizabeth retorted back. "He didn't have to return me to you. He didn't have to come back to regain his honor. He chose to do both, against my better wishes. But he chose to do so. That's the kind of man he is. If you wish to come see us, then you are welcome. If you do not wish to come, you are still welcome. But we are going! We will make our home on our plantation just outside of New Providence."

"Plantation? You are a land owner?" Lord Howard sputtered.

"Aye," Henry said. "Are you surprised? You shouldn't be. My plantation is almost three to four times that of your land grant, including what you have stolen from your less affluent neighbors and I have more wealth than many small governments. Your daughter will be well provided for!"

"Elizabeth, I demand you get down right now!" Lord Howard said as he began to turn beet red.

Suddenly another voice broke through. It was that of Sarah Howard.

"My dear husband," she said. "*Shut up*!"

" Elizabeth, remember us and we will come to see you after you are settled. Perhaps within a year or so?"

"I demand....." Lord Howard began in a strangled voice.

"And I demand that you *shut up*!" Sarah Howard interrupted. "You have already done more than enough to Elizabeth and Henry. Let them live their lives in peace. They deserve it."

"Thank you Lady Howard," Henry replied almost reverently. I have two things to do before we leave. Neither will take long."

Elizabeth wrapped her arms around Henry and kissed him with such passion that even Lady Howard turned away just for a moment, although she watched the kiss covertly with great attention. One can tell much from a kiss, or a touch, or even a gentle caress. Elizabeth's kiss was very telling.

"Very well then," Lord Howard said. "At least make use of my carriage, so you are not a spectacle to the entire village."

It was then Lady Howard spoke.

"Elizabeth dear, *under the circumstances*, perhaps you should indulge your father's fancy!"

Elizabeth caught her mother's concern and instinctively touched her lower abdomen.

"Could we Henry? I'm just so tired. A carriage would suit me better."

"Certainly my dear," Henry replied. "If that makes you feel better."

Once the carriage presented itself, Henry removed the saddle from the Black and stored it in the boot of the carriage and tied the animal to the rear. He helped his fiancé into the carriage and then started to get in himself. He stopped and walked up the steps where the Howards stood waiting.

He held out his hand to Lord Howard who took it hesitantly.

"I never really thanked you," Henry said. "Yes you refused me that which I admired most. But you took care of me as a child, schooled me, and saw to it that I had everything I needed and most things I wanted. I feel like I need to acknowledge that to both of you!"

He then stopped and gave Lady Howard the hug a son would to a mother.

"Thank you mum," Henry said. "Good-bye."

"Where are we going?" Elizabeth asked.

"First to Kensington, and then to the *Bathsheba.*" Henry replied. "I wish to pay my respects to my father before we leave and to the lady I knew as my mother. My father had her remains brought to Kensington from *The White Monastery of Our Lady* in Kent. He felt it fitting she be buried in the family cemetery. I owe him again for that."

"Henry, I have an idea, if you won't think it foolish."

"What is that, my dear?

Elizabeth managed a wicked womanly laugh and grasped his maleness.

"Take me now, here in the carriage. The shades are drawn. The driver won't ever know as bumpy as the roads are."

She pulled up her skirts and lay back on the seat.

"It's from the bouncing silly," Elizabeth said. "Come on then Captain. Come get your plunder!"

"Aye," Henry said in a husky voice as he entered her. "Privateers rut better, and longer for sure!"

Chapter 85

"A father is a man who expects his son to be as good a man as he meant to be."

Frank A. Clark

Henry and Elizabeth were greeted warmly at Kensington. Lord Rockfort took great pleasure in getting to know the son he had shunned for many years. Henry Jennings felt the same way. The world stopped when they were together. Elizabeth recognized they needed this time for healing and gave it to them.

Henry and Lord Rockfort often took walks across the property, stopping when the walk became too strenuous for Lord Rockfort and then progressing again. Elizabeth could tell something was wrong with the older man and he did not want either of them to notice.

The time for their leaving was growing near. *Bathsheba* had already come into port and was now docked at the Port of London. She was taking on supplies for the long trip to Nassau. They would soon depart England and Elizabeth doubted she would ever see its shores again. It did make her a little sad, but she knew letters would come and she would respond. At least these would keep her in touch with her family, such as it was. She still harbored ill will against her father, but knew she would miss her mother greatly.

This morning was a special day for both Henry and Lord Rockfort as they visited the family cemetery. Lord Rockfort brought a single English rose, which he placed solemnly on Josephine's grave and stepped back silently.

"We were so young, Henry," Lord Rockfort said. "We both knew what we were doing was wrong, but it wasn't just the throes of passion. I truly loved her. Perhaps it was because it was the one thing I couldn't completely have. The day she died, a piece of me died along with her. I was never quite the same. It greatest pleasure

I had were my visits to see you and watch you grow up as best as I could. I know you despise Lord Howard in many ways, but he did me a great favor at a time when many other Lords would have taken the babe to the nearest stream and drowned it. You were a part of her and I loved you because you were part of her. I simply wish I had named you my son before my wife and son died. It would have given you a better life."

Henry placed his hand on the older man's shoulder.

"Trust me father," Henry said. "I know only too well the ways of the wealthy, as well as the ways of the impoverished. What you did for me was the most unselfish thing any parent could do for a child. I had a wonderful childhood. I had Lizzie my entire life. How many men can say that? So this was my birth mother?"

He pointed to the stone that read simply *Josephine.*

Lord Rockfort nodded and for a moment a smile crept across his face, remembering.

"Aye, she was a bonny lass, she was," Lord Rockfort said. "She was as beautiful as an English sunrise and as soft as the petal of that rose."

Henry knelt beside the grave that bore the name *Ellen Jennings.*

"This was the woman I knew as my mother," Henry said. "She suckled me as a babe and gave me comfort as only a mother can give. I shall never forget her."

He turned a little and looked up at the older man.

"I hope that doesn't displease you!"

"Why should it?" Lord Rockfort exclaimed. "Why do you

think I had her brought here? Twas' time she had peace. It was the only thing I could do for her, except check on her from time to time."

"You visited her?" Henry asked incredulously.

"Oh yes, almost every month," Lord Rockfort said. "She loved coffee and sweets. I saw she had both, and enough to share with the nuns."

"I never knew anyone else was aware where I took her." Henry said sadly.

"Don't you remember lad?" Lord Rockfort laughed. "Your little argument with Lord Howard over Elizabeth's hand. You told him then. He told me and I told him to stay away or I would kill him. It was one of the last things I could do for you. I brought her sweets and she gave me details of your life that I would have never known. She was a most special woman!"

Henry rose and embraced his father.

"That you for that sir," Henry said. "I always worried about her. No offense, but she was the only real parent I ever knew."

Lord Rockfort waved him off.

"No offense taken son. Shall we return? I'm getting tired."

They began their walk back.

"How much did my freedom cost you?" Henry asked.

"Oh, only a bit o' this n' that," Lord Rockfort replied. "That's all!"

"You are not being truthful. I wish to pay you back!"

"Kensington should have belonged to you upon my death. The dear Lords and Ladies would never have allowed it to happen.

So, I traded what should have been your legacy for your life." Lord Rockfort said, as he seemed to ponder his decision.

"I would say it was a fair trade," he continued. "At least my bloody cousin won't have it. Maybe they will make it into a monastery, or perhaps a couple of hundred years in the future, they will show people through it to let them know how we *used* to live. Either way, remember one thing son. A house, estate, or a piece of ground is just that. It's just a bunch of rocks, dirt, and wood. It's blood that really matters. And blood takes care of their own."

Henry looked back at the graves and slightly shook his head.

"And then there are those that should have been blood! Do you hear me son? It's blood and people that makes us what we are and look over us. Never forget that. Promise me you will teach my grandchildren the meaning of it all. That will be my greatest legacy!"

"I promise father!" Henry said as he tried to ease the elder man's temper.

Lord Rockfort's chest had begun to rise and fall quickly. They stopped for a moment until he was able to remove his hand from his chest.

Suddenly, a grand idea came to Henry. It was one that made perfect sense.

"Come with us father! If there is nothing left to hold us here, come with us to New Providence!"

"It's a good thought lad," Lord Rockfort said as he dismissed it with a wave of his hand. "But there's the foundry to think of."

"Give it to the man that has done so much for you in your employment," Henry suggested. "I'm never coming back to England."

Lord Rockfort laughed.

"I thought you might feel that way," Lord Rockfort said. "It will be done as you have asked. But I can't go."

"Why not?" Henry demanded. "You have nothing left here!"

They stopped again. The main castle loomed before them. Lord Henry was panting. Finally he regained his breath.

"Because, I am dying son," Lord Rockfort replied. "I don't know how long. It could be days or months. But my heart is giving out. I would never make the trip."

"We can postpone leaving," Henry said gently. "We'll find the best doctors!"

This time, it was Lord Rockfort who placed his hand on his son's shoulder.

"Lad, I'm dying," he said quietly. "There's nothing you can do about it and there's nothing I can do about it. I simply thank the Almighty that he has given me the chance to redeem myself in your eyes and in mine, and that I have finally been given the gift of knowing my son. You need to prepare to be on your way. We'll take my carriage to the dock."

"Alright then," Henry said sadly. "I'll let Elizabeth know. I wish you would change your mind."

"It is God's will," Lord Rockfort said. "I am now happy!"

Chapter 86

"You and I will meet again, When we're least expecting it, One day in some far off place, I will recognize your face, I won't say goodbye my friend, For you and I will meet again."

Tom Petty

The ride to the dock was a quiet one. Lord Rockfort did not know what to say and neither did Henry. Elizabeth tried her best to raise their spirits, but it did not work.

Finally the carriage pulled onto the dock, close to *Bathsheba.* Scurvy had done a supreme job in refitting her. She was as close to new as a refurbished ship could be. Henry asked his father to come on deck, but he politely refused, insisting he spent his military career on foot and on foot was where he meant to stay.

While Henry checked the ship and spoke to the crew, Elizabeth had a few moments alone with Lord Rockfort.

"When are you going to tell him, my dear?" Lord Rockfort asked.

"I'll tell him after we are out to sea, when it is hard for him to turn the ship around," Elizabeth replied. "He may decide he wants his child to grow up amongst its grandparents. You can never tell what Henry will do."

"Don't underestimate him child," Lord Rockfort exclaimed. "His hatred of England is as strong as his love for you, although his allegiance will always be to his homeland."

"I wish you would go with us," Elizabeth whispered. "He's a different man when he's with you. He's not nearly as careless with his life, or as quick to make rash decisions."

"Ah," Lord Rockfort said. "That will change in time and certainly with the birth of his first child. You will see an entirely different Henry. I hope you will love the new one as much as the old. Much of the mischievous and rash behavior will disappear."

An excited Henry, who rushed to them from the ship,

interrupted their conversation.

"She's all ready to go," Henry quipped. "She's in better shape than she was when I got her!"

"Lord Rockfort, it was a pleasure," Elizabeth said as she gave him a peck on the cheek. "I will let the two of you say your goodbyes."

"And for me as well, my dear," Lord Rockfort replied.

"Are you certain you will not change your mind?" Henry asked his father.

"No son," he replied. "It is not meant to be."

"Then I guess this is goodbye," Henry said quietly.

"Yes, it is," Lord Rockfort replied as he hugged this boy who had grown into a fine, strong man. "Be happy my son. Make her happy. You are a pirate no more!"

"I will father!"

"Henry?" the old man's voice faltered.

"Yes father?"

"I love you son," Lord Rockfort said as he tried to keep his voice from quaking. "I love you. I am proud of the boy you were and the man you have become. Make me proud of my grandchildren!"

And with that, Lord Rockfort turned and walked toward the carriage. Henry stood there for a moment, looked back and then boarded *Bathsheba*. His father could hear him calling commands to his crew and he stood there for a moment, glowing with pride as he watched the sails fill and the ship leave port.

"Aye, loose the ropes at the bow and stern," Henry cried.

"That's it lads! Here we go now. We are off the dock. Raise the mainsail. Let's get her underway. Scurvy, take the wheel. I'll be in my quarters!"

Lord Rockfort stood on the dock for a full half hour, watching *Bathsheba* depart. Finally a long steam of tears slid down his face as he watched his son, his daughter-in-law-to-be and unborn grandchild sail out of his life forever.

London's more dignified crowd could not understand why this elegantly dressed old man would stand so still on a dirty dock with tears streaming down his face watching the sea. Lord Rockfort, the Eighth Duke of Kensington didn't give a damn. Finally he turned and stepped into his carriage.

"Home," he said simply.

This day was more than he could bear. The servants would find Lord Rockfort dead, the following morning, from a massive heart attack. He had passed quietly in his sleep with a smile on his face. The sins of the past were forgiven and that which was wrong had been made right.

Chapter 87

"A successful marriage requires falling in love many times, always with the same person."

Mignon McLaughlin

Bathsheba was deep into the Atlantic, within 3 weeks of her final destination at New Providence. Henry rose quietly as he did every morning, so as to not awaken Lizzie. But this morning to his surprise she was already awake.

"Good morning my love," he said giving her a gentle kiss, while savoring her sweet, lush lips.

"Wouldn't it sound better to say, *Good morning my wife*? " Lizzie asked.

"Well, of course," Henry replied.

"I seem to remember you made an offer of marriage to me under the large tree at the edge of the common, did you not?" Elizabeth said, chastising him.

"Well, of course I did," Henry stammered. "And I bloody well meant it too!"

"I seem to remember I accepted, Mr. Jennings," Lizzie retorted. "Is it your intent to make good on your promise or to have me remain an unattached woman to be made sport of when she walks down the street?"

"Well, of course," Henry began.

"Then I would suggest you be quick about it," she replied rolling to her side. "I want to be married by a priest."

"Scurvy can marry us as the Captain at sea," Henry said.

"Isn't Father O'Donnell on board?"

"Well of course," Henry said. "He's a priest that's been in prison though. Is that what you want?"

"Are you to be holding it against the poor man that he was imprisoned for averting a terrible act upon a child?" Lizzie spat.

"Why no, I was just thinking. . ." Henry started again.

"Then stop thinking," Elizabeth retorted. "I want to be married. I've waited long enough, don't you think?"

"I'll check into it right now," Henry said, immediately beginning the mental calculation most men are aware of. It is the time when men may tread lighter than usual and good deeds often head off disputes. What was the time of her last monthly? He racked his brain. Dammit, it must have occurred while he was in prison. That is why he did not remember. But by gosh, if she wanted a wedding now, then she was going to have it.

He quickly donned his best trousers, jackboots, shirt, and jerkin.

"I'll return shortly," Henry said.

"No need, you may knock on the door. Send Cassie down if you can find her. It is bad luck for the groom to see the bride before a wedding."

"Aye love! I'll start working on it right away!"

Henry hit the upper deck in frenzy.

"What in the bloody hell is the matter with you?" Scurvy inquired.

"It's Lizzie and she wants to get married. Today. I mean right now!" Henry replied.

Scurvy chuckled.

"Yeah, she and Cassie have had their heads together for the last several weeks," he observed.

"Can you send Cassie down to help her," Henry observed. "And where is that bloody chest of jewelry, we took off that Spanish ship afore we stopped being pirates." Henry demanded.

" You mean the box of jewels headed to the colonies from the Queen of Spain to her cousin?"

"Yes dammit! That's the one! Where is it?"

"It's in the forward hold Captain," Scurvy said, holding back his laughter. "Would you like me to find Father O'Donnell for you?"

"Damn your eyes Scurvy! You are a part of this!" Henry chided. "All of this sport at my expense!"

"Call it a welcome home present," Scurvy noted.

"Get the bloody priest and I'll go get a bloody ring. I wanted this to be special, not aboard some ship in the middle of the ocean!"

"We are coming up on the Camel's Hump, if my math is right," Scurvy observed. "No ships in sight. Would you like us to drop anchor and the sails?"

Camel's Hump was the name for an undersea mountain range in the Atlantic where ships could often drop anchor for a short time.

"Yes, do whatever you need to do!" Henry said quickly. "I've never seen her this way."

"Oh, it can get worse," Scurvy noted.

"And I guess you are the authority, since you and Cassie were married afore we left London," Henry said through gritted teeth.

"Maybe," Scurvy admitted nonchalantly as he sauntered off.

It took Henry ten minutes to find the large diamond and ruby ring he wanted to give Lizzie as he wedding ring. Being a pirate could have its benefits. There was usually some type of plunder available, especially if the ship had not put into port to sell it.

Henry arrived on deck, disheveled and not a little angry that the men who were supposed to respect him were all standing with smiles on their faces, alongside the railing of the ship.

"Don't you have work to do?" Henry said testily.

"Now is this the way you treat your honored guests and witnesses," Father O'Donnell chided. "You may be the Captain of this ship, but you are the groom and I am the priest, so at least for the moment I outrank you. You may have me cut into pieces at your leisure. Henry, stand over here. That's a good lad! And now for the bride!"

Elizabeth slowly climbed the steps from the Captains Quarters to the main deck. She was dressed in a rich white satin gown. Cassie came behind her, also dressed for the occasion in an equally stylish light green gown. As she passed the men against the railing, each dropped their head, and if they wore a head covering, removed it in her honor. Finally she came to stand to Henry's left.

The sunlight and blue sky added to the beauty of the day, but she was truly stunning. This was her day.

"Turn and take each other's hands," Father O'Donnell said.

"Brothers and sisters, let us praise our Lord Jesus Christ, who loved us and gave himself for us. Let us bless him now and forever. We know that all of us need God's blessing at all times; but at the time of their engagement to be married, Christians are in particular need of grace as they prepare themselves to form a new family."

He stopped for a moment, looked at Henry and noted, "Some need more blessings than others. However, let us pray, then, for God's blessing to come upon this couple: that they will grow in mutual respect and in their love for one another; that through their companionship and prayer together they have prepared themselves rightly and chastely for marriage. Love is patient, love is kind. It is not jealous, love is not pompous, it is not inflated, it is not rude, it does not seek its own interests, it is not quick-tempered, it does not brood over injury, it does not rejoice over wrongdoing but rejoices with the truth. It bears all things, believes all things, hopes all things, and endures all things. Love never fails. We praise you, Lord, for your gentle plan draws together your children, Elizabeth and Henry, in love for one another. Strengthen their hearts, so that they will keep faith with each other, please you in all things, and so come to the happiness of celebrating the sacrament of their marriage. We ask this through Christ our Lord."

Lizzie looked at Henry, smiled, and squeezed his hand.

Father O'Donnell looked them both sternly and began to finish the marital ceremony.

"Henry Jennings, do you take this woman, Elizabeth Howard to be your lawfully wedded wife, to have and to hold from this day forward until death do you part?"

"I do," Henry replied.

"And do you Elizabeth Howard, take Henry Jennings to be your lawfully wedded husband to have and to hold from this day forward until death do you part?"

"I do," Elizabeth said as she squeezed Henry's hand again.

'Then what God has joined together, let no man put asunder! By the power of the Lord God and the Catholic Church, I pronounce you man and wife. You may kiss your bride, Captain Henry Jennings!"

Henry bent forward, pulled Lizzie tight, and kissed her passionately on the lips.

"Huzzah!" the men shouted.

"Congratulations!" Scurvy said as he pumped Henry's hand. "I always knew you were destined for greatness. Shall I begin calling you the Lord and Mrs. Governor now?"

"Kiss my arse," Henry growled.

"Ok, lads," Scurvy cried. "Ceremony's over. Get that anchor up and these sails into the wind. We are a sitting duck out here!"

The men scurried into action. They knew their job and they knew it well.

In their cabin, the newlyweds celebrated as only a newly wedded couple can. The sun had already begun to slide toward sunset. There was not much time.

"I love you Lizzie," Henry said as he brushed his fingers long the shape of her breast.

"I love you Henry Jennings! I always have and I always will. By the way, the ring was beautiful. In fact it was so large, it is almost indecent!"

"A mere trinket," Henry replied.

"I have a gift for you as well," Lizzie said slyly. "But we must get dressed to see it."

"Alright," Henry replied. "Formal or informal?"

"Informal," Lizzie replied. "I want to save that gown!"

"Alright let's go then," Henry replied as he tucked his shirt into his trousers.

They came out onto the open deck.

"To the stern," Lizzie said. "Quickly!"

"Ok," Henry said, "Where is the surprise?"

"Hold me, and I'll show you," Lizzie replied. "Face the setting sun."

"It is a beautiful night," Henry said. "But not as beautiful as you."

"I know you think I don't pay attention to everything you tell me." Lizzie said. "But most of the time I do. This is something you showed me after you almost came back from the dead. I talked to Gazini about it and he gave me another explanation. Father O'Donnell gave me another."

"What are you talking about?" Henry asked.

"Watch!" Lizzie replied.

It came. They quickly took in the sun's ball of red as it continued to slip below the horizon. Just before the sun changed from red to orange, there was a brilliant green flash that lasted for almost two seconds, and then was gone.

"It never ceases to amaze me," Henry said.

"Scurvy told me that although the sea holds many secrets in her depths, there will be a time when she will yield her secrets, all of them and lay them before all mankind. Someday, the entire world will know who you are and when you are gone, who you were. Father O'Donnell told me another one. He said the Bible says *"And the sea gave up the dead which were in it; and death and hell delivered up the dead which were in them: and they were judged every man according to their works."*

"I guess that means I'm in my neck up to shite then," Henry replied solemnly.

"No, I like Gazini's story the best," Lizzie replied. *"The sun only flashes as two hearts beat as one and only where there is great love."*

"I rather like that one too," Henry replied.

Lizzie took Henry's hand and placed it on her expanding abdomen that was beginning to show.

"Do you feel that Captain Henry Jennings, my husband," Elizabeth asked.

"Feel what?" Henry said as he gently felt her abdomen.

A man must never tell a woman she has gained weight.

"Your child, my husband. I am after all, quite pregnant!"

Chapter 88

"For me, a happy ending is not everything works out just right and there is a big bow, it's more coming to a place where a person has a clear vision of his or her own life in a way that enables them to kind of throw down their crutches and walk."

Jill McCorkle

Their arrival in New Providence brought much commotion. News had already reached them via some means that a new Governor was coming. Henry and Elizabeth arrived in New Providence just in time to witness the final sale of three slaves on the auction block. There was a man, a woman, and a young boy of roughly eight. It was obviously a family.

Henry was dressed in usual island attire, with no jerkin and a loose fitting, airy linen shirt.

"Just a moment," Henry told the driver. "Stop!"

"Now Henry," Elizabeth said.

"Now Henry nothing," Henry said as he walked to the slaver.

The male slave was nude to the waist. The woman's clothing was open, revealing her breasts and her pubic area. Several men walked around her, grasped her body and laughed.

"Leave her alone," the man cried in broken English. "She is my woman, not yours!"

"She is whoever I say she is," the slaver cried as he began to lay the cat on the black male. The man hunkered to his knees, blood beginning to run from the cuts on his back.

The slaver was surprised as the whip was jerked from his hand and the tip of a sword touched his throat. It was Henry who now held both.

"Do you like whips?" he asked.

"Who the devil are you? Yes sometimes it takes the cat to bring a man back to his senses!"

"Like this?" Henry replied as he threw the whip away and

tore the back of his shirt to reveal the badly healed scars.

"You were a mariner. He's a mariner and he dishonoured his Captain. Take him!" the slaver cried.

"Not likely," Henry said. "How much for the lot of them?"

"Well, they are prime meat, just in from Jamaica," the slaver said. "I'll take 100 pieces of silver."

"How much is your life worth?" Henry asked.

"I see, perhaps we can make a deal," the slaver said hopefully.

"Here is your deal," Henry said sternly. "My name is Captain Henry Jennings and I am the new Governor and head of His Majesty's Privateer Navy. We no longer sell slaves here and if I find any man laying a whip on a man's back for defending his family or what is rightfully his, he'll get Moses law which is forty minus one. Do you understand?"

The slaver nodded.

Henry turned to the family, "Pull your clothes on. You are not pieces of meat and no man shall ever treat you as such again."

"We are your property Master," the man said. "What do you want us to do?"

"First, my name is Captain Jennings or Mister Henry, not Master or anything else. You may address my wife as Miz Elizabeth or Lady Elizabeth. If you wish to come with us, we have a large plantation down the road. I could use a good family to help run it. We can decide on your wages after we arrive, if you are interested. If you are not, then good day to you sir!"

Henry turned to go.

"How we going to get there, Mister Henry? We can walk, ifn' you can tell us the way."

"You are Maa, are you not?" Henry asked.

"We are! How did you know Mister Henry?"

"Just did. One of my best friends was Maasai. He has gone home now. Perhaps ***Enkai Na-rok*** was with you today. At any rate you may ride with us, if you like. There is room in the carriage. It's open top anyway!"

The man looked at his wife, who was embarrassed because of her recent display.

Elizabeth took her arm and handed the woman her shawl.

"It's all right my dear and perfectly safe. If my husband has given you his word, that is it."

The woman pulled her dishevelled clothing around her, nodded and all climbed into the carriage.

"Forward to the plantation," Henry said.

The carriage drove through miles and miles of countryside, teeming with crops growing in the fields.

"Where's your house at Mister Henry?" the man observed.

"We'll be there in a few minutes," Henry said.

"Where does your land start?" the little boy asked in broken English.

Henry smiled and tousled his hair.

"Lad, you've been riding on it for the last two hours!" Henry replied. "There, there it is!"

The main house was a large as any castle with stone and white washed wood. The landscaping was perfect and attended to by several hired workers. A large metal arched frame extended from one side of the driveway to the other, giving entry to a cobble stone drive.

"Why ain't you got no name up, Mister Henry? Ever big house has a name." the man asked, surprised this expression of wealth should not be named.

"I could never think of one," Henry said quietly.

"I think it already has a name," Elizabeth said matter-of-factly as she gently held her bulging stomach and the child within her. "Its name is Kensington and we are finally home!"

Epilogue

Henry Jennings is a somewhat mystical character in the world of piracy. Captain Henry Jennings was an 18th century British privateer, who served primarily during the War of Spanish Succession and later served as leader of the pirate haven or "republic" of New Providence. Although little is known of Jennings' early life, there is conjecture that he was indeed the illegitimate heir of a member of British nobility. Although bastards were common, acceptance or "claiming" of bastards was not a common practice.

After protecting his childhood love from calamity, he was forced to the high seas to escape the gallows. He was first recorded operating from Jamaica, then governed by Lord Archibald Hamilton.

There is evidence that Jennings owned enough land in Jamaica to live comfortably, thus leaving his motivations for piracy to conjecture. His first recorded act of piracy actually took place in early 1716 when, with three vessels and 150-300 men, Jennings' fleet ambushed the Spanish salvage camp from the 1715 Treasure Fleet. After forcing the retreat of around 60 soldiers, Jennings set sail for Jamaica carrying back an estimated 350,000 pesos. While en route to Jamaica, Jennings encountered another Spanish ship and captured another 60,000 pesos.

When Jennings met "Black Sam" Bellamy, he allegedly teamed with him to commit more piracies against the French. When Bellamy double-crossed him, Jennings' ruthlessness was evidenced in the brutal slaying of more than 20 Frenchmen. This was at a time when Britain and France were at peace, although political tensions were running high. The very governor of Jamaica, who had commissioned him, declared Jennings a pirate. Strong evidence points to the fact the governor acted out of anger as he did not get his cut of the treasure.

Jennings was forced to flee from Jamaica and eventually established a new base of operations in New Providence in the Bahamas. Based out of Nassau for a time, Jennings became an unofficial mayor of the growing pirate colony and retired from piracy.

In early 1718, Jennings surrendered to authorities in Britain following the amnesty declared by the newly appointed Governor of the Bahamas, Woodes Rogers and supported by wealthy members of Parliament. Circumstances surrounding his pardon and release are not clearly documented.

Jennings retired as a wealthy plantation owner in Bermuda, after receiving his pardon. He never forgot his true love and some history tells us he risked the gallows again to return her to England in 1717. We can only surmise Elizabeth's love for Henry was as strong as his love for Elizabeth.

We do know that he lived out his days with his one true childhood love, a woman of British aristocracy that gave up her title, her inheritance, and her dull life of leisure. For life on a plantation in the Bahamas. Henry Jennings stayed well beyond the reaches of British aristocracy, France, and Spain. It is reported Elizabeth bore Henry several strong male and female children. Henry and Lizzie remained inseparable until Henry's death many years later, after growing old with his family in Bermuda. Although she was several years his junior, Lizzie, followed Henry in death only a few months later. Her lifelong friend and handmaiden said Elizabeth was a very healthy woman, but died of a broken heart. Her final words were "Henry and I will not be separated again."

Henry Jennings is one of very few pirates said to have enjoyed a successful retirement.

The question remains. Did they really live and love? The answer is yes! Guided by their North Star a part of their lives will always belong to the mystery of the oceans and remains a Secret of the Sea. And there it shall stay.

The End

Author's Notes

1. **<u>Slave Ship Adelaide.</u> According to maritime history, the slave ship Adelaide may have actually sank off the coast of Cuba on October 10, 1714, not 1717. Although historical dates vary, both counts agree that during the night of 10th October, she was thrown onto a reef by a hurricane and sank within an hour. The frigate broke in two parts: its bow was washed ashore with some survivors and its stern sank. Only 45 men were able to escape, with the wreck causing 106 fatalities. Strangely, listed among the survivors was the Captain, M. Champmorot, who was later held responsible for the disaster before a French court - but found not guilty.**

2. **<u>Spanish Galleon.</u> A typical Spanish galleon had a number of decks: forecastle, upper or weather deck, main deck, lower or orlop deck, poop deck, and quarterdeck. The crew's quarters were in the bow while the officers and passengers lived in cramped cabins in the waist or center section of the galleon. Provisions were stowed near the galley. Larger galleons also had a surgeon aboard. In addition to the sailors and soldiers that made up the crew, there were also the carpenter, sail maker, cook, and cooper. The captain or admiral lived in the Great Cabin, earmarked by large windows, greater space, and more comfort. While his was above deck, the crew slept and ate on the gun decks where it was dark, damp, and odorous. Insects and rats abounded and foodstuffs often spoiled. The crew of a Spanish galleon with thirty guns might number 180 men. In battle, sixty-six worked the guns, fifty manned small arms on the upper deck, and fifty sailed the ship. Four were stationed in the powder room and as many as four carpenters repaired damage below deck. The surgeon commanded several men who served as assistants in tending the wounded. The remaining crew kept watch for fires. Few galleons sank from enemy attacks, though. The enemy's guns more often damaged the rigging and masts, and inflicted serious wounds on the crew from flying splinters when shot crashed through wood. The enemies that inflicted the most devastating damage on the treasure galleons, though, were the sea and wind. In spite of its seaworthiness, the galleon was a fragile structure. Hurricanes and rough seas sank more than one treasure ship during the years the galleons sailed. The "superstructure" or tall rear of the ship that provide additional quarters and storage space proved to make the vessel top heavy causing many of them to topple during a heavy storm.**

3. **<u>Bellamy and Jennings.</u> Bellamy, Williams, Jennings and a young Charles Vane teamed up to take a French frigate in April of 1716. Bellamy and Williams double-crossed Jennings, however, stealing much of the take from the French vessel. They teamed up then with Benjamin Hornigold, a well-known pirate who refused to attack English ships, preferring French of Spanish vessels. One of Hornigold's officers was a man named Edward Teach, who would eventually gain great fame under another name: Blackbeard. Bellamy continued to haunt the Caribbean for a few months and in February he made a major**

score, capturing the slave ship WHYDAH carrying valuable cargo including gold and rum. As a bonus, the WHYDAH was a very large, seaworthy ship and made a great pirate ship, after mounting 28 cannons on board. On his way to plunder the rich shipping lanes off of New England. Bellamy continued north. On April 26, 1717, another major storm hit: the vessels were scattered. The WHYDAH was driven onto shore and sank: only two of the 140 or so pirates on board somehow made their way to shore and survived. Bellamy was among the drowned. It is rumoured the storm may not have been the only thing that caused him to sink. Henry Jennings was a good man and a gentleman, as pirates go. However, like many men of his time, he never forgot a traitorous deed. It was rumoured that Bathsheba's cannons found The WHYDAH during the storm and that aided significantly in her demise.

4. Maasai Tribe of Africa. The Maasai are a Nilotic group. They inhabit the African Great Lakes region. Nilotes speak Nilo-Saharan language, and came to Southeast Africa by way of South Sudan. Most Nilotes in the area, including the Maasai, the Samburu and the Kalenjin, are pastoralists, and are famous for their fearsome reputations as warriors and cattle-rustlers. As with the Bantu, the Maasai and other Nilotes in Eastern Africa have adopted many customs and practices from the neighbouring Cushitic groups, including the age set system of social organization, and circumcision. According to their own oral history, the Maasai originated from the lower Nile valley north of Lake Turkana (Northwest Kenya) and began migrating south around the 15th century, arriving in a long trunk of land stretching from what is now northern Kenya to what is now central Tanzania between the 17th and late 18th century. Many ethnic groups that had already formed settlements in the region were forcibly displaced by the incoming Maasai, while other, mainly southern Cushitic groups, were assimilated into Maasai society.

5. Kanya. Kenya was often referred to as "Kanya" in the 1600s. It was a frequent trading ground for Greek and Arab traders who travelled south from Egypt. It was also a feeding ground for slave traders until it came under British influence many years later that discouraged the practice.

6. Chemise. The term chemise or shirt can refer to the classic smock, or else can refer to certain modern types of women's undergarments and dresses. In the classical use it is a simple garment worn next to the skin to protect clothing from sweat and body oils, the precursor to the modern shirts commonly worn in Western nations.

7. Pardon of Henry Jennings. Under the direction of the pro-stuart Governor of Jamaica, Archibald Hamilton, Jennings armed his 80-ton sloop Bathsheba and at the end of 1715 sailed out to salvage loot from the wrecks of the Spanish treasure fleet. Instead, he launched an all-out assault on the Spanish salvage camp at Palma de Ayz, Florida, stealing £87,000 in gold and silver. He then put in at Nassau, where he offended Hornigold, before returning to Jamaica on January 26, 1716. Although

his raid was illegal -- Britain and Spain were at peace -- Jennings was unmolested by Jamaica authorities. He set out again in March, sailing to Cuba where, on April 3, he illegally seized a French merchant ship with the help of a motley group of pirates lead by Samuel Bellamy. Bellamy subsequently stole a large portion of the treasure and slipped away to join Hornigold, who happened to be operating in the area. This attack on neutral French shipping triggered a diplomatic storm that ultimately resulted in Jennings being declared a pirate by King George. He moved his operations to Nassau, where he would remain a leading figure for the next two years. Like Hornigold, he did not target English ships. When word of the King's pardon reached Nassau in late December 1717, the pirates split into two camps, one wishing to take the amnesty, the other intending to carry on to the bitter end. Jennings was one of those who chose clemency, though curiously he and his close followers chose to surrender in Bermuda, not Jamaica, a decision that fuels speculation that Jennings had family ties there.

8. Triple Alliance. January 4 (December 24, 1716 Old Style) – Great Britain, France and the Dutch Republic sign the Triple Alliance in an attempt to maintain the Treaty of Utrecht (1713), Britain having signed a preliminary alliance with France on November 28 (November 17) 1716.

9. Blackbeard. Crews on two ships commanded by Benjamin Hornigold and Edward Teach attack and capture the British-built French Guineaman Concorde in the eastern Caribbean. Hornigold soon accepts a British amnesty for all pirates, but Teach rejects it and subsequently becomes known as Blackbeard. A rift between George I of Great Britain and his son the Prince of Wales leads to the latter being banished from the royal household. December – Blackbeard teams up with Stede Bonnet but later takes his ship and demotes Bonnet to guest. The Queen Anne's Revenge and Revenge take several ships as prizes in the Caribbean. Blackbeard eventually adds two more ships to his party and sails north to the North American coast.

10. Queen Anne Pistol. The Queen Anne Pistol is also known as the "turn-off" pistol due to the fact that the barrel unscrews from the chamber for loading. It takes the name "Queen Anne" from the era in which it first appeared in numbers. While any gun from the 1702-1714 period could technically be called a "Queen Anne", it is the turn-off pistol that has become synonymous with that name. The ability to have the barrel unscrew allowed for a tighter fitting bullet that would develop more power and greater accuracy in use. Most period pictures of Black Beard show him with lots of pistols that seem to be of the Queen Anne style.

11. Words of the Massai. Maa – the name of the tribe that separates it from the rest of the world. Death is known as En-keeya. House or homestead is known as enkang'. En-jung'ore or En-jung'go is known as the amn's inheritance. Since the Maasai do not believe in life after death, women receive nothing and simply die, never to return, and with no reward.

12. Execution at Execution Dock - The legal jurisdiction for the British Admiralty was for all crimes committed at sea. The dock symbolised that jurisdiction by being located just beyond the low-tide mark in the river. Anybody who had committed crimes on the seas, either in home waters or abroad, would eventually be brought back to London, and tried by the High Court of the Admiralty. Capital punishment was applied to acts of mutiny that resulted in death, for murders on the High Seas and specific violations of the Articles of War governing the behavior of naval sailors, including sodomy. Those sentenced to death were usually brought to Execution Dock from Marshalsea Prison (although some were also transported from the Newgate Prison.) The condemned were paraded across London Bridge past the Tower of London. The procession was led by the High Court Marshal, on horseback (or his deputy). He carried a silver oar that represented the authority of the Admiralty. Prisoners were transported in a cart to Wapping; with them was a chaplain who encouraged them to confess their sins. Just like the execution procession to Tuburn, condemned prisoners were allowed to drink a quart of ale at a public house on the way to the gallows. An execution at the dock usually meant that crowds lined the river's banks or chartered boats moored in the Thames to get a better view of the hangings. Executions were conducted by the hangmen who worked at either Tyburn and Newgate Prison. With a particular cruelty reserved for those convicted of acts of piracy, hanging was done with a shortened rope. This meant a slow death from strangulation on the scaffold as the drop was insufficient to break the prisoner's neck. It was called the Marshal's dance because their limbs would often be seen to 'dance' from slow asphyxiation. Unlike hangings on land such as at Tyburn, the bodies of pirates at Execution Dock were not immediately cut down following death. Customarily, these corpses were left hanging on the nooses until at least three tides had washed over their heads.
13. The North Star. Exactly where you see Polaris in your northern sky depends on your latitude. From New York it stands 41 degrees above the northern horizon, which also corresponds to the latitude of New York. Since 10 degrees is roughly equal to your clenched fist held at arm's length, from New York Polaris would appear to stand about "four fists" above the northern horizon. At the North Pole, you would find it overhead. At the equator, Polaris would appear to sit right on the horizon. So if you travel to the north, the North Star climbs progressively higher the farther north you go. When you head south, the star drops lower and ultimately disappears once you cross the equator and head into the Southern Hemisphere. And always keep this fact in mind: Polaris is more accurate than any compass. A compass is subject to periodic variations and can only show you the direction of the lines of the strongest magnetic force for a particular spot and for a particular time. But even Polaris isn't positioned exactly due north. Only about 0.7 degree separates Polaris from the pivot point directly in the north – called the North Celestial Pole – around which

the stars go daily. Aside from the North Star the two stars at the front of the Little Dipper's bowl are the only ones readily seen. These two are often referred to as the "Guardians of the Pole" because they appear to march around Polaris like sentries; the nearest conspicuously bright stars to the celestial pole except for Polaris itself. Columbus mentioned these stars in the log of his famous journey across the ocean and many other navigators have found them useful in measuring the hour of the night and their place upon the sea by their position relative to Polaris.

Revenge of the Pandora Project

"If you prick us do we not bleed? If you tickle us do we not laugh? If you poison us do we not die? And if you wrong us shall we not revenge?"

William Shakespeare

The well-dressed man carefully opened the cardboard file box, noting the labels read TOP SECRET. TO BE OPENED WITH PRESIDENTIAL APPROVAL ONLY. He grunted and smiled as he slit the red tape that bound the box and began to sift through the folders. He flipped through them until he came to the end, noted the name on the folder and removed it. He added it to the two folders on his desk, opened them and after a few minutes of review, picked up the phone and placed a call.

After a few moments, the line was answered.

"Petrov here."

The man leaned back in his chair.

"Petrov, it's General Ben Carson."

"I thought I told you never to contact me," Petrov snarled.

"Things have changed. We have an emergency."

"What kind of emergency?" Petrov snarled back.

"It's the old project," Carson snapped.

"Which one?"

Petrov was curious now.

"*The Pandora Project*, you idiot. It is rearing its ugly head again." Carson replied.

"I thought we had that taken care of," Petrov said. "Packard has been dead for over two years. He was the last."

"Yeah, at the cost of ten of our best agents. He may not have been young, but special training comes through quickly when needed. His home was a blood bath. He went down covering his wife, even though it was too late." Carson retorted. "But it's more than that. His son Brock has been digging. He left DEVGRU a little over a year ago and he's been raising hell ever since. Claims he found an old journal that belonged to his father and it describes everything in detail. Says something else was done to his father and a couple of other members of the team. He's asked for a Congressional Subcommittee Hearing."

"You left loose ends," Petrov said icily.

"Yes."

"See they are taken care of," Petrov replied.

"I have agents already working on it," Carson said uneasily. "The girl is missing as well."

"Chapman's daughter? I thought you had her under control."

"Don't you understand?" Carson snapped back. "Something Packard and Chapman received was somehow passed on to their children. They are more intelligent, faster, and stronger than our best agents! She escaped!"

"I don't give a shit," Petrov snarled. "Find them and kill them! The world must never know!"

More Novels by Michael Letterman

Sins of the Father

JACK

The Prophet

Lea

TWIN

The Pandora Project

Blood Moon

Secrets of the Sea

The Author

Michael Letterman

Michael is a resident of middle Tennessee and lives with his beautiful wife Jan; sons Jeremy and Brett; and Aleah, a Belgian Malinois trained as a K-9 and the family's most vigilant protector.

Michael often draws on his travels and personal life experiences as material for his novels. His wife Jan provides valuable input in the areas of human behavior, psyche, and profiles of female characters.

Michael is an avid firearms advocate and has achieved black belts in multiple disciplines. He is an active supporter of law enforcement and our nation's military.